INKER AND CROWN

GUILDS OF ILBREA, BOOK ONE

MEGAN O'RUSSELL

Ink Worlds Press

Visit our website at www.MeganORussell.com

This book is a work of fiction. Names, characters, places, and incidents either are products of the author's imagination or are used fictitiously. Any resemblance to actual persons, living or dead, events, or locales is entirely coincidental.

Inker and Crown

Cover Art by Sleepy Fox Studio (https://www.sleepyfoxstudio.net/)

Editing by Christopher Russell

Interior Design by Christopher Russell

Printed in the United States of America

For the ones who have survived the flames.
You are strong enough to topple kingdoms.

WHITE MOUNTAINS
Royal Palace
Map Master Palace
BARRENS
Ilara
Arion Sea
Barrens Bay
Frason's Glenn
Harane
Ian Lioche
ILBREA
Ian Mithe
Ruthir Mountain
Mountain Road
Ian Ayres
Southern Citadel
Pamerane

N

Spice Trail

Spice Trail

EASTERN
MOUNTAINS

WYRAIN

Mountain Road

Spios

KINGLESS
TERRITORIES

Acalia

Golden
Sea

The Horn

INKER AND CROWN

ENA

There is a moment when the first spark of a fire appears and it is still possible to ignore the coming blaze.

There is no smoke tainting the air. No damage has been done.

Just a little flash that seems harmless and beautiful.

You can't see the raging power of the fire, but it is there, hiding its danger and waiting for its moment to ignite.

That one spark will consume the world.

It does not care if you are too blind to see the destruction racing toward you.

We will all burn in the coming blaze.

I perched in the rafters above the crowd, wondering if any of the people below could see the spark or sense how near our doom we stood.

"The paun will starve us." Cade stood on a crate, looking out over his followers. His eyes gleamed as he took in the silent horde. "They will watch our children die and not raise a hand to save them. For too long, we have let the Guilds build their glory on the corpses of our fallen brothers. Their time is coming to an end. How many of you will be brave enough to stand with me when the battle begins?"

A rustle of murmurs fluttered through the crowd.

"Watch and see what decrees the King sends down for Winter's End," Cade said. "He won't order the healers to stop letting those who can't pay die. He won't order the soldiers to put down their swords and help the common farmer in the field. The King cares only for glory and riches. We are worthless rodents to the Guilds."

He stood still for a moment, basking in the crowd's rapt attention. With his curly, blond hair, handsome face, and broad shoulders, he looked like the hero the common folk had been waiting for. The savior of the tilk standing on a crate as he made grand plans to change Ilbrea.

Cade looked up at me.

My heart stuttered, but I didn't shrink back into the shadows. I held Cade's gaze as he spoke.

"A new day is dawning. The blood of the Guilded paun will slick the streets. Fire will consume anyone who stands in our way. There is only death or freedom. There can be no other path. Who will answer when I give the call to fight?"

"I will!" a voice shouted from the back of the crowd. The same voice that had shouted first the last time Cade held court.

"I will fight with you!" A man stepped up to the front of the horde.

"I'll fight!"

"I will!"

I stood up on the rafters and made my way back to the open window at the front of the stable. The shouts of the horde were still growing as I grabbed the thick rope hanging off the side of the building and swung myself down to the street.

The people passing by paid no attention to the roaring shouts in the stable. It was Winter's End, after all. A day of celebration for everyone in Ilara.

Cheering, dancing, drinking, a raucous mess would swallow

the streets by nightfall. Why should anyone care if some started their celebrating before midday?

I forced my shoulders to relax as I followed the crowds toward the cathedral square. But even as I pressed a careful smile onto my face, I couldn't drive the horrible images of blood and fire from my mind.

Cade wanted a rebellion. He wanted blood to slick the streets of Ilara.

It would be easy to cause chaos and death in Ilbrea's capital city.

It would be impossible to protect the innocents of Ilara if Cade got the battle he craved.

"Mama, mama, look!"

I nearly tripped over the little girl who had stopped in the middle of the street to point at me.

The child gazed up at me, her eyes wide with wonder. "Are you a fairy?"

"There is no such thing as fairies." The girl's mother frowned as she eyed me.

I bent down to be level with the girl and pulled my hair over my shoulder, letting her touch the technicolor strands. "But it is Winter's End, so I suppose anything's possible."

The girl giggled as I winked and strode away.

I could feel others staring at me, but it didn't bring me any fear or make me blush.

I wanted them all to stare.

A dozen colors streaked my hair. More decorated my skirt. I offered them all a grand display as I fluttered through the streets of Ilara.

Armor comes in many forms. Mine is forged of pigments and beauty. Better to know why I drew the gaze of those around me than to wonder if they'd discovered the secrets I'd hidden in the shadows.

The pace of the crowd slowed as we neared the cathedral square and the people packed more tightly together.

I weaved through the throng, offering smiles to the men who let me pass, winking at the women who glared disapprovingly.

"Keep moving forward." A soldier stood on the steps of a shop, waving the horde onward. I caught his gaze, and he smiled down at me. "Happy Winter's End, miss."

He was young and handsome. He had a glimmer of hope in his eyes as he smiled at me, as though speaking to a pretty girl might bring evening enjoyment.

A laugh escaped me before I could stop it. I tucked my chin and hid behind the curtain of my hair, hoping the soldier would think I was shy rather than disgusted at the thought of ever letting a filthy paun touch me.

The line of people stopped as we reached the cathedral square.

"We should have stayed home," an older man grumbled.

A woman smacked him on the arm. "We should have left home when I wanted to."

I ducked around them and dove deeper into the crowd, aiming for the statue of the seven-pointed star that rose up in the center of it all.

A hand grazed my waist as I climbed up onto the statue's pedestal. I didn't bother looking for whoever had been so brazen. The crowd nearest the cathedral had already begun cheering, and I hadn't the time to spare.

The bottom two arms of the star were set into the white marble of the pedestal. The next pair up had already been claimed by men.

"Give a girl a hand?" I reached for the man sitting above me.

"I don't mind the company." He grinned, wrapping his calloused hand around mine as he helped me up.

As soon as I got a toe onto his arm of the star, I let go and climbed onto the level above him.

"I thought we were going to be friends," the man called up to me.

"I only asked for a hand." I gripped the center arm of the star and looked toward the towering, white cathedral.

A line of soldiers in black uniforms stood in front of the cathedral steps.

Fear flickered through me. Only a chivving fool would be brazen enough to climb above the crowd in front of so many paun soldiers. But it was Winter's End. I would no more be whipped for climbing the statue than a fiddler would be for taking coins for their songs.

And, even if the soldiers wanted to get to me, they would have to slog through hundreds of others to reach me.

I forced myself to breathe.

The crowd at the front gave a fresh round of cheers as the Lord Soldier climbed the cathedral steps. Two lines of men in black uniforms marched behind him.

The golden doors of the cathedral opened before the soldiers reached them and closed as soon as they'd passed through, keeping the common folk from peering into the Guilds' precious sanctuary for too long.

The sailors in their blue came next. They didn't march in neat columns as they entered the cathedral. A young man with black hair moved at the center of their unruly pack, and even the Lord Sailor laughed at whatever joke the young man had made.

I tried to find a bit of sympathy in my chest for the sailors. They looked almost like common men, like they'd rather drink ale with you than see you dead.

But the healers started up the steps, and any flicker of pity I might have felt vanished.

The Lady Healer turned and waved to the crowd as though she actually thought herself to be a savior of the common folk.

I gripped the star, biting back my urge to scream that the

healers were no better than murderers. How could anyone be grateful for a healer who left the poor to die?

The Lady led her red-clad killers through the golden doors.

The map makers in their green entered next. At least the Lord Map Maker didn't stop to wave at the people. He led his flock straight to the doors. A girl with red hair wore the same map maker's uniform as the men. She walked taller than the rest, though she was the shortest among them. She kept her shoulders thrown back and her chin held high.

At least there was one paun I could feel true pity for. Poor thing had lost herself to the world of men and didn't even have the sense to revel in the power it gave her.

The doors shut again. I squinted through the sunlight glinting off the metal but couldn't see the fancy carvings in the gold from my place on the star.

I'd only been near enough to see the carvings once, when I'd come by late at night and offered a smile to the soldiers guarding the cathedral in exchange for a chance at a closer look.

A soldier had tried to tell me about the scenes and saints the images honored, but all I'd been able to think of was the number of children that could have been fed off the gold the paun had molded into a door.

I'd run away from the soldier and been sick in an alley.

The crowd cheered again as a flock of white-robed scribes climbed slowly up the steps. At the front of the group, two men clasped each other's arms. The older had a shining bald patch. The younger, dark blond hair so neatly groomed I wished the wind would give a great gust just to muss it up. I thought the younger man had been helping the older up the stairs until they reached the top and the hint of a limp marred the younger man's stride.

I had heard of that scribe before. Born on the bastards' island of Ian Ayres and now the heir to the Scribes Guild. Too young for the position, too talented to be unseated—even the common folk liked to chatter about the Ian Ayres-born scribe. The whispers in the shadows called him the Guilded Cripple. I wondered how many in the crowd were disappointed to see a young man with a limp rather than a mangled beast.

Before the door had closed behind the scribes, a golden carriage stopped in front of the steps.

High up on the cathedral walls, horns blared, welcoming the King.

He stepped out of his gilded carriage and smiled for the crowd, waving at his people like the benevolent ruler he pretended to be. His clothing glinted gold in the light, and sour rolled up into my throat.

The Queen stepped out of the carriage next, her gown sparkling like her husband's coat, though she did not smile as the King had. Her face was pale, and the King gripped her hand as though keeping her on her feet.

The King helped the Queen up the steps, leaving the young Princess to face the crowd on her own. The girl was beautiful, and her silver gown made her look like something out of a fairy story. But her smile flickered away as she watched her brother abandon her to the crowd. She nodded to the horde and followed her brother up the steps.

Last to arrive were the purple-robed sorcerers.

The Lady Sorcerer led her pack. She didn't look to the common crowd or to the soldiers as she climbed the steps and sauntered to the door, completely secure in her position. Completely certain that no danger could touch her.

The purple lady was above us all, her power made untouchable by the strength of her magic. She held the throat of the Guilds in her hand as the paun crushed the common folk beneath their fancy boots.

The golden doors closed behind the sorcerers, and the soldiers tightened their ranks around the cathedral.

All the most powerful people in Ibrea packed into one place.

They'd spend hours locked inside, plotting new ways to grow Ilbrea's might.

If a fire could start, flare to life right in the middle of the cathedral, then the paun would burn and Ilbrea would be free.

But only the gods could set a fire like that, and none of them have ever seen fit to be so kind to the common folk.

A fiddle started playing on the far end of the square. A pipe and a drum joined in.

Men rolled out barrels of ale and frie, and the whole square turned to chaos as the celebration of Winter's End truly began. The common folk would dance, and drink, and sing, and laugh while the Guilds decided what new torments to unleash upon the people of Ilbrea.

I could see the spark of the fire that would devour Ilara hiding beneath the celebration. It was in the leering of the soldiers and the red faces of the men who drank to forget their troubles.

The inferno would not come quickly, but it was beyond my power to stop.

I was not strong enough to save the people dancing below from the coming flames.

2

NIKO

Light shone through the stained glass windows, sending dazzling colors glinting off the golden, seven-pointed star inlayed in the center of the white marble floor. Fresh, cool air swept through the cathedral, making the space far more bearable than it had been at the summer council Niko had been dragged to. The stuffy heat of that afternoon had been as tiring as Lord Gareth droning on for three hours about how the other Guilds needed to be more responsible in providing records to the Scribes' Hall.

"Welcome Lords, Ladies, and proud members of the Guilds." The King's voice rang around the cathedral. With nothing in the room but people to stifle the sound, the force of the King's voice boomed loudly enough to ensure even the eldest present would be able to hear. "We have come together to celebrate Winter's End and to plan for Ilbrea's great future."

Applause followed the King's words. Nothing like the raucous cheering of the crowd in the square. Such a rowdy display could never have been allowed inside the cathedral.

Of course, there were times when the grand place was empty. Late at night when the cathedral could be snuck into.

"This great day marks the 775th anniversary of my family's reign over Ilbrea."

Niko shook away daydreams of nights filled with meaningless promises and passionate kisses as the King held out his hand and his sister dutifully stepped forward to join him.

Each of the seven Guilds stood on the same level ground in the cathedral, each at the point of the star that represented their place in Ilbrea. The King's and royals' place was at the tip of the star beneath the largest and grandest of the stained glass windows. The sun streamed through the image of a beautiful woman. Standing below her grandeur, the Princess looked like a child, far younger than anyone who should be allowed in the Guilds' enclave.

"The 777th anniversary is rapidly approaching. An auspicious year for all of Ilbrea and the year my sister will come of age," the King continued. "While we have eternally striven for the protection of Ilbrea and progress for all her people, the time has come to move forward more quickly."

A faint murmur fluttered around the space.

Niko stared at the back of Lord Karron's head, wishing he could read the Lord Map Maker's thoughts.

"Two years from this day, Princess Illia will marry Prince Dagon of Wyrain."

The princess swayed, her pale face pinking for a moment as those staring at her applauded.

Niko clapped with the rest, resisting the urge to run forward, ready to catch the Princess should she faint from nerves.

Mara stood next to him, a smile plastered on her face.

If Niko hadn't known her so well, he might not have noticed the pink flushing Mara's pale skin to a shade closer to the vivid red of her hair.

"A marriage to Wyrain will bring our two great kingdoms closer together, opening paths of commerce that will ensure prosperity for the people of Ilbrea!"

The loudest round of applause yet came from the Guilded.

If the King was seeking new trade routes through the eastern mountains, that would mean work for the map makers.

Niko rocked on his toes, the scroll at his hip near burning in its want to be filled with places yet to be seen.

"I have given each of the Guilds a task as we prepare Ilbrea and her people for the royal wedding and the future of our great country." The King bowed and took a step back, looking to Lady Gwell of the Sorcerers Guild.

Niko let out a silent sigh, resigning himself to the torture of listening to the sorcerer talk.

"The King, in his great wisdom, has assigned these tasks." Lady Gwell's voice grated Niko's ears. It wasn't even the pitch of it, just the sanctimonious air of the woman behind the words. "It is the will of the King that the Soldiers Guild build up their forces. The trouble in the south must be calmed to ensure the safety and ease of the wedding."

The Lord Soldier nodded.

"To do so, the King wishes to swell the soldiers' ranks by accepting unguilded men…"

Niko closed his eyes, letting the hum in his mind drown out Lady Gwell's words. Adding unguilded soldiers would be a disaster. A complete and utter disaster. For every common man the soldiers gained, they would lose a Guilded warrior to displeasure with the Guilds and the King.

A wide valley, that's where he should be, far away from kings and royal weddings and politics.

The valley south of Ilara where the river cut a deep swatch of land away every year when it surged over its banks. He'd mapped that valley twice already, making sure the width of the river was properly recorded.

A faint tickle in the back of Niko's mind was the only sign the sorcerer-made scroll at his hip had begun to draw. It had taken him years to even notice the tiny sensation—the magic that connected map to mind.

He pictured the details of the rocks caught within the flow of the river but still resisting its pounding force, holding steady in their fight against the current.

And flowers.

Bright flowers always flourished on the field in spring. Tiny, golden blooms and great bushes of vivid violet.

Far to the north, the white mountains peeked up, claiming the sky. Their jagged outline marking the northern border of Ilbrea and the end of civilization.

And a beautiful girl sitting beside the river, holding fresh spring flowers to her nose. The girl hadn't been there with him in more than a year, but as long as he thought it convincingly enough, the scroll would sketch her as perfectly as it did each tall blade of wild summer grass.

Perhaps he could give the picture to the beautiful girl later.

A sharp pain in his ankle yanked Niko from his daydream.

Mara glared at him before looking to Lady Gwell.

"The exploration of the southern islands has been beneficial to Ilbrea," Lady Gwell said.

Lord Karron gave a nod, acknowledging her praise.

"While their exploration cannot be halted, the map makers must also turn their efforts closer to home," Lady Gwell pressed on. "The white mountains must be properly charted. For too long we have taken for granted that no person could survive the deadly northern snows. We cannot enter into an alliance with the east without knowing if our northern border leads to unknown foes."

A shiver ran up Niko's spine, not in fear of the mountains to the north, but in dread of the constant snow and ice such exploration would bring.

"The eastern mountains must be mapped as well. As a wedding gift to Princess Illia, the King of Wyrain has agreed to allow our map makers to explore new paths that might lead to his country's borders. If we are to grow with Wyrain, access between the two countries cannot be limited to one trade road. It is the King's wish that you find new paths to bring commerce and harmony with our eastern neighbor."

Lord Karron bowed.

The King stepped forward again. "It is my wish that the Sorcerers Guild ensures the progress of each command. Helping to forge new arms for the soldiers of Ilbrea, creating new medicines for the healers, and rendering aid to any other Guild that should require assistance from our magical brethren."

Lady Gwell bowed deeply.

It was revulsion rather than surprise that twisted in Niko's gut. The sorcerers dug their talons into every facet of the other Guilds, no matter how unwanted their interference might be. Why should the King's plans be immune? But the faint smile on Lady Gwell's lips as the King acknowledged each of the other Guilds was worse than her placing a crown on her own head.

Another sharp kick from Mara reminded Niko to relax his jaw and look pleasant. At least there was a chance he would be sent to map the eastern mountains. It would be better than endless snow.

"Tonight, we celebrate with the people of Ilbrea. The people each of us toils to serve and protect. By the will of Dudia and the grace of the saints, may we all meet here at next Winter's End with joyful news of bountiful progress to share with the people of this great land." The King turned his back on the Guilds to gaze up at the massive, stained glass window of Morelan, the Patron Saint of the royal family.

The rest of the Guilds turned to face the window at their points of the star. Aximander, Saint of the map makers, towered over the cluster of green-clad Guilded.

Aximander's depiction in the glass was much the same as everywhere else. Dark-haired, proud-faced, standing on top of a high mountain. He'd been the first of the Ilbrean map makers, finding a path through the southern mountains to the kingless territories, and sailing west to the Barrens when no other dared risk crossing the Arion Sea.

Niko reverently bowed his head and closed his eyes.

Aximander, watch over us on this year's journeys. Bring the map makers home safely with new wonders to share with the Guilds and Ilbrea. Help us each to journey with a steadfast heart and a mind to our task.

Niko opened his eyes and looked back up at the saint.

And if you could see to it I get sent east instead of to the white mountains, I'd be very grateful. May the will of Dudia be done.

His silent prayer was over before the rest of the map makers', whose heads were still solemnly bowed. Niko had never been particularly taken with the saints of the Guilds or Dudia, the god the Guilds preferred. Even as Lord Karron's apprentice, he'd never been pushed away from the common gods of his childhood. None of the Lord's wards had. Niko was grateful, though it did make long silences for prayer rather boring.

He glanced over to the cluster of blue uniforms.

Kai had stopped praying, too, and stood fidgeting in the midst of the sailors. He winked when Niko caught his eye and gave a smile before nodding toward Adrial at the front of the pack of scribes.

Adrial stood by Lord Gareth's side, looking appropriately somber as he prayed.

They should've both been given chairs. A fellow with a bad leg and a man who'd reached his sixth decade shouldn't have been made to stand for hours while Lady Gwell prattled on.

Niko clenched his hands and took a deep breath, looking back up to Aximander.

Grant me the patience to work alongside the sorcerers for the good of Ilbrea.

"It is time to deliver the news of our great endeavors." The King's voice rang out, breaking the solemn silence.

The royals led the way back out of the cathedral, each of the Guilds filing in as the party before them passed. Sorcerers, soldiers, map makers, sailors, healers, and scribes, all in clumps of matching colors with their Lords in the lead.

The golden doors flew open at a nod from the King, and a wave of noise crashed into the cathedral.

The commoners hadn't wasted the time the Guilds had been locked away—dancing and music filled the square.

The chaos of it, the clashing of sounds and twirling of colors, filled Niko with a kind of excitement nothing inside the council had managed. He peered over the people in front of him, trying to catch sight of the nearest barrel of frie.

"Patience," Mara hushed in his ear. "You can frolic soon enough."

"I don't frolic," Niko whispered. "I revel."

The horns high on the cathedral walls cut over the tumult, silencing the crowd with their first note.

"People of Ilbrea!" the King called to the square. "I bring great news of wondrous things to come. Today, we begin preparations for an alliance with Wyrain. Two years from today, Princess Illia will wed—"

The cheers of the crowd swallowed the rest of his words. The King didn't try to silence them. There were too many details to be shouted from the steps, and some orders were best left to the commoners' imaginations. The unguilded would find out what the King wanted them to know when he wanted them to know it, if they even cared to listen.

After a full minute of bellowing approval, the King finally raised a hand.

"A Happy Winter's End to you all!"

The doors of the golden carriage swung open, waiting for the royals to escape the hordes.

Lord Karron turned to his map makers. "I expect all of you in the hall early tomorrow. I don't want to hear about any of you getting into trouble." He fixed his gaze on Niko before looking to Mara.

Mara's bright red eyebrows shot up, and Niko laughed.

Lord Karron gave him a clap on the shoulder.

"Happy Winter's End." Lord Karron strode down into the crowd, following in the wake of the golden carriage with the other Guild Lords. They would walk together to the palace for the true meeting of the Guilds, where fighting and negotiating would accomplish the real work of the day.

"You two children keep safe," Head Map Maker Seamus said in a mocking, mothering tone, twisting his already lined face into worried wrinkles. "We wouldn't want you to get trampled underfoot."

"We'll be fine," Mara said.

"As long as you're sure." Seamus held up his weathered hands in surrender and backed away.

"Come on." Mara seized Niko's sleeve and dragged him down the steps to where Adrial stood close to Lord Gareth.

"I'm quite sure, Adrial"—Lord Gareth waved a hand to quiet Adrial—"and I won't hear another word about it. I am, after all, the Lord Scribe."

"Yes, sir." Adrial nodded.

"Now, away with you." Lord Gareth shooed as Kai joined their group. "I'm too old to manage Karron's flock. Go enjoy Winter's End. Who knows what chaos will come before there is music to be heard again?"

3

ADRIAL

"Sorry," Adrial muttered as he slowly maneuvered his way through the crowd. "So sorry."

Servants carrying trays of bubbling chamb, sweetmeats, and rich cheeses weaved through the Guilded revelers.

The people in the ballroom weren't separated by Guild color anymore. It was all a confusing mass of mingling and laughing.

Paintings of beautiful landscapes and great lords lined the walls, their golden frames glinting in the light of the sparkling chandeliers. All the finery of the Gilded Hall, from crystal glasses to ornate bannisters, had been polished for the occasion.

A troupe of musicians had been brought in for the Winter's End Ball, and the center of the room had been taken over by dancing.

"Pardon me." Adrial sidestepped a girl in healer red as she dragged a soldier onto the floor.

Pain shot through Adrial's bad leg. He struggled to keep his gait even and face pleasant as he plunged deeper into the crowd.

Standing in the cathedral for hours had been torture, but he couldn't say it. Couldn't allow himself the luxury of going home to sleep. Weakness could not be accepted from Lord Gareth's second, not when so much responsibility fell on the head scribe. Not when Lord Gareth was counting on him.

Not when everyone in Ilara agreed Adrial was too young for the position.

"A faster tune!" Kai shouted from the center of the dancers as the song ended. The people around him cheered as Kai grabbed a girl in white, scooping her into his arms and twirling her around.

"Adrial"—a hand slipped into his—"come on."

Keeping his gaze on the dancers, Adrial let himself be led away.

"Kai's lucky the Sailors Guild has very loose expectations of their men." Allora nodded to the revelers who parted ways to grant her and Adrial a path. "Honestly, he shouldn't be making such a spectacle. And even if he seems to be getting away with terrible decorum, he ought to know better. I should know. I'm the one who worked for years trying to teach that boy manners. "

"He's only having a good time," Adrial said when they reached the edge of the horde and the crowd swallowed the surging mass of dancers. "He's young. Let him enjoy himself."

"What am I, an old maid?" Allora tossed her long, blond hair over her shoulder. "Kai's barely younger than we are, and we know how to behave properly."

"Some of us are made older."

Allora stopped so quickly, Adrial nearly toppled over trying not to run into her.

"A limp and old age are two very different things, Adrial Ayres." She brushed imagined dust off the shoulders of his white robes. "Don't let a bad leg take credit for good manners."

"Thank you, Allora."

"Now come along." Allora smoothed the folds of her green and gold gown. "The others will be waiting for us."

A wide, stone staircase cut up from the corner of the room. A few people leaned over the railings, either watching the party below or trying to hide how much chamb they'd drunk.

A young man in healer red gripped a glass of frie as he dangled precariously over the crowd. The pungent smell of the strong liquor emanated from the man as much as from his glass.

Allora glared at the man as they climbed the stairs, keeping Adrial's hand firmly in hers as they weaved past a sorcerer trying to fend off the affections of a healer.

Adrial didn't need the help to dodge the couples on the stairs. He could manage the steps on his own, even make better speed than Allora allowed. But she'd been helping him for years. Shaking her off would have been a cruel slight at Winter's End.

And, if he really dared to be honest with himself, he enjoyed the comfort of having someone to walk with. He might not be dancing in the crowd below, but at least he wouldn't be spending his evening alone.

"Are you really hauling us all away from the dancing?" Kai bounded up the stairs to catch them.

Mara followed behind him at a statelier pace, her lips pursed as she hid her smile.

"I'm not hauling anyone away from anything," Allora said. "I'm merely trying to spend time with *my family* before they scatter to the winds on the King's command. If you'd rather cavort with someone you've never met before and will probably never see again—"

"There's nothing I would rather do than spend the evening with the lovely Allora Karron." Kai beat them to the top of the stairs, grabbed Allora's free hand, and gave it a dramatic kiss. "Just promise me there will still be dancing."

"I'll dance with you, you getch." Allora breezed past him. "But only out of pity."

"And you, Mara?" Kai caught her around the waist, twirling her down the hall. "Will you dance with me?"

"I will always dance with you, Kai." Mara laughed as he spun her under his arm.

"Do you want to see what I've planned for us or not?" Allora's severe tone did not match the glimmer in her eyes.

"Of course we do, Allora." Adrial bowed, unable to keep from laughing as Kai lifted Mara high overhead.

"Don't break her!" Allora squealed.

"Not everyone is as fragile as Lady Allora Karron." Kai set Mara back on her feet. "Please forgive me and show us your surprise, miss."

"I don't know why I bother trying to do anything nice for the lot of you." Allora poked Kai's nose and beckoned them all down the corridor.

One side of the hall was lined with doors, but the other was painted with a glorious mural of the southern countryside, an image broken only by one, wide double door set with glass panes.

Allora flung the glass doors open. "Welcome to the Karron clan party!"

A balcony looked out over the thousands of common revelers in the square and the shining white cathedral beyond. Shouts and cheers rose from the crowd below, but the balcony was empty.

"Allora," Mara breathed, stepping past her to take in the view, "what have you done?"

Tiered trays of cakes, fruits, and other delights sat on one round table. Bottles of chamb chilled in the spokes of a compass-shaped ice sculpture. Couches draped with warm blankets to guard against the night chill sat next to candelabras with brightly burning candles.

"And how did you do it?" Niko asked from the doorway.

Tham stood behind Niko's shoulder. While Niko radiated delight, Tham's brow furrowed as he took in the lavish display.

"I know all the best people." Allora grinned. "Sometimes being nice means people are thrilled to help you. You might consider trying it sometime."

"Having coin to pay doesn't hurt, I'm sure." Kai grabbed a bottle of chamb and began pouring a glass for each of the six.

"It's wonderful, Allora." Adrial moved toward the rail.

Torches on poles that reached high above the crowd shed light on the square.

"A toast then?" Kai pressed a glass into Adrial's hand.

"But of course!" Niko grabbed a glass. "A drink for everyone. Even Tham."

"I'm fine." Tham stood in the doorway, hovering on the edge of the group. There wasn't a hint of merriment on his face, but then his dark hair, complexion, and eyes had the effect of making him appear somber at the best of times.

"You must have a drink for the toast." Allora flitted over, glass in hand. "Adrial and I are about to be abandoned in Ilara while you all adventure yet again. Be kind and toast with us. Give me a perfect night to remember when I'm lonely all year."

Without a word, Tham accepted the glass.

"To the Karron clan." Allora held her glass high. "May we bring honor to Ilbrea and the name of Karron wherever we go!"

"To Lord Karron." Mara raised her glass.

"To Lord Karron!" Adrial joined in with the rest of the pack.

"It really is remarkable." Mara sipped her chamb, wrinkling her nose at the taste. "Lord Karron manages to collect one daughter—"

Allora curtsied.

"—two apprentices—"

Mara raised her glass to Niko.

"—and three wards—"

"To the motherless children!" Kai cheered.

"—and look how well each of us has done," Mara finished.

"I really thought one of us would have ended up in prison by now." Niko poured himself another glass of chamb.

"I really thought it would be me." Kai threw himself back onto a couch. "Or maybe Tham."

"I'm quiet about the trouble I make." Tham gave a rare smile. "It would have been you."

"And we always knew who would rise the highest." Mara pulled two sandwiches from the tray, passing one to Tham before biting into her own. "To Adrial, the future Lord Scribe of Ilbrea."

"I was always certain our sweet Adrial would achieve greatness." Allora leaned on the railing by his side. "From the day my father dragged a ragged boy from Ian Ayres into the Map Master's Palace, I was quite sure there was utter brilliance beneath those caked-on pounds of mud."

"To our brilliant prodigy, Adrial Ayres!" Kai raised his fresh glass of chamb.

"I'm not brilliant. I'm just the only one of us not to have caused any trouble." Adrial smiled. "And perhaps becoming a lord isn't what it should be." He sipped his chamb, letting the dry sweetness flood his mouth.

He could say it to them. They were his family. They'd all been raised by Lord Karron, though none but Allora shared Lord Karron's blood. They'd seen each other at their worst and best and still held fast to their little clan. "Master Gareth wants me to make the vellum. He thinks it will be a good way to show my worth. To prove to the Scribes Guild that he was right to name me as his heir."

"What vellum?" Niko asked as the rest of them looked somewhere between awed and sympathetic.

"Didn't you listen in the council?" Allora asked.

"Of course he didn't," Mara said. "I had to kick him to make him look in the right direction."

"The King wants a new vellum made." Tham finally stepped onto the balcony, joining the rest of the group. "A new, fully illuminated volume detailing the history of the royal Willoc family in Ilbrea. A wedding gift for Princess Illia to take with her to her new home in Wyrain."

"And you're to make it?" Allora clasped Adrial's hand. "That's wonderful, Adrial. Just fantastic!"

"A book like that will have to be a real work of art," Kai said.

"He'll be brilliant." Allora shot a glare at Kai.

"If I'm not, if I fail, all of Ilbrea will know." A lump formed somewhere between his lungs and throat as he said the words. "A project this large will take the full two years."

"The vellum will be magnificent." Mara set down her glass and pulled Adrial into a tight hug. "Lord Karron will be so proud of you. We're all so proud of you."

"To Adrial." Niko raised his glass.

"To Adrial!" the others chorused.

"What about the rest of you?" Allora asked. "Where are you going, and how soon are you abandoning us?"

"No idea," Kai said. "The King wants a fleet of new ships and a path plotted around the horn at the southern tip of the continent. Who knows where in that I'll fall? Though I do hope I'll get to sail around the horn. See the great southern storms, fight the wind herself."

"Don't talk like that, you terrify me," Allora chided.

"Like you've never been shipwrecked before," Kai laughed.

"Hush, you." Allora blushed and sipped her chamb.

"I've no idea where I'll be sent," Mara said. "We're meeting in the Map Makers' Hall tomorrow. I suppose your father will tell us where we're to be assigned then."

"And our stalwart Tham?" Allora asked.

"I don't know." Tham's eyes flitted to Mara for a moment. "I've experience guarding the map makers' journeys, and with the amount of work that needs done, they can't venture into uncharted lands with new blood who can't tell a compass from a sword."

"I'm sure my father will request you, as always." Allora raised her glass to Tham, giving a not so subtle wink to Mara.

"It takes time to organize a journey," Niko said. "No matter what the King wants, we won't be able to leave for a week at least, more likely two."

"Two weeks of company, Adrial," Allora cooed. "How very lucky are we?"

"Exceptionally." Adrial nodded.

"A lot can happen in two weeks." Niko sat forward on his couch. "You could plan a whole wedding in two weeks if a certain girl who knows all the right people set her mind to it."

"Are you planning on getting married, Nikolas? I must meet the lucky girl." Allora took a long drink of chamb.

"Oh, Allora." Mara poured herself another glass.

"For the love of Aximander's greatness, just marry me, Allora." Niko dropped to his knees. "I'll beg in front of those we like best, just marry me."

"Will he bark like a dog, too?" Kai whispered loudly.

"Marry you?" Allora laughed.

If he hadn't spent years with her, Adrial might not have noticed the hurt in Allora's tone.

"Marry you and spend two weeks in your grand company? Leave my father's magnificent palace on the cliffs to move into a small house where I can console myself in your long absences that at least I'm a wife? I'd rather not."

"You break my heart with every rejection." Niko slumped dramatically to the ground.

"Then stop asking." Allora tossed her hair over her shoulder and turned toward the square.

"And what will you do, my beautiful Allora? Marry a merchant? A commoner?" Niko asked.

"She'd never lower herself so," Kai said. "None but a Guilded man for Allora Karron."

"Perhaps I'll marry Adrial," Allora said. "Be the Lord Scribe's wife."

"Careful, Allora," Adrial said. "Tease one too many times, and poor Niko might believe you."

"No, I refuse." Niko ran to Allora, sweeping her into his arms, leading her in a dance to match the music coming from the square below. "I will have you or no one. You have held my heart for years, Allora Karron. I have learned patience none but Dudia can match."

"I will not have a husband whose breath smells of frie." Allora laughed, leaning into Niko's arms as he spun her.

"Tham, will you dance with Mara?" Kai asked.

"Not tonight," Tham said.

"Then it is my happy duty." Kai pulled Mara from her seat, leading her in a rather more athletic dance than the one Niko and Allora swayed to.

Adrial turned back out to the square, closing his eyes, trying to memorize the laughter of his friends.

Allora was right. It would be a long, lonely time before they were together again.

The music changed, and the crowd cheered as the new song began.

Adrial opened his eyes, wanting to bask in the joy of the people below.

A girl danced at the center of the throng, spinning as she flitted from partner to partner, never staying near one man long enough for him to wrap his arms around her, though most of them tried. Her hair shimmered in the torchlight, one moment seeming pale purple, the next deep blue, matching the tight bodice she wore. Tiers of fabric cut into slices, like fish scales of every color imaginable, made the layers of her skirt.

She twirled between two men, and her skirt swirled around her like a cloud.

It was as though a fairy had escaped a children's tale and landed in the middle of the cathedral square. She tipped her head back and laughed.

Adrial wished he could hear the sound over the music.

A man dressed in the dull brown and yellow of the Guilds' servants waved as he wound his way toward her, his gaze fixed on the fluttering of her hair.

Adrial gripped the rail, not letting go even when pain snuck into his bad shoulder. Surely, the girl hadn't done anything wrong. There was no reason for her to be in trouble with the Gilded Hall. There was no rule against dancing in the square on Winter's End.

The girl smiled as the man reached her, letting the servant lean in to speak in her ear.

Her eyes flicked up to the balcony, landing on Adrial.

Heat rose to Adrial's face. He shouldn't have been watching. Not that there was anything wrong with watching the dancers.

The girl cut through the crowd, keeping her gaze locked on Adrial, not pausing as a man offered her a drink, or as a child poked at her flowing skirt.

Adrial tried to pull his hands from the railing, tried to look away from the square. But there was an enchantment about the girl, an undeniable pull as she reached the front of the building.

She finally looked away, examining the columns that held up the stone balcony.

Air flooded back into Adrial's lungs. It was only a coincidence the girl had looked at him, nothing more. Still he couldn't pull his gaze away from her.

She was only twenty feet below him now, and the light from the front of the building showed her hair as it truly was—not one color that changed in the light, but a dozen beautiful colors spread haphazardly through the strands.

Adrial's heart stopped as the girl looked up at him and winked.

She grabbed on to the stone flowers that coated the column and began to climb. The movement was as easy as that of a cat scaling a tree. The girl pulled herself up, rose by rose, her toes finding purchase on the spirals cut deep into the stone.

"Adrial, what are you..." Allora began before gasping, "By Aximander's greatness," as the girl pulled herself over the railing and onto the balcony.

"Hello, scribe." The girl smiled.

Tham stepped forward, pulling his knife from its sheath.

"Going to stab a girl for climbing a balcony?" The girl raised an eyebrow at Tham. "Didn't know the soldiers had sunk so low."

"How dare—" Allora began, but the girl turned back to Adrial and pulled three glass vials from deep within the folds of her layered skirt.

"I'll be by in the morning to discuss your order, scribe." She pressed the vials into Adrial's hand and started toward the glass doors. "But fair warning, my work is very expensive."

Without a backwards glance, she strolled into the hall and out of sight.

"What?" Allora squeaked indignantly.

"Who was she?" Kai stared after her.

"More importantly, what did she give you?" Mara peered over Adrial's shoulder.

Adrial held the vials up to a glowing candelabra.

The first held a black so deep, the light couldn't pass through it. The second, a pale lilac to match the most prominent color woven through the girl's hair. And the third, a vibrant red that seemed to hold a spark of fire hidden just out of sight.

"Ink," Adrial said after a long moment. "She's brought me ink."

"An inker climbed the balcony to give you samples?" Allora shut the balcony doors. "Commoners can't seem to understand their place in the world these days."

"Marks for determination though," Niko said. "That was a bit of a climb."

"I suppose this will be your life from now on," Kai sighed. "Beautiful, technicolor women fighting to win your business. Perhaps I should have chosen a more scholarly path. Too late for me, I suppose. Ah, well. A toast to Adrial. May many women scale our beloved scribe's balcony."

4

MARA

"I have to go." Tham's whisper pulled Mara from sleep.

She curled into the warmth of his chest, wrapping her arms around him as though she could push back the sunrise through mere defiance.

"Mara."

She could hear the smile in his voice. The easy, gentle tone he so rarely used with anyone else.

"What if I say no?" Mara kissed his chest. His thick muscles built from a childhood at sea and years of training with the Soldiers Guild relaxed at her touch. "What if I say you can't leave me? That you have to stay here with me forever?"

"Then I'll gladly accept your decision." Tham pressed his lips to the tangles of her curly, red hair. "But in an hour, my commander will start looking for me. Soon after, Lord Karron will start looking for you."

Mara threw the covers back with a huff, letting the cold of the morning steal the last of her happy dream. "Fine. You're right. Duty and importance, and all those wonderful things must outweigh my will to stay happily in bed."

Tham crawled out over her, not even bothering to try and

make her get up first. With a twist of the key, the lamp lit, filling the room with its dim glow. The dull light cast shadows across the deep scars on Tham's back. Ancient reminders of his punishment for the first time he'd saved her life.

Mara caught Tham around the middle, kissing the deepest scar before pressing her cheek to his back. "Are you meeting with Lord Kearney this morning?"

"We've all been called to the barracks hall." Tham lifted Mara's hands, kissing her palms before releasing himself from her grasp.

"Do you know what he'll say?" Mara found her green pants on the floor, giving up any pretense that she might go back to sleep once Tham left. "Do you know where you'll be sent?"

The question hung in the air as Tham dragged on his black pants and thick leather boots. "The King wants peace in the southern country. Most of the soldiers will probably be sent there. He wants unguilded trained as soldiers, too, so some will stay in Ilara to help with training, or maybe be sent out to recruit. But I don't think I'll be wanted for either of those."

"Because you should stay with the map makers." Mara fought to keep her tone even. "You've been guarding the journeys for two years now, ever since you were given your mark. We have three journeys going out by the King's orders. Two to territories we've never explored. I know Lord Karron had other plans as well—"

"Mara." Tham caught her hands. She hadn't even realized she been flinging them about. "Lord Kearney knows my experience. He knows my strengths. He'll send me where he will."

"You could ask—"

"It doesn't work for soldiers the way it does for map makers." Tham pulled her into his arms, letting her bury her face against his bare chest. "If I asked to stay with you, they would know."

"Let them." Mara tipped her chin up to look into Tham's dark eyes. It was so easy to remember when they'd met a few short years ago, when the thought of being separated was only a distant nightmare. "I don't care if they know about us. What will it do, ruin my chance of catching a proper husband?"

It was the wrong thing to say. She knew it the moment the words fell from her lips.

His whole body stiffened as he let go of her.

"You chose to be a map maker, Mara. You knew going in you wouldn't be allowed to marry." Tham yanked on his shirt, hiding his dark skin beneath the smooth, black fabric.

"I know." Mara caught his hand. "I wanted to be a map maker. I gave up the protection of marriage. I made that choice."

"And I stay." There was no anger in his voice, only sadness, which hurt Mara worse than any fury. "I crawl into your window at night, hiding in the shadows, so no one knows I've been here. The only time I ever pray to Saint Dannach is when I pray to be sent wherever you go. I want to fight by your side, Mara. I would gladly die to defend you."

"Tham—"

"I will climb into your window whenever you'll have me for the rest of my days." Tham took Mara's hand and placed her palm on his chest. "But never forget I would marry you in an instant. I would have married you the day you came of age. You chose to be a map maker. I never had a choice in loving you."

Mara rose up on her toes, wrapping her arms around Tham's neck.

"I know." She brushed her lips against his cheek, reveling in the roughness of his early morning stubble. "I love you. More than anything in Ilbrea, I love you. If there were a way—"

"There's not." Tham kissed her forehead. "You're a map maker. I'm a soldier. The best we can do is pray the Guilds keep us together."

"And if Allora demands Lord Karron assign you as my guard?"

"Only a fool would try to stop Allora Karron from doing anything her heart desires."

"And if I begged Allora to demand you be assigned to me?" Mara kissed Tham's neck.

"There is nothing in Ilbrea that can stop Mara Landil when she wants something."

She could hear the smile in his voice as she kissed his cheek.

"And if I'm on the journey to the white mountains," Mara teased, "would you be trapped in the snow for me?"

"Mara"—Tham took her face in his hands, interrupting the trail of her kisses—"I have faced death and danger by your side. I will spend my life keeping you safe, even if it means facing a terrible wall of snow."

Mara leaned in, catching his mouth in a kiss before he could speak again. "I love you," she whispered as he pulled away.

"And I love you, Mara. More than the stars."

Before her heart could find a steady rhythm, he'd stepped away and grabbed his jacket from the chair.

"Just a few more minutes," Mara begged, though she knew it would do no good. "Please, just a little longer."

"If I don't go now, I never will." A cold gust of air flew through the room as Tham slid the window open. "And if I'm marched out of the Soldiers Guild, there will be no hope of my following you as you map our world."

"I hate it when you're sensible." Mara stole one last kiss as he threw his leg over the windowsill.

"Light the candle." Tham brushed a curl off Mara's forehead and disappeared into the early morning darkness.

Mara held her breath, waiting for the dull thud of him reaching the ground. A moment later, a figure darted through the shadows. Taking a shuddering breath, Mara fought back the tears that burned in her eyes.

She had chosen this life. There was no going back. It had all been decided years ago.

Her fingers found the compass mark on her left forearm. Too well she remembered the pain of the marking the day she became a map maker's apprentice. The needle in the mark twisted, pointing due north. A gift of magic to be sure she could always find her way home.

But home always moved when it was a person and not a place.

The first red rays of sun peered up over the sea. Soon, the servants of the Map Master's Palace would slip through the halls, preparing everything for Lord Karron to wake.

Mara shut the window and finished dressing in a minute, quickly forcing her hair into a braid as she slipped out into the hall.

She was the only one of the map makers to live in Lord Karron's home. There were no barracks for the map makers as there were for the soldiers. Most of the male map makers were married with families of their own, living in Ilara.

As a female map maker, Mara was a rarity. Marriage and children could never be allowed for her. How could the Guilds endorse a mother abandoning her children to trek on dangerous journeys?

A father could leave, but a mother...

Anger surged through Mara's chest. Leaning into the shadows of the hall, she pressed the heel of her hand to her heart.

Fair doesn't matter. It is what it is, and there's nothing to be done.

The sun peered in through the windows of the long hall, shedding gray light onto the portraits of the long line of Lord Map Makers to have ruled the Guild. They were her lineage—the height to which each map maker strove to ascend.

Pushing herself off the wall, Mara crept down the hall, nodding at the servants as they appeared. She had lived in the palace since she'd become Lord Karron's ward when she was just a little girl. It was no strange sight for her to be wandering into the family's wing of the house, past the ornately carved wooden door that led to what had been her room until she'd insisted on being moved.

Allora had fought the change. So had Lord Karron, for that

matter. But at least Lord Karron understood. It was one thing for everyone to know she had been raised his ward, another for them to know she ate breakfast with the Lord Map Maker every morning.

Allora had insisted Mara at least stay in the house. So Mara had moved as far away as the palace would allow. Hers was the only room in the guest wing to see regular use. The other bedrooms were only ever occupied when parties were thrown. The seclusion offered her peace and freedom from the bustle of Lord Karron's home. Her room's proximity to the orchard made Tham's coming and going much simpler.

At the end of the family wing, four doors surrounded a grand bay window that looked out over the cliffs and down onto the city of Ilara. Only the far edge of the city was visible from this angle. The rest stayed hidden beneath the height of the cliff.

Ships had already started moving away from the docks, the only sign of life visible from so far above.

Mara closed her eyes, remembering the scent of the sea surrounding her as the wind burrowed through her hair.

The thrill of adventure swirled lightness through her limbs. Then she thought of journeying alone, and dread crashed back into her chest.

Mara turned toward Allora's door and didn't bother knocking before swinging it silently open.

The new sun fought valiantly through the curtains, giving just enough light to silhouette Allora sleeping peacefully in her bed. Her blond hair splayed around her, catching the dim bits of light like a dazzling star.

"Allora," Mara whispered, shutting the door behind her. "Allora."

"Mara, have you come to wake me before dawn?" Allora mumbled without opening her eyes.

"It's past dawn." Mara grinned.

"Still much too early."

"I need to talk to you." Mara crept toward the bed.

"Don't you dare put your filthy boots in my bed, Mara Landil," Allora groaned, throwing back the covers to make room for Mara.

A giggle escaped Mara as she kicked off her boots and climbed into the warm sheets.

"What's wrong?" Allora finally opened her eyes.

"Nothing's wrong. I just wanted to talk."

"Does it have to do with a brooding soldier and where he's going to be assigned?" Allora sighed dramatically.

"They could send him anywhere—to the south, or out to sea…" It could be years until she saw Tham again. This time, she didn't fight the tears that spilled onto Allora's silk pillows.

"Shh," Allora hushed, wriggling over to wrap her arms around Mara. "You've never been pretty when you cry, and there's no need for it besides."

"Allora—"

"Father was still awake when I arrived home last night, waiting up for me as though I were a wayward child. I arranged it all before I let him sleep. You're going to the white mountains, and Tham will be your personal guard."

"Allora, thank you!" Mara held her tightly.

"Only *thank you*? No anger at my interference? I thought you might at least be cross about the snow. But father and I agreed it has to be a small expedition and you or Niko would have to be one of the two map makers sent."

"And Niko's familiar with the east," Mara said. "I don't care where Tham and I go, as long as we're together."

"It really wasn't hard, you know. Father knows about the two of you. Maybe he doesn't really *know*, but he understands separation would be devastating to you both. And the dear sweet man loves you enough that destroying you would break his kind, old heart."

Mara laughed, brushing the tears from her cheeks. "I don't

know if I should be appalled your father knows about Tham and me or relieved he isn't furious."

"A bit of both, I suppose. It would be so much simpler if you could just marry him."

"I know." Pain crept back into Mara's chest.

"But it's against Guild laws, and you can't leave the Guild." Allora turned toward Mara so their faces were only inches apart, just the way they used to share secrets when they were young. "You and Niko can't leave the Guild. Father relies on the three of us in ways he can't trust the rest of the map makers. I don't know what he'd do if you or Niko abandoned him."

"Find two other map makers foolish enough to cross the Sorcerers Guild?"

"I don't think two such fools exist. But as I'm the one who's stuck here guarding our deadly secrets, I'm sure the three of us will hang nicely together when the day of our execution arrives."

"Your father will be strung up beside us for letting Niko and me explore such forbidden secrets," Mara added. "And Tham for helping on the journeys."

"Kai and Adrial will be a sad sight, alone at our funerals." Allora smiled. "But our path is set, and we all must follow where it leads."

"I wouldn't change it," Mara said. "Maybe small things, but I wouldn't change our little clan or the wonders we've seen."

"It would be nice if you could just marry Tham, though," Allora sighed. "Every time you come creeping into my room, I worry he's put a child in you. Then I would have to fake some terrible illness that would make it utterly impossible for you to leave my side. We'd have to spend months on end in seclusion to prevent contagion. It's the only way we could hide you well enough to keep you from being sent to Ian Ayres never to return."

"Have you truly been plotting to hide me?" Mara laughed.

"I could never let you be sent to that horrible island, illegitimate child or not." Allora pinched Mara for laughing. "And I wouldn't let your child be raised on Ian Ayres either. Once the child was born, I would have to announce my early spinsterhood by taking on your secret child as my ward."

"What?"

"I couldn't let them take your baby from us," Allora chided. "It would have to stay with me."

"Spinsterhood might not be your only option. You could marry Niko and pretend the child is truly yours."

"A child with dark skin and flaming red hair? I'm sure no one would question the honesty of it."

"But you could marry him. He really does love you, you know."

"I do know." The teasing slipped from Allora's face. "And it makes saying *no* so much harder."

"But you love him, too." Mara squeezed Allora's hand. "I know you do."

"It isn't loving him that's the problem." Allora bit her lip, an old trait she used to scold Mara for. "I spent my childhood waiting for my father to come home from his journeys. He'd triumphantly return, tell me wonderful stories of adventure, and abandon me all over again. Then he piled wards into the palace and being left behind wasn't so dreadful anymore. Father would leave, but at least I had all of you beside me.

"Now we've all taken our places in the world, and my place is to stay here. I don't mind it, really. I know the work I do here is important, even if it would see me hanged. But I'm back to being left behind. I love Niko, more than my heart can stand, but I don't think I could survive being a wife who's always waiting. It would break me beyond repair."

"Oh, Allora." It was Mara's turn to hold her friend as silent tears trickled down her cheeks. "I don't think he'll ever stop trying to convince you to marry him."

"Good," Allora laughed through her tears. "I don't think I could survive that either."

"What a sorry clan we are." Mara wiped Allora's tears with her sleeve.

"You can't marry Tham. I won't marry Niko."

"Kai loves everyone a little too much. And Adrial—"

"Loves his work," Allora said. "Think of how many unhappy fools can't even claim that."

"We'll be all right, won't we?" Mara held tight to Allora's hand. "The lot of us?"

"Of course we will. We're Karrons. We're survivors."

5

ADRIAL

"It's not as hard as you're making it out to be," Natalia said. "If you think something is impossible, it will be so."

"I am trying, though." Taddy's voice cracked as he spoke. "Please don't think I'm not trying."

Adrial leaned against the wall of his workroom, just outside the main office of the scribes' shop. He could go out and look at whatever Natalia had decided didn't obtain Guild perfection, but there was no need. She could handle the shop's apprentice as well as he could.

"There's already spots on the corner," Natalia said.

A whimpering groan followed her words.

"I know you're trying, Taddy," Natalia said, "but you're going to have to get it right eventually. So go on and start it again."

Taddy gave a shaky sigh, and the scratch of his pen sounded a moment later.

Adrial clicked his door closed and crept back to his desk as quietly as his limp would allow.

It was almost noon. Soon, the servants would bring food for the scribes in the office, and poor Taddy would have a break.

Nearly half the day had passed, and Adrial had spent all his time staring at the sheets of paper laid out on his oversized desk.

His workroom was nearly as large as the whole outer office, where eight scribes took on the daily tasks needed to keep the city running—writing official notices, entering information into the Guilds' records, creating documents for marriages and taxes. Normal scribes' work for the scholars who maintained order in Ilara.

But the paper on Adrial's desk was not meant for posting commands from the King or granting names to newborns.

This paper was perfect. Thick and supple, made by sorcerers' hands. Adrial trailed his finger along the edge of the parchment and, whether it was only his imagination or not, could feel traces of magic the sorcerers had left behind.

The six best-loved histories of Ilbrea lay on a table to one side of his office, each opened to the first page.

He wasn't to make a copy of any existing book. That could easily be done by many other hands. The King's command was to create a new work, combining the best of each volume with illuminated illustrations worthy of a gift for a princess.

Adrial buried his face in his hands. He had the paper and the books. There was nothing for it but to start working. He opened his eyes and stared down at the sheet of paper propped up on the tilted portion of his desk.

In the light streaming down from the high window, the pigments were even more remarkable than they had been by candlelight the night before. Three streaks of color marked the parchment. The truest black he'd ever seen, a pale purple so lyrical it seemed to swim of its own accord, and a red so violent, fire would be jealous of the ink's complexion.

A beautiful madwoman had delivered the most perfect inks he'd ever seen and had sworn to visit him this morning. The fear of her not coming to the shop warred against his reasonable desire to keep insanity as far as possible from the Princess's vellum.

Chimes sounded from the front of the shop.

Adrial's door muffled Natalia's cheerful greeting. He held his breath, waiting for the new arrival to answer. A low, gruff voice sounded.

Adrial sank into his chair and leaned back, letting the wood dig into his bad shoulder.

The girl had probably gone to the library. That was where the scribes' most detailed work was usually handled. The best of their trade spent their time in the library workshops with giant skylights, dozens of desks, and plenty of guards to keep the outside world from bothering them.

But Adrial was the Head Scribe of Ilara. The head scribe's duty was to do his work and manage the business of the scribes' shop where common folk could come for their needs. It was meant as a way to train the head to manage the Guild while maintaining his own work, but the chimes at the door made thinking impossible. Especially when any ring might mean the arrival of the inker.

"Waiting will do you no good, Adrial Ayres." He straightened his cuffs. "Start on the work, and get it done."

"Head Scribe," Taddy called through Adrial's door. "Head Scribe, there's a woman come to see you, sir." The touch of frightened excitement in Taddy's young voice left no room for doubt as to who the woman was.

"Yes, Taddy." Adrial rose quickly from his chair, ignoring the pinch of pain in his leg. "I'll be right out."

The door to his workroom flew open before he could reach for the handle.

The girl stood in the door, technicolor hair draped over her shoulder, a teal basket hanging from her arm. She wore the same skirt made of hundreds of swatches of fabric and a bodice tied tight enough Allora would have been shocked at the girl's lack of modesty.

"I didn't tell her to open the door, sir." Pink devoured Taddy's cheeks.

Adrial's heart stuttered as he wondered if his face had betrayed him as well.

"Don't worry, love." The girl tousled Taddy's hair and gave him a wink. "I'm sure the scribe has been waiting for me."

"Actually, he has spent…" Taddy's voice trailed away at a glare from Adrial.

"Thank you, Taddy."

"Yes, sir." Taddy backed away, keeping his eyes on the girl.

"Have you decided on your ink order?" The girl closed the door, shutting out the still-staring Taddy.

Adrial opened his mouth to speak but couldn't find words.

"Are you a scribe or a fish?" The girl trailed her fingers along the edge of his shining wooden desk, stopping at the portion that was tipped up, displaying her inks. "You clearly like the colors, so what's the trouble? The crown keeping you on a tight budget?"

"No." Adrial fought to keep his tone level.

"So you've promised the work to another inker?" She picked up the parchment and held it to the light.

"No."

"Then what's the problem?" The girl tipped her head to the side. Her hair shifted with the movement, displaying the pale skin of her neck.

Adrial dug his nails into his palms, willing his eyes not to drift any lower.

"This vellum is important," Adrial said, gaining confidence from the firmness of his voice. "You climbed into a private party and gave me three good—"

"Exquisite." The girl planted her hands on the desk and leaned toward Adrial. She smiled at him as though she knew exactly how hard he was trying not to look at her chest fighting to break free from the confines of her bodice.

"They are exquisite colors." Adrial held up his hands as she opened her mouth to speak. "I can't let you make the ink for the vellum. I want to use the same inker for the whole project. Everything needs to match. I don't know you. I don't even know your name. How can I be sure you can maintain this quality of work, or if you can even make any other colors?"

He held his breath, waiting for her to storm out or worse, cry.

Instead, she reached into her basket. "My name in Ena Bairn. It's a pleasure to meet you, scribe. Of course you don't know me, I'm not from Ilara. My home is farther south. Which means"—she pulled a jar of pure map maker green from her basket and held it up to the light. The color sparkled like emeralds. Before Adrial could reach for the jar, she'd set it on the table with a satisfying clunk—"I make southern ink. It's brighter to start out with, harder to smudge, and won't fade like your northern-made, chivving rot. I'm the only one in the city who knows how to make this quality ink." She pulled a deep-blue jar from her basket. "And, as you're nigh on drooling over it, I'm sure you're smart enough to know just how good my work is."

"I-I'm sure it's fantastic, but—"

"How many inkers came by this morning hoping for the job?" Ena lifted a bottle of violet ink from her basket.

"Five." Adrial's fingers itched for a quill. The pigments matched the colors of the Guilds so perfectly, if he used each hue to outline a portion of the star…

"Did you take any samples from them?" Ena stepped closer, a sly smile twisting her rose-pink lips.

"No, but I've seen their work before." Adrial swallowed as she stopped six inches from him. He forgot to breathe as the scent of wildflowers swirled around him.

Ena was barely shorter than Adrial. Her bright blue eyes were nearly level with his.

"Don't lie, scribe. You haven't a talent for it. You didn't take their samples because you were waiting for me. Because you knew whatever I brought you would be far better than any ink those slitches could hope to make." She held a jar of gleaming gold in the breath of space between their faces. "You know you want it. I'm the only one who can make it. And you're going to pay dearly for it."

"Fine." Adrial forced the word past the unnatural dryness in his throat. "You can make the ink for the vellum."

"Good. I was worried I might have to convince you." Ena winked and turned to Adrial's worktable, stacking his papers to make room for her basket.

"I was working on those."

"And I'm sure you worked very hard on each of those empty pages. Don't worry. I won't harm your precious parchment."

Adrial's heart flipped as he caught a glimpse of the inside of the basket. Nestled in the colorfully stained fabric were another dozen jars. Cerulean blue, dazzling sapphire, and blazing yellow were scattered in with nine jars of pitch black.

"Do you like them?" Ena whispered.

His shoulder grazed hers. He'd moved forward without even meaning to.

"Yes." Adrial limped back a step while heat flamed in his cheeks.

"Good." Ena lifted the jars out of her basket one by one, holding each up to the light from the high window for Adrial to examine before setting it on the table. "I thought these would get you a good start. You can tell me what colors you need from here."

"I'm not sure what I'll need." Adrial wished he could swallow his words the moment he spoke them. He was the head scribe, set to be the youngest Guild Lord in a century. Indecision was a luxury he could not afford.

"Are these the books you're supposed to be copying?" Ena

swept toward the table of books, the colorful layers of her skirt whispering around her as she moved.

"Not copying." Adrial followed her, carefully keeping his distance. "I'm combining and adding, writing new text and drawing completely original illustrations."

"They're beautiful." Ena leaned over the oldest of the vellums. "I've never seen a book like this."

"There aren't many to be seen outside the library and the Royal Palace." Adrial gingerly turned a page in the book. An illustration of a magnificent bird covered the next page. With sweeping feathers in the colors of the Guilds, the bird soared over a map outlining the shore where Ilbrea met the Arion Sea.

"You're going to make a book like this?" Ena looked to Adrial, a tiny wrinkle pinching between her eyebrows as she studied him.

"I've a bad leg, not an unsteady hand." Heat rose in Adrial's face.

Ena crossed her arms and leaned back to perch on the table with the books.

The scribe in Adrial wanted to shout at her not to lean on the table that held the priceless volumes. But she held his gaze, and the words drifted soundlessly from his mind.

"I don't think I've ever met a person capable of creating something that beautiful," Ena said as though stating a simple, unimpressive fact. "What colors will you need?"

"All of them."

"You might need to give me a little more than that," Ena laughed.

The sound was free and beautiful.

Adrial's heart twirled in his chest.

"I'll need a deep blue and a bright blue for the first pages." A sky, that's how he needed to show the beginnings of Ilbrea. A crisp, blue sky over a land longing to be discovered.

"Gods and stars, scribe, you're going to have to do better than that. Between bright blue and deep blue there are a hundred shades waiting. Here." She pushed herself off the table and took Adrial by the shoulders.

His skin burned beneath her touch as she backed him to the center of the room.

"We'll do this the easy way."

"Easy way?" Adrial's voice squeaked like he was no better off than Taddy.

Ena leaned in, her cheek brushing against his as she whispered. "Don't worry. I can be gentle."

Before Adrial could think past the delicious mix of wild-flowers and new flames in her scent, she'd pulled away, her eyes dancing with mirth.

"Pick a color from my skirt." She turned in a slow circle. "I don't just wear the thing because I like being every color in the world. It helps unsophisticated customers make a decision."

Adrial watched the colors as she turned once, and then again.

"There." He pointed to a swatch of blue so warm it seemed trapped between sky and sea.

"Where?"

"There." Adrial pointed to the patch that sat on her right hip.

"You'll have to be a little clearer than *there*, scribe." Ena slid toward him.

There was something in the laughter in her eyes that made Adrial want to scream, disappear, and whoop in giddy joy all at once.

"Go on, scribe," Ena whispered. "Touch it."

Adrial hated his finger for trembling as he reached out and touched the swatch of perfect blue fabric.

"That one's easy. I can have it to you by tomorrow."

"And that one." Adrial pointed to a grayish-green patch farther down her thigh, grateful she didn't ask him to touch that one, too.

"I'll have to wait for a few things to bloom." Ena wrinkled her brow. "But if spring goes as it should, I might have it in two weeks."

"Two weeks?" There wasn't time to wait that long. Not with a project this large.

"Never rush perfection, scribe. Don't they teach you that when they trap you in your white robes?"

"I'll need that one, too." He'd just spotted it. A blue so light the color could barely be seen. It was fine and bright, like fairy dust sprinkled on a gentle summer wind.

"I knew you had decent taste buried somewhere beneath your robes." Ena tenderly brushed the patch by her knee. "That one won't be ready till the warm weather comes. You wouldn't believe all the work that ink takes. Some might even call it magic."

It wasn't until she winked that Adrial realized he'd forgotten to breathe.

"I'll be back tomorrow. I expect a bag of coins waiting for me." Ena grabbed her basket on her way toward the door. "And wear clothes you can leave your little scribe's hole in. I'll be needing your help."

"I—what?" Adrial limped after her. He felt his eyes go wide and his jaw drop open but somehow couldn't school his face into a more respectable expression.

"I need help tomorrow, and you can't work until you have the ink you need." Ena turned and patted his cheek. "Sweet Taddy is too small, and from the look of it, you could use a little sunshine and fresh air. Having a limp is no excuse for locking yourself inside."

She threw open the door to the outer shop. Taddy toppled over by the doorjamb, landing with a thunk and a squeal.

"There's a whole world out there, scribe," Ena called back as she strolled through the line of desks toward the front door. "You can't hide from it for the rest of your days."

Adrial didn't dare to breathe until the door closed behind her.

"Head Scribe, who is she?" Taddy scrambled to his feet.

"The inker for the Princess's vellum." Craning his neck, Adrial watched as Ena turned her face up to the sun for a moment before striding down the street.

"Where is she taking you?" Taddy asked.

"I've no idea."

6

NIKO

The wretched stench of fish permeated the air. Laughter and shouting echoed through the streets, bouncing between the stone buildings. The combination was enough to make Niko wish he'd stayed in the Guilded section of Ilara, but not quite enough to stop his feet from carrying him forward.

"New coats in the best Guild colors!" a brazen man called from his stall. "Find a sorcerer purple for a lovely lady!"

Niko swallowed the words he longed to shout back at the vendor and crossed the road to walk right past the man's stall.

"A lovely green for those who want adven..." The man's words faded as he caught sight of Niko's green uniform.

Niko bit back his grin. If he were one to anger easily, he'd call the soldiers and have the man hauled away for daring to copy the hues of the Guilds for commoners' clothes. But there was no need for fighting and unpleasantness over a specific shade of green. The man would run and hide for the night and, if he was smart, be more careful about selling his wares tomorrow.

Niko gave the vendor a nod before moving on.

Stalls of food, candles, scents, and frie lined the streets. The poorer merchants and commoners moved from seller to seller, searching out the best prices.

Niko's pockets rattled with more coin than most commoners could hope to earn in half a year's time.

I should be afraid. I should be terrified of the lot of them tearing me apart to steal every coin I have.

But his map maker green protected him. Only a fool would attack a Guilded man, even as the night grew dark.

"To the King!" a voice shouted in the distance.

"To the King's fleet!" a dozen men answered.

"To the King's sword!"

"To the Arion Sea herself!" Niko shouted, though he hadn't reached the crowd.

The men erupted into cheers as a fiddle struck up a lively song.

A group of men clad in blue stood under a sign that read *The White Froth.* The sailors swayed as they sang to the fiddler's tune.

"If the crossing's going rough,

And the storm's tossed you about,

And your belly's not so tough,

And your lady's thrown you out."

The lack of talent amongst the sailors didn't stop them from singing along with enviable enthusiasm.

Niko dodged through the door, ducking between the sailors and commoners.

The stink of sweat and spilled ale overpowered the stench of fish inside the pub. A harassed-looking man and a woman with breasts pushed up level with her collarbone stood behind a long counter, doling out ale and frie to the horde of men.

A few brave women dressed in Sailors Guild blue or plain, unguilded sailors' clothes had joined the chaos, shouting over the tune to be heard by their drinking mates.

Niko was the only one dressed in another Guild's colors, and the stares of those around him were plenty of warning that he was out of place. Not that he'd been fool enough to expect any different.

"Niko." Kai stood up from his table at the far end of the bar and waved a hand in the air. His black, curly hair bounced in his exuberance.

Head down, Niko weaved toward Kai, ignoring the tingling on the back of his neck as the stares of the crowd followed him.

"I thought you might've forgotten your way down to the docks." Kai clapped Niko hard on the shoulder and pressed a glass of frie into his hand.

"Or maybe the fine map maker doesn't want to be seen in such low company." Drew raised his pint toward Niko.

"There is never low company at the White Froth." Niko clinked his glass with Drew's.

The sailor winked and took a swig of his drink. Drew was barely older than Niko, but a life on the sea as an unguilded sailor was harder than even a map maker's lot. Scars cut across his cheek, and shining spots dotted the back of his left hand where his skin was still healing.

"And how was the shipyard today?" Niko took a swig of the frie, relishing the burn as it slid down his throat.

"Depends on who you ask." Kai shrugged. "If you ask the sorcerers, the ship builders are a pack of lazy slitches unworthy of spitting in the sea. If you ask the sailors, the ship builders aren't building the boats we need for what the King's asked us to do."

"And if you ask the ship builders?" Niko raised an eyebrow.

"Then the lot of the Guilders are fools and have no business telling the ship builders how to work their trade." Drew raised a glass.

"And they may have a point," Kai said. "I can tell you I need a ship for twenty men that will hold up to a storm with speed to reach the horn in less than two weeks, but I can't tell you how to shape a hull."

"The sorcerers want a fleet ready to sail south by fall, but it won't happen if they keep lording over the builders." Drew took a long drink of his ale. "The sorcerers should have learned by now that it's best to leave sea folk to themselves. The waves have magic even the Lady Sorcerer herself can't master. They should keep themselves to their tower and let the rest of us manage the real work."

Niko's neck tensed at the layer of anger in Drew's voice. Sitting up straight, as though looking for another friend to join their chat, Niko slid his gaze around the room, searching for Guilded who might turn Drew in for speaking ill of the sorcerers. The sailor could lose his place on the ships for talking like that.

"And have they told you where you'll be sent?" Niko asked rather more loudly than he'd meant to in his determination to not seem suspicious.

"To the horn if the ships are ever ready," Kai said. "Running envoys round the coast in the meantime."

"Sorry," Niko said.

Two men in soldier black swung open the door to the White Froth, tightly wrapped scrolls clutched in each of their hands.

"Don't be sorry." Kai shook his head, sending his black curls bouncing. "It's not exciting work, but I'll get to run some of the tight little schooners. And I'll be in and out of Ilara to keep an eye on Allora."

"Right."

The soldiers headed to the walls on either side of the bar, tacking up the papers without so much as a word to the White Froth's owners, who glared at the intruders.

"Where are you going to be mapping?" Kai leaned sideways, blocking Niko's view of the bar.

"Eastern mountains. Finding a new path through. The King's right—the one road to Wyrain we have won't be enough if they want to start trading in earnest."

"So Mara's going north then?"

Niko forgot to answer as he stood to look over Kai's head.

The men in the bar had begun gathering around the notices. There weren't faces of criminals sketched on the sheets. Just words.

Niko barely had time to read *A Call to Commoners to Join the Soldiers' Ranks* before the gap in front of the papers closed completely.

"I think we may want to take our drinks elsewhere." Niko carefully maintained his smile as he turned back to Drew and Kai. "A quieter place to discuss our new adventures."

"What's this supposed to mean then?" an angry voice spoke from the bar.

"It's a notice written by the scribes at the King's command," one of the soldiers answered.

Niko didn't know the soldier, couldn't even say if they had ever met before. But he recognized the set of the man's jaw. That soldier didn't want to be standing next to the notice any more than Niko wanted to stay in the pub.

"They're offering Guilding to common folk?" a hopeful young man asked from the back of the pack.

"I think a quieter place sounds wonderful." Kai dropped a few coins onto the table.

"They don't want us to join the Guilds." A man with curling blond hair and broad shoulders shoved his way through the crowd toward the soldiers. "They want to set us up in a line and let whatever monsters the King's angered kill us first."

"The Soldiers Guild is offering fair wages—" the younger of the soldiers began, but the blond man shouted across him.

"Fair wages and a new pair of boots? Is that what the King offers us to betray our people?"

"We need to go." Niko grabbed Kai and Drew by the elbows, steering them toward the door.

"The Soldiers Guild serves all the people of Ilbrea, as all the Guilds serve this great country."

"And what of those starving in the south?" The blond man leapt up onto the bar. "The ones who rebel against the King's taxes. Who refuse to watch their children starve so the Princess can have a new pair of golden slippers. Do the Guilds serve them?"

A group of common men stepped in front of the door to the street, blocking Niko and the others dressed in Guild colors from leaving.

"Will the King ask us to kill common folk whose only crime is refusing to starve?" The blond man surveyed the crowd. "Is conscripting boys when they're only children no longer enough for the Soldiers Guild? Has the Lord Soldier grown tired of stealing our sons and twisting their minds so they believe the Guilds' lies? Now grown men should offer themselves as living shields for the paun? It would be better to slit our own throats than to draw common blood for the glory of the Guilds who don't even want us as members, just extra bodies to rot in the field."

"Let us out." Niko kept his voice even as he spoke to the common men blocking the door. "We have no quarrel with you."

"The color of your uniform says different," a man sneered. His breath stank of frie, and his splotched red face shone with drunken sweat.

If he were sober, would he be bold enough to block my path?

"I'm giving you one warning to get out of our way." A friendly smile shone on Kai's face. "You seem like a nice enough fellow, and I'd hate to have to hurt you just to get through a door."

"We will not allow Guild paun to drag us through the mud so more common folk can starve!" A roar of approval greeted the blond man's words. "If they want us to fight, then we'll do it. But we will bleed and die fighting those who have ground the common folk into the mud!"

"What a chivving night," Niko sighed as Kai shrugged.

"Don't say I didn't ask nicely."

Mayhem devoured the pub in an instant.

One soldier shouted, "Rip that getch off the bar!" at the same moment one of the commoners hit the other soldier with a chair. A pack of men charged the sailors, and Kai punched the man who'd refused to move in the ribs.

"Kai!" Niko shouted as a fist hit him in the jaw. Before he could truly wonder who had punched him, something hard struck him in the back of the knees. Pain shot through Niko's legs as he hit the floor.

"Leave him be." Drew rammed his shoulder into a man holding a rough chunk of wood.

"Are you really pulling a knife on me?" Kai laughed.

Niko scrambled to his feet in time to see Kai kick the knife out of an older man's grasp.

"We need to go." Niko grabbed a heavy wooden chair and swung it at the men blocking the door as bells rang in the distance.

The soldiers would be rallying. In a few minutes, they'd be on their way.

The chair in Niko's hands shattered as he slammed two men into the wall.

A few minutes to wait for the soldiers seemed like far too long.

"Kai, Drew!" Niko ducked as a bottle of frie flew past his head.

"Are the paun too frightened to fight?"

The question spun Niko around.

The blond man had climbed down from the bar. The shouts and clatter of the fight at the back of the pub nearly drowned out the man's words. "Want to run back to the safety of your expensive bed and wait for a flock of soldiers to come handle us?"

"I'm not afraid to fight you." Niko had reached the table right next to the door. His hands fumbled across its sticky surface. "But I am fond of the White Froth, and I hate to see damage done to such a fine establishment." Niko's fingers found something solid and metal. "But as you've given me no choice." He swung the candlestick toward the man's face. The flames streaked through the air, leaving a blur across Niko's vision as he hit the man in the side of the head.

The man roared as blood stained his pale hair.

"Niko, get Drew!" Kai's shout carried over the bedlam.

Niko easily spotted Kai who had a knife in each hand as he backed toward the door, flanked by others in sailor blue. But Drew wasn't with the Guilded sailors.

The blond man shouted and lunged for Niko, who leapt to the side, shoving the man in the back so his forward momentum sent him face first into the wall.

Niko caught sight of Drew.

Blood coated Drew's knuckles. He bared his teeth as he swung at a commoner who had backed him against the window.

Cursing under his breath, Niko leapt up onto the table between them, his feet barely touching the surface before he jumped down on the other side. Raising his candlestick high, Niko swung at the man closest to Drew.

He only caught a glimpse of his opponent's face before his poor weapon struck.

He's practically a boy. He shouldn't be here fighting.

But two other men waited behind the boy to strike as he faltered.

"Sorry about this." Niko grabbed Drew around the middle and leapt back, throwing them both through the window.

The pain of glass slicing his skin as the window shattered was only a pinprick compared to hitting the stone street on the other side.

"Niko!" An arm wrapped around him, dragging him to his feet.

The clomp of heavy boots thundered from the end of the street.

"Is Drew all right?" Niko blinked as his eyes drifted in and out of focus.

"I'm fine," Drew grunted.

Niko's feet fumbled on the cobblestones as Kai dragged him away from the soldiers.

The shouts inside the White Froth had gotten worse in the few moments they'd been outside.

Kai pulled him into the shadows between two cracked and shabby stone houses. "Everyone still breathing?"

"For now." Drew leaned against the house opposite Niko.

Niko rubbed his eyes with his sleeves, but the red covering Drew didn't go away.

"We need to get to the healers." Niko pushed away from the wall, gritting his teeth against the pain that seared through his left side where he'd struck the street.

Kai bled from a gash across his shoulder, and even his tan skin couldn't hide the bruises forming on his face.

Niko didn't even want to know how bad he looked.

"You two go on." Drew gripped the wall as he swayed. "I think a nice rest and a bottle of frie is what I need."

"You need healing," Kai said.

"If you go now, you'll be clear of the common streets before word of the fight spreads," Drew said. "The last thing you'll want is to be caught around here in Guild colors tonight. I don't think they'll even be friendly to sailor blue."

An itch of worry gnawed at Niko's stomach. They were in no shape to fight again, and asking the soldiers to escort them back to the Guilded streets was more than his pride could bear.

And, if the soldiers saw him, word of his being in a brawl would reach Lord Karron and trickle right down to Allora.

"Best to move quickly then." Niko took a step forward. Pain shot through his right leg. "Maybe not too quickly."

"Come on, Drew," Kai said as he joined Niko at the end of the alley, his gait showing no harm from the fight.

"All I need is a bottle of frie." Drew waved a blood-covered hand. "You head to the healers. I'll see you at the docks in the morning."

"Don't be daft," Niko said. "You're bleeding from more places than I can count. Come with us, and they'll fix you up."

"No, they won't." Drew shrugged, wincing in pain from the movement. "If I had been hurt on the ship, the Healers Guild would fix me up in a flash, but I got hurt throwing punches."

"So did we—" Niko began.

"But I'm not Guilded," Drew cut him off. "They'll want nothing to do with me. I'm not going to limp across Ilara to be turned away by a bunch of scarlet-clad slitches."

"Drew—"

"I'm glad you'll get help. But the best help for me is to get off the streets and away from the two of you." Drew gave a half-hearted laugh. "The last thing I need is to be caught with two bloodied-up Guilders. Caught by common folk or soldiers, I'll be stuck up a chivving pole either way."

Niko opened his mouth to argue, but Kai spoke first. "Be careful on the way home. And if you need anything, send word." Kai pulled a silver token from his pocket and pressed it into Drew's hand. "If the soldiers give you trouble, tell them you saved me."

Drew smiled, creasing the drying blood on his face. "You be careful, too. The tilk in the White Froth might be louder than the rest, but they aren't the only ones who are unhappy. Guild colors will be as good as a target soon, and even your fancy saints won't be enough to save you."

Drew limped through the shadows and out of sight.

"Wasn't expecting a brawl when I came out tonight." Niko shifted his weight onto his injured leg. The pain carried up from his knee as though something were out of place. "We all knew bringing in unguilded soldiers would cause trouble, but I thought it would start farther south."

Kai wrapped Niko's arm around his shoulder, helping him limp out onto the street.

"It's bigger than unguilded soldiers." Kai spoke softly. "You don't see the common folk as much as I do. I work with tilk every day on the ships. I live in their district. The rumblings of trouble have been coming for a while. On the ships, in the streets, the common folk are angry. I don't think this will blow away with the summer wind."

"And what are we supposed to do?"

"We survive." Kai gave a low and humorless chuckle. "We're Karrons. It's what we do."

7

ADRIAL

"How the lot of us do our work is not up to you." Natalia's voice carried through Adrial's door.

"It's how things need to be done," Travers growled in response.

Adrial sighed, placing his thick mug back down onto the tiny table in the corner of his workroom. He hadn't even gotten to take a sip of his tea before they'd started in on each other.

Longingly, he looked to the page on the tilted section of his desk.

A Royal History of Ilbrea to Honor Princess Illia Willoc.

The intricate script adorned the center of the parchment. A delicate swirl looped along the bottom of the page in map maker green. The side borders were a woven pattern of purple birds flying up toward the sky. But the top of the page was still left blank, waiting for Ena to bring the new batch of blue.

"He's not *your* apprentice," Natalia half-shouted.

Adrial rubbed the knot of tension between his eyes and opened the door to the front office.

Five of his scribes sat with their heads down, studiously ignoring Natalia and Travers, who stood on opposite sides of the shop, glaring at each other, while poor Taddy cowered in the middle, clutching a sheaf of parchment.

"Taddy," Adrial said, "I need you to run to the library and fetch more parchment for the vellum."

"Yes, Head Scribe." Taddy tore out the front door without stopping to set down the stack of parchment already in his hands and was out of sight before the chime stopped ringing.

"What seems to be the problem?" Adrial asked.

Natalia and Travers didn't bother to stop glaring at one another long enough to look at Adrial.

"Scribe Gend seems to think his primary duty is to issue orders to Apprentice Baiton." Color crept up into Natalia's tan cheeks as her voice shook in poorly concealed anger.

"Scribe Tammin thinks coddling the apprentice is the way to teach him to be a proper scribe." Travers looked like an angry bear as his lips curled in a sanctimonious smile.

Adrial took a deep breath, letting Lord Gareth's words fill his mind.

It doesn't matter if the scribes under your authority are younger than you or older. I chose you as the Head Scribe of Ilara. You are my heir. To doubt your ability to do the job is to doubt my wisdom.

The Lord Scribe's eyes had twinkled as he spoke. As though he knew how terrified Adrial was of failing his mentor and his Guild.

"Scribe Gend, Apprentice Baiton is not your personal apprentice or servant," Adrial said to Travers.

Travers clenched his jaw, the ridges on his neck displaying themselves as he nodded curtly.

"Good." Adrial looked toward Natalia. "And Scribe Tammin, you can't coddle the boy. I know he's young, but he needs to learn being a scribe isn't just an easy life of playing with pens and papers. He'll never be Guilded if he doesn't improve. I want to inspect his work myself every evening from now on."

"Yes, Head Scribe." Natalia gave a little bow.

"I want all of you to take it in turns to teach Apprentice Baiton." Adrial addressed the other scribes. "It's all of our responsibility to ensure he's ready to take his mark. I know we all like Taddy, but liking the boy won't be enough to get him through. If anyone has any questions on how to instruct him, I would be happy to advise."

Not waiting for questions, Adrial turned and strode back to his workroom, hiding his limp as best he could.

He didn't breathe until he'd shut the door behind him.

He was used to things not being easy. His appointment as head scribe and Lord Gareth's heir hadn't been popular. There were scribes twenty years older than Adrial who longed for the Lordship. Travers Gend desperately wanted the position and took every opportunity to show as much. Though posturing and muscle were hardly things Lord Gareth had looked for when choosing an heir.

Lord Gareth wanted young blood. New eyes for the Guilds Council. Someone who had absolutely no interest in power or politics. As a prodigy who rarely noticed anything outside his work, Adrial fit the mold Lord Gareth wished to fill.

Adrial turned back to his tea, trying to rid his mind of all imaginings of how different his life might be if only he had the power to pluck out a few moments of his past and erase them entirely.

A quick tap sounded on the door before it opened.

"Hello, scribe." Ena breezed into his workroom, teal basket in hand.

"You're here." Adrial's heart stopped as she turned to face him.

A fiery red streak had been added to the front of her hair.

"Good morning to you, too." Ena smiled as he stared silently at her. "Is that tea?" She lifted the mug right out of his hand and held it to her nose. "They give you Guilded fancy tea." She took a sip, closing her eyes with a sigh. "And you don't make it too sweet, either."

"I'm not fond of sugar." Adrial blinked, trying to figure out what in his surroundings he might be misunderstanding. Perhaps he'd developed a fever. Or maybe he hadn't even gotten out of bed yet. He dug his nails into his palms to try and right his senses, but Ena still sauntered to his worktable, his tea still clutched in her hand.

"You've actually done some work. And it's good." Ena glanced over her shoulder. "You weren't lying when you said you were brilliant."

"I never said I was brilliant." Adrial joined her at the table. "It still needs more work. I want to add more depth to the birds. Maybe some of that red."

The image of the colors in his head was perfect. Birds with fire in their wings soaring over Ilbrea.

"You can't do that," Ena laughed. "An orange red with a purple won't come out the way you think. Honestly, scribe, the things you don't know about your craft could fill more books than you could ever stuff into that handsome head of yours."

Heat rose in Adrial's cheeks. "Are you saying I can't layer the inks?"

"No." Ena poked him in the chest. "I'm saying it was a lucky day for you when I decided I was desperate enough to take Guild coin. You'll have to have a blue-based red for the birds to look the way you want. But, as you look desolate at having to wait, I suppose I can be a kind girl and help."

The jars of ink she'd brought the day before sat on one side of the table, arranged by color.

"Do the Guilds demand all their scribes keep everything in strict order?"

"Your coin." Adrial pointed to the small pouch next to the jars.

Ena lifted the pouch, weighing it in her hand before tucking it into her pocket. "I'll have to be very kind to you if you keep paying like that."

Adrial blushed.

Ena laughed again. "You really do make it too easy, scribe."

She set the mug on the table, and Adrial snatched it the moment it touched the desk. "Not on there. Please don't set it on the work desk." The words came out harsher than he'd meant. "It might…it might spill."

"Very well, scribe." Ena laid a hand over her heart. "I won't set stolen tea on your worktable."

"Thank you," Adrial mumbled as he carried the tea back to the tiny tray. His roll sat untouched, and his tea was half-drunk by a mad woman with ink.

"It should be a simple enough thing," Ena said. "Just a dash of blue, and it should fit perfectly with the purple."

Ena knelt next to the table, dipping her finger into the tub of blue ink.

A shock shook Adrial's spine at the sight of the color on her hand. She moved deftly over to the jar of red, letting two blue drops fall from her finger.

"That should do it." She replaced the tops of both jars before giving the red a shake.

Squinting, she held the jar up to the light.

The color had deepened. The fire inside of it hadn't disappeared but had darkened to an ember.

"It's exquisite," Adrial whispered.

"I know. But don't try mixing the inks on your own. It's not just the colors, but what they're made of that makes that sort of thing work."

Adrial nodded, not trusting himself to say something intelligent.

"Now look at the match." Ena pulled off the top of the red and dipped in a clean finger, swiping the color onto the back of her pale hand before doing the same with the purple.

Adrial forced his jaw to unclench so he could speak. "Do you have to do that?"

"Do what?" Ena looked from Adrial to her hand.

"I do have regular parchment," Adrial said. "And I could...I could find you pens."

"Does it bother you? Me having ink on my skin." She wiggled her fingers in the air. "Does it make you nervous, scribe? Should I put some on your hand?"

"Please don't." Adrial shook his head, fighting the childish temptation to hide his hands behind his back. "Scribes' hands are always supposed to be clean."

"You work with ink, but you shouldn't touch it?"

"Perfection, not correction," Adrial repeated the phrase that had been pounded into his head as an apprentice. "The ink should never spot nor spatter."

"And they make you wear white to prove you haven't made a bad stroke of the pen?"

"It's a symbol of purity of word and truth of speech..."

Ena turned back to her basket and began pulling out new jars of ink.

"Come, scribe. I think we should get your robes a bit dirty. You can pay me as much for this batch as you did the last." Her basket empty, she strode to the door. "Aren't you coming?"

"Coming where?" Adrial asked like a child lost in the market.

You are the heir to the Scribes Guild, not a pitiful child, Adrial Ayres.

"I told you I needed your help for an errand, scribe. Did you think I was joking?" The corners of Ena's mouth curved up in a smirk.

"Yes."

"Well, now you'll know for next time. Come on." Ena flung

open the workroom door with a bang. "I've work to do, you've history to write. Time is coin, scribe."

"Right." Adrial squared his shoulders, ignoring the ache of pain in his right side.

"Head Scribe." Natalia stood the moment he entered the outer office. "Is everything all right?"

"He's fine," Ena answered. "Just helping me with an errand."

Natalia's eyes widened. "If she needs assistance, perhaps she can wait for Taddy."

"That dear little pudgy boy?" Ena laughed. "I'm afraid he can't help."

"I would be happy to assist." Travers stood up behind his desk. "I'm sure the head scribe would be better suited to stay in his office."

"You weren't here yesterday." Ena slunk over to Travers's desk.

"No." Travers gave a winning smile. "But I'm sure I can assist you in any way you need. If it involves traveling outside"—he looked to Adrial, staring at his bad leg while he spoke—"I'm sure I would be better suited to the task."

Ena planted her elbows on the top of Travers's tilted desk and leaned closer to him.

Travers's gaze slid down to Ena's chest.

"Did you drink a little too much frie on Winter's End?" Ena whispered loudly enough for the whole room to hear. "Or maybe you don't drink the strong stuff. Maybe it's too much for you to handle. Did you get sick on chamb? Is that why you weren't here?"

Travers's face turned to stone.

"Come, scribe." Ena swept to the front door. "Poor weak-stomach might still be recovering. I'd hate to make noise that might hurt his precious little head." Ena held the door open, waiting for Adrial to follow.

"I'll be back in a bit," Adrial said, carefully keeping his gait even as he walked outside.

It wasn't until the chimes sounded as the door closed behind him that a touch of panic set in. He'd followed a mad woman onto the streets, disregarding the monumental work that had been left in his care.

"Are you all right, scribe?" Ena asked after a long moment.

"Fine," Adrial answered a bit too loudly. "I'm fine."

"Good." Ena threaded her arm through his. "I wasn't sure if you looked pale because you aren't used to the sunlight, or if you were going to be sick on your shoes in terror of going outside."

She set an easy pace down the busy street.

The scribes' shop sat on the border between the Guilds' section of the city and the merchants' rows. Guilded in colorful robes mixed with merchants in fine brocades and richly patterned clothes. Even with the bustle on the street, Ena still drew stares from the people she passed.

The men gaped at her like they wanted to devour her. The women, like they were jealous of whatever magic had created a creature of such perfect beauty.

A beautiful girl in a rainbow of colors on the arm of a crippled scribe.

Adrial kept his eyes to the ground, avoiding the questioning glances of the passersby.

"How bad is that leg of yours?" Ena asked as she led him down a side street and east toward the towering cliffs that blocked Ilara from the inland of Ilbrea.

"How do you mean?" Adrial asked. The ache in his leg was getting worse by the minute. Hiding his limp was painful and never quite worked.

"Can you walk a distance, or should I have brought that weak-stomached letch who likes to leer?"

"My leg is fine for distances." Adrial turned his face away

from Ena, fixing his gaze on the windows of the fine dress shops they passed. "It's speed I'm lacking."

"Good." Ena knocked him in the stomach with her basket. "That other scribe would have stared at my breasts while plotting to lift my skirt. Just imagine the trouble I'd get in for gutting a Guilded scribe."

The buildings grew higher as they weaved through the rows of fine houses where wealthy merchants lived alongside the lower-ranked members of the Guilds.

Smooth stone fronts and wide windows graced every home. Shrubs and stalks where flowers would soon bloom took up the orderly patches of dirt in front of the houses. Lampposts dotted the street, ready to ward off the darkness come evening.

"You don't have to hide your limp, you know," Ena said. "You're sweating just from trying."

Adrial reached instinctively to his brow. Beads of sweat had indeed formed from the effort.

Shame curled in his stomach, but there was no point trying to disguise what she'd already noticed. With a sigh, he let his good leg take more of the weight of his stride. His gait wasn't as even, but the pain lessened.

Ena trailed her fingers along a low bush that had just begun to show signs of life. "Does it always hurt?"

Adrial opened his mouth to say no. "Yes."

"I thought so." Ena stepped in front of him, taking his face in her hands. "That explains why you don't smile very much."

"How do you know if I smile?"

Her hands were soft on his cheeks. Her skin smelled of something sweet and fresh. "You've got sad eyes." She ran her fingers along his temples. "And you've no lines from laughing."

"I'm not old enough for wrinkles." Adrial took her hands in his. Only the width of her basket separated them.

"It's not a matter of age," Ena said. "It's a matter of what your face is used to."

She stayed that way for a moment, her hands beneath his as she stared into his eyes.

"Come on. We've work to do," she said as if she hadn't done anything strange. She slipped her hands out from beneath Adrial's and tugged on his sleeve, making him follow her.

"Do you often tell people things about themselves?" Adrial asked.

"Is that what I did?" Ena said with a hint of humor in her voice.

It wasn't until they'd passed the last of the tall stone houses and moved on to the shorter, less manicured homes that lived in the shadow of the cliff that Ena spoke again. "Not all of us have the privilege of being protected by a Guild, scribe. I survive on my own in Ilara, by warehouses and docks, no less. If I weren't good at reading people, I wouldn't know who wanted to hurt me, who wanted to roll me, and who only fancied a chat."

"Is it that bad by the docks?" He'd only ever been to that part of the city to see off journeys for the Map Makers Guild or to visit Kai when he was in Ilara. But it had never seemed a frightening place.

A different sort of people spent their time down that way. The smell of the sea and the stench of fish were stronger, the voices were louder, and the chaos of commerce wasn't hidden behind thick stone walls. The mood of the place seemed joyous and free, not dark and dangerous.

"It's that bad everywhere, scribe. Some of us are just forced to stare straight at the shadows." Ena stopped between two close-set houses.

The homes weren't as well maintained as those around them. Proximity to the cliffs made sunlight a scant commodity in this corner of the city, and a musty odor permeated the air.

"Are you up to giving a girl a boost?" Ena eyed Adrial.

"A boost?"

"Well, I could try and lift you, but I don't think you'd know what to do once you were up there." Ena pointed five feet overhead.

A layer of black had crusted the side of the building, filling in the tiny cracks between stones, and hiding the gray of the house.

"You want to go up there?" Adrial asked, hoping perhaps he'd misunderstood.

"What looks like filth to you looks like things I need for ink to me." Ena took Adrial's hands, stacking them one on top of the other to make a sort of step. "I could run all the way out to the woods in the east to gather the grime I need, but you'd run out of black before I could make it back with more. So if you want to keep working, give me a boost."

She reached down and, with a flick of her wrist, pulled a knife from her boot.

"Do you always walk around with a weapon in your shoe?" Adrial glanced down the alley. There was no one in view. And he had no chance of outrunning the mad inker.

I'm going to be assassinated, and no one will know why I was here.

"I've just told you I live by the docks." Ena placed her non-knife hand on Adrial's shoulder. "Don't drop me, or who knows which of us the sharp bit of the knife might stab?"

Gritting his teeth against the effort, Adrial took Ena's weight as she stepped up onto his hands. "Couldn't you just climb the wall?"

The scrape of metal on rock pulled Adrial's gaze up.

"Careful now," Ena warned as he swayed. The movement only disrupted her work for a moment. "I can't climb a thing that has nothing to hold on to, scribe." She shoved her knife into a crack between stones, prying free a chunk of black and dropping it into the basket that waited below.

"Of course." Adrial's bad shoulder seized, sending pain shooting through his neck all the way into his ear.

"There we are." With a clang, Ena dropped her knife onto the cobblestone street.

Adrial stumbled forward as she leapt out of his hands, landing so their faces were nearly touching.

"That wasn't bad, now was it?" Ena didn't step away from him.

"No." Adrial searched desperately for more eloquent words. "It wasn't."

"It hurt your shoulder, though." Ena laid a hand on his shoulder, like she could see the pain radiating off it.

"A bit."

"You'd think the sorcerers and healers might try and help someone who's going to be a Guild Lord." Ena turned away, sticking her knife back into the top of her boot and folding the bits of black she had tossed into her basket in a white square of fabric.

"It was decided the attempt would be ill-advised." The familiar taste of bitter disappointment flooded Adrial's mouth as he recited the words. It had been years since the healers sent the note denying him any aid, but he still hated the memory of that morning. Hated the little boy he had been for crying too hard on Allora's shoulder.

"You've got a bit of filth on you." Ena pointed to the front of Adrial's robes.

Black spots of the stuff Ena had pried loose flecked the white chest of his robe, and dirt had stirred up from the street, coating his hem in brown.

Adrial's heart twisted for a moment as a terrible vision of Lord Gareth rounding the corner with scorn etched on his face flew through his mind.

"You should have worn something fit for being out of your perfect, plain little world." Ena winked. "I assume you can find your way home?"

"Of course." Adrial brushed the black off his chest.

"Good. You wouldn't want to follow me on the next errand."

Ena strode down the street far more quickly than she'd walked with Adrial.

"When are you bringing more ink?" Adrial called after her.

"Why, scribe? Afraid you might miss me?" Ena turned the corner and was out of sight.

Adrial's breath caught in his chest as her laughter drifted behind her.

8

ALLORA

The rain was trying enough to be getting on with. Not that Allora feared getting wet. Or even being cold and covered in mud should it come to that. But there was a time and place for looking like a filthy, drowned kitten, and a trip to the Royal Palace was not one of those times.

"Are you sure the Princess requested to see me immediately?" Allora felt quite pleased with herself. She hadn't sounded at all like she was whining. "Wouldn't it be better to wait until the storm passes?"

"The Princess requested you be brought to her directly," the matron said, not looking away from the carriage window.

"As the Princess desires."

Of course, Allora had already let herself be herded into the carriage, so it was much too late to avoid a soggy trip to the palace.

If only I'd had the sense to hide. I could be comfortable in my bed right now. Warm, dry, not worrying about the whims of the young royal.

But she had obediently answered the knock on her bedroom

door, and now she would spend her day at the mercy of the Princess.

The carriage bounced along the twisting road as it trundled down from the cliffs where the Map Master's Palace sat high above the city.

The Royal Palace was nestled at the far northern edge of Ilara where the cliffs gave way to gentle hills. The royals of Ilbrea had long since given up on the cliffs as a measure of defense, choosing instead a barricade of walls and warren of tunnels for their protection.

The Guilded streets were nearly empty. A few Guild members hurried along with their heads low and cloaks wrapped tightly around their shoulders. The commoners Allora spotted did not dodge through the rain. They walked with an air of resignation, as though the rain were nothing more than a new inconvenience.

There were no commoners or colorfully cloaked Guilded near the royals' home. Only the ranks of soldiers patrolling the outer wall of the palace braved the deluge.

The rattle under the carriage's wheels changed as they crossed from the street to the stone bridge that spanned the wide moat. The bridge's very existence was, by non-magical standards, impossible. Without any struts reaching down into the water far below, the wide expanse appeared ready to collapse at any moment. The stones were barely a foot thick with no visible mortar holding them together.

Allora closed her eyes tight as they reached the center of the bridge.

It's the work of the sorcerers.

She wasn't sure if the thought should be comforting or not.

The sorcerers' magic could hold up the stones, but the sorcerers' magic could send her falling to her death as well.

The sound of the wheels changed again as they reached solid ground.

The carriage paused for a moment while soldiers' voices rumbled outside, their words muted by the pounding rain.

Has Lady Allora been summoned to be trapped inside by a petulant child?

Yes, we have the Lady Map Maker.

Bring her in and lock her up for the rest of her days. Allora Karron will make a fine pet.

Allora bit back her smile at the imagined conversation.

Caring for the woes of a princess could hardly be considered the worst position for a person to be trapped in. At least with the Princess, there was bound to be a hot cup of tea waiting for her.

The pounding of the rain against the roof of the carriage stopped for a moment as they passed through the outer wall, then again as they passed beyond the inner ring and into the palace proper.

A wide lawn stretched out on either side of the road. Perfectly trimmed hedges and carefully curated flowerbeds dotted the wide swath of green. Had the Princess summoned her on a sunny day, they could have strolled through the early blooms, letting the cool spring wind invigorate them.

But even the Sorcerers Guild could not banish the rain. And the royals would not be ruled by the weather.

The carriage stopped at the bottom of the wide stone steps, and a servant in yellow and gray livery trotted down the stairs, umbrella in hand.

"I will escort you home when you are finished." The matron gave a simpering smile.

Escort me home when I am freed. Allora swallowed the retort.

"Thank you, madam." Allora gave the woman a nod and ducked out into the rain, grateful for the protection of the umbrella even as the downpour soaked the hem of her skirt.

She didn't know the matron's name, though she had seen the woman at least a dozen times. A flutter of guilt nibbled at her as she hurried up the steps. She didn't like the woman who dragged her out in the rain, but it did seem a little vapid to sit in silence with a person without knowing her name.

Then again, she didn't know the name of the liveried man who was now soaking wet after having carried her umbrella.

"Thank you," Allora said as they stepped into the grand entryway of the palace.

The man gave a tiny bow.

There was no point in asking his name. She might never see him again and probably wouldn't recognize him if she did.

He disappeared through a discreet door that led to rooms she would never see. His place was in the narrow corridors that led from one part of the palace to another. Allora's place was in the immense front hall.

The light of the glittering chandeliers reflected off the shining marble floor and golden filaments woven through the pale tapestries that covered the walls. Flames crackled in the two fire-places that flanked the space. Both were large enough for several people to stand in, but the fires hadn't pushed back the damp chill of the morning.

Allora looked at the puddle her dress had dripped onto the floor, hoping whichever poor maid would have to scrub her mess away wouldn't blame her for dragging in the storm.

"Lady Allora!" the Princess's bright voice called from the top of the grand staircase. "I was hoping you would come."

Allora smiled and gently bowed her head. "I am always thrilled to see you, Princess Illia."

"Please come up." The Princess beckoned.

The wide marble stairs swept up to the second floor, which housed the royal apartments. Most in Ilbrea would be honored beyond belief to be taken to the Princess's private parlor. But the grandeur of the Map Master's Palace rivaled that of the Royal Palace. The only true differences being the lack of soldiers constantly patrolling and other public persona endlessly invading the royals' home.

"How are you this morning, Your Highness?" Allora asked as she reached the second floor.

Portraits of the royal family lined the long hall, each grander than the last. Jewels studded the frame of King Brannon and Queen Carys's wedding portrait. Allora bit the inside of her lips to keep from giggling at the gaudy display.

"Quite well." The trill of the Princess's voice faltered a bit. "The rains should be helpful in washing the city. And everything must be at its best in Ilara."

"Of course," Allora said as Princess Illia opened the white double doors to her parlor. "The city must always be at its best. The capital is the pride of Ilbrea."

Princess Illia closed the doors, letting her hands linger on the knobs for a moment, as though she were afraid someone would throw the doors back open.

"Is there a reason the city should be made even more beautiful?" Allora asked.

The Princess glanced around the room before letting her customary smile slide away. "So many reasons, or maybe no reason at all."

A fire had been lit in the parlor, and the room was small enough that the flames actually did some good. Still, Allora was grateful when the Princess led her to the two seats closest to the stone fireplace.

Every shred of the parlor's decorations had been chosen with the Princess in mind. Pretty pictures hung on the blue and white walls. An easel, paints, and a harp waited to entertain the Princess. A tiny shelf of books hid in the corner. None of the spines looked as though they had ever been bent.

Allora's nails bit into her palms at the thought of Adrial toiling for two years to make a book for a girl who cared so little for the scribes' craft. But perhaps Princess Illia's children would care to learn of their mother's homeland.

Allora waited until she was settled in her seat by the fire, and the silence had become unbearable, to speak. "Your Highness, may I ask why you're particularly interested in having the city look perfect this spring? If I'm not overstepping, of course."

"Of course not, Lady Allora." The Princess took Allora's hand. It was in moments like this when it became easy to see that Illia was barely fifteen. The girl clung to Allora as though she held some magic greater than any sorcerer's, which could wipe away whatever troubles plagued her beautiful blond head.

"The Queen has lost another child," Illia began.

"Oh no." Allora pressed her free hand to her mouth.

"We all knew it would happen," Illia said. "It's the sixth in as many years, and with each, she becomes more frail."

"The poor Queen."

"The child held on through Winter's End, but now the Queen's fallen back into mourning. My brother won't even speak of it. None of us are meant to."

"Of course." Allora couldn't stop herself from glancing toward the door, waiting for the matron to come bustling in to scold the Princess for daring to mention forbidden things.

"I can't help but wonder if she wouldn't feel better if she left the palace," Illia said. "She sits all day in the nursery she prepared. If she would only walk through the gardens, maybe she would feel better. The new blooms the rain brings might tempt her outside."

"We all grieve in our own way," Allora said, "and the Queen has had so much to grieve."

"She has." Illia let go of Allora's hand and began fidgeting with her skirt, smoothing it as though preparing for her portrait to be painted. "And it seems she may never carry a child to term. My brother might never have a true heir."

Tension gripped Allora's neck as understanding trickled through her.

"Ilara must have an heir," Illia said. "If the Queen cannot

produce one, and I am to be sent to Wyrain, the throne will leave the Willoc name."

"I'm terribly sorry." The words seemed hollow even as Allora spoke. "I'm sure the King—"

"I should be allowed to stay," Illia cut across Allora. "If my brother's heir will not be his child, then he should look to me before any of our cousins. If he thinks I'm not fit to take his place, I should at least be allowed to stay and help, or marry the chosen heir to keep our bloodline in Ilbrea. Dudia gave our family to the people of Ilbrea to protect His great land. I cannot abandon my home."

"You aren't abandoning Ilbrea." Allora ached to take the girl's hand, but it couldn't be allowed. The Princess could reach for her, but not she for the Princess. "Ilbrea and Wyrain need to come together. Our people have been at odds for too long. Wyrain blocks us from the Golden Sea and all the goods from the eastern lands. Your wedding will open trade routes and bring prosperity to the Guilds."

"So trade routes are the price for selling me?" Illia stood and paced in front of the fire. "I don't know the prince I am to marry. I've never even met him. Wyrain is to be my new home, and I've never been allowed to cross the mountains to see it."

"Your Highness…"

You can't tell her it's awful and unfair. You can't tell the Princess her place is in Ilbrea, protecting her brother's throne.

"The weight of the Willoc name is a heavy burden to bear."

Illia shrieked a laugh.

"But Dudia would not have borne you into the royal family were you not strong enough to bear the weight."

"You mean to bear children for a prince I've never met." Tears streamed down Illia's face. "Lady Allora, what if he's terrible?" Collapsing to her knees, the Princess buried her face in Allora's damp skirt. "What if he smells like cattle or does nothing but drink frie?" The Princess's words came out in muffled gasps.

"He's a prince, not a common sailor." Allora petted Illia's hair.

They could be sisters. Their bright blond hair and pale faces were so similar. Somewhere, a few generations back, their families had been intertwined. Allora was a simple twist of fate away from being in Illia's position. Promised to be sent to a land far from home.

"What if he hates me?" Illia dabbed her cheeks with a finely woven handkerchief. "What if he thinks I'm vapid and stupid and spends all his days dreading to be near me?"

"How could anyone hate you?" Allora dared to brush the hair from Illia's brow. "You are lovely and kind. Prince Dagon will see that."

"Are you sure?" Illia sniffed.

"Absolutely." Allora smiled. "You know…you really needn't wait until the wedding to get to know Prince Dagon."

"Because my brother will let me cross the eastern mountains to see my new home? You can't possibly believe there's any chance of it until after the wedding."

"No, I'm certain the King won't allow you to leave Ilbrea. I'm quite certain Prince Dagon won't be allowed here either."

"Then it's impossible."

"Not if you write to him." Allora stood and led Illia to the writing desk in the corner. "Letters are carried through the mountains by traders all the time. Ask him of his home in Wyrain. Ask him of his horses, or if he likes to sail."

"And what if he hates horses and sailing?" Illia sank into the chair, her fingers trembling as she reached for the finely pressed paper.

"Then we'll find out what he does like. And if he was raised to be as princely as he should, he'll ask what things bring you joy."

"Do you really think so?" A glimmer of a smile kissed Illia's lips.

"I do, Your Highness."

"Will you help me write him?" Pink crept up Illia's cheeks. "I've never written to a man before."

"Of course I will." Allora sat on the upholstered chair next to the desk, carefully looking away from the table to give Illia her privacy.

This was the price of her delaying marriage. Were she a married women, even if her husband were away on a journey, she would not be expected to come running at the Princess's bidding. Her place would be in her home and her mornings meant for more than sitting beside a young girl's desk.

Please let the Prince write her back.

Illia was completely right. Prince Dagon could be a wretched beast who cared more for drinking and women than the good of his own country. But Princess Illia didn't need to know that. She would have to marry him, whether he was terrible or not. There was no need for the girl to spend the next two years dreading her fate.

And they had no reason to give up hope. Perhaps he would be lovely and send her a letter back. Maybe Illia would be lucky and grow to like the Prince enough she might look forward to her wedding day.

Men on journeys couldn't send letters. There weren't the resources to spare. Niko would be gone for months, charting the eastern mountains, at least until winter came. Mara and Tham would be off in the white for ages. Kai would be far away on a ship.

And Allora and Adrial would be stuck in Ilara, praying to Dudia and Aximander that everyone would come home safe.

"Will you read it?" Illia's words pulled Allora from her reverie.

"If you like."

Illia's nerves showed in her writing. The usual smooth curve of her penmanship had been replaced by angular script.

My Dear Prince Dagon,

I hope Winter's End has found you in good health. Our celebrations of the spring have ended in Ilara. Are there such festivals in Spios? Do you celebrate Winter's End or some other festival?

I do hope to learn more of my new home before I join you across the eastern mountains.

King Brannon's chief joy in the spring is riding through the forests that surround Ilara. He finds the fresh air does him good after a winter confined in stone to avoid the chill of the season.

I have heard winters in Spios are kinder than winters in Ilara. Are you able to ride through the country even in winter? Do you enjoy riding at all?

Please give my regards to His Royal Highness and whomever else you hold dear.

Yours in highest regards,
Princess Illia Willoc

"Is it a good letter?" Illia asked as soon as Allora's gaze reached the bottom of the page.

"It's a fine letter." Allora slipped it back onto the desk. "And I'm sure he'll be grateful for it. Think of the comfort he'll feel when he knows he's getting a kind wife."

"Oh, Lady Allora, I knew you would help. You've always such a level head, and I never feel embarrassed to talk to you." Illia bit her lips together. "I was thinking, and I'm sure I could convince my brother, but what would you think of moving into the palace?"

"Your Highness"—Allora's mind raced through a dozen different rejections—"I'm sure your brother wouldn't want me invading his home."

"Is it not my home, too?" Illia asked. "My mother passed years ago. My brother's wife should by all rights be my guardian, but she's always so sullen she hardly speaks to me."

"And what of the matron who came to collect me?"

"Sara is a dowdy old thing." Illia waved a hand through the air.

"She never would have suggested writing to Prince Dagon. She speaks only of duty. I don't think the old crow knows anything else."

"Your Highness, I am always at your service, but I cannot live in the Royal Palace." Allora took a deep breath. "My place is in the Map Master's Palace. My father has no wife to care for his house. I cannot abandon him."

"But he's so often gone." Illia took Allora's hand.

"And it is my place to keep everything safe for him in his absence." Allora's mind flew to a stone room and a hidden secret.

"Is that why you still haven't married, so you may care for your father?" Illia's brow wrinkled as she spoke, as though she were a child confused about the making of supper.

"There are many reasons," Allora said, "but I cannot abandon my father. Not when the map makers have so much to do before your wedding."

"I suppose I should be pleased a daughter of the Guilds is so attached to her duty." Illia sighed. "Wouldn't it be wonderful if we could do as we pleased, and live where we pleased, and marry whom we pleased?"

"Perhaps, but the Guilds require sacrifice. And who are we to refuse?"

9

MARA

Long ago, before the light of Ilbrea entered the world, great beasts roamed the white mountains. Bears that could devour a man in one swallow. Wolves that could outpace the wind as they ran across the snow. The horrors that filled the white kept even the bravest of men away from the snows of the northern mountains.

Every once in a while, a brave man would glance north, dreaming of adventure. An icy chill would race down his spine at the sight of the mountains that pierced the clouds in the sky. The man would remember why the white belonged to the beasts, and his dreams of adventure would vanish.

Men cannot survive in the land where winter never leaves. The lady born of the ice has—

"I'm not sure if you didn't get the better end of the deal."

Niko's words pulled Mara's attention from the book in her lap.

"Really?" Mara leaned back against the stone wall of the mausoleum. "So far in my reading, I have horrible monsters, ice that holds spirits, naked women dancing through the snow, and I've just gotten to a bit about a woman born of ice."

"You automatically won with the naked women dancing in the snow," Niko said.

Adrial gave a low laugh from his corner of the mausoleum. He'd laid a tan blanket down before sitting on the floor, but even still, his pristine white robes seemed absurd against the swirling pink and gray of the polished stone walls.

"See, Mara, even our innocent Adrial agrees with me." Niko picked up the next book in his stack. "Naked women always win for best journey."

"It's not that." Adrial looked up from his own reading. "I was laughing as I imagined what Allora would say if she heard your excitement at the possibility of magical naked women."

"At least they would give me something cheerful to look at," Niko said. "If the myths and legends of the eastern mountains hold any truth, then I have ghostly bandits, mountains that eat people, and shadow monsters to look forward to."

"Are you saying you'd rather not go on your journey?" Allora stood in the door of the mausoleum. The hinges hadn't even squeaked when she'd come in, and the door shut soundlessly behind her, blocking out the chill of the night wind. "If you wanted to stay in Ilara and work with the apprentices, I'm sure I could convince father—"

"I want to go to the eastern mountains." Niko picked up a new book. "I crave adventure, long to explore, and have given my vow to Lord Karron that I will spend my life finding the magic hidden in the shadows even if it means risking the Lady Sorcerer hanging me from her black stone tower."

"Don't be dramatic." Allora set her basket down and sat beside Niko. "If the King or the sorcerers found out you were hiding evidence of magic outside the Guilds' control, you wouldn't be hanged from the sorcerers tower."

"Do you really place that much faith in my undeniable charm?" Niko asked.

"No," Allora laughed. "But if you were caught and hanged, they would display you in the cathedral square. It's tradition."

"No one is going to be hanged anywhere," Mara said.

"She's right," Niko said, "we'd just disappear in the middle of the night. A public hanging might make people wonder what we'd done wrong, and the sorcerers can't afford that sort of scrutiny."

"The sorcerers aren't going to come after anyone," Mara said, "because we won't give them any reason to. Niko and I know how to be careful. No one on our journeys will notice us hunting for magic, and we keep our true maps hidden from anyone who might turn us in. Allora is guarding the maps we've already made, and Adrial—"

"Don't worry about me," Adrial said. "I didn't even have to sneak the books of myths and stories out of the library this time. I've been trying to find a way to make the vellum for Princess Illia something she might actually be grateful to have. I've been hunting through old stories for ideas for making the illuminated illustrations more appealing to her while maintaining the history of Ilbrea."

"Have you had any luck?" Niko reached into Allora's basket.

Allora swatted his hand away.

"Not really," Adrial said, "but it gave me a good excuse for taking every book I could find with any hint of magic that pointed to the eastern or white mountains."

"The Princess is fifteen," Mara said. "Does she really find fairy stories to be more interesting than the history of the country her family rules?"

"Probably," Niko said.

"Be kind, Niko," Allora said.

"When you were her age, you'd taken over the running of your father's house and established yourself as the Lady of the Map Makers Guild," Niko said.

"You'd taught a bastard orphan to read and battled against the Guilds to get him apprenticed as a scribe," Adrial said.

"And saved your best friend from despair and stood against your own father to help her fight for her dreams," Mara finished.

"Thank you all very much for your praise." A faint blush rose to Allora's cheeks. "But you're being unfair to Illia. You can't judge her by our standards. We had each other, and were able to travel, and were given freedom the poor Princess can't even properly imagine. The girl is engaged to a man she's never met and has never slept a night outside the Royal Palace. You can't expect her to be grown up and grand, she's never had a chance to spread her wings."

"You're right." Niko kissed Allora's hand. "But don't let your compassion make you forget how spectacular you are, Allora."

"I won't." Allora looked away from Niko as her blush shifted to a brighter pink. "It's going to be a long night, so I smuggled us some provisions." She pulled a bottle of chamb, four glasses, a box of sweetmeats, and a box of cheese from her basket.

"You are the most brilliant girl to have ever lived." Niko pulled open the bottle of chamb.

Mara looked to Adrial in time to see him wince at the presence of food and drink so near the books.

"Do you ever wonder if they'll write stories about us?" Niko poured Allora a glass of chamb.

"About our betrayal of the Guilds?" Allora sipped her chamb. "I hope they don't."

"I don't mean fables of our executions. I mean about all the wonders we've discovered." Niko passed Mara a glass.

"That would depend." Adrial closed the book he'd been reading and set it on his lap. "In order for a scribe to record the wild magic you've seen, the Sorcerers Guild would have to admit that there is, in fact, magic in the world that is not under the control of the Lady Sorcerer. Which, in an ideal Ilbrea, would be easy. Welcomed even.

"By discovering animals with unnatural abilities, you would be offering the sorcerers resources they don't currently have. The same could be said of stones that hold magic, people who hide their magic, places that shield magic. Every bit of power that hides in the shadows holds untapped potential a practical person would be thrilled to discover. But to accept that any of those resources exist, the sorcerers would have to admit they are not the only source of magic in Ilbrea."

"Which would make them vulnerable." Allora shuddered.

"They are vulnerable." Niko took her hand. "The Lady Sorcerer pretends we all have to grovel at her feet, but she's wrong. Someday, the Guilds and all Ilbrea will figure that out, and when they do, the true maps that your father, Mara, and I have been creating—the wonders you've been guarding—will make everyone see just how much Ilbrea has to offer."

"You're right. The sorcerers won't lord over us forever." Allora didn't let go of Niko's hand even as she set down her glass and reached across him to take a book from the stack Adrial had brought him.

The mausoleum settled back into silence as they all began reading again.

Men cannot survive in the land where winter never leaves. The lady born of the ice has...

Mara couldn't make her mind focus on the story of the deadly queen who stained the northern snows with blood.

She liked reading the old stories and guessing what bits of the legends might have been born of truths. She needed to know as much as she could about what might wait for her and Tham in the white mountains.

But sitting in a mausoleum reading fairy stories always felt wrong to her, no matter how many times they'd hidden together while poring over books.

Sorcerer-made lights hung in each corner of the gray and pink marbled room, casting away any shadows that might have lurked amongst the dead. The walls held places for a dozen people to rest, but only one place had been claimed. Only one Karron had fallen since Lord Karron built the palace before Allora was born.

Mara looked up to the plaque that marked Allora's mother's resting place.

Alloretta Karron had died before Lord Karron had first discovered magic beyond the sorcerers' control. She'd been gone for years before he started creating two different maps on every journey.

One map held the detailed drawing of the landscape the Guilds were willing to accept and the sorcerers were willing to allow. The other map, the true map, marked each of the places where wild magic existed, preserving their discoveries for a time when the truth could be told to all the people of Ilbrea.

"If this book is to be believed," Allora said, "you might very well be trapped in an underground labyrinth."

"Really?" Niko leaned close to Allora to peer over her shoulder.

Allora tensed for a moment before leaning closer to Niko, letting her shoulder rest against him. "If you happen to discover the Dark Hall, you might wander for a hundred miles and never see sunlight."

"A hundred miles isn't so bad," Niko said. "Take that at a good pace, and you could cover the ground in well under a week."

"But there might be ghosts stalking through the hall, trying to trap you for all eternity," Allora said.

"I'll just have to kindly explain to the ghosts that I can't stay." Niko tipped his head toward Allora's.

She sank even closer to him, letting his cheek rest against the top of her head.

"I have people waiting for me in Ilara," Niko said. "No amount of adventure, no horde of ghosts, could ever keep me away. I'll always come home. No matter what it takes."

Mara glanced to Adrial. They shared a smile before she looked back to her book.

Men cannot survive in the land where winter never leaves. The lady born of the ice has claimed her domain and will kill to keep it.

At the heart of the white mountains, beyond the peaks no man can climb, the lady lives in her palace of ice.

When she was born into the cold, there was no shelter for her. She spent her childhood always shivering in the snow.

But the white mountains would not let the snow child die. The cold protected her even as it stole every ounce of hope she'd been born with. Icicles weighed down her hair, and the frost that coated her body cracked and grew as the years passed and she left childhood behind.

At the dawn of her fifteenth year, the lady felt the first spark of magic fly through her veins, offering her deliverance from her solitude.

First, she let out a great shout, calling the largest and fastest of the wolves to her side.

Second, she beckoned the bear with the softest fur.

Finally, she summoned the most daring snow hawk.

The wolf, she made her mount, so she could charge south over the impassable peaks and to the lands of sunlight and warmth. The bear, she skinned to make herself a white coat so she would not be seen unclothed. The hawk, she bade fly south to bring her news of what waited for her beyond the edge of the white.

When the lady climbed onto her wolf, the mountains trembled. When she charged south, the stars grieved, for they knew only death could come out of the white mountains.

ADRIAL

Aximander and Farrin standing together on the prow of a ship, the sail whipping in the wind as a fierce storm gathers behind them.

For the greatness of Ilbrea and at the order of King Gransen Willoc the First, Aximander set forth on the first map making journey on a ship captained by Farrin, the great seafarer. The journey led them east across the Arion Sea to the Barrens, then south to Ruthir Mountain.

That would be the next image Adrial would have to illuminate—Saint Aximander, Patron Saint of the Map Makers Guild, standing atop Ruthir Mountain. Most of the images of him showed a grassy mountaintop like those to the northeast of Ilara, but that wasn't the first mountain Aximander conquered in King Gransen's name. Ruthir Mountain had proven to King Gransen that Ilbrea needed the Map Makers Guild, and the perils Aximander survived had secured him his place as Patron Saint of the map makers.

If this vellum was to travel to Wyrain with Princess Illia, it should tell the true story, not the pretty tale told by the stained glass.

Unless the King wants it to match the stories Princess Illia has grown accustomed to.

Adrial pinched the bridge of his nose. He would need to ask Gareth what he wanted before he could move on to the next illustration.

Our duty is to honor truth. But our duty is also to bring understanding. And how can you make them understand if they won't turn past the first page? Gareth's voice sounded perfectly in Adrial's mind, as though the old man stood behind his shoulder.

Will I still be able to hear him when he's gone and the Lordship weighs on my shoulders?

In a movement too quick for his own body, Adrial stood, knocking his chair to the ground.

"Are you all right, Head Scribe?" Natalia called from the front room.

"Fine," Adrial said. "I'm not an invalid."

"What?" Natalia spoke through the crack in the door.

"Nothing. Just knocked over a chair." Adrial dug his knuckles into his eyes, willing his heart to slow.

Gareth was wrong to choose Adrial as his heir and a fool to trust Adrial to make the vellum.

Adrial belonged in the library, hidden amongst the shelves of books as he dove into scholarly pursuits. He was not a leader. No one would ever want to obey the Guilded Cripple. No one would think him capable of protecting his Guild.

"I'm not built for this." Even whispering the words sent a sickening guilt rolling through Adrial's stomach.

Hands shaking, Adrial moved to the tea tray in the corner.

Two mugs and a tray with two rolls sat next to the teapot. But what was the point in requesting an extra mug so Ena wouldn't steal his if the girl never showed up?

The sun had shifted enough that the midday chimes would ring through the streets any moment.

And he still hadn't eaten.

You're a getch of a fool, Adrial Ayres.

Breathing deeply, Adrial steadied his hands and poured himself tea. A bit of sugar, a leaf of bitter herb.

"I'm not sure this is the best time." Natalia's voice carried through the door. "Maybe if you come back tomorrow—"

A laugh bubbled over Natalia's words as the door swung open.

"I told you, now isn't—"

"It's fine," Adrial spoke over Natalia as Ena breezed into the room.

She dropped her basket onto the table before strolling to the tea tray and tossing a wink over her shoulder at Natalia, as though daring her to argue.

"I have very important merchandise for the head scribe." Ena took the mug from Adrial's hand and a roll from the tray. "From the looks of it, he's been horribly distressed waiting for the new batch of ink." She nodded at the tipped over chair. "Or maybe you weren't driven to madness at having to wait a week to see me. Maybe you've gotten stuck on the vellum and had a tantrum like a weaning babe."

"Is there anything else I can do for you, Head Scribe?" Pink crept up Natalia's neck.

"No, thank you." Adrial nodded.

Ena grinned and took a sip of his tea as the door to the shop swung shut. "Sorry for the wait. I hope you haven't been pining for me."

"No. I've been getting work done," Adrial said, his tone harder than he'd meant it.

"Well, don't be angry with me." Ena shook her head, sending her hair flying around her shoulders. Deep green had taken prominence in its coloring.

"I'm not." Adrial filled the second mug with tea. "You could have fixed yourself a fresh cup. I have one here."

"But I like the way you do it." Ena winked and took a bite of her roll before moving to the worktable. "I really didn't think you'd catch on so quickly."

"Catch on?"

"You've already had them send over extra breakfast so I wouldn't steal yours. I'm impressed."

"Really?" Heat rose in Adrial's face. "How long did you think it would take?"

"A few more visits at least."

Adrial dumped too much sugar in his tea and moved toward the table, walking as steadily as he could.

"Don't hide the limp. It only causes you pain." Ena didn't turn to look at him as she spoke. "This is beautiful."

"Thank you." Adrial righted the knocked over chair.

"So you didn't toss your chair because you were mad about your work being awful." Ena turned to examine him, her face only inches from his as she stared into his eyes. "You aren't mad at me, or you wouldn't have put up with my teasing and stealing your tea."

"Of course I'm not mad at—"

"What then?" Ena tossed the rest of her roll into her basket and took Adrial's chin in her hand. "And don't say *nothing*. You're a terrible liar, scribe."

"I've never lied to you."

"But you've thought about trying." Ena leaned in and whispered in his ear. "You're not going to get out of telling me."

The smell of something wild floated from Ena's hair. The scent filled his lungs and made his head swim.

He should have been livid. An inker pressing the head scribe for information. Invading his space, stealing his food.

"Lord Gareth isn't doing well." The words slipped from Adrial's lips before he knew he'd decided to speak.

"I heard." Ena stepped back, a tiny wrinkle creased between her eyebrows.

"How?" Adrial faced his drawing table.

At least the paper and ink make sense. At least I'll still have something to hang on to.

"Lord of a Guild takes ill, it won't stay quiet." Ena shrugged. "Especially not in a city packed as tightly as Ilara. It would be sad to see him go. Losing an honest head of a Guild is a terrible blow for the common folk."

"He is a very good man." Tears stung in the corners of Adrial's eyes. "But he'll be fine. He's strong. He'll be well soon enough."

"If death does claim him, at least there's another good man waiting to take his place." Ena took the mug from Adrial's hand, leaving both cups on the tea tray before starting to empty her basket. "Just imagine what a horrible thing it would be if that chivving paun Travers were in line for the Lordship. We'd be in an even worse mess than we are now."

The jolt of shock that shot through Adrial at hearing the word *paun* spoken in his office was swallowed by the flare of pride that surged in his chest. "You shouldn't talk like that about him. He might hear you."

"I've dealt with worse than him." Ena pressed a vial to Adrial's chest. "All bluster and nothing else."

"We can hope." Adrial held the vial up to the light—a black with purple coursing through it. "It's beautiful."

"I know. And it is nice to know someone worthy is using my ink for once. You would be amazed how many untalented people come sniffing around for my pigments. Like good ink will help with the chivving messes they make." Ena held another jar up to the sunlight. Her sleeve tumbled down her arm, revealing her pale skin. Pink and blue ink marked her flesh right above a deep-set bruise. "I had a man offer me coin for fine black ink so he could pen a love letter. The oaf probably couldn't spell *love*."

"Ena, what's that?" Adrial took her arm.

"I took his money anyway, but—"

"Ena," Adrial cut across her.

"Worried about a bruise?" Ena laughed. "It's nothing, scribe. But this pink is perfect for sunsets."

"It's not nothing." Adrial snatched the jar from her hand without looking at it. "Did you fall down a mountain, get thrown from a horse?"

"Strangely enough, both of those things have happened recently." Ena yanked her arm from Adrial's grip and dug back into her basket. "The mountain fall was terrible but worth it for what I found. If you're lucky, maybe I'll make you tromp out with—"

"Ena!"

Ena spun to face Adrial, her eyes gleaming with something between loathing and mirth.

"Do they tell you nothing, scribe?" Ena whispered. "Do you just stay locked in your land of pure white and assume the rest of the world is just as perfect? Because that's far from the truth."

"What happened?" Adrial held his hands forward, not daring to actually reach for her.

"The chivving Soldiers Guild happened." Ena ran her hands through her hair. The bottom layer shimmered a bright pink.

"The soldiers hurt you?" Adrial took another step forward. "If they did, I'll go to Lord Kearney myself."

"What a defender! Do you think the Lord Soldier would care about a rotta inker?"

"Ena—"

"It wasn't the soldiers themselves anyway." Ena turned to the table, straightening out all the inks, placing the ones she'd brought in the line with what Adrial already had. "The soldiers decided to kick up the muck. Asking common folk to fight against their own in the south and not even giving them a fancy uniform for the trouble of having tilk blood on their hands."

"That's not why the King—"

"Don't pretend to understand things you don't, scribe. Ignorance doesn't suit you."

Helplessness swooped through Adrial's stomach. "All right. If I don't understand, then explain it to me. It's not as though I'm a complete fool."

"There are too many years of pain for you to understand." Ena looked up at Adrial, and for a tiny moment, he thought he saw tears glistening in the corners of her eyes. "And the people who know that pain won't let the Guilds slather common folks' blood on their hands."

Before Adrial could reach for her, the tears were gone.

Ena searched Adrial's eyes. "The common folk, the tilk, are tired of the Guilds' tyranny. And anyone who helps the Guilds, well, we're just traitors."

"And you're helping me." Adrial looked to the ink on the table. Such a simple thing, but he couldn't make the vellum without it.

"That I am." Ena pulled up her sleeve to show the bruise. "They took my basket and smashed every vial and jar. I made a few of them bleed, but ink isn't worth hanging for murder. And why should I come around here if I don't have anything to bring the head scribe?"

"Did you tell the soldiers someone had hurt you?" Adrial's mind raced to Tham.

He was busy getting ready for the journey, but he would find time to help Ena.

"Are you sure you're not a chivving fool?" Ena asked. "Do you really think the soldiers care if thugs rough up common folk? If they had trod on a sorcerer's hem, they'd all be hanged, but they can smash everything a tilk has and the chivving paun don't care."

"If you tell me who it was," Adrial spoke slowly, keeping his voice calm against the anger that thudded in his chest, "I'll be sure the soldiers care. I'll make sure they're arrested."

"And hanged?" Ena took Adrial's hand in hers and swung it

back and forth, as though they were children playing in the garden. "It would only make it worse. Handsome men with dangerous words, they rouse the folks around them to brave and daring deeds. Fight the Guilds, protect your people, rid the land of traitors. It all sounds so wonderful when lantern light dances across their faces and their words ring out over a hushed crowd.

"But then the blood starts raining down. And the handsome men die. The people who follow them die. And the ones unlucky enough to wade through the blood and fire and come out alive, they're stuck trying to live in a world that should be better than it is. Trying to forget there's blood all over their hands."

"Ena—"

"But then another handsome man decides to change the world for the better, and you're on the wrong side of the line. Or maybe the world has just turned into a darker and meaner place." Ena took Adrial's face in her hands. "Getting rid of one will only give whoever comes next a reason to be crueler. To fight harder and hurt more people."

"But they hurt you," Adrial said. "You can't just let them get away with it. What if they attack you the next time you bring an order? Unless you won't be bringing any more ink."

Ena laughed and turned back to her basket. Whatever quiet moment of truth she had shared was gone, replaced with a glint in her eye and a smile on her lips that Adrial did not know how to see through.

"And if I don't bring ink to you, how will I eat?" Ena asked. "I can barely keep a roof over my head with only the common ink orders."

"I'll come get the ink from you," Adrial suggested. "Then you won't have to come to the shop."

"Oh, what a treat that would be! The Guilded Cripple walking to the docks to gather ink. I'm sure Travers would love that."

"Travers works for me." Adrial walked to the tea tray and

picked up the bag of coins he had ready for Ena. "I don't care what he thinks of how I do things."

"Liar."

Adrial grabbed the few coins he had in his pocket and slipped them into the bag.

"Your coming to me would be worse than my coming here," Ena said. "To some, it might be worth the risk of being hanged if they could bloody the head scribe."

"Then what are we going to do?" Adrial tossed the bag into Ena's basket, hoping she wouldn't count the coin and notice the extra until she was well away from the shop. "You can't keep coming back."

Saying those simple words lodged a shard of ice in Adrial's heart.

But if it wasn't safe to work for the Guilds, she shouldn't be doing it. And he barely knew her, had only met her a few times. So there was no reason for him to worry about not seeing the mad inker anymore. His life could go back to its usual state of unchanging peace.

She won't come to the shop bothering me. Stealing my tea.

The shard of ice dug deeper.

"Don't worry, scribe." Ena reached into the pouch and pulled out several coins, tossing them onto the table with a clatter. "I've learned my lesson. I know who to avoid, and I know how to be careful."

"Are you sure?" Adrial swallowed the bubble of hope that flitted up into his throat.

"I'm always sure." Ena poked him in the chest, all trace of worry and fear gone. "And if you want to help me, don't try to slip me extra coin. You haven't the skill for sleight of hand."

"What can I do then?"

"I'll need your help in a few days." Ena winked as she breezed toward the door. "Just be ready for another little adventure."

MARA

The beast bared its fangs at Mara, snarling its dislike of everything she was.

"Nice dog," Mara cooed, careful to keep her fingers out of the animal's reach as she tossed meat into its bowl.

The beast snapped its teeth at her once more before tearing into its food.

"You can't let the dogs know you're afraid of them," Carrow spoke from behind her. "They'll start to think they're in charge, and that's a fine way to get left behind in the white."

"I'm not afraid of them," Mara said. "I just don't like being snarled at."

"You wouldn't like freezing to death, either." Carrow turned Mara around, took her shoulders, and looked into her eyes. "The dogs are what will keep you alive in the white."

It was meant to be a kind gesture, but Mara hated the pack master touching her.

He wouldn't pander to the men.

"I'm sure I'll find a way to manage." Mara smiled.

"Managing won't be enough in the white mountains." Carrow shook his head sagely. "You're asking these animals to risk their lives for you. I'm not saying they have to love you, but if the dogs don't respect you, they'll leave you to freeze in the snow."

A chill licked the back of Mara's neck, as though the white mountains wanted to consume her so badly, they'd sent their icy breath to lure her onward.

"Well, give me a few days' travel with the dogs, and I'm sure we'll learn to get along." Mara stepped out of Carrow's reach.

"To tell the truth, going deep into the white mountains might be better than being in Ilara soon enough."

"What?" Mara laughed. "Why? Are warmth and summer flowers too much for you?"

"Sometimes I forget how far away the Karrons really are, living up on the cliffs." Carrow shook his head.

"I'm not a Karron—"

"'Course you are." Carrow reached into the kennel, stroking the ear of the dog that had been near taking Mara's hand off. "You may walk through the mud like a common man, but all of Karron's brood have Guild colors on their backs and the Lord Map Maker's title to shield them from the uglier bits of Ilbrea. Still, I thought you would have heard of the trouble stirring up what with Map Maker Endur getting into a scuff."

"You mean Niko fighting at that pub?" Mara dropped her voice.

The whole of Ilara knew things had gotten rough at the White Froth, but Lord Karron had been careful to keep word of his former apprentice's involvement quiet. If Niko were disciplined for fighting—not that he should be, but if he were—someone else would be assigned to the journey to explore the eastern mountains.

If a foolish brawl ruins Lord Karron's plans...

"—and it's worse for us unguilded," Carrow finished darkly.

"I'm sorry," Mara said, trying to sort through what she had missed while her mind had wandered, "but how is the fighting in the White Froth worse for the unguilded?"

"'Cause I work for the Guilds." Carrow's voice dropped to barely above a whisper. "The common folk are chivving furious with the Guilds. Last winter was bad—too cold, food prices high—and they've had enough. And when the common masses decide they don't want any of our kind working for the Guilds, folks like me will have to choose between meeting the hard end of a stick and making a living."

"Surely it won't get that bad." Mara stepped back as the dog snarled again.

"Down, Bayna," Carrow said. "I hope you're right, map maker. And if you're not, then I hope you find a fairyland in the snow where you can live away from this mess."

Mara gave a small, awkward laugh and nodded, unsure of what to say.

"And if you get Lord Karron's ear before you leave," Carrow said as Mara started down the long row that cut between the dogs, "ask him for more guards for the stables and kennels. I'd hate to see what angry people could do to these animals. And up the pay for the lot of us who'll be risking our necks for the Guilds, too."

"I'll do my best." Mara waved over her shoulder, not turning around as the dogs yipped and barked as she passed.

Twenty dogs had been chosen for the journey to the white mountains. Their job was to haul the supplies for the two map makers and ten soldiers. It would be nice if they could pull the party and not just the supplies, but venturing into the snow was not a thing commonly done, and only twenty dogs were dubbed fit and trained enough for the job.

"They really are nice, you know," Tham said from inside one of the kennels. Dressed in his soldier black, he sat on the floor with a gray and white dog.

The animal didn't snarl or snap at Tham. The dog had laid his head on Tham's lap, panting contentedly.

"Not all of us can be as naturally brilliant with animals as you are."

"Well, you'd better learn to like them. Starting tomorrow, they'll be our best friends."

If Mara hadn't known Tham so well, she might have missed the hint of teasing in his voice.

"Yes, I'll spend all my nights curled up with a snarling ball of fur to keep from freezing."

Tham gave the dog one last scratch behind the ear and stood, brushing fur and dirt from his pants. "I hope you're not too lonely on the cold nights."

Mara bit the insides of her cheeks. "The thought of freezing winds howling through my tent is terrifying. Perhaps I'll light an extra candle tonight to keep the fear at bay."

It was Tham's turn to bite back a smile. "May the night bring you peace before your journey."

She longed to reach out and touch his face. To feel the tiny creases of his smile and the faint hint of stubble on his chin.

Don't be a fool, Mara. If you let the others on the journey know about the two of you, your time in the white will be miserable. If they let you go at all.

"See you in the morning." Mara nodded and strode to the kennel doors.

Bright, clean air greeted her outside the kennels. She took a deep breath, freeing her lungs of the stench of dog.

"I suppose it would be wrong of me to brag that the only animals coming on our journey are horses?" Niko called as he strode across the courtyard. "Though your way is bound for more glory, at least I'll be traveling on horseback."

"Such a gentleman, as always." Mara shoved his shoulder. "If I freeze to death, you'll feel very guilty for mocking me."

"And if the ghosts of the eastern mountains swallow me whole, you'll be glad you've been stomping around in snow shoes." Niko gave a deep bow. "Though I do promise to give the ghosts your regards."

"How kind."

The courtyard at the map makers' compound buzzed with activity. Both journeys were to leave tomorrow. Common workers loaded wagons of supplies under Lord Karron's watchful eye. His journey to the southern islands wouldn't begin for at least another two months.

The approach to the islands was impossible until the sea storms passed. So he lorded over the preparations for the other two journeys, ensuring perfection in every detail. Failure could not be allowed when the journey was under command of the King.

Niko tipped his head for Mara to follow him. They strolled along the stables and passed the statue of Aximander. Both bowed their heads for a moment before stepping through the high gates to the street beyond.

"Are you ready for your journey?" Niko asked, stopping at a stall selling sweet bread.

"You mean have I taken a moment to appreciate my ten toes in case I come home with fewer?"

"Two please." Niko gave coin to the woman running the stall.

She couldn't have been more than twenty, barely older than Mara and Niko, but bags hung heavy under her eyes, and her face had the sallow look of one who had seen too much work and too little food.

"Thank you." Mara laid an extra coin on the wood as the woman handed them bread dripping with honey and fine sugar.

"There are other preparations to be made that don't involve a fond farewell to your toes," Niko said as Mara bit into her bread.

The pure sweetness was better than chamb.

Enjoy it now. All luxuries will be gone come morning.

"I've packed extra scrolls." Mara glanced around the street, as though she were looking for a shop. "Tham knows to take them from the lining of my pack if anything happens to me."

"I envy you having someone to trust so completely." A bitter sadness crept into Niko's voice.

"You have a whole clan to count on." Mara looped her arm through Niko's. "They just won't be traveling with you."

"Well, if the ghosts gobble me up, there won't be anyone to keep the true map I've made safe. If I even find anything to make a second map for." Niko tipped his face toward the sky. "The stories of spirits in the eastern mountains could really just be old wives' tales."

"Of course," Mara laughed, "and the tales of magic in the Barrens are just children's stories. And we can't forget the lies about the floating islands."

"Does it ever make you hate the Guilds?" Niko stopped so suddenly, Mara nearly dropped the meager remains of her sweet bread.

"Hush," Mara warned, dragging Niko down a side street where tiny clusters of flowers separated the passersby from the houses' front windows. "You need to remember yourself, Nikolas Endur. Having been Lord Karron's apprentice can only save you from so much pain."

"I'll take that as a no then." Niko shrugged and began walking down the street, half-dragging Mara behind him.

Mara glanced up to the windows of the houses surrounding them. "I never said that. Sometimes I do think we'd all be better off without the Guilds' laws."

"Who should hush now?" Niko chuckled.

"I shouldn't have to hide extra map scrolls in my pack," Mara spoke softly, the lilt of her voice more like she was talking about the weather than treason that could see half the Karron clan hanged. "I shouldn't be making true maps to be hidden in case the Guilds ever realize they're fools to fear everything they can't control. There is magic in the world that is not controlled by the

Sorcerers Guild. That's a fact neither of us can deny, and a secret I hate to carry."

"I shudder to think how incredibly wealthy we would be if we could only claim the bounty on the wonders we've seen."

Mara hit Niko in the arm.

"What? It's true. We should be swimming in coin and have our portraits hanging in the Map Makers' Hall to boot. Instead, we're Lord Karron's former apprentices who have only moved up so quickly in the map makers' ranks because of favoritism and unearned positions."

"We are rather useless, aren't we?" Mara sighed dramatically.

"The King deserves better." Niko nodded solemnly.

"Are you heading up to see her?" Mara asked. "You know she'll be furious if you don't."

"Am I walking all the way up the cliffs to visit a girl who has refused to marry me more times than Rance Miter has sunk the Sailors Guild's ships? Yes, I suppose I am."

"Good," Mara said as they began climbing the road to the top of the cliffs.

They hugged close to the stone side of the road, letting the infrequent passing carriages take the outer edge. The road twisted up the solid rock of the cliff, doubling back on itself several times to keep the switchbacks from getting too steep to be easily climbed.

Every turn in the road had been carefully fortified by the Sorcerers Guild, jutting too far out into the open air to be stable by non-magical means.

The sorcerers wouldn't have helped a normal Guilded man build a road to their estate, but for Lord Karron, they had made an exception.

Mara tried to cast aside her worries of what would become of the road to the cliffs if the sorcerers ever discovered what Lord Karron had been so carefully hiding.

She took a deep breath as they reached the fourth leg of their walk. "She really does care for you, you know. More than she'll ever admit."

"I know." There was no joy in Niko's voice at the words. "If she didn't, I would have stopped trying a long time ago."

"It really is the cruelest to her, not being able to talk about the wonders we've found. We, at least, get the memories of finding lights flashing inside mountains and valleys filled with magic so small we barely noticed it. All she gets are the scrolls that would see her hanged if the King ever found them."

"That is the problem with treason." Niko scratched his chin. "It doesn't seem wrong when you're the person doing it. I can't imagine destroying the true maps. It would be a sin against Saint Aximander himself not to chart the wonders we've found. But to the King and the sorcerers..."

"We're tiny birds pecking away at the foundations that protect the Guilds and all the lies Ilbreans hold most dear."

They walked in silence, the cool spring breeze growing stronger as they climbed. They passed through the gates and onto the palace grounds, stopping at the very edge of the cliff to look out over Ilara.

The city sparkled in the afternoon sun, the top of the cathedral glistening and the white slanting roof of the library shining like a beacon. From this height, the great walls surrounding the Royal Palace didn't block the spires and gardens from view.

"How many times did we stand up here, mapping the streets of the city?" Niko asked.

"A hundred." Mara laughed. "Maybe two hundred or three. And mine were always better than yours."

"*Better* is in the eye of the beholder." Niko flicked her arm. "From up here, even the wharfs look pretty."

"Distance and fair weather can hide a great many flaws. Do you ever miss it when you're gone?"

"Ilara?" Niko tucked his hands into his pockets, looking for all the world like the boy he'd been at sixteen. "I miss the people. I miss warm baths and cold chamb. Every once in a while, I even miss clean clothes. But I prefer the mountains to the city."

"Me too. Perhaps that's what's doomed us." Mara leaned up on her toes, pulling Niko into a tight hug. "Journey well, my friend. I'll miss you at the northern gate in the morning."

"You're not coming up to the house?" Niko asked.

"Not yet." Mara shook her head and backed away. "I've got to stop by the mausoleum."

"Well, then"—Niko squeezed Mara's hand—"until next Winter's End."

"To the map makers." Mara nodded.

"And the maps."

Niko continued up the road through the wide, sweeping lawns that led to the Map Master's Palace while Mara followed the smaller foot trail.

Wide trees, whose branches were just forming their new spring leaves, closed in on either side of the path. Mara shut her eyes and imagined them at the peak of summer, dripping with fine white petals. Their scent would fill the grounds, covering the stench the heat brewed in the city below.

A small building waited at the end of the path. A mix of pink and gray polished stone formed the walls of the mausoleum with black slabs covering the top. A golden compass marked the heavy, wooden door.

Mara laid her hand on the mark. The same mark she bore on her arm. The mark that gave her purpose.

The door didn't squeak as it swung open, no rush of chill air met her skin, no darkness sent horror tingling in her spine.

The sorcerer-made lights cast an even glow around the small room, ensuring that, even though Mara was alone, the mausoleum did not feel like a place claimed by death.

Mara stopped in front of the only resting place that had been filled by a fallen Karron.

Alloretta Karron—born to the Soldiers Guild, loved by the Map Makers Guild, perished Lord Map Maker's Wife.

Mara's heart ached at the simple inscription. She had never even met Alloretta. She had died long before Mara came to live with the Karrons. But Alloretta guarded all of them in death, protecting them as none other could.

"Thank you," Mara whispered, running her hands along the side of Alloretta's stone. Her fingers met a tiny indentation, barely large enough to be noticed.

Pulling a pin from her hair, Mara pressed it into the tiny dent.

A crack as quiet as the snapping of a twig sounded as the stone loosened.

Mara's breath caught in her chest as the stone swung out. No matter how many times she had opened Alloretta's tomb, Mara could never rid herself of the childlike visions of skulls and rats that flashed unbidden through her mind.

But no specter of death lurked behind the stone.

She let out a shuddering sigh.

A stack of neatly arranged scrolls waited for her. Mara's fingers ached to pull each of them out. To see the maps Niko and Lord Karron had drawn of places she'd never been, or to remember the wonders of the true maps she'd created herself. But there wasn't time for such things.

Mara pulled a tiny scroll from her pocket and placed it on top of the others. It seemed out of place with the maps, but Alloretta's grave was the safest place she had and the one place Allora was sure to look if the white took Mara forever.

NIKO

The crowd was smaller than it should have been. The King and Lord Karron were at the northern city gate, seeing off the journey to the white mountains. Princess Illia was the only royal to come to the southern gate to bid farewell to the journey to the eastern mountains.

Wagons laid heavily with supplies lined up behind eight horses, waiting at the closed city gate.

Niko studied the loads of supplies, wondering how many bottles of frie he might have been able to stash if only he'd been fool enough to try.

"I have your horse ready for you, sir." A small boy nearly squeaked at his boldness in speaking to Niko. The boy was young, not yet old enough to have been chosen to study with the map makers, but he wore the green trim on his sleeves that distinguished him as a child of the Map Makers Guild.

"Thank you." Niko nodded.

The child didn't leave.

"Are you really going to go into the eastern mountains?" the boy asked.

"That is the journey the King commands." Niko scanned the

crowd. It was selfish, but he had hoped someone would come to see him off. He'd said all his goodbyes, but still...

"And they aren't taking any apprentices on this journey?" the boy asked with the air of one dreaming of adventure.

"Not this time." Niko smiled kindly. Too well he remembered longing to go on his first journey, and too well he knew this venture was not one children could attend. "Two map makers and eight soldiers."

"Brilliant," the boy breathed. "You must be going someplace very, very dangerous."

"Are you afraid of danger?" Niko said as a head of brilliantly blond hair moved through the crowd and Allora joined the Princess on the platform.

"No, sir." The boy pulled himself up to his full height. "I am always ready for adventure. Even if it is dangerous."

"Give it a few years." Niko ruffled the boy's hair. "There will be journeys left when you come of age."

The boy glanced around before speaking. "But what if everything's been explored by then?"

"The first thing you learn in map making is there will always be something more to explore. Sometimes, the things are small. Sometimes, they are whole mountain ranges. But the world changes far too often for the Guilds not to need new maps."

The boy bounced on his toes, his face beaming with excitement.

"Now go mind my horse, or I'll be walking to the eastern mountains," Niko said.

The boy ran back to Niko's horse and took hold of the reins.

Niko's mount was accustomed enough to standing with wagons waiting for journeys, he could have been left alone. But the child beamed with pride as he guarded Niko's horse.

"Everything set?"

Niko held back his groan as Jerick Ballak, the head soldier on the journey, appeared out of the common crowd.

"Of course," Niko said perhaps a little more brightly than he'd meant to. "Everything's packed, the weather is fine, we're one speech from being on our way."

"Good. The sooner the better." The short, stocky man barely reached Niko's shoulder, but something in his manner made every word he spoke a decree. It was not a trait Niko enjoyed.

"You know, I think you might be addicted to traveling with the map makers." Niko tucked his hands into his pockets. "You've journeyed with us one too many times, Jerick. I think you've grown attached."

"I do my duty." Jerick gave a curt nod that might have been meant as a bow. "Be ready to go as soon as the rigmarole is through."

Jerick melted back into the crowd before Niko could form the words *slitching getch* in his mind.

"Niko," a familiar and much more welcome voice called from behind as Adrial limped his way out of the crowd.

"Come to see me off?" Niko clapped Adrial on the back, careful to aim for his good shoulder. "I'm surprised they let you out. Such important work you're doing, Head Scribe."

"Well, nothing I can do at the moment but bring an old friend some comfort for his journey." Adrial pressed a leather pouch into Niko's hands. The finely etched leather had years of wear scarring its surface, and the weight felt more like stones to carry than anything that could be of comfort.

"I know it's heavy," Adrial said, as though reading Niko's face, "but promise to keep it with you. And don't open it until you're truly desperate for comfort."

"Hmm." Niko weighed the bag in his hand again before stuffing it into his pocket. "Mysterious gifts don't seem much like you."

"I wasn't alone in this." Adrial pointed up to the royal platform where Allora had joined Illia.

Niko wanted nothing more than to run to her. To sweep her

into his arms, kiss her with a passion that had burned for years, and carry her far away.

But they had already said their goodbyes, and his pride couldn't stand a public rejection at the city gate.

"You know, I think she's softening," Adrial said. "It burns my heart to say it, since it betrays a friend's trust, but not saying anything would harm another friend's chances."

"Saying what?" Niko whispered as a hush fell over the crowd and Princess Illia began to speak.

"Map makers," Illia began, nerves shaking her voice, "the journey you begin today—"

"Allora came to me in tears before dawn this morning," Adrial spoke softly, hiding his mouth behind his hand. "You and Mara leaving on the same day tore her apart."

Pain struck Niko's chest. He should stay. Relinquish his place in the Guilds and damn the shame it would bring.

But they needed someone to make a true map of the eastern mountains. Lord Karron was to sail south, and Mara would already be on the road to the north. Someone had to be brave enough to record the things the sorcerers didn't want them to find.

"The ties that will bring us closer to Wyrain will bring prosperity to Ilbrea." Princess Illia seemed near tears.

"She said she didn't think she could stand watching you ride away again," Adrial whispered, "especially not knowing if you were going to take up with some southern woman and bring her home as your bride."

"What?" Niko said louder than he'd meant to.

Jerick turned his sharp blue eyes to Niko, giving him a vicious glare.

"I told her you had every right to marry whomever you like if she kept turning you down," Adrial continued once Jerick had turned back to the Princess. "She looked like I'd stabbed her in the heart and sobbed hysterically."

The loathing of anything making Allora unhappy mixed with a surge of joy at her being distraught at the thought of Niko choosing someone else. Cruel, half-formed plans flitted through his mind.

Finding a common woman from the south and bringing her back to Ilara just to prove to Allora that he could. Rolling his way through every woman he happened to meet on his journey. But his gaze met hers as she glanced at him from the royal platform, and everything inside him melted.

"Am I supposed to take tears as a sign of promising things to come?" Niko said under the applause of the crowd.

"The winds could blow us all away before you return." Adrial gave a one-shouldered shrug. "But somewhere beneath the tears, I distinctly heard her say she loved you, and whoever thought anyone but Mara would hear her say that out loud?"

"She said she loved me? Are you quite sure?" Niko clenched his hands into tight fists as he fought the urge to leap onto the royal platform and kiss Allora.

"Oh, I am very sure." Adrial smiled. "Go and find some glory and honor, and for the stars' sake, bring a ring with you the next time you propose."

A bugle sounded at the front of the caravan. The young boy holding the reins of Niko's horse nervously waved to him as the gate swung open.

"I should talk to her now." Niko glanced back at the stage.

Allora gave a tiny smile and nodded at him.

But he couldn't do anything now. They had already said their goodbyes, and the journey wouldn't wait for him to propose again.

"Take care of her." Niko grasped Adrial's shoulder. "And if any man comes within ten feet of her, remind him she is spoken for by Nikolas Endur."

"I will," Adrial said. "Be safe, old friend. The city will be lonely without you."

"Be safe, brother," Niko said. "Guard the gates until I return."

Niko ran to his horse and swung easily up onto his saddle. Cheers rose as he waved down at the crowd.

The leaving had always been one of the grandest parts of journeying. Reveling in the adoration of the people. Bolstered by the hopes and confidence of the Ilbreans. But his heart didn't float with joy as the caravan took the first steps forward.

Niko forced air into his lungs, promising himself he was only being a lovesick fool, and then screams rent the air as a crack sounded behind him.

"Allora!" The shout tore from Niko's throat before he'd even turned around.

Smoke coated the street near the royal platform. Flames licked the bottoms of the houses and reached toward the Princess.

Soldiers in black uniforms lay on the ground in growing pools of blood, but others were still on their feet.

"Allora!" Niko moved to leap down from his horse, but the soldier riding next to him grabbed his reins, dragging his mount into a run. "Stop. We have to help!"

A soldier grabbed Allora, pulling her down from the platform and bundling her into the waiting royal carriage with the Princess.

"We can't risk the caravan. Ha!" Jerick screamed at the horses, making them run faster. The wagons behind them blocked the road from sight as they broke free of the last of the city and were out on the wide road.

"We can't just abandon them." Niko's hands shook as he snatched at his reins.

"Do you think going back would help?" Jerick said. "What could you do that the soldiers left at the gate can't? The start of our journey was attacked. The best thing we can do is get our party away from the city as quickly as we can."

Niko buried his face in his hands. Only years of riding kept him in the saddle. He wished they hadn't. He wished he could fall to the ground and crawl back to the city.

Allora hadn't looked injured when they'd bundled her into the carriage. Terrified, but not wounded.

It was a blessing from Dudia that the Princess's carriage had been so close. And the soldiers so quick to act. And that there were so many of them.

"Did you know?" Niko's eyes snapped open. "Did you know the journey was going to be attacked?"

"Had we known, we would have left in the middle of the night." Jerick tossed Niko his reins.

"But you suspected."

They passed the last of the outlying houses. An old woman worked in her front garden, no sign of fear showing in her manner as she pulled weeds.

"There have been rumblings from the common folk," Jerick said. "The journeys starting today are the biggest events Ilara will see until the King's birthday in two months and Lord Karron's sailing after that. If anyone wanted to cause problems, today was their best chance."

"And the Soldiers Guild decided to let Guilded and commoners, and even royals, gather anyway?" Niko spoke through gritted teeth. The smoke of the blast was barely visible from here. No more than a cook fire gone wrong. "Has the Soldiers Guild gotten so lazy they've decided to just let the commoners run wild and hurt people? Murder a few as morning fun?"

"We had no proof," Jerick said, unfazed by Niko's insults. "And the orders came from far above. I don't even know who gave them. If it were up to me, there would be no ceremonies when the map makers leave. No one gives speeches when soldiers march out of the city. Why should it be different for those dressed in green?"

"So we just ride east to the mountains and hope the city

doesn't burn while we're gone?" A horrible ache settled in the back of Niko's lungs.

"The King has given us our task for the good and safety of Ilbrea," Jerick said. "We must trust in the wisdom of the Guilds to protect those whose duty it is to stay behind."

Jerick didn't sound comforted, or even very sure.

Aximander, Dudia, mother—whoever might be listening—take care of them. Protect the city. Protect my family. Protect Allora. Give me the strength to ride away from them. And the promise of something to come back to.

ADRIAL

Pain. Sharp, terrible pain in his shoulder.

The pain in his head was worse.

The screaming voices ignited the pain in a wave of piercing agony that made thinking impossible.

Instinct told Adrial he should find out what everyone was screaming about, but there were far too many people speaking at once. If they could all just be silent for a moment, maybe he could work out what they were shouting about and be able to help them.

Adrial pushed himself to sit up. The world blurred around him.

Red tainted his vision. His hands shook as he fumbled in his pocket for something to wipe his eyes. His robes had been stained. Black, red, and brown marred the white.

Praying for Saint Alwyn's forgiveness, Adrial wiped his eyes on his sleeve. Clearing his vision didn't make the scene any more manageable.

Smoke billowed from the buildings behind the platform where the Princess and Allora had been standing.

"Allora!" Adrial coughed. Pain wracked his lungs. "Allora!" A golden carriage disappeared from view.

If they had taken the Princess, surely they would have taken Allora as well.

But what if they hadn't?

Patches of blood smeared the singed wooden platform. Black covered the people who lay unmoving on the ground.

Adrial swallowed the sour in his throat. "Allora!"

He stumbled toward the platform.

A woman in torn merchant's clothing ran past, knocking into Adrial's shoulder. His bad leg buckled, but he fought to stay standing.

Four men lay on the ground. Their clothes hadn't been burnt black by the flames. They were wearing Soldiers Guild uniforms.

"Help." Adrial ran forward as fast as his legs could manage. "They need help!" But the chaos of the street drowned out his shouts.

Half-collapsing to ground, Adrial knelt by the nearest soldier. His eyes were stuck open. Frozen in terror. Adrial pressed his fingers to the man's neck, searching for some sign of life.

The man hadn't shaved that morning. Rough stubble greeted Adrial's fingers. But the soldier was still. Blood pooled around him, leaking from a wound Adrial couldn't see.

"I'm so sorry." Adrial crawled away, moving on to the next soldier.

This one was young, barely old enough to wear the black.

Something sharp sliced into Adrial's palm. He lifted his hand. Blood dripped down his fingers, some of it definitely his.

The sharp thing stuck out of his hand. The jagged cut on his palm bled freely. But he had crawled through the soldier's blood. The soldier's blood would mix with his.

Adrial gasped as he pulled the sharp shard from his skin.

Shouts and the pounding of hooves carried from down the street.

"The Healers Guild are on their way," an extraordinarily tall soldier barked to the others. "Move everyone who can walk out of the street."

Adrial knew the man's name. He had met him before. At a party?

No, it wasn't at a party. Allora would have introduced the soldier if Adrial had met him at a party, and she was good at making sure he remembered people's names.

"Can you walk?" a short soldier with blood smeared on his cheek shouted at him like he had been saying the same words to Adrial for a very long time.

"Yes," Adrial said, shocked by the calm of his tone. "But that man is dead."

"Well, you're not, and we need to get you away from here." The short soldier looped his arm around Adrial and hoisted him to his feet. "The healers will be here soon."

"Where are you taking all of us?" Adrial asked.

Soldiers herded the spectators of the ceremony who hadn't already fled, shifting them farther down the street to where the buildings hadn't been damaged.

"Someone has attacked the Map Makers Guild and the Princess," the soldier said. "We have to move everyone away until we can find out what happened."

"I can't stay here to wait for healers." Adrial pulled away from the soldier. "I need to get to the scribes' shop. They need to know I'm safe."

"Everyone is going to wait for the healers—"

"I need to be sure the shop is safe!" Adrial had not expected the shout that tore from his throat.

"I have orders to keep everyone here." The soldier reached forward to seize Adrial's arm.

"I have—"

"Head Scribe, are you all right?" The tall soldier's voice cut across Adrial's.

Rictor. That's his name.

"I'm fine." Adrial nodded, the small motion sending his head spinning again. "But I need to get back to the scribes' shop. If someone tried to attack the start of the journey…"

Mara. Mara and Tham's journey began at the northern gate.

"The other journey"—Adrial gripped Rictor's sleeve—"were they attacked as well?"

"Not that I've heard of." Rictor took Adrial's elbow and led him toward the line of soldiers' horses. "When we were sent out, there was no word of any other trouble in the city."

"I have to get to the scribes' shop."

The library was protected. Soldiers and scribes' guards constantly patrolled the thick walls of the white stone fortress. But the shop was simply a shop.

"Every soldier in Ilara is being sent out to protect the Guilds." The soldiers parted at Rictor's approach, whether from intimidation of his rank or his size, Adrial didn't know. "We need to get you to the Sorcerers Tower. They'll take care of healing you yourself."

"I'm fine." Adrial tried to step away, but Rictor's grip on his arm was too firm. "I've been much worse, believe me."

"Take him straight to the Sorcerers Tower," Rictor ordered two men who still sat atop their horses.

"No, I refuse—"

Rictor didn't seem to care what Adrial refused to do as he hoisted him onto a horse.

"Do not stop until you've reached the tower." With that order, Rictor turned and strode away.

"Can you ride on your own, Head Scribe?" One of the two soldiers that flanked him asked.

"Yes," Adrial said.

A common man scrambled through the debris near the front of one of the houses just behind the platform, pulling broken bits of wood away. A filthy hand showed through the wreckage.

"You should take someone else," Adrial said as the soldiers moved forward, urging Adrial's horse along with them. "I'm not badly hurt. Someone else should go."

"It's not about being hurt, Head Scribe," the soldier said. "It's about keeping you safe."

Adrial wanted to protest, but they were right. It was his duty to protect the Guilds, and that included allowing himself to be protected. Tears stung his eyes.

A few streets north of the gate, the air cleared, and the sun glinted off the windows of the houses. If it weren't for the soldiers riding beside him, it could have been a completely normal morning.

The sun caught on something silver at the soldiers' sides.

Swords. They're riding with weapons drawn. How did the morning come to this?

He should be in his shop in a few minutes' time. Tea and rolls would be delivered.

He'd asked for an extra cup to be brought in for Ena. A note had arrived the night before.

Don't forget you promised to help, scribe. Be ready for our little adventure tomorrow.

She didn't say what time she'd be arriving. What if she'd already come and gone? What if Ena had been caught waiting outside the scribes' shop by whomever had hurt her before?

Surely, she'll be safe in the Guilded section of Ilara.

But the journey had been attacked.

Poor Taddy would be terrified.

"The scribes' shop is protected?" Adrial asked as they reached the wide thoroughfare of Farers Way and the soldiers pushed the horses to move more quickly. "Do they even know what happened?"

"The entire city is protected. And the scribes' shop will know the head scribe is safe," the soldier said as they passed the cathedral and aimed their horses toward the shining dark tower of the Sorcerers Guild.

"If the entire city is protected, how did this happen?" Adrial asked.

His gaze caught on a group of four soldiers patrolling the streets, weapons drawn and ready to attack.

The soldier riding next to him didn't answer.

The base of the sorcerers' home came into view. The dark stone of the tower shimmered in the sun. It was built of obsidian, Adrial knew it had been. He'd studied it in books—the sorcerers finding the stone far across the sea and sending dozens of ships to ferry it to Ilara.

But there were no masonry marks on the tower. No joints to show where one slab ended and another began. Saint Gyntra herself had formed the tower. Using magic beyond the reach of her peers, she had melted the edges and sewn the rock seamlessly together.

In the morning sun, the stone shone with a purple hue, setting it apart from anything else in Ilara. The impossibility of the tower sitting between the wealthiest of the merchants' houses and the shops selling the finest jewels in Ilbrea was unbelievably breathtaking.

But the tower was very real and decidedly planted in the middle of the street.

"We have Head Scribe Adrial Ayres," the soldier shouted at the stone walls, though there was no sign of anyone being present to hear. "He was injured at the southern gate and needs sorcerer aid."

With a crack that shook Adrial's lungs, a door appeared in the side of the tower. His horse backed skittishly away as the door swung, not open as logic suggested it should, but down, leaving an entry large enough for Adrial to pass through while on horseback.

"Head Scribe, are you all right?" A woman dressed in purple robes appeared at the entry.

"I'm fine," Adrial tried to answer, but the soldier spoke over him.

"We have orders from Rictor Nance to bring him to your care." The soldier ushered Adrial forward. "He needs to be healed. We'll wait out here until he's fit to be brought back to his post."

"Thank you," Adrial said as the woman reached up and lifted the horse's reins from his hands.

He tried not to bristle. They were helping him, giving him assistance none of the others injured in the blast would receive. But he was more than capable of guiding his own horse through the newly formed doorway into the interior of the Sorcerers Tower.

"We'll see to him immediately." The sorcerer nodded to the soldiers as the door sealed itself with a sharp crack.

Adrial shut his eyes and took a shuddering breath, shoving down the horrible feeling of being buried alive in a stone vault.

"Do you need help down?" the sorcerer asked.

Adrial opened his eyes.

A dazzling glow surrounded the sorcerer as she reached up to him.

Light poured down from the ceiling, as though the sorcerers had managed to trap the essence of the sun itself and forced it to do their bidding. The floor was not made of the dark stone Adrial had expected. Lush, green grass, more vibrant than even the lawns of the Map Master's Palace, coated the ground.

Fountains surrounded by white stone dotted the grass, their water sparkling like diamonds as it soared through the air. The edges of the massive room were lined with beds of deep violet flowers, backed by wall-climbing vines.

Sorcerers dressed in purple robes lay on the grass, reading books or chatting to their fellows. On the far side of the largest fountain in the center of the space, an older man instructed a young boy who held fire in his palms.

The sorcerer who'd taken his reins smiled kindly up at Adrial. "Haven't been in here before?"

"Never." Adrial slid down from the horse, biting back his moan as pain shot through his hip. "It's different than I expected from my reading."

The sorcerer offered Adrial her arm. "We don't let low ranks in this way. Very few are lucky enough to be greeted in the gardens."

"There's another way in?" Adrial asked, glad his voice sounded sure.

"There are a hundred ways." She shook her head, sending her soft brown hair flying around her shoulders. "I often forget how little outsiders know."

Adrial mouthed for a moment, searching for a response. But the farthest section of the circular wall came into view, and all thoughts of insult or lack of information drifted from his mind.

A staircase glided up the wall, the steps constantly rising as though pulled up by some unseen giant. With barely a whisper, the steps changed their path, twisting down instead.

Lady Gwell, the leader of the Sorcerers Guild appeared at the top of the steps, her bright red hair shocking against the deep green of the leaves behind her.

"Wonderful." The sorcerer who had greeted Adrial smiled a bit too brightly. "I was afraid I would have to search for her."

"What chaos has descended upon Ilara?" Lady Gwell said as soon as she stepped onto the grass. "First, I hear the journey to the eastern mountains was attacked. Then I hear Princess Illia and Allora Karron were rushed to the palace for safety, and now I have the bleeding head scribe in my garden."

The grit of her voice cut over the gentle hushing of the fountains. The glistening of the water changed, as though in response to the disruption of the calm. The diamond-like clarity disappeared, overtaken by an orange glow.

"Lady Gwell." The brown-haired sorcerer bowed. "The soldiers delivered the head scribe here to be healed by us."

"Of course they did." Lady Gwell studied Adrial. "We cannot risk an already weakened heir to a man who's well past his prime, especially not to the hands of the red-clad butchers. Willa"—the sorcerer on Adrial's arm gave a little bow—"see him up to the mending room. I'm sure they'll be able to patch up the head scribe."

"Thank you, Lady Gwell." Adrial nodded.

"It is always a pleasure to be of help to one of Lord Karron's pack." Lady Gwell smiled. The expression seemed so foreign on the woman's face, it was almost frightening.

Willa gave another little bow and began leading Adrial to the moving staircase.

"Wait." Adrial kept his feet firmly planted even as Lady Gwell turned away. "You said Allora Karron had been taken to the palace."

"She has," Lady Gwell said.

"Was she hurt?" Adrial asked, refusing to budge even as Willa pulled on his arm. "They were closer to that blast than I was."

"The message from the King said nothing of either of them being injured," Lady Gwell said. "I've been summoned to the King's side. If I see Allora Karron, I will inform her of your concern."

"Thank you." Adrial nodded, finally letting Willa drag him away.

The grass cushioned his steps with unnatural softness. As they passed each of the fountains, their pattern changed, as though showing off for their guest. The water flew up in crisscross patterns one moment, then soared fifteen feet into the air the next.

It should be beautiful.

But Adrial couldn't shake the gnawing fear from his lungs.

Lady Gwell summoned to the King's side. A terrible thing happened, and people had died. But protecting Ilara was the duty of the soldiers, not the sorcerers.

"I'm sure Lady Karron is fine," Willa said as they reached the staircase. "We heard about the Princess and Lady Karron before we received word you were on your way."

"How did you know?"

Willa stepped onto the shifting stairs as though there was nothing strange about a whole staircase moving like cogs in a clock.

Taking a breath, Adrial followed. He had expected the movement to be sharp and jarring, throwing him off his precarious balance. But the stair felt completely stationary. If the ground hadn't been getting ever farther away, he wouldn't have known he was moving at all.

"We have ears all over the city," Willa said as the garden slipped out of view.

"But you never see sorcerers on the streets," Adrial said as they emerged onto the next level.

A stone corridor, brightly lit with golden torches, greeted them. Deep red doors, polished to shining, lined each side of the hall as it curved out of sight.

"Do you spend much time on the streets, Head Scribe?" Willa asked.

"More than most sorcerers do," Adrial said.

"We have found the natural possession of something others can never hope to achieve breeds hostility." Willa tapped on the closest door. "It's better for all in Ilbrea if those who have been born with magic in their blood keep to themselves. We are, after all, an utterly unique resource. There is no magic without the Sorcerers Guild, and what would be left of Ilbrea without the protection of magic?"

KAI

It was almost disappointing, how easy slipping away from the docks would be.

The order had come from Lord Nevon himself. All sailors were to stay by the docks and guard the shipyard. The fleet in the water and the new fleet under construction could not be allowed to be damaged.

Damaged. What a funny way to say blown up.

The waves lapped against the rock wall by the docks. The Arion Sea didn't feel the need to be violent, even if violence was what the people who lived on her shores crept toward.

The near full moon gave off more light than Kai would have liked.

Lines of men in sailor blue and common work garb roamed the planks of the docks, searching for anything suspicious. Anything that might mean the ships were the next target of whoever had decided the journey was bad for Ilbrea.

Kai clenched his fists. It would be nice to not be angry at a *they* for trying to kill part of his family. Having a face to throw punches at, or worse, might quell the fire that burned in his chest enough for him to be able to properly breathe.

"I'll take the spot, Kai." Drew limped down the stone walk that bordered the sea, the bruising on his face utterly apparent in the moonlight.

Another reason to be angry.

"You grab a bite and a seat." Drew laid a hand on Kai's shoulder. "There'll be plenty of time for all of us to prowl in the dark."

"Thanks, friend." Kai squeezed Drew's hand then headed down the stone pier, toward the noisiest place on the dock.

Even when sailors were meant to be defending their ships, they couldn't manage to be quiet. The massive room where the sailors were usually fed their midday meal was stuffed to the brim. The plain wooden tables lined with crooked benches overflowed with people demanding food.

Five harassed women scuttled through the dining room, bearing trays of meat and bread. Frie and ale had been banned from the docks until the soldiers declared the city safe.

No wonder everyone's in such a foul mood.

Kai slipped to the far end of the room. The women were too busy serving to watch the door to the kitchen.

He bent double to slide through the door.

The kitchen fire burned brightly, heating the room to boiling despite the chill of the evening. Other than a mangy dog sleeping by the door to the street, the space was empty.

A staircase angled out the far side of the kitchen, cutting up to the storage rooms above. If the sailors in the dining room knew barrels of the ale and frie they had been denied sat right above their heads, there would be a riot on the docks unlike any the Guilds had ever seen.

But the others hadn't bothered searching the nooks and crannies that surrounded the docks like Kai had. As a Karron ward, he'd found too many hidden treasures to allow any shadow to go unexplored.

Soundlessly, Kai crept up the wooden steps, skipping the stair that always creaked horribly, and pressed himself into the shadows that covered the landing.

Silence.

No chatter. No barrels being dragged across the floor.

Keeping his head low, Kai peered around the corner. The storage room was empty. Of people at least. Barrels of flour, salt, frie, and ale sat below hanging racks of dried meat. Crates of apples and tubers ready to be packed onto ships lined one whole wall.

Kai cut along the other side of the room, past the shelves of spices and packets of hardtack, heading directly toward the open window on the north side of the building. The breeze from outside did little to fight the heat drifting up from the fire below, but Kai was grateful someone had thought to open it. Winter storms had warped the wood of the building so the window made a terrible squeal when forced to move and took more time to shimmy open than he had to waste.

Giving one last glance behind, Kai crawled through the window and onto the slanted roof beyond. Fresh sea air greeted him. He had only been inside for a moment, but even that short time trapped in wood had made the fire in his chest burn hotter.

He had to do something.

His feet carried him quickly across the pitched roof, and leaping to the next barely required thought.

I should be finding out who did this.

That would be the most satisfying option. He knew the faces of the men who started the fight in the White Froth, but starting a brawl in a pub was a far cry from setting off an explosion so near the Princess.

And Allora.

Kai's foot slipped as he leapt to the next roof. The pain shooting through his knee as he stumbled was the price for his drifting thoughts.

Kai shook his head, forcing himself to focus. Holding his arms to his sides, he made it to the far end of the roof faster than most would have traveled on the ground.

But if the men from the White Froth were angry, perhaps they knew who else might hate the Guilds enough to attack in Ilara.

"One foot at a time," Kai whispered into the salty wind.

The roofs leading away from the docks were as familiar to him as the streets below. For a man raised on the ropes of a ship, scaling unswaying roofs was easy. The tricky bit came in puzzling out how to move from one to the next.

The tannery roof sat above the herbalist's roof, but he could slip from one to the other without making a sound. A leap to the edge of the milliner's roof was simple enough at this time of night when the streets were near empty and chances of people looking up and noticing his dangling feet were low.

The stables were where his path ended. Merchants who owned a horse, but hadn't room at their home for their animal, all kept their horses together. The stench was plenty to tell passersby what the building held. A long rope dangled from the side of the stable, strong enough for hoisting feed, and an easy path to the ground for a sailor.

A line of water barrels hugged the side of the building.

Kai swung wide, landing on the cobblestone street, avoiding the dull thunk of his boots hitting the wood. He already missed the freedom of the rooftops. But there was no time to linger. The emptiness of the streets made them all the more dangerous.

"Come on, Gelda, don't let a fellow down." Kai reached into the darkness behind the row of water barrels, hoping his fingers wouldn't meet animal muck. With a sigh of relief, he grasped a glass bottle and coarse wool. "That's my girl."

The bottle of frie Gelda had left him was two sips from full—a favor Kai felt sure she would remember—and the wool cloak had just the right amount of filth on it.

Kai tossed the cloak around his shoulders, hiding his sailor blue.

Wrenching the cork out of the bottle, Kai let a little frie spill onto the cloak. With a smell like that coming off him, no one would wonder why he roamed the streets.

Adding a bit of a wobble to his step, Kai headed out to the main roads of Ilara, taking the fastest route to the Guilded section of the city.

"Need a place to rest, love?" a woman's voice called from down the street as Kai turned onto Mason Lane.

"Not tonight, dearie." Kai waved over his shoulder without turning back. "Best not to linger on a night like this."

"Next time then."

Kai gave another wave as a group of common men came into view. Metal workers from the look of them. Their stumbling put Kai's to shame.

"Brother!" the man at the front of the pack shouted. His voice bounced off the stone of the houses. "Are you enjoying the freedom of the night air?"

"It's a fine night." Kai nodded. "A wonderful one."

"Then come and celebrate!" a second man spoke. "We are at the dawn of a new day."

"Not quite dawn yet." Kai stopped when the men were twenty feet away. Better to let them approach than walk into the middle of them. "And best to keep it down. There are soldiers all over the streets."

"Paun soldiers?" the first man asked. "Or unguilded traitors?"

"Come here, little paun!" the smallest man in the group called, as though summoning an animal. "Come here, mewling little paun!"

"I'd best be on my way," Kai said as the thump of boots sounded from the nearest cross street.

"What's going on down here?"

Kai cursed under his breath as seven soldiers appeared behind the common men.

"We're enjoying the fine night air in the common part of town." The smallest man turned and bowed to the soldiers. "Don't see why it should matter to you. There's no princesses to worry about here. Only us sewer rats."

Kai slipped into the nearest alley. The space was barely wide enough for him to squeeze through sideways, but it was better than being caught on that street.

"The soldiers are commanded to protect all citizens of Ilbrea, and that includes the people who live here."

A damp, rotting stench flooded Kai's nose as a rat scurried past his feet.

"And who protects the people of Ilbrea from you?"

"Just run, you slitches," Kai muttered as he shimmied his way out onto the far side of the buildings.

"Stop right there."

Kai's shoulders sagged as a voice spoke from behind him.

"What sort of man has business creeping between houses in the middle of the night?"

Kai turned slowly, careful to keep his hands well clear of his cloak.

Two soldiers glared at him, both looking as though they wanted nothing more than to take out their fatigue and frustration on his ribs.

"I'm trying to get clear of whatever is about to happen on Mason," Kai said. "I'm Guilded. I just didn't want to walk around the streets in blue tonight."

"Really?" One of the soldiers raised a thick, black eyebrow.

Shouts carried from the other side of the houses.

"Can you blame me?" Kai shrugged.

"Let me see your mark." The soldier grabbed Kai's wrist, yanking up his sleeve to see the twisting breath of wind permanently inscribed on Kai's skin. "All right then."

"What are you doing out here?" the second soldier asked. "I thought all sailors were watching the docks."

"I have a friend who was near the damage done today. I need to be sure they weren't hurt."

"Best get there and back fast then." The thick-eyebrowed soldier nodded. "You know, I never thought we'd be looking at Guild marks to see who to worry about on the streets of Ilara."

"It's a dark time." Kai pressed the mostly full bottle of frie into the soldier's hand. "In case you need it on the long night's watch."

"Thank you, sailor."

Kai didn't wait for the conversation to continue. He was nearly to the Guilded part of the city. Slip past the cathedral, and he'd be up the cliffs in no time.

As soon as he stepped past the first row of Guilded homes, he shed his cloak, draping it over his arm for the return journey.

A mark on my arm gives me leave to walk freely. Not what I expected when the sorcerers seared my skin.

The uniform was a help, but stealing a sailor's blue was as simple as waiting outside a bath house for someone to be careless. A Guild mark could only be given by a sorcerer.

Kai vividly remembered the sorcerer's stylus pressing into his arm. The horrible burning sensation, as though the woman in purple had taken a hot iron to his flesh. And then the childish disappointment that his mark didn't move. Mara's and Niko's compass marks had moving images of needles that would always help them find north. Kai's was a motionless twist of wind.

The cathedral rose up like a ghost in the night, surrounded by soldiers who didn't give Kai more than a glance.

They should be checking the marks. I'll tell Tham.

But Tham wasn't in the city. Another weight to add to the fire in Kai's chest. His family should be all together if horrible things were going to happen. It was how their little clan survived.

Two soldiers had been placed at the bottom of the twisting road leading up the cliffs.

"What business do you have up the road?" a soldier asked. Dark bags under the man's eyes showed even in the moonlight.

"I'm Kai Saso, former ward of Lord Karron. I'm here to check on my sister by home, Allora Karron, who was with the Princess this morning." Kai kept his chin tilted up, looking as regal and stern as someone would expect of Lord Karron's wards had they never met them.

"Very well." The soldier nodded for Kai to pass. "And I saw her through the carriage window when they brought her home this evening. She looked fine. Tired, but fine."

"Thank you." Kai clapped the man on the shoulder and headed up the cliffs at a jog.

His legs should have been exhausted. He'd been at the shipyard, working on the new fleet when word of the explosion came. Then the world had started to spin, and the flames in his stomach had flared.

He pushed himself to run faster, letting the pain of uselessness force heat into his limbs.

Another line of soldiers waited at the top of the cliff.

"Kai Saso, former ward of Lord Karron…"

Another at the gates to the Map Master's Palace.

"Kai Saso…"

Men in map maker livery waited at the front door of the house.

"Kai?" one of the men called as he ran up the lawn.

"Is Allora here?" Kai asked. He didn't know the man's name, but he recognized his face. Recognized all the men's faces.

A tiny bit of the twisting in his stomach loosened.

"She's here." The man nodded. "I don't know if she's awake, but if she is, I'm sure she'd be glad to see you."

Kai nodded and swung open the giant front door.

He expected to have to go to the family wing of the house to find her and shake her awake, but a moment after he closed the door, Allora appeared in the hall, wrapped in a long, white robe.

"Kai," she breathed, running to him and flinging her arms around his neck in a most un-Allora-like way. "You're safe. Thank Dudia I know at least one of you is safe."

"Allora." Kai rocked her back and forth in his arms. "What are you doing down here?"

"Waiting for you or Adrial." Allora didn't let go of Kai. "Or for my father to come back from the council, or for a letter to come from Niko."

"Poor, dear Allora, you've been going mad, haven't you?"

Tears poured down Allora's cheeks. "The world caught fire and Niko left, and Adrial's locked in the Sorcerers Tower and I can't get to him. Mara and Tham are headed north, and they may not know anything has happened. The Queen fell ill when she found out about the explosion."

"Come on." Kai took Allora's hand, leading her to the front parlor.

Her immaculate writing marked the envelope clasped in her other hand.

Nikolas Endur. Map Maker. Eastern Mountains Journey.

Even after a day of panic, Allora's handwriting slanted and curled perfectly.

"I—" Allora pressed the letter to her chest. "I just need to send this to him. I'm the Lord Map Maker's daughter. I know how impossible getting a letter to a journey can be."

"But they only just left." Kai took the letter and slipped it into his pocket. "And they're not sailing on the Arion Sea. I'll find a way to get it to him."

"Thank you, Kai." Allora brushed the curls away from his forehead as she had when he was only a boy. "Please don't leave tonight. I know it's awful of me to ask you to stay away from the ships to sit here with me while I worry."

A dozen soft seats lined the parlor, but by habit Kai pulled Allora down onto the most comfortable couch with a view of the front lawn. "This is my home, Allora. You are my family. I love the Sailors Guild and the ships, but…"

He wasn't sure what the *but* was.

"But our little family is what sees us through." Allora nestled her head onto his shoulder, and together they sat, watching the great lawn bathed in moonlight.

ADRIAL

"We need to be more careful with you." Lord Gareth's wrinkled face reddened in concern. "You are my heir. The Guilds cannot afford to lose you."

"There was an attack." Adrial kept his tone steady even as sweat glistened on Lord Gareth's brow. "I wasn't the only one who was hurt."

"It doesn't matter." Gareth's tea trembled as he raised the mug to his lips.

"I'm better now than I was before the attack," Adrial said. "I promise you that."

Morning had passed before the sorcerers finally let him out of their tower. An entire day and night of poking, prodding, spells, and healing. It hadn't been a pleasant experience, but at least the pain had been worth it. The damage from the explosion was entirely gone, and his shoulder felt better than it had in years.

The man who had spent a full day working on him looked at Adrial's leg as well, but there was nothing to be done. No way to mend bone out of the shape into which it had grown.

The old disappointment had only stung Adrial's heart for a few minutes.

After the exhausting affair, all Adrial had wanted was to sleep. To slip into his bed and rest without anyone hovering over him. But as soon as the sorcerers' carriage reached the front of the shop, Taddy ran out, nearly knocking Adrial over in his glee, and passed him a letter from Ena.

Meet me at the top of the Map Master's cliff an hour before sundown if you're still alive.

And before he could wonder why Ena would want to meet him near the Map Master's Palace, Lord Gareth's carriage had arrived. Gareth had shooed the others away and escorted Adrial to his workroom for tea and a thorough talking to.

Adrial's head began to ache as Lord Gareth talked himself around in circles for the fourth time.

"The world is a dark and dangerous place, Adrial." Lord Gareth set his cup down on the tea tray and tented both wrinkled hands under his chin. "We who keep the records of the best and worst of this world understand that better than most. And you, who have suffered so much, understand it better than I.

"The tide is changing in Ilbrea. It's natural, just like the sea. Darkness and light sweeping over us all. I am lucky. I have lived my life in one of the greatest times of brilliant light Ilbrea has ever seen. And as my twilight comes, the darkness creeps back around."

"Sir—"

"But you cannot forget the good one good man can do. Adrial Ayres, you came from the worst of all places and have become the best of men. There are those in the Guilds who don't understand that there are people who live without the privileges and protections of the Guilds.

"The Guilds are leaning further and further toward forgetting that our purpose has always been to serve, not ourselves, but the people of Ilbrea. If someone like Travers took the Lordship, the scales would tip so far toward those who care only for power, it would take at least a generation for sanity to return to the cathedral floor, if it found its way back at all."

Gareth paused for a moment, sweating as though he'd just walked a long way.

"Sir," Adrial began, "I know the place you've given me is important. But are things really that desperate in the Guilds? The commoners are upset about unguilded soldiers—"

"If you think that is where the root of the problem began, you have more to learn than I thought." Gareth worried his lips together so they disappeared. "You're going to have to move back to the library. Natalia can run the shop, and you can work on the vellum from within the great room. You'll be more comfortable there anyway."

Adrial's stomach shattered.

I'll never see her again.

Even if Ena were willing to brave the gates of the library, the scribes' guards would never let her in. They would take her ink and pay her on the street. She would never be allowed to enter the sanctity of the library or to disturb the head scribe as he worked at the King's command.

You would work faster without her distraction.

Adrial pictured her waiting at the top of the Map Master's cliffs for him, her rainbow hair fluttering in the breeze. Would she be disappointed if he never came? Angry maybe? Or perhaps relieved she would never have to see the Guilded Cripple again? Then she could earn her coin in peace.

Adrial tightened his grip on his mug. "I'm sorry, sir, but I can't. The duty of the head scribe is to run the scribes' shop. If I leave, it will only allow for more questioning of my ascension as Lord Scribe than I am already bound to receive."

"There can be no questioning. You are my heir."

"An heir everyone believes is too young and inexperienced for the position. I can't give up the running of the scribes' shop. It will sew too much doubt. You want me to lead the Guild in the right direction, but what good is being a leader if no one believes in you enough to follow?"

Gareth gave a coughing laugh. "Lord Karron did well with you. That's the problem with surrounding yourself with smart people—you can't always win against them."

"Thank you, sir." Adrial gave a little bow.

"But there is no rule saying the head scribe must live above the shop. It's a convenience, not a necessity. You'll move back to the safety of the library and be brought to the shop by carriage each day."

"Is that really necessary, sir?" Adrial's room above the scribes' shop was simple—nothing compared to the marble floors and wide windows of the library—but it was quieter here. Only the scribes from the shop were allowed to live in town. The housing at the library constantly buzzed with people. Meals were eaten surrounded by people.

No peace to breathe.

"Having you unguarded would be a terrible mistake. If people with dark deeds in mind wish to cause fires, a wooden building filled with paper, and the head scribe asleep in his bed, would be too easy a target."

Adrial opened his mouth to argue, but Gareth was right.

"What about the others?" Adrial asked. "If I need to change my residence to the library, then surely they do, too."

"They'll be safer here without you." Gareth pushed himself to his feet. His face paled from the effort. "I'll send guards to defend the others. They can take your room. If things go as I fear they may, it won't be long before the shop shuts down and all scribes retreat to the library."

"Sir"—Adrial took Gareth's arm, helping him to the door—"do you really think this is necessary?"

"Absolutely." There was no fear in Gareth's eyes. Only terrifying resignation.

"Are the other Guilds doing the same?" Adrial asked. "Are they gathering their people?"

"Not yet." Gareth gave a sad smile, which added another decade to his face. "They do not cherish history as we scribes do. They don't breathe it through the books every day as we do. And they don't recognize it when the patterns begin again. I'll see you at the library tonight."

"Yes, sir."

Gareth patted Adrial's hand and opened the door. Two white-clad scribes waited to escort him back to his carriage.

Adrial watched their slow progress through the shop. All the scribes stood as their Lord passed. Gareth nodded to each of them, the movement of his head seeming to cost him more than it should. Then the trio passed through the shop doors and were out of sight.

A familiar dread swooped through Adrial's stomach.

I am not ready to lead.

Adrial shut his eyes tightly. He didn't have the luxury of time to contemplate his failings. Not now.

"Taddy," Adrial called the apprentice over.

Taddy's pudgy face creased in worry as he trotted to Adrial.

"Everything all right, Taddy?" Adrial asked, bowing the boy into his workroom.

"Yes, sir," Taddy said a bit too quickly, but Adrial hadn't time to pry.

"I need you to go to my room and pack up all my personal belongings." Adrial held up a hand as Taddy opened his mouth to speak. "People from the library are coming to collect me at the end of the day. It's the Lord Scribe's desire that I take up residence at the library."

"But you're still going to be in charge here?" Taddy's brow grew more wrinkled still.

"Yes. Now, when they come in the carriage to collect me, I need you to tell them I was called away on urgent business and will meet them at the library. Give them my things and tell them not to worry, I've arranged for my safety."

"You've arranged for your safety to meet Ena at the cliffs?" Taddy's eyes widened in fear as soon as the words left his mouth.

Adrial bit the inside of his cheeks to hide his grin. That look of mischievous terror was too familiar to rouse any anger in Adrial. "If you tell them where I've gone, I'll have to ask how you know where I'm going, Taddy."

Taddy hung his head in appropriate shame.

"Close up your desk in the shop, then see to my room." Adrial moved toward the back door of his workroom. He would need to change his clothes if he wanted to reach the cliffs without being stopped, and he would have to move quickly to make it there in time to meet Ena.

"Are you really going to be safe?" Taddy asked. "I mean, that part is true?"

"Or course it is, Taddy." Adrial smiled. "Now run along."

Adrial was up the narrow stairs to his room in a minute. The sparse space had been his home for two years, but there wasn't time to reminisce about the white wood walls or the worn gray chair. It only took him a few moments to put on the one set of ordinary clothes he owned.

Lord Gareth's insistence on his keeping a set of common clothes on hand had never made sense to Adrial before. His hands froze on the buttons of his plain shirt. What whispers from history had warned Lord Gareth that scribe white could be a danger?

Carefully folding his white robes, he slipped them into a bag and tossed it over his good shoulder. He would have to find a place to change back into his whites before arriving at the library. There would be too many questions to be tolerated if he didn't.

Moving as quickly as he dared, Adrial snuck down the stairs and to the back door of the shop. He'd hardly ever used the door, but he knew the street that lay beyond. Shops for wealthy merchants to sell their wares to each other. Chamb, fine clothes, pastries—all respectable businesses.

Still, he froze with his hand on the door.

He wasn't doing anything wrong. He was an adult. A high-ranking member of the Guilds. He had every right to walk about the streets whenever he liked.

The thumping of his heart told a different story. He was a child escaping into the night, breaking the most sacred of rules. Sneaking around like a thief.

"Don't be a getch, Adrial." Steeling himself, he swung open the door and walked out onto the street.

He didn't dare walk too fast, not with soldiers patrolling. He was too easily recognized. Who in Ilara hadn't heard of the Guilded Cripple?

But none of the soldiers gave him a second glance. The only ones who seemed to notice him at all were small children and a few old women who gave him sympathetic smiles.

The air blowing in from the sea carried the promise of rain in its scent. Adrial let the fresh air fill his lungs, and pain didn't throb through his shoulder in protest.

The walk through town was brief, and even the ache in his leg didn't drain the joy of his anonymity.

Nobody bowed. Nobody whispered.

A merchant in a finely carved carriage drove right past him and didn't pause.

No one wanted to bend his ear or beg him to ask Lord Gareth to change his opinions on the business of the Guilds Council.

The wind whipped up the cliffside. Adrial swallowed the whoop of joy that soared into his throat. Sweat beaded on his brow at the effort of the climb, but even as his leg trembled and begged him to stop, he pushed on. Pass after pass, scaling the cliff with nothing but his own two feet to carry him.

It wasn't until he reached the top of the cliff that he saw Ena perched high in a tree, staring out toward the Arion Sea.

Adrial swallowed, willing his words to come out strong. "Nice view from up there?"

Ena looked down at him, her gaze sliding from his shoes to his plain coat. "Traveling in disguise, scribe?"

With a leap that sent Adrial's heart soaring into his throat, Ena jumped out of the tree. As she fell, the layers of her skirt fluttered around her, as though she had become an exquisite bird. She landed two feet from Adrial without even a stumble.

"I was hoping you'd be in your scribe white." Ena tipped her head to the side. "But you lived with Lord Karron for a long time, didn't you?"

"Yes, but what has that got to do with wearing white?"

Ena looped her arm through Adrial's, leading him toward the gates of Lord Karron's palace. "I want to get in there." She pointed to the wide stand of trees with weeping branches pressed up against the cliff on the far side of the gates. "I need those pretty pink petals, and you're going to get me into the Lord Map Maker's grounds. It's either that or I walk two days out of the city to get them and you wait another two weeks for your pale pink ink."

Adrial didn't know what to say. Didn't even know if he wanted to say anything. He looked toward the storm darkening the sky over the Arion Sea. Soon it would hit the shore and pour rain upon them.

"They will recognize you at the gates, won't they?" A frown curled the sides of Ena's mouth.

"I'm sure they will."

"Then what's the matter?" Ena poked him in the ribs. She hadn't brought her basket with her. There was nothing to indicate they were doing anything other than going for an evening stroll.

"Allora," Adrial said when they neared the gates. "She'll be furious I haven't come to see her, and I doubt she'll be too pleased to see the girl who climbed onto the balcony she arranged so well for her party on Winter's End."

"Allora's the possessive blond? We just won't tell her we're here."

"These are her father's grounds." Adrial shrugged. His right shoulder moved with his left. "I don't know if we'll be able to keep her from knowing."

"So it's true then." Ena glanced at Adrial's shoulder before turning her face away. "They did take you to the Sorcerers Tower."

"Yes," Adrial said, trying to catch a glimpse of Ena's face as she hid behind her bright blue and violet hair. "The sorcerers took me in after the attack. While they were healing me, they did a bit of work on my shoulder."

"And it's better?" Ena asked as they approached the gates.

"For the first time in years, it doesn't hurt." Adrial couldn't keep the smile from his lips.

"But nothing for your leg?"

"Same answer as before," Adrial said as a line of guards in green-trimmed uniforms stepped in front of the gates. "Too much damage to be fixed by magic."

"So, the sorcerers won't save the Guilded Cripple." Ena pulled Adrial to stop ten feet shy of the high gates. "For the glory of the Guilds."

16

ADRIAL

"What's your business?" called the guard at the center of the formation.

Adrial's heart thumped at the man's rough voice, though he kept his face from flinching. "I'm Adrial Ayres, raised a ward of Lord Karron."

"Head Scribe?" The guard squinted at Adrial. "I didn't recognize you out of your robes, sir."

"With the trouble in town, I thought it best to be discreet while walking on my own." Adrial led Ena the last few feet to the gates. "I have a vendor with me. She's working on inks for the vellum the King ordered. I need her to match the petals on the lady's heart trees, and there are no others in the city."

"Of course, sir." The guard gave a little bow and a nod to the other guards.

Silently, the gates swung open.

Adrial stepped back, stopping just out of range of the ornately carved metal.

How many times had he climbed to the cliff after a day of training in the library? How many worries had fluttered out of his mind as soon as he crossed through the gates and entered the sanctuary of the Map Master's Palace?

My first true home.

Allora had insisted all the Karron wards live at the Map Master's Palace as long as their apprenticeships would allow.

Adrial knew the gates and the grounds. Had memorized the pattern of the floor in the great ballroom and all the best corners for a timid and afraid child to hide.

"Shall I tell Lady Allora you've come?" the guard asked as Adrial led Ena through the gates.

"I'm afraid I haven't time for a visit." A tiny curdle of guilt bubbled in Adrial's stomach. "I'm to report to the library this evening."

"Of course, Head Scribe."

Adrial gave another nod to the guards, not knowing how to end the conversation.

"It's beautiful," Ena said as Adrial veered her onto a side path away from the wide road that led to the main house.

Allora could be watching through those windows. If she saw him here with Ena, her welcome would be far less generous than the guard's had been.

"It's not as grand as the mountains, but still, it's pretty." Ena trailed her fingers along the bushes that lined the path.

It was one of a dozen walkways that cut through the grounds. To the mausoleum, to the house, to the walled garden, and so many other places a child could lose himself.

"I was very lucky to be brought here." Adrial stooped and picked a bright orange flower from the side of the path.

"So early in spring for such brightness." Ena studied the bloom.

A fit of daring seized Adrial. He reached over and tucked the flower behind Ena's ear.

His heart tumbled and crashed into his lungs, stealing his breath away, as a gentle smile curved Ena's lips.

"And why were you so lucky to be brought here, scribe?" Ena tugged on Adrial's arm, steering him down the path toward the wide swath of pink-laden trees along the cliffs. "What else would the Lord Map Maker have done with the Ayres born?"

There was no malice in her words, but they still stung as childlike shame reddened Adrial's cheeks.

"He could have left me where he found me," Adrial said. "He came to Ian Ayres to fetch Mara Landil. Lord Karron had been friends with Mara's father. When he died, they sent Mara to the bastards' island."

"No one would take her?" Ena tightened her grip on Adrial's arm.

"I don't think they looked very hard. Lord Karron was furious when he found out what had become of Mara and sailed straight away for Ian Ayres. When he got there, he found me, took pity on the tiny cripple boy, and brought me here."

"You're not his bastard then?"

"Why would you think that?" Adrial asked. "Is it the striking family resemblance?"

"A bastard Ayres child not only being Guilded, but chosen as the heir to the Lord Scribe?" Ena shook her head, sending her hair fluttering around her shoulders. The flower fell from behind her ear, and she caught it before it reached the ground. "I just assumed you must be his. I think most people do."

Ena handed Adrial the flower and tucked her hair behind her ear before leaning toward him.

"You're far from the first person to have assumed I was Lord Karron's bastard. It was always a wonder to me that he kept me around, what with all the whispers." Adrial tucked the flower back in its place, and Ena took his hand, drawing him farther down the path. "Though I don't suppose Allora would have let him get rid of me anyway. She's the one who taught me to read, you know."

"I suppose I'll have to try and forgive her for being a paun princess then."

They had reached the edge of the cliff. To one side, great spring thunderheads gathered in the distance, turning the Arion Sea a steely gray. To the other, a sweeping line of trees blocked the palace from view, their weeping branches dripping with pink blossoms.

"Here you are," Adrial said, his heart sinking as Ena let go of his hand.

Don't be a fool, Adrial Ayres. You may be Guilded, but you are still a broken man.

Ena ran to the nearest tree, grabbing a low branch and launching herself up. She seemed to fly for a moment before finding her footing on a higher limb.

I want to watch her fly through the trees forever.

There was no joy in the thought. Only the empty echo of impossibility.

In less than a minute, Ena reached the top of the tallest of the branches and pulled down a bunch of flowers. She held the blooms to her nose for a moment before shoving them into one of the many pockets hidden in her skirt.

"Won't that ruin them?" Adrial asked.

"Some things are better broken." She grabbed a branch and dangled by her hands for a moment before dropping to the ground as though falling from great heights were the most natural thing in the world.

"You should be careful," Adrial said as his heart righted its rhythm after her fall.

"I didn't even lose my flower." Ena displayed the orange bloom. "You worry too much, scribe. If you fuss over every little thing that might kill you, how will you have time to enjoy the things worth living for?"

Lightning split the sky over the Arion Sea.

"We should go before the storm hits." Adrial reached for Ena's hand as a low rumble of thunder carried above the rustling of the wind battering the leaves.

"No." Ena tucked her hands behind her back, her eyes dancing with mirth. "Let the storm come. What are you afraid of? You aren't wearing your pretty white robes."

Another streak of lightning lit the graying sky.

"If we go back now, we might get most of the way to the city before it rains."

"Why should we run from the storm?" Ena stepped forward, taking Adrial's face in her hands. "The storm will come whether we stay on the cliff or not. The storm can kill us in our beds if Death has decided to claim us. So why flee from the rain?"

"Ena."

Her eyes sparkled, not with teasing or laughter, but with something else. A fierceness Adrial had never seen in them before. Her face was only inches from his, and the wind whipping around them surrounded Adrial in her scent.

"Say you'll stay through the storm, scribe," Ena whispered as thunder cracked. "Say you'll stay through the pounding rain and unending winds."

"I'll stay."

"Good." Ena let go of Adrial and tipped her face to the sky as drops began to fall. "I love the rain. I love to revel in it."

"To revel in the mud and muck?" He wanted to reach out and brush the raindrops away from her cheek. To touch her hair and see if the color would rub off on his skin.

"The rain doesn't make the mud. The dirt does that. When the rain touches us, it's clean, perfect. It doesn't care if we're common or Guilded. It pours upon us all just the same. I want to dance in it. To stand in the middle of the storm and scream my rage at the sky." Ena looked to Adrial as the rain began in earnest. "There are some wounds too deep for mortal men to understand. But I think the sky might.

"It feels like the whole sky is crying with me. The rain feels everything I feel. And touches every part of me as it weeps. It makes me feel as vast as the mountains and as tiny as a raindrop all at once." Ena walked to the edge of the cliff, her face unafraid as her toes touched the ledge. "I want to fly away on the back of the storm. See how desperately far from here it's possible to go."

"I wish I could see the world as you do," Adrial said. "If only for a moment."

"You could, scribe, if only you'd look beyond the tip of your quill." Ena reached for his hand.

"I wish I could believe that. But the pen is my place." A pang stung Adrial's chest as he took her hand. His was a world of walls and rules. Not flying into freedom.

Ena pulled him forward to stand next to her at the very edge of the cliff.

There was nothing between him and falling to his death. The winds of the storm raged past him as thunder cracked in the air.

"You've never thought of burning your pen and running from the Guilds?" Ena didn't look at Adrial as she spoke. Her gaze stayed fixed on the storm as rain battered the edge of the city.

"I can't. I've nothing else I can do to be useful in this life. And even if I could, the scribes need me."

"Then we'd better go." Ena took his arm as she had before and led Adrial back to the path as the rain picked up. "We can't afford to have you fall to your death. If you're not alive to take the seat as Lord Scribe, I can't imagine what sort of slitch they'll give the spot to."

"The worst kind of getching paun." Adrial shivered, not from the chill of the rain, but from the thought of someone like Travers taking the role of Lord Scribe.

"Language, scribe. Does the worst paun have ink spots on his cuffs? Or bad penmanship, perhaps?"

"He hates the commoners." Adrial tried to swallow the words. He didn't know why he was telling Ena, but he couldn't stop the words from tumbling out. The weight of Gareth's lecture still hung too heavily on his mind. "He hates that he has to work in the shop to serve the people. Honestly, I think if the soldiers wanted to rid Ilara of all commoners, he'd think it a grand idea."

"That chivving slitch of a paun." Ena rounded on Adrial. "And you, scribe? What do you think? Do all common folk deserve to be slaughtered?" Ena's eyes darkened to a more frightening gray than the storm.

"No," Adrial said. "A life is a life, Guilded or not. If I had been one room farther down the hall when Lord Karron came to Ian Ayres, he never would have seen me. I would have stayed stuck on that awful island. Would I not still be human then?"

"But what about when the next attack comes? And this time it's more than four in black who die?"

"The soldiers are guarding the city—"

"If you believe that was the end of it, you're a chivving fool. A worse fool than the men who thought they could make things better for the masses by attacking in the open."

"The people of Ilara shouldn't be punished for the work of a few madmen." Rain streamed down Adrial's face. "The soldiers will do everything they can to find the attackers and protect the city."

"The soldiers think it was common folk who set the explosions. If they prove it, will you stand on the council—"

"I'm not on the council."

"You will be." Ena laid a finger on Adrial's lips as he began to argue. "You'll be one of seven to cast a vote on whether the tilk should be driven from the city to starve in the south." She moved her finger from his lips to his chin.

"The entire city would starve without the unguilded. Clearing the commoners out of Ilara would be bad for everyone," Adrial said. "I would have the men who attacked found. I would fight to keep the peace. The world isn't split into Guilded and killers. It doesn't matter if a bad man wears the seven-pointed star or not. We can all do harm."

"So you'll protect the common folk when they give you your fancy robe?" Ena asked.

"I'll do whatever I can to make life better for all of us."

"And you won't let the common folk starve when the city burns?" Ena placed her hand over Adrial's heart.

"The city won't—"

"It will, and when it does, there's no other Guild Lord who will care for anything beyond his walls."

"I won't let people starve. Not while there's food to be found."

Ena leaned in, pressing her lips to Adrial's cheek. She lingered for a moment, her body next to his. "Then you might be the one to save us all."

She took Adrial's hand in hers, for the first time not walking ahead dragging him, but walking beside him as the rain poured down.

"Travers doesn't think I'm strong enough to lead," Adrial said. "He thinks I'll be the death of the Guild."

"You're stronger than all of them, Adrial."

Adrial's heart leapt as she said his name.

"Why do you say that?" Adrial asked.

"Because you're still alive," Ena said as they reached the road to the gate. "Can you ride, scribe?"

"Yes, but I don't have a horse up here." Adrial wished he had as the rain turned colder. "I could ask at the stables—"

"I don't mean to get down the road. I mean to carry you up to the mountains. I can walk, but it would take you a week."

"Why would I be going to the mountains? I had to sneak away just to get here."

"You're coming to the mountains because I've told you to get two horses and enough food for two days' journey and meet me beyond the northern gate two weeks from tomorrow," Ena said.

"Why two weeks from tomorrow?"

"If you want to learn to fly, scribe, you'll have to dare to take the first leap. Don't you trust me?"

"Yes." The word swallowed Adrial whole.

17

NIKO

Mud squelched up around Niko's ankles, pouring over the sides of his boots. "It is rather rich that the sorcerers can mark a working compass on my arm, make a light that breaks even the thickest darkness, and give us scrolls that will draw maps from the thoughts in my mind, but boots that repel frigid mud are beyond their measure."

"Come, Niko, it's not that bad." Jerick used his pole to batter the brush down, making them a path. "We could be in the frozen north. Then you'd have no toes."

"Fair enough." Niko paused, closing his eyes to listen past the rustling and thumping of the three men moving around him.

Birdcalls echoed through the dense trees of the forest. More to his right than his left. A faint bubbling sounded to his right as well.

"I think there's a stream that way." Niko spoke loudly enough for the men to hear.

"Cut over now?" Amec asked from his place thirty feet in front of Niko.

"No, keep heading down." Niko looked up to the rise behind them. Through the small, new leaves on the trees, the jagged tops of the mountains were barely visible in the fading light. "We'll come back up and plot the water tomorrow."

"You know," Amec said, "when I was assigned to this journey, I didn't think I would be climbing the mountains every day."

"Six days out of the city, and he already misses making endless circles around the palace," Jerick said.

"It's easier when the terrain isn't covered in trees." Niko stopped for a moment, examining a rock formation that rose strangely from the slope. "When the ground is bare, I can see it all at once and let my scroll do its work." The boulder was ten feet tall, ending in a rounded peak. "With all these trees, it's impossible to know if I've found something of interest until I'm right on top of it."

The tingle of magic itched in the back of Niko's mind, though the leather tube at his right hip gave no outward sign that the sorcerer-made scroll was adding the dark stone to his map.

"Is it something of interest, Niko?" Jerick cut back up the path to stand next to the boulder.

Niko took a deep breath, pressing down his flicker of frustration.

Don't blame them for not recognizing the world for being what it is. It would only make your job harder if they did.

"It's a good landmark if nothing else." Niko walked to the boulder, carefully sizing it against the trees. He placed a hand on the boulder's smooth surface. "Fascinating."

Niko circled the stone, letting his fingers enjoy the delicate texture. Time hadn't cracked the stone, and even the moss so common in the dense forest had left its face untouched.

"What's fascinating, Niko?" Amec asked, feeling the stone as Niko had.

"The stone doesn't match the forest around it." Niko peered through the trees, searching for something, though he didn't know what.

"Then how did it get here?" Amec said. "Did someone haul it up the mountainside?"

"I doubt it." Niko patted the stone. "My best guess is the land herself carried it here far before the Guilds claimed Ilbrea. Come on, I don't fancy tramping back to camp in the dark." Niko started down the slope. They would have to wake before sunrise to do another climb back up and down the mountain.

It had always seemed strange to him that the peaks of the eastern mountains had never been named. Hundreds of map makers had walked the valleys far below, plotting the jagged lines of the mountains on the horizon. But in all the time of Ilbrea and Wyrain, they'd been so busy keeping out of the mountains—to avoid the very real threat of war between the countries and the mythical threat of ghosts and bandits lurking in the woods—no one had dared claim the peaks by naming them.

Wyrain needed Ilbrea's magic. Ilbrea needed goods Wyrain could bring them from the Golden Sea to the east of Wyrain's coast. But if a truce were solidified through the Princess's marriage, perhaps the time to name the mountains would soon be upon them.

Allora's Peak.

Niko smiled at the same moment a voice behind him screamed in terror.

"Amec!" Jerick shouted a moment later.

Niko spun, searching for the young man, but he was nowhere in sight.

"Amec." Tarrum dove to the ground, reaching into a hole that hadn't been there a moment before.

"I'm—I'm all right." Amec's voice carried out of the hole as Niko ran to the others.

"What happened?" Niko knelt beside the gap in the earth. A hole four feet around and ten feet deep had swallowed Amec.

"I was walking, and the ground split," Amec said, only a touch of fear sounding in his voice.

"What do you see down there?" Niko asked.

"What does he see?" Jerick looked to the sky. "The boy fell into the earth, and you ask what he sees?"

"Well, I can already tell he's breathing and standing." Niko pulled his criolas from the thick leather pouch on his belt. The sorcerer-made orb glowed brightly, a pale bluish tint glimmering from deep within. Niko held the light as far down in the pit as he could reach.

"Seems like a bit of a cave maybe?" Amec said. "A bunch of damp rock."

"Probably a spring." Niko twisted his legs over the edge of the hole.

"What do you think you're doing, Niko?" Jerick caught hold of Niko's arm.

"I'm hopping down to see if there's anything of interest." Niko inched closer to the edge of the hole.

"Amec's just said there's nothing down there but dirt and rock," Jerick said.

"And it's my job as a map maker to make sure the dirt and rock aren't anything interesting." Niko pulled his arm free from Jerick's grip, trying not to be angry over the bruise to come.

"Well, we're soldiers, and it's our job to protect the map makers." Jerick sat next to Niko. "So I'll go down and—"

Niko pushed himself forward and dropped into the pit, stumbling as he landed.

At least you stayed on your feet.

"You're a slitch, Niko." Jerick didn't sound amused.

"Don't worry. You can be nice and helpful when you haul me out of here in a moment." Niko held his light up to the stone walls. They were smooth, undamaged by Amec's fall.

"If you're not careful, I'll haul Amec up and leave you down there," Jerick said.

"And what would the King think of that?" Niko moved to the eastern end of the pit. The ground under his feet gave slightly as though he had, in fact, fallen into an underground spring. But the passage leading east was tall enough for him to stand in.

"What is it?" Amec asked, leaning over Niko's shoulder.

"Not a trade route to Wyrain." Niko pressed one hand to the thin sheath on his left hip, holding up his criolas in the other.

Flat stone walls stretched into the blackness beyond the reach of his pale blue light.

"Strange looking for a spring, though."

Why did the observant soldier have to fall through the earth? Niko silently asked Aximander as he walked to the west side of the pit. Here, the ground sloped up, and the passage grew too short for a man to stand upright.

But the walls were still smooth. Too perfect to have been buried by nature.

"Find a passageway to a fairyland?" Tarrum called down. "If you have, ask the fairy princess for dry weather and a barrel of frie."

"I don't think there's any frie down here." Niko stepped into the stream of evening light that pierced the earth.

"Are we all going to have to jump down after you and trek along, hoping not to be squished by massive stones?" Tarrum asked.

"No. I'll mark it on the map in case we ever need to go chasing underground springs, but it's nothing to do with the journey the King ordered," Niko said. "Haul Amec up first. I'd hate to leave him down here when he's only recovered from the fright of falling."

"I wasn't afraid." Amec boldly waved a hand through the air in a way that made Niko quite certain the soldier had been terrified. "And shouldn't we follow the passage east and see how far it goes?"

Be quiet, fool.

"Passage?" Tarrum laughed. "Like a fairy princess dug it?"

"Shut it, Tarrum!" Amec shouted up.

"A spring like this could lead for miles," Niko spoke loudly as Tarrum opened his mouth to mock Amec again. "We haven't the time to trace it, and it isn't what the King's searching for besides. I'll submit the spring to Lord Karron when we finish our journey. If he thinks it's of interest, he'll send a map maker out to follow the path."

"As you say, map maker." Amec reached up and seized Tarrum's and Jerick's hands. "Though it does seem a pity not to at least see where it goes after the earth let us find it."

"There are too many things in these mountains to explore them all at once," Niko said as Amec's feet disappeared aboveground.

He desperately longed to walk into the darkness, to see where the smooth stone led. Someone had made this place. Perhaps an expert hand had carved it when Ilbrea was still new. A way to easily access pure water underground.

But if the softness under Niko's feet wasn't the remnants of a spring past its prime. If there was some other reason a person had smoothed out the walls…

The sorcerers would erase it from your map as soon as you reached Ilara.

Niko clutched the sheath on his left hip and closed his eyes, willing the parchment hidden inside to form the rock on the mountainside and the passage sweeping east toward mysteries that were not in his power to solve.

"Have you decided to sleep underground for the night, Niko?" Jerick asked. "Because I prefer my tent if you wouldn't mind coming up so we can get back to a hot bowl of stew."

"Will it really be hot?" Niko clasped the hands that reached down for him, letting the soldiers haul him out of the pit. "Or will it be bland and mildly warm as I'm fast becoming accustomed to?"

"I think they spoil the map makers." With one jerk of the arm, Tarrum yanked Niko to his feet. "Demanding three meals a day and a tent to sleep in? What would the southern folk say if they knew?"

Niko knocked the stocky man on the shoulder. "Careful there, soldier. If the southern folk hear you, they might hang you by that pretty black hair of yours."

The whole crew laughed as Tarrum carefully patted his hair back into place.

"The raven preens." Amec elbowed Niko in the ribs, proud of his jibe.

"Be careful talking of ravens," Jerick warned. "We may be tramping up and down the same mountain day after day, but we're still outside the safety of Ilbrea. If the woods hear you talking of ravens, they just might send one of their birds to answer."

"Old man Jerick worries about the whisperings of trees," Tarrum said with a laugh like a bark.

"Old man?" Jerick said. "Old man? Last I counted, you were on track with me for how many Winter's Ends you've drunk away."

The two kept bickering as they moved down the hill, sounding more like old men with gout than Guilded soldiers.

Every so often, Niko would stop and examine a landmark to add to the ever-growing map on his right hip, all the while trying to ignore the sting in his gut.

He was an explorer. His first duty was to discover new things.

But the passage might only be a spring.

The sun crept down in the sky. Soon, it would disappear, leaving the party in darkness.

But you've seen enough to know strangeness is rarely random.

Sounds of horses sighing and pots being stirred over fires carried through the brush below them.

But if it is something, really truly something, the worst thing would be for a pack of soldiers to go fumbling through the dark after you as you tried to figure out what you've found. The soldiers can't be a part of mapping the true Ilbrea.

Making the King's maps and mapping the true Ilbrea were two entirely different endeavors. Splitting himself between the two pursuits often felt like he was straddling an ever-growing chasm. His fall was inevitable as long as he tried to keep a foot on each side.

Would those you journey with hang you themselves if they knew your secret?

Resentment rose like bile in Niko's mouth as the camp came into view.

Rollands was already sitting, boots off, by the fire. His pack of soldiers sat near him, eating and drinking as the night faded to gray.

"Late coming in, Niko?" Rollands said as Niko sank down by the fire.

"Amec fell into a spring." Niko clasped his hands firmly under his chin, resisting the urge to reach for the sheath that held the true map. How wonderful it would be to follow the darkness and see where it led. "It took us a bit to fish him out."

"You know"—Rollands glanced over his shoulder before continuing—"I've never understood why they let the young soldiers come out with journeys. The soldiers are the most plentiful among the Guilds. There are thousands of them. How hard could it be to find a few older ones who want to trade in fighting for mud and trekking?"

"Amec's a fine soldier," Niko said. "The ground just decided to eat him is all."

"Niko," Inger called, waving something over his head. "A letter's come for you."

"A letter?" Niko rolled the words around in his mouth, as though they came from a long lost language.

"A messenger came from Ilara to be sure all of us were all right after the rotta scum tried to blow us up." Inger pressed the letter into Niko's hand. "They came while I was watching the camp today. I told him everyone was just fine when I'd seen them right after dawn, and then he gave me this to give to you."

Perfect handwriting worthy of a scribe's robes marked the outside of the envelope.

Nikolas Endur. Map Maker. Eastern Mountains Journey.

"Is it news of the city?" Amec asked.

"I doubt it." Niko stood and stepped outside the circle of travelers before slipping his finger into the folds of the envelope.

What would Allora have to say that warranted chasing him on the journey?

That she hates you for leaving her, and that if you ever had a fleeting hope of winning her, it's disappeared forever.

"But if it's not news of Ilara—"

"Leave him," Jerick cut Amec off. "Don't you have food to be making anyway?"

"Yes, sir." Head hung low, Amec made his way to the cook fire.

Niko almost felt sorry for him. The youngest soldier on the journey, given all the tasks no one else wanted, and he'd fallen into a hole to boot.

"Are you going to read your letter or just keep clutching it?" Jerick thumped Niko on the back. "Waiting to read it won't change its words."

Niko nodded and cut through the trees, not stopping until he was beyond the farthest of the tents.

"Amec fell down a well!" A laugh split the twilight as Niko tore open the letter.

Niko,

The perfect script tore Niko's breath away. He scrunched his eyes up tight, trying to sear the image of that word into his memory.

Niko,

I'm not sure if this letter will find you or, if it does, how long it might take. For me, the explosion was only this morning, though I suppose for you it's now weeks away.

I wasn't hurt. My dress was barely marked by the flames. I didn't even know what had happened when the soldier lifted me over his shoulder and ran me to the Princess's carriage. I nearly shouted at him for treating me in such an awful way. But then I saw the flames, and my ears recognized the noise as screams.

I caught a glimpse of you on your horse. You were staring back at me. I could see it on your face, the urge to run back and rescue me. But the soldier beside you forced your horse to run, and I'm glad he did. I don't think whoever made the street explode wanted to hurt the Princess. I think it was the journey.

The Princess could be attacked in a hundred different ways, each of them more dramatic than what happened this morning. And if it was the journey they wanted to hurt, then you would have been the one to strike. I don't think I could survive seeing you burned and bloody, Niko. I know I am stronger than Ilbrea will ever give me credit for, but I am not strong enough for that.

The Princess is safe. The Queen collapsed when she heard the news. Our sweet Adrial has been locked in the Sorcerers Tower to be healed, but the King himself has promised me Adrial will be well by morning. Mara and Tham left the city before news of the attack had even spread to their ears.

I know you, Niko. As well as I know any heart. I know you must be furious with yourself for riding to safety. You aren't sleeping for fear that those you left behind hate you for going.

You're wrong. I'm not angry. You did what duty demanded, and I am safe.

But promise me you will be safe as well. If I am right, if it was the journey they attacked, then the darkness might seek you again. And I will not be there to know if you're safe. Promise to come home to me, and every time you have ridden away will be forgiven.

I cannot bear that look of terror being the last time I see your face.
I will wait for you,
Allora

Tears stung the corners of Niko's eyes as he pressed the letter to his chest. They were safe. All of his family, safe.

And Allora…

A smile that ached his cheeks spread across Niko's face.

"Is the messenger gone?" Niko called as he sprinted back into the circle of tents. "Inger, is the messenger gone?"

"Left right after he dropped the letter." Inger nodded. "Truth be told, I was shocked he managed to find us in the woods. Can't blame him for wanting to get back to the road and on his way."

"That's fine." Niko folded the letter, tucking it safely into the sheath at his hip.

Allora will wait.

18

ALLORA

The sweeping lawns had changed much in the early weeks of spring. Flowers bloomed brightly in every garden bed. Lush indigos, pinks, and violets burst through the emerald leaves. Even knowing the sorcerers had a hand in the gardens didn't pale their beauty.

Fruit trees grew along the walls, their branches pressed flat against the stone, feeding the trees extra warmth from the sun. It was still too early in the season for fruit to drip from their branches, but leaves had appeared, giving a promise of pleasant things to come.

"It's more a matter of what Ilbrea needs."

Allora continued to studiously ignore the King's words, focusing instead on the sculpted hedges. The groundskeeper claimed he did the work himself, but staring at the perfect replica of the Ilbrean Star, Allora suspected sorcerer involvement.

"Ilbrea needs the southern islands," Lord Karron said. "I know we've suffered heavy losses sailing that far into the storms before, but there are whole stretches of islands that lay beyond. I've seen a few of them from the decks of the ships."

INKER AND CROWN | 167

"And have only been able to land on one." The King waved a flippant hand through the air.

Allora closed her eyes, willing herself to be strong enough not to listen. She was there as an ornament, not as a thinking being.

Father won't blame you for listening. But the King will. Do not displease your King, Allora.

"And that one island brought us knowledge and riches beyond what the dozen journeys to the Barrens have given," Lord Karron said. "That is why I have chosen to lead the journey myself."

Allora clenched her fists, digging her nails painfully into her palms. Knowing her father planned on leading the dangerous expedition and hearing him speak of it to the King were two entirely different matters.

"No."

Allora's eyes flew open at the King's pronouncement.

"Your Highness," Lord Karron said. "The journey needs to be made—"

"Lady Allora"—the King bowed to her—"please do join us as we walk."

Allora smoothed her green skirt and stood, leaving the safety of the carved stone bench to take the King's arm.

"Lady Allora, I assume you heard your father volunteering to lead a year-long journey attempting to break through the southern storms to explore the islands and whatever might lie beyond."

Allora glanced at her father for a split second, just long enough to see his tiny nod.

"Yes, Your Highness," Allora said.

"Do you think your father is a good man?" the King asked.

Allora's breath caught in her throat. "My father is the best of all men."

"A daring thing to say while walking on the arm of your King." The King raised an eyebrow at her, though his teal eyes twinkled with mocking, not anger.

"I might call you an exquisitely close second." Allora held her breath until the King laughed heartily, shaking her arm in his. "I do hope you'll forgive the bias of a daughter."

"Were I ever blessed with a child, I would hope for nothing less from them. You've raised her well all on your own, Lord Karron." The King led them down a path of tall shrubs that blocked the views of both the high wall that surrounded them and the palace.

"I would say she did most of the work on her own," Lord Karron said. "I was so often gone."

"And was it a detriment when your father was gone?" The King stopped to examine a bush of crimson flowers.

"A detriment?" Allora smiled, the expression tight on her lips.

"If your father is the best of all men, is Ilara not a better city for having him within its limits?" The King let go of Allora's arm.

"To me, of course," Allora said as the King picked the largest of the red blooms. "But my father is the best Map Maker Ilbrea has seen since Aximander himself. He has brought knowledge and riches to this country. It would be a waste of his gifts to beg him to stay by his daughter's side."

Allora froze as the King took the end of her blond braid in his hand and slipped the stem of the flower between its folds.

"But what if it were not for his daughter's sake?" The King looped Allora's arm back through his and continued down the path as though he'd done nothing strange. "What if it were for the good of the kingdom that he stay?"

"The good of the kingdom?" Allora said.

The high hedges gave way to white-barked trees. The sunlight glimmered down through the bright green leaves that fluttered with the afternoon breeze.

"Who is your second, Lord Karron?" the King asked.

"Seamus Traim," Lord Karron said. "You've met him."

"He's experienced and ambitious, I remember." The King

stopped at a bench carved of white wood. He sat and drew Allora down to sit beside him. "But he's not a very stately figure. He's not particularly pleasant. And he has yet to bring in enough bounty to build himself a fine house, let alone a palace fit for entertaining guests from Wyrain."

"If you would like to impress guests with my home, I think Allora would be a better host than an old man who's more suited to the wild than a ballroom," Lord Karron said. "I am known for my accomplishments in journeying, not charming dignitaries."

"And you, Lady Allora?" the King turned to her, the bright teal of his eyes more startling than beautiful. There was a keen intensity behind his gaze, a power that often made Allora forget the King still had a few years before he'd reach his thirtieth birthday. "Would you be willing to leave behind your hours of leisure to entertain the dignitaries Wyrain is sending to inspect our fine city?"

"I have never been one for leisure, Your Highness." Allora gave a small bow of her head, grateful for a reason to look away from the King's piercing eyes. "If you think I am fit to take my father's place as host so he might travel to the southern islands, then I would be honored to do my duty for Ilbrea."

Fool. You could have kept him safe.

It was a childish thought. Even if she had told the King foreigners terrified her and then vomited on his shoes, her father still would have found a way to go to the southern islands. Neither King nor daughter could keep Lord Karron from a journey once his course was set. That power lay with Dudia alone.

"I am glad to see I will have a Karron by my side when the masses from over the mountains descend upon us." The King took Allora's hand in his, pressing his lips to her fingers. "It brings me great comfort."

Allora froze, a pleasant smile locked upon her face, waiting for her father to say something. To take her by the arm and lead her away. To tell the King there was a pressing matter that required his attention. But no help came.

"You do understand why the truce with Wyrain is so important?" the King asked, with no hint he had done anything embarrassing or intimate.

"We need a better route to the Golden Sea," Allora said, grateful when the King stood, again looping her arm through his and leading her down the white-wooded path. "The Spice Trail is the only road we have right now, and Wyrain taxes everything that crosses through their side of the eastern mountains. If we could use the road freely or form a shorter path to the Golden Sea, goods could be brought in with less expense."

"Very good," the King said. "You are as clever as I had hoped."

Clever, like a child reciting a rhyme.

"And Wyrain has no magic within its borders," Allora continued, not needing to look at her father to feel his disapproval stinging the back of her neck. "Those with the gift of sorcery have only ever been born within the borders of Ilbrea. No other country has been blessed with the magical gifts Dudia nurtured within the Sorcerers Guild. We want gold and spices. Wyrain wants magic. But magic can't be shared with enemies. The result could be disastrous. Giving them an advantage if their men should ever pour over the eastern mountains to burn our country."

"Really?" the King said.

"The only solution is to lock the countries together so closely war could no longer be considered." Allora stopped, turning to face the King. "And to make sure if the truce ever did crumble, Ilbrea would be strong enough to push Wyrain's army off the eastern mountains. To move the mountains themselves should the time come."

The King examined Allora, looking from her eyes to the red flower in her hair.

"You are far brighter than I have ever given you credit for, Lady Allora." The King smiled. "I think you will stand up very well to the Wyrain delegation. Lord Karron, if you wish to journey to the southern islands, so be it. But do be sure your affairs are in order so Lady Allora can represent the Map Makers Guild and manage your estate in your stead."

"Represent the Guild?" The words tumbled from Allora's mouth.

"Things are changing in Ilbrea." The King kissed Allora's hand again. "We cannot behave as we have in the past. A strong leader while tramping in the dirt will do us no good with diplomacy. Traim may be a fine hand at plotting a river, but Allora will have the seat at the table in front of Wyrain."

"In ceremony only." Allora forced air into her lungs.

"In whatever capacity best serves Ilbrea," the King said. "I do hope I can always count on you for that."

"Of course, Your Highness." Allora bowed.

"Safe journey, Lord Karron." The King strode away, leaving Lord Karron and Allora in the trees.

"Allora." Lord Karron seized his daughter's arm, dragging her down the path. "Allora."

"What?" Allora asked as they passed back into the high hedges.

"For once in your life, could you not have remained silent?" Lord Karron growled with anger in his voice that sounded foreign to Allora's ears.

"He asked me to speak," Allora whispered. "He asked you to bring me here. You want to go to the southern islands. You've been saying as much since you returned from your last journey. I made sure you could go. How was I wrong?"

"You don't understand. The last thing we need is for you to attract the King's attention." The anger disappeared from her father's face, replaced with lines of fatigue and worry that seemed just as foreign. "You think you're normal, Allora. You see yourself as a pretty girl who's been left behind to keep our home and our secrets safe. But you are so much more than that." Lord Karron took his daughter's face in his hands. "And you've just shown the King exactly how valuable you are."

19

MARA

"A day in the white is more than a thousand score,
For once you've climbed to the white, you see spring nevermore.
Nevermore summer, nevermore spring,
Nevermore feel a pleasant young thing."

"Enough," Mara called to the wagon rumbling along behind hers.

"Sorry, map maker," Smitter shouted back over the clatter of the wheels and grumblings of the dogs. "Didn't mean to offend the lady."

Mara clenched the rough wooden edge of her seat. "I'm not offended, Smitter. It's just making me cold already. Can't we enjoy the last bit of color left to us?"

"Best enjoy it fast," Smitter called back.

"Right you are." It was impossible to ignore the white, even if Mara had wanted to.

Even here, thirty miles from where the permanent snow began, the white mountains towered in front of them. Reaching so high into the sky they kissed the clouds, the white mountains coated the entire northern horizon. Just looking up to their peaks sent Mara's head spinning.

They weren't to climb to the top. Such a feat would be impossible even if the sorcerers cared to help. The King's orders were to explore the mountains for signs of life. No creature could survive where the summits met the sky.

"Afraid of freezing, map maker?" Tham asked.

Mara. I wish he could call me Mara.

Her fingers ached to touch him. To graze his palm or caress his cheek. The tiniest hint of his skin against hers would satisfy her, or at least make the longing better for a few hours. But if any of the expedition party saw, there would be hell to pay back home.

"I'm not afraid of freezing any more than I would be of burning." Mara didn't look at Tham as she spoke. She wouldn't be able to keep a smile from her lips. It was hard enough to hide her sheer joy at riding through the crisp air beside him when she couldn't see his dark eyes.

"Two days from now, we'll be on the snow," Tham said, "and the wagons will be on their way back to Ilara."

"It is rather rude of them to abandon us." Mara gripped the side of the wagon as a wheel thumped into a divot in the road. "But I do suppose a wagon would be useless in an hour and the horses dead in a week."

"Whitend ahead!" The shout echoed back from the front wagon.

Trusting Tham not to let her fall, Mara stood on her seat.

A clump of low houses with faded wooden sides had appeared over the rise. The cluster held no more than twenty dwellings, all built around a wide stone circle at the center.

"Not much to see, is it?" Smitter said.

"It's the end of the world as far as most are concerned." Mara could see where the belief came from.

Beyond the drab cluster of houses, a span of scruffy tundra reached into the distance. Near the village, the turf had been touched by the green of spring. But farther north, the green gradually disappeared, swallowed by dead, brown scrub bushes. Beyond the brown, white took hold as the ground became permanently coated in snow.

A cold wind whipped down from the north, lifting the hairs on the nape of Mara's neck.

The white is waiting for us.

Mara batted away the childish thought and jumped back down to the floor of the wagon.

"And the King thinks there might be people living in the mountains?" Tham said.

"Let's hope for all our sakes he's wrong."

"Shall we trundle right into the village, Lamac?" a voice called from the front of the line.

Mara turned to watch the wagon's canvas drape pull aside as Lamac peered out into the sunlight for the first time that afternoon.

"May Aximander bless all our souls." Lamac stood on a supply crate, cutting a daring figure despite the wrinkles on his green uniform. "I don't suppose we have a choice."

"Careful, Lamac." Mara kept her tone cheerful and bright. "The soldiers don't pray to Aximander. Let them keep their own saint."

"Why?" Lamac reached into the canvas shelter and grabbed his scroll tube and boots. "Do you think Saint Dannach watches soldiers while they're on journeys?"

"What you and I believe isn't the point. We're about to go into the cold and—"

Tham pressed his arm against Mara's, cutting off her words.

"If we're all going to be living in tight quarters"—Mara forced the cheerfulness back into her tone—"it's best to let the soldiers keep to their own beliefs. It keeps the peace."

"Following orders keeps the peace," Lamac laughed. "Everything else is just politics."

"As you say, Lamac."

Movement stirred in the village—people coming out of their houses, barely visible from this distance. The brown of their clothes matched the dull colors of their homes, making it difficult to tell the difference between person and dwelling.

"Are we really to stay here for the night?" Lamac said. "If we're going to sleep in the mud, I'd just as soon do it without curious locals prowling around."

"Hadn't we best learn from them?" Mara said as the first wagon stopped at the edge of the village. "They hold more knowledge of the white mountains than all the books we've studied."

"Because they've stuck their toes into the ageless snow?" Lamac lowered his voice as their wagon stopped. "I somehow doubt that."

A man with bright white hair moved slowly toward the wagon, head cocked to the side.

What Mara had taken for filth on the clothes of the people was actually the fur of some brown animal.

"You the map makers?"

The white-haired villager was not a man as Mara had thought, but a woman with closely cropped hair and pants made of fur.

"We are." Mara jumped from the wagon and approached the woman. "We've been sent by order of the King to map the white mountains."

"Pity." The woman worried her wrinkled lips.

"Did you not receive word of the King's proclamations at Winter's End?" Lamac asked, his voice raised as though the woman were deaf.

"That?" the woman pointed to a tattered piece of parchment tacked to the side of a house. The ink had been washed away by rain and the corners torn by the wind. "Man came up on a horse and hung it."

"And could you read it?" Lamac said, his voice still raised.

"What Map Maker Lamac means"—Mara stepped in front of Lamac, reaching out to shake the woman's hand—"is we hope we aren't inconveniencing your village by stopping here for the night. We made better time than we'd planned on the way north, and you may not have expected us yet."

"Last good time you'll make." The woman laughed, the rasp of it like dry brush rubbing together. "Makes no difference to us when you're here. Don't break into the houses, and don't go wandering off and get lost. We don't rescue strangers around here."

"We are map makers," Lamac said, stepping up to stand beside Mara. "Wandering is what we do."

"I like it better when the girl talks." The old woman glared at Lamac. "I'll speak to her from now on."

"If that's what pleases you." Mara bowed. "May I ask where we should camp for the night?"

"North side since that's where you'll be going." The woman pointed through the houses to a patch of tundra beyond. "Give the mountains a chance to get your scent. Maybe then they'll know not to devour you."

"This way," Tham called to the wagons, leading them through the narrow strip of bare dirt between houses.

"May I ask your name?" Mara said.

"Bernate." She grasped Mara's hand with shocking strength.

"Thank you for allowing us in your home, Bernate," Mara said.

"You'll be wishing I hadn't soon enough." Bernate waved for Mara to follow her.

"You shouldn't undercut me like that in front of the locals, Map Maker Landil," Lamac murmured as they followed Bernate toward the stone circle.

"Since when do you care to speak to the locals?" Mara asked.

"Fair enough, but I will not be made to look a fool in front of the soldiers."

You need no help from me.

"You been in the white before?" Bernate rounded on Mara so quickly, she had to jump back to keep from running into the woman.

"Not quite. Only to the foot of the white mountains," Mara said, pressing away the horrible cold that nipped the back of her neck. "I've traveled this way with Lord Karron."

Lamac's eyes widened in surprise. He opened his mouth to speak, but Bernate held up a hand to silence him.

"The white must like you then." She took Mara's chin in her hand.

Mara held steady, not flinching at the touch of the Bernate's wrinkled and frigid fingers.

"You should be the first to go in." Bernate tipped Mara's chin down so she could examine her eyes. "The wind must like your scent to let you leave her home."

"Thank you. I'll do as you suggest."

"It's customary for map makers to rotate who takes the front when there are two equals leading an expedition," Lamac said.

"Lead wherever you like, boy." Bernate didn't look away from Mara as she spoke. "The white will kill you before you reach the heart of the mountains. If you have a letter to your loved ones, best to leave it with us. We don't get messengers coming here much, but I'll give it to them when they do."

"Ma'am, we are Guilded map makers," Lamac said, anger sounding in every word. "I don't think it is for you to judge the success of our journey before it has even begun."

"Saint Aximander?" Bernate said.

Mara took a deep breath as Bernate let go of her chin and turned to Lamac.

"What of him?" Lamac asked.

"Is he who will see you through the mountains and back? Is he who will make sure you have fire to heat and food to eat? The mountains and the wind care nothing for your measly saint. The forces that run through the endless winter are deeper and more magical than any saint could fight against." Bernate seized Lamac's wrist and dragged him toward the great stone circle.

Mara hadn't noticed the people surrounding them until they began following Bernate and Lamac. There were at least sixty villagers. Some young, some old. The bushy beards of the men was the only distinction between the sexes.

"Look upon it."

Bernate's voice carried through the crowd to Mara.

A pile of stones rose up from the center of the rock circle.

Mara weaved her way through the pack of onlookers, following Bernate's voice.

"We have kept watch over the mound for centuries. Protecting all who dwell south from Kareen. You wander into the white looking for things you don't want to find, and you don't even understand what danger could ravage all of Ilbrea if we in Whitend didn't spend our days upon the tundra protecting you."

Mara reached the front of the crowd. The villagers all looked silently on as Bernate pointed a trembling finger at Lamac.

"Rocks?" Lamac said, his tone somewhere between entertained and furious. "You protect all of us from a pile of rocks?"

Mara could see no significance in the massive pile. Thousands of stones about the size of her fist had been shaped into a mound twelve feet high and thirty feet around, with no visible break in the structure.

"It's not the rocks. It's what's under them."

At Bernate's words, all the villagers seemed to tense.

"Well, now that you've buried whatever it is you think could ravage Ilbrea under a few thousand rocks, I'm sure we'll all be safe," Lamac said. "If you don't mind, I have important duties to attend to. I am, after all, a Guilded map maker on a journey ordered by the King."

Bernate spoke before he'd taken four steps. "Your letter, map maker."

Lamac shook his head and weaved through the crowd.

Murmurs floated through the villagers. A few sounded angry at Lamac's slight, but most were mournful. And their sorrow was more terrifying than if they had tried to drive the journey away by force.

"I'm sorry." Mara's voice carried over the crowd. "We are grateful for the hospitality of Whitend."

"Hospitality." Bernate shook her head. "Call it what you like. We have people here all the time. They wander up to see the mountains. Most don't even know how dreadfully far away they are. Think they can reach the edge of the white in a day."

"I've told them it will be longer," Mara said. "The ground isn't properly frozen, not all the way to the surface. Trying to get horses and dogs through will take time."

"At least they sent one with sense." Bernate shooed the villagers away. Even the largest of the men slunk back into their houses. "It'll be getting dark soon. That's one of the tricks of being so far north. This time of year, it looks like the sun will never go down, then she vanishes, leaving you to the wind."

"I should get to my camp then." Mara gave a small bow. "Thank you for—"

"You aren't going to ask about Kareen?" Deep creases furrowed Bernate's already wrinkled brow. "You know there are things in the white that can't be explained by the Guilds. I can see it in your eyes."

Mara opened her mouth to argue, but there was no point. Not if Bernate could see the truth.

"Do you know of something hiding in the white?" Mara asked. "Do you know where I can find it?"

"There's nothing you can find, girl." Bernate pointed at the summits of the mountains.

The sun had nearly reached their peaks. The last light of the day threw the ridges into sharp relief.

An entire world could be hidden up there, and she'd never be able to reach it.

"But if you spend long enough looking," Bernate said, "something will find you."

Mara's shoulders shook against her will.

"Tell me about Kareen," Mara said.

Bernate stood by Mara's side, watching as the sun kissed the tops of the mountains.

"Many centuries ago, when Ilbrea and magic still joined freely, a great warrior came down from the north. Her heart burned for the magic of Ilbrea. To find it all and gather it for herself so none other could compete with her power. Sword and shield in hand, she rode a great white wolf down the side of the highest peak. The people of Whitend saw her beastly mount and knew they had to stop her. Knew drawing all the magic from Ilbrea was a crime against Dudia himself. So the villagers fought."

As if on Bernate's command, the sun turned the white peaks of the mountains red, casting a tragic glow on their beauty.

"The people of Whitend fought with sticks and fire, but Kareen was too strong for men to defeat. So the great wind blew and burned all the forests between Whitend and the mountains, scorching their trees so badly they would never again take root in the frost. The fire burned Kareen and her wolf, and they fell. But they could not be killed. Not the way you and I die.

"Kareen holds the magic of the unending winter in her. If she rises, and the winds don't see fit to save us, Kareen will ride her white wolf through Ilbrea and kill everything with a beating heart."

"And the rocks hold her?" Mara asked.

The sun passed behind the mountains, leaving the sky a bloodied gray.

"Each of us must journey to the mountains and bring back a stone. The power of the mountains keeps her buried." Bernate took Mara's hands. "Ferrying a stone will show the mountains and the winds you mean to help their cause. Carry a stone, girl, and may the stone be enough to keep you alive."

20

MARA

The ground squished beneath Mara's boots, sucking her down into its muck with every step. With a yank, she pulled her foot free, careful not to tip under the weight of her pack. The next step was the same, and the next.

Had it been only Tham with her, Mara would have asked to find a mound of less sopping tundra to perch on and rest for a while. But the sounds of Lamac struggling behind her were satisfying enough to keep her pressing forward.

"Can you shut those beasts up?" Lamac snapped at Kegan, who walked far to the left of the rest of the journey, surrounded by a pack of twenty barking dogs.

"Why would I?" Kegan shouted over the chaos. "You're not trying to sneak up on anything. They're all staying together, making it through the muck better than you. If they want to make a bit of noise, what's the harm?"

"It's driving me insane," Lamac growled.

"If the beasts you're trusting to keep you alive in the white are driving you crazy before you even get to the edge of the snow, how do you think you'll fare in the freezing months ahead, map maker?" Kegan asked.

"I don't need the opinion of a commoner who is little better than a stable hand," Lamac said over the muffled laughter of the soldiers.

Careful, Kegan, he's a nasty one. Mara bit back her smile.

"Stable hand," Kegan said slowly. "Stable hand? If you find a comfy stable, you let me know, eh? I'd be pleased to hole up someplace warm and wait for the lot of you to come back. But seeing as I'm the only one who's run a sled before and, unless one of the soldiers is hiding a talent for training animals, the only one who knows how to manage the dogs, I think I'd prefer the title *All Mighty Purveyor of All Things You Need to Stay Alive.*"

"It's a good title," Smitter laughed.

The noise set the dogs to barking again.

"Don't encourage him, Smitter. He'll have a rude awakening when we get back to Ilara if he starts imagining himself grand out on the ice." The thread of a threat ran through Lamac's words.

"Let those who make it through the white decide what happens when we get out," Kegan said. "Best not to dwell on getting home before we've weathered a single storm."

"If you lack confidence—"

"Will they bicker the entire journey?" Tham spoke only loudly enough for Mara to hear.

"Probably." Mara wrenched her foot out of a particularly deep patch of soggy sod. A fresh wave of freezing water flooded her boots.

"They sound like Niko and Allora."

Mara glanced over to see the tiniest smile glimmering on Tham's face. Such a rare expression to see outside the company of their closest friends.

He's always been happier on the move. Heading toward something.

Mara looked back to the path ahead of them, if what they were traveling could really be considered a path. The maps from those who had journeyed this way before pointed to this route as their best option, and the locals of Whitend agreed. But the way forward was far from the ease of traveling a road. A slightly tamped down strip of wet tundra was really all they'd found.

The wagons had been abandoned within the first two hours of trying to move north of Whitend. The horses had been loaded with as much as they could carry, and the rest fell to the travelers to haul themselves.

At least it will get better when we get to the snow.

Mara squinted, trying to judge how much longer it would be before they could load the supplies into the sleds for the dogs to haul. The travelers would have to trudge through the snow, but at least they wouldn't be laden with horribly heavy packs.

"At least an hour," Tham said as if in response to Mara's thoughts. "I think we should camp and dry off as soon as we hit the ice pack. No point in risking losing toes so soon."

"I agree," Mara said. "The trick will be convincing Lamac not to argue."

The back of Tham's hand brushed Mara's.

She longed to cling to him. To breathe in his scent and surround herself with the sure knowledge that no matter what the white brought them, they would be together.

Because you're dragging him along with you.

Mara glanced behind, making sure the rest of the party remained out of earshot. "Thank you, Tham. Thank you for coming to the white with me."

"Where you go, I go. As long as the Guilds allow."

"As long as the Guilds allow." The words tasted sour in Mara's mouth.

The pattern continued for an hour. Step in the muck, pull your foot free, try not to fall. Try not to wonder what waits ahead.

Try not to wonder if you're leading everyone with you to their doom. Try not to remember the thrill of magic, in case you never find it again.

Brown covered the tundra, speckled with large swatches of

snow. Blue, so bright it seemed absurd, appeared in the distance. Mara forced herself to keep her pace steady even as the cliff of ice shone a dazzling cerulean, slicing through the pure white of the horizon.

"We should head for that cliff to camp for the night," Lamac said, his words the first break in the solid trudging forward in an hour.

Mara steeled herself to argue, but Kegan spoke first.

"We won't make it there by dusk. And running the dogs in the dark is a risk you shouldn't take unless the white demons are at your heels."

"What under Dudia—"

"It's ten miles at least," Kegan said. "I'd say more like fifteen. We've got an hour of true light left."

"That's utterly absurd," Lamac said.

"We should camp here," Mara called back, stopping where she stood.

A solid sheet of white stretched out in front of her. The lowering sun glimmered on its surface with sparkles of palest pink. Not a tree or animal broke the terrain leading all the way up to the blue cliffs in the distance.

"We should press on." Lamac joined Mara, standing at the very edge of the ice.

"The party should stay together," Smitter said. "If we keep going, the two with the horses will be alone for the night."

"And horse thieves will creep up in the dark and raid them?" Lamac asked. "Slit their throats and run off into the night?"

"People won't come for the horses, but wolves might." Smitter stepped out onto the white. "We camp here for the night and send the horses back in the morning."

"Have you become a map maker?" Lamac said.

"No." Smitter stomped on the snow, testing his footing. "I'm a soldier. We're the folks in charge of keeping you and Mara alive.

But we're also in charge of keeping each other alive. I won't see those two men heading into the dark alone."

"I agree." Mara stepped out onto the snow, the crispness of it foreign under her feet. "We need to warm up and dry off at any rate."

"The dogs agree as well." Kegan dropped his pack onto the snow and pulled out a bundle of thin, silver stakes.

"This journey is never going to get anywhere if we don't move." Lamac walked twenty paces beyond the rest of the journey before dropping his pack onto the ice.

"If you're worried about getting somewhere, spend your night plotting how to get the dogs to the top of that glacier." Kegan walked in a wide circle, pressing the silver stakes into the ground. "These are the best trained sled dogs Ilbrea has to offer, but I can promise you climbing cliffs of ice isn't a thing they like to do."

Lamac's shoulders tensed for a moment, but he said nothing.

"Let's get the horses unpacked." Tham moved to the horses, and the other soldiers followed suit.

Tham wasn't the ranking soldier, but he so seldom spoke, people tended to listen when he bothered.

"Elver, get the tents set up and the fires started," Smitter said, as though wanting to be clear that he was, in fact, the soldier in charge.

"I'll help." Mara grabbed one of the fire bags as Lamac moved toward her. Better to have something to do with her hands. Busy work made it easier to hide her frustration.

"We should head to the ice cliffs first thing in the morning." Lamac loomed over Mara as she pulled a set of silver disks out of the bag.

"Straight in and then cut west?" Mara placed the first disk on the ground. It was two feet wide and polished so well, it might have been made as a mirror. The few weeks on the journey had already changed her face.

Gray circles showed under her eyes, and her cheeks had hollowed out. Freckles dotted her face and lips.

Allora would never approve.

"We should go up the cliffs," Lamac said. "Get as high as we can and see where our path should take us."

Mara struck the flint, letting a tiny, purple spark leap onto the silver disk. Lavender flames tickled the surface.

"We'd have to get the dogs and equipment up the cliffs," Mara said. "And if there is no path farther in, we'd have to haul them all back down."

"Are you afraid of work now?" Lamac said. "I'm sure Tham could do the lifting for you."

Mara kept her eyes trained on the violet flames that now filled the dish.

"I'm not afraid of hauling the dogs up or down." Mara moved on to the next silver disk. "I'm afraid of wasting time. We only have half a year until there's too little sunlight to keep plotting by and the storms become too fierce to risk the elevation. There are easier paths to get up to the base of the mountains that will take far less time and involve far less danger."

"That ice will be the tip of a glacier." Lamac stomped his foot.

Mara looked slowly up at him, willing her face into placid calmness.

"We should follow the glacier up. It will give us a path," Lamac said. "There can be no glory for the Guilds without daring. I say we climb and follow the ice."

Mara bit her bottom lip, hating herself for letting the nervous habit creep up.

The ice wall sparkled gloriously in the setting sun—a thing of exquisite beauty begging to be conquered. The views from the top would show them the terrain, even if it didn't offer a path into the heart of the mountains.

Allora would be horrified at the very thought of you climbing that.

"We'll send up two climbers in advance." Mara turned back to the fire trays, striking a spark and watching the purple flames grow. "They can test the ice and be sure it'll hold, let the party know if it looks like there's a path beyond or nothing but more sheer ice."

"And let me guess, you and Tham should be the ones to climb?"

"You can climb if you want. And take whomever you like with you." Mara moved on to the third tray.

"I'll take Edder with me." Lamac's smile sounded in his voice. "Best to take the most daring when working for the glory of the Guilds."

"Of course." Mara lit the fourth disk. Sitting in the center of the fires, her skin warmed for the first time in weeks.

Lamac hovered over her for another moment before striding away.

"Come get fires!" Mara called as she lit the fifth and final disk.

"The sorcerers are wonderful things." Elver crouched in the snow, dancing his fingers through the fire. "Flames that won't set the world ablaze." He dangled his sleeve in the purple flames. "What a wonder."

"Don't trust the wonder too much." Mara's laugh sounded hollow and tired even to her own ears. "You never know when magic might fail you."

"Right you are, Mara." Elver picked up the tray and carried it to the tent at the farthest end of the camp.

Six tents dotted the snow. After tomorrow, there would only be five. Five tents out on the white. The thought was both thrilling and terrifying.

"Elver, get the food going," Smitter shouted from inside his tent.

"You should make the food, Smitter," Rowls laughed as he grabbed one of the fire trays. "You've the most experience in eating."

"I think I just heard Rowls volunteer to make food for the next week," Smitter said.

"I only meant you have the most refined palate with all the culinary experience you've had," Rowls said.

The men laughed in response.

Mara stood and lifted one of the fire trays. The bottom of the metal was frozen with no trace of the heat of the flames.

A true wonder of magic.

Elver had set up Mara's tent at the center of the camp. The safest place for the one person who would be sleeping alone. The men all packed in together, sharing space, but the Guilds wouldn't allow Mara that comfort.

If they'd only let Tham join me.

"Mara." Kegan loped toward her, his gait comically similar to the dog walking at his side. "I've penned the others in for the night." He waved a hand at the circle of silver stakes. The dogs all prowled between them, not venturing past the perimeter, though there was nothing visible stopping them.

More wonders from the sorcerers.

"Elle here doesn't like to sleep with the others." Kegan patted the dog's head. "She's a fine girl, but she'll keep us up all night. You've got a bit of extra room in your tent, and I was hoping you might keep her."

Mara looked down at the dog. Her fur was snow white, except for circles of charcoal around her bright blue eyes. Elle tipped her head to the side as Mara examined her, as though judging Mara for a tent mate as much as the map maker judged her.

"I can always try to squeeze Elle in with us." Kegan shrugged. "Though I don't know how the soldiers will like it."

"She can stay with me." Mara reached out a hand, letting the dog sniff her. "No point in crowding the others."

"Right enough." Kegan bounced on his toes. "You stay with Mara, Elle." He ruffled the dog's ears.

Obediently, the dog stood and transferred herself to sit at Mara's feet.

"Best get back to the lot." Kegan ran back toward the other dogs, who howled their approval.

"Just you and me, Elle." Mara opened the tent flap, and the dog sauntered in, immediately claiming the center of the space for her own.

21

ADRIAL

"Are you sure you don't want me to go for you?" Taddy's forehead wrinkled as he frowned. "I don't mind riding out of the city, and I'm good on a horse."

"I'm a fine rider too, Taddy." Adrial pulled on the fastenings of the saddle, more to prove his point than because he thought the stable hands hadn't done their work properly.

"But Master Gareth will be furious if he finds out you've left." Taddy dug his nails into his pudgy cheeks. "And what if something happens to you? What if—"

"Taddy." Adrial cut off the boy's list of worries. "We made an agreement. I bring you to live at the library to help me get to and from the shop every day so you don't have to live in the same building as Travers."

Taddy shivered at the mention of Travers's name.

"In exchange," Adrial continued, "you tell everyone I've locked myself in my quarters to focus on the vellum for a few days."

"They'll know you're gone." Taddy shook his head, his eyes wide.

"You'll accept all the food that's brought to me and send out the letters I've written to Natalia and Travers explaining my absence. You'll stay in my quarters, studying until I return."

Taddy hadn't stopped shaking his head.

"Do you understand, Taddy?"

"No," Taddy squeaked. "I mean, yes, I know what I'm to do, but no, I don't understand why you're leaving the city before dawn."

"I'm going to collect things for the vellum." The words were true enough, Adrial felt no regret in saying them. "I'll be perfectly safe, I promise you."

"I know Ena can take care of you, sir." Taddy wrinkled his nose. "But if the city isn't safe, then how will the woods be safer?"

"Because, Taddy"—Adrial took the boy by the shoulders—"it's not the wild the soldiers are protecting us from. It's bad people. The forests don't have those sorts of people. Just be a good lad and stay in my room. Do as I've told you, and no one will ever need to know."

"But what if they find out?" Taddy asked, his tone near a whimper.

"Then tell them I'm the one who ordered you to say I was in my room." Adrial grabbed the saddle and dragged himself painfully onto the seat. "They can't blame you for doing as I ordered. I am the head scribe. You had no choice but to obey."

"All right, sir." Taddy handed Adrial the reins of the second horse. "But do be careful, sir. It's been quiet living in the library away from Travers, and I would hate to have to go back to living with him if you die."

"I'll be fine, Taddy." Not bothering to hide his smile, Adrial guided the horses to the stable door.

The scribes' guard outside paid no attention to Adrial as he rode out onto the dark street.

Crisp morning air greeted him, filling his lungs with reckless joy. How long had it been since he'd ridden out of the city?

Years.

The stables let out on the backside of the library, away from the merchant's street. With no shops in sight, his path was abandoned.

The clopping of the horses' hooves echoed off the stone buildings. But no one ran out to gape at the Guilded Cripple. Even if someone peeked out a window, they wouldn't recognize him in the dark coat and pants Taddy had scavenged for him.

Adrial pushed the horses to a trot, relishing the wind on his face. The breeze lifted his hair, sending a chill tumbling down his spine.

And Ena would be waiting for him.

He guided the horses past bakeries, taverns, and inns. The scents of a hundred different breakfasts baking wafted around him. Adrial took a deep breath, drawing the delicious aroma into his lungs.

As he neared the northern gate, people appeared on the streets. All with the same dull look of early morning, as though the orange kissing the horizon held no thrall.

Adrial sat up as straight as he could, keeping his eyes front as he approached the gate.

Twelve guards flanked the exit of the city, their gazes searching each of the early morning travelers that passed.

"What's in the cart?" a guard stepped in front of a handcart entering the city.

The man pushing it sounded more resigned and fatigued than afraid. "Food to sell. Same as yesterday and the day before that."

The soldiers began pulling everything out of the man's cart, tossing it none too delicately onto the ground. The man kept silent as the soldiers ruined a full third of his goods.

Stop them. Call out, tell them who you are, and stop them.

But then they would know the head scribe was attempting to ride unchecked through their gate. They'd stop Adrial just as soon as they'd stopped the farmer. Though they'd be less rough about it.

Adrial kept his eyes down until he'd passed through the arch in the stone wall and reached the outside of the city.

A hint of terror trembled in his chest. He'd done it. He'd left Ilara.

You're not a child stealing sweets, Adrial Ayres.

He dragged his gaze away from the back of his horse's neck.

The houses of those who hadn't been lucky enough to build within the protection of the city walls were packed in on either side of him, as though the homes were huddling together for safety.

"You actually came." Ena's voice drifted out of the shadows.

Adrial didn't bother searching the ground. He looked up to the low rooftops of the houses surrounding him.

Ena leaned against a chimney, wrapped in a deep red shawl. It was the most muted color he'd ever seen her wear.

"Did you think I wouldn't?" Adrial said as Ena climbed off the roof and onto the second horse.

"I did wonder a bit." Ena clicked to her horse to move. "They've got that library so wrapped up in guards, I didn't know if you'd be daring enough to slip away, let alone find two such fine horses."

"Truth be told, I made Taddy help me."

"The poor boy, he must be terrified." Ena tipped her face to the sky.

Pink overtook the gray of the morning as Ena led him north, beyond the last of the houses. To the west, the new rays of light sparkled off the Arion Sea.

Adrial watched the waves gleam red until the path took them inland and trees hid the water from view.

Neither of them spoke as they traveled. A hundred questions tore through Adrial's mind, but the gentle calls of the birds and Ena's quiet humming as she rode in front of him were too blissfully perfect. To speak would be to shatter the moment.

An hour's ride north of the city, Ena guided her horse off the road and into the trees to the east.

"Ena," Adrial said, even as he let his horse follow her, "where are you going?"

"I thought you trusted me, scribe."

"I do." Adrial ducked beneath the low hanging branches. "There's just not a road here."

"When you've seen where I'm taking you, you'll be glad there's no road leading to it."

Ena steered her horse without stopping or hesitating as they skirted around stands of trees too thick for their mounts to pass through.

"If there's not a road or path leading to where we're going, then how did you find it?" Adrial asked as they reached a stream. He let his reins go slack so his horse could drink. The clear water bubbled over the rocks. Adrial wanted to touch it. To feel the chill on his skin.

"The truth, or the fairy story?" Ena asked.

"The truth."

Ena took a shuddering breath. "When I came north, I wasn't ready to live in Ilara. I knew a trade but had no supplies, no coin. A girl on her own is an easy mark, and I was too tired to defend myself against every man who fancied himself my savior. So, I walked north and lived in the woods for a bit. I found a lot of places I don't think even your map makers have seen."

"You were all alone in the woods?"

"For a few months. But the snows came, and I had enough flowers stored to begin mixing inks. So, I went back to the city, found a place to live, and started working." Ena nudged her horse to walk. "I do miss it out here. So much quieter. You know which animals to eat and which will eat you, and the rest is just surviving. If it weren't for the snow, I'd have been tempted to stay."

"I'm glad you didn't." Blood rushed to Adrial's cheeks. For a moment, he thought the sloshing of the horse's hooves had masked his words, but before his heart could find a normal rhythm, Ena twisted to look at him.

"Your vellum wouldn't be half so pretty."

She stared into Adrial's eyes as her horse cut through the trees. The intensity of her gaze burned like a dare.

Adrial took a steadying breath. "I would have made do and wouldn't have known the difference. But I would be awfully sorry not to have known you."

Ena winked. "Too right, scribe." She turned to face front as the trees opened up onto a wide, sweeping plain.

Spring wildflowers coated the ground. Pale pinks grew beside bright reds and oranges. Moss-green butterflies flitted through a swatch of deep-blue blooms, wider than the grounds of the library.

In the distance, low mountains covered in emerald trees stretched out over the horizon, with only the white mountains to the north hinting there was anything in the world beyond the forest.

"It's beautiful," Adrial said.

A raven swooped overhead, cawing his approval of the wide valley.

"If I had known you were so easy to impress, I wouldn't have planned on taking you all the way to the mountains. I forget how much of your life you've spent locked indoors. But I need the petal, so you'll just have to ride through the pretty valley with me to get it. Unless you'd like to stay here and play with the butterflies?"

"No, I'll ride with you." The beauty of the valley was undeniable. But Ena smiled, and he couldn't bring himself to look away from her.

If magic or Dudia had somehow granted him the power, he would have stopped the world, freezing time with the sun kissing his skin and Ena's smile filling his soul.

I'd follow her to the white mountains.

The little voice at the back of Adrial's mind whispered, *She wouldn't want you to.*

"Best keep up then, scribe. We'll have to ride faster to get there in time." With a kick, Ena took off through the field, her hair streaming behind her.

"Come on," Adrial urged his horse onward.

He'd been taught to ride, made to practice by Lord Karron. Though the bouncing of the horse ached in his hip, he had confidence in his seat.

"Come on." Adrial rode up next to Ena.

Mirth danced in her eyes. "Well done, scribe."

This is bliss. This is paradise.

The sun pressed away the bite of the spring wind.

Ena laughed as a flock of birds shot up from the ground in terror at their approach.

Let this last forever. Let this ride be how I spend my days.

But the mountains grew ever closer, and before the horses had tired, Ena slowed as they approached the woods. These trees weren't a flat forest like the one they'd ridden through earlier. Here, the woods scaled the slope, climbing the side of the mountain.

"Best to get down now." Ena slid easily from her horse and took the reins from Adrial. "The walk's not long, and the branches get awfully low."

Adrial looped his good leg over his horse, dropping down so it could take the brunt of his weight.

If Ena noticed him stumble, she had the kindness not to mention it as she handed him back his reins.

"I didn't think you'd be so comfortable riding." Ena ducked into the trees.

"It's nice to go fast." All fear of sounding childish vanished as he stepped into the woods.

The thick green leaves painted the light from above, giving the air an ethereal glow. A heavy scent of damp earth carried through each breath, but it wasn't stifling.

If life has a scent, this is it.

"Could you ever run, scribe?" Ena asked.

"Run?"

"When you were little? Or were you born with the bad leg?" Ena stopped by the edge of a gully and, gently shushing her horse, tied his lead to a tree.

"I…" Adrial began after a long moment. "I wasn't born with a bad leg. I think I remember running, when I was very little."

Ena didn't say anything as she tied Adrial's horse near hers and pulled the bags from both mounts. Ena hadn't asked him to bring much. Blankets and a bit of food. She handed him one of the bundles before taking his arm.

"I don't know which would be worse," Ena said, "remembering what it feels like to run and be free, or to have never known the feeling at all."

"I wasn't running to play and be merry. The only time I can remember running was when I was running from someone who wanted to hurt me."

Ena tensed on his arm.

"It was a long time ago," Adrial said, "and I've done just fine for myself."

"You have." Ena kept her arm through his as she led him slowly down the gully, letting him take his time to find his footing on the loose rocks. "Head Scribe. Soon to be the youngest Guild Lord in who knows how long."

A rumble of water cut through the rustling of the wind in the trees.

"We're nearly there, scribe."

A mound of boulders blocked the path ahead.

Before Adrial could find the courage to say he wouldn't be able to climb them, Ena let go of his arm and slipped through a crack between the stones.

He twisted sideways, following her path. Though Adrial was

far from being a burly man, he had only a few inches of space to spare.

The rumbling of the water grew louder as they slithered between the stones.

Adrial hoped the sound was loud enough to cover the thundering of his heart.

Ena stopped at the narrowest point in their path.

Stone touched Adrial's ribs as he breathed in. He could see nothing but cramped passage in either direction.

"Does it make you nervous?" Ena grinned. "Like perhaps the rocks will collapse in on you and trap you forever so the Guilds will never find your bones?"

The thought hadn't occurred to Adrial until she said it, but suddenly the horrible idea of the rocks pitching in on them seemed very real.

If one boulder moves a few inches, we'll never get out.

"So, just a touch of panic then?" Ena snaked sideways again.

Patches of moss appeared on the rock face as mist touched the air. And in one glorious movement, Ena stepped free of the rocks, pulling Adrial out behind her.

High walls dripping with moss and vines butted up against the boulders, blocking out the rest of the world. A waterfall fifty feet high fed a pool that gleamed in the afternoon light. Trees peered over the cliffs high above, offering shade to the rocky shore. There was no sign of where the water from the pool might go. No stream to break the perfect seclusion of the falls.

"Do you like it, scribe?"

"Of all the words I have known, I have none to describe this place."

"Good." Ena took the bundle from his hands and tossed it onto the flattest section of the shore. "I can't let you tell your map maker friends about this place. Not that you'd be able to find your way back here. But if those map makers you're so fond of discovered it, they'd destroy it."

"Destroy it? They only chart places. And I doubt many would travel here, even if it appeared on the maps."

"There are some things too precious to be shared with the masses, and plenty of treasures the Guilds would destroy if they couldn't find a way to control." Ena tossed her burgundy shawl onto the ground and unlaced her boots. "Come on then, scribe. Don't want to get your fine borrowed things wet."

"How did you even find this place?"

"I've a talent for finding hidden things." Ena tossed her boots and knife aside. "If you think I'm a fine inker, you should see what other skills I have." She untied the laces at the top of her bodice.

Before Adrial could think to look away, she shimmied free of her bodice, unbuttoned her skirt, and dropped it to the ground.

22

ADRIAL

"Ena, what"—Adrial shielded his eyes, examining the rocks by his feet—"I—I should wait by the horses."

"But you haven't seen what I've brought you here for." Ena's shift landed on his boot. "Now take your clothes off and come on."

"Take off my clothes?" His words came out with a roll of laughter.

"We have to swim a bit, and you'll have an awful night if you try to sleep in wet clothes." Ena pulled his hands away from his eyes.

She was perfect, her technicolor hair draped over her shoulders. Alabaster skin and round hips. The only thing she wore was a black stone pendant that hung between her breasts.

"Don't tell me you've never seen a naked woman before, scribe. If we don't get up the falls, you'll miss it."

Adrial stood frozen as she unbuttoned his shirt, her fingers brushing against the bare skin of his chest.

"Can you do your pants on your own, or have the Guilds left you too helpless?"

"I can undress myself." Adrial took a step back and turned away.

"As you say, scribe, but come on."

Splash.

Adrial glanced toward the water in time to watch as she dove deep beneath the surface.

His fingers froze on the buttons of his shirt. "Saint Alwyn, help me." He dropped his coat and shirt to the ground as Ena broke through the surface of the water.

"Jump in, scribe. It's not that cold." She treaded water, watching him pull off his boots and socks, a mischievous grin glinting in her eyes.

"I could just swim with my pants on."

"And freeze when night comes? Would that be a fair price for modesty?"

Adrial took a breath, willing his hands not to shake as he unbuttoned his pants. "Is this a normal thing among the unguilded?"

"Afraid there's a bunch of naked rotta scum running through the alleys in Ilara?"

"I would never call an unguilded person such a thing."

"If you're going to be such a gentleman, I suppose I should be kind as well. Take off your pants in peace. But hurry it up or I'll climb without you."

She dove beneath the water and swam toward the falls as Adrial whimpered, "Climb?"

You're the head scribe of all Ilbrea. Groomed to lead the Guild and face any foe who threatens the sanctity of the Scribes Guild. You cannot run away from a naked woman.

Adrial dropped his pants and stepped free, slipping into the water before Ena could surface and look back.

The cool water didn't match the spring air. Adrial had expected the cold to knock the breath from his lungs, but the chill of the water was more invigorating than painful.

"Well done, scribe," Ena called from a boulder at the base of the falls. She'd climbed on top of the rock and stood, brazen in her nakedness.

Adrial dove beneath the water, letting his eyes take in the rock bottom of the pool instead of Ena's perfect form.

What would Allora say?

Ena grabbed his hand as he reached the boulder, hauling him up onto the rock.

"Not so bad is…" The words faded from Ena's lips as her gaze fell on his shoulder.

Adrial tipped his chin up, steeling his jaw as she examined the shining red patch of skin that marred his right side.

He shuddered as her fingers trailed along the scar that ran from his shoulder to his ribs.

She lifted her hand away, and Adrial thought it would be done. She would jump off the boulder and swim away from the horror of his flesh.

His breath caught in his throat as she traced the half-moon scars on his ribs.

He closed his eyes as her touch found his hip. No scars marred his flesh there, but the bones beneath were misshapen, and the muscles bulged in strange places as they tried to compensate for the deformed bones.

"I thought if you hadn't been born like this, you must've gotten sick," Ena whispered. "I thought an illness had stunted your bones. Who did this to you?"

Adrial looked to the bright blue sky overhead. The fierceness of noon had passed, and the gentle late afternoon sun caressed the sky.

"Who did this to you?" Ena took Adrial's face in her hands, forcing him to look into her eyes. Her arms grazed his bare chest, pressing skin to skin.

"I don't remember," Adrial said. "I have no idea who did it. I remember pain. Lots of pain. But not a face. It could have been another child on the island or one of the matrons."

She let go of Adrial's face and turned away. A black bird marked the side of her ribs.

He wanted to touch the bird's wings.

"We'll take the easy path and climb slow."

"Ena," Adrial said as she climbed onto the next level of rock. "Ena."

"Yes, scribe?" She leapt sideways, moving closer to the falls.

"Ena, look at me."

Slowly, she turned around.

You're a monster. A deformed beast.

He waited for her face to change. The moment of sympathy would pass, and she would see him for the twisted weakling an evil island had left him.

"You think I haven't seen a naked man before?" Ena's mouth curled into a smirk.

"Ena—"

"You think I haven't seen a scarred, naked man before?" Ena cocked her head to the side. "Sorry, scribe, but I've seen much worse. If you ever remember who did this to you, I'll kill them myself. But don't expect me to cower and cringe. I've seen too much for that."

They stood staring at each other for a long moment. The waterfall rumbled behind Ena, not caring for the troubles of the people who had invaded its home.

"Are you coming or not?" Ena held out a hand.

Adrial climbed onto the next boulder, more conscious than ever of the awkward movements of his bad leg.

"I promise it'll be worth the effort." She pulled Adrial onto the high stone with her and turned to the rock wall beyond. "You'll be on your own for the next bit, but I have faith in you." Reaching high overhead, she grasped a stone. The movement showed the black bird more clearly than he'd seen it before.

The beautifully drawn bird had its wings spread wide. Fine strands of black exquisitely etched out the details of the feathers.

"Where did you get the mark?" Adrial reached up to the high stone. Gripping the rock was simple and painless. Getting both legs to scramble up to the next level was a different matter.

"Mark?" Ena patiently waited to show him the next place to grip. Always one step ahead, never leaving him entirely behind.

"The bird." Adrial leapt across a gap between two rocks, silently thanking Alwyn for not letting him fall. "I've never seen a mark outside of a Guilding brand."

"It's not a normal thing among common folk." Ena perched on a stone jutting out from the rock wall that looked as though it might snap off at any moment. "It's the mark my family gave me." Ena moved on to more stable footing and left the protrusion to Adrial.

"It's beautiful."

Ena laughed over the roar of the waterfall. The low rumbling did nothing to diminish the beauty of her laugh. It made it fiercer, more defiant.

"It was never meant to be a thing of beauty, but I suppose it's better than having a slug marked on my side."

"Why a bird?" Adrial's fingers slipped from his handhold, and his good foot slid out from under him. He snatched at the rock wall with his other hand and, with a shout, pulled himself back toward the cliff, smacking his torso against the stone.

Panting, he leaned against the cold cliff. It was cooler than the water, though the sun must have touched it during the morning.

"Nice save, scribe." Ena stood on a rock ten feet above him. "It would be a pity to have to start all the way from the bottom when you've nearly made it."

"It would be a bigger pity to die," Adrial panted.

"You wouldn't die if you fell. How do you think we're going to get down?"

The world spun for a moment. Adrial closed his eyes and

pressed his forehead to the slick stone. "Tell me about the bird. Please."

"It's a remnant of another life."

Adrial focused on Ena's words, forcing himself to climb up one more step.

"The mark has little meaning now." The melody of Ena's voice held a hint of sorrow.

Adrial needed to get to her, to look into her eyes and find where the sadness came from.

"How old were you when they marked you?" Adrial asked.

"Older than when the Guilds branded you."

"But why would your family give you a mark?" Using his knee as leverage, he climbed up to the ledge right next to the waterfall and landed face first at Ena's feet.

"Families come in all different kinds, scribe. You should know that as well as anyone."

"You're right." Adrial kept his eyes down as he stood. "I did find myself in a very strange little clan."

"And see what they've made of you." Ena tipped his chin up to look into his eyes. "You're an adventurer now. Climbing waterfalls to find hidden things. Who'd have thought it from the head scribe?"

"No one," Adrial laughed, the absurdity of standing naked beside a waterfall giving way to pure joy. "Absolutely no one."

"Can you trust me just a little bit more?" Ena twined her fingers through Adrial's.

"Yes."

She drew him to the very edge of the rock where the roaring falls splashed on their skin.

How badly would it hurt for that water to pound me into the ground?

"Take as big a leap as you can, and aim for just about there." Ena pointed a few feet below them, right in the center of the falls.

"What?"

"Best not to think too much about it. Just jump and hope for the best."

"But, Ena—"

She dropped his hand and leapt into the falls.

Adrial's heart soared into his throat.

She's going to die. The beautiful bird will be smashed by the water.

But her colorful hair disappeared through the falls before Adrial could scream.

His heart raced in his ears, drowning out the roaring of the water.

Jumping was a foolish, deathly thing to do. It would be wiser to climb back down and find his pants.

Taking a step back, Adrial jumped with all the strength he had.

Cool water pounded down upon him, but before the sensation had time to become unpleasant, he landed with a splash.

Water surrounded him. His feet touched bottom a moment later and he kicked up.

"That's the way, scribe." Ena cheered as his head breached the surface.

"We're not dead," Adrial gasped.

"No, scribe."

Ena stood ten feet away from him, the water lapping right below her breasts.

Adrial looked away, examining the cave he'd somehow leapt into. He was in a pool twenty feet long. Water fed in from the falls, kissing the edge of the pool, but there was no current trying to carry Adrial out.

Slices of sparkling blue stone cut through the gray of the cavern. Overhead, a tunnel of light peered through the earth, casting its beams on the small boundary of dry stone between the pool and the walls.

The blue stone had formed sweeping circles on the ceiling

overhead, more like a painter's work than anything to be found in nature.

"Dive down and look." Ena smirked.

Taking a breath, Adrial dove into the water. The entire bottom of the pool was made of blue crystal. It looked sharp, vicious even. But his feet had touched it, and he hadn't been hurt.

Kicking his legs, he swam to the very bottom of the pool and ran his fingers gently along the stone. But it didn't feel like stone. It had the texture of fresh flower petals, and radiated warmth.

Letting the air in his lungs pull him up, Adrial rose to the surface. "What is it?"

"Magic, scribe."

"Magic." The word tasted dangerous and thrilling in Adrial's mouth.

"Yes, magic." Ena pushed herself out of the pool and sat on the stone side so only her legs were covered by the water. "And if you tell the sorcerers what I've shown you, you might as well tie the noose around my neck yourself. So don't even dream of making pretty pictures in your book about this place."

"I won't." Adrial swam over and leveraged himself up onto the ledge next to her. "How did you find this?"

"I told you before, I'm good at finding things." Ena scooted closer to him and nudged him with her shoulder.

"But something like this…" Adrial took a long look around the room. "How many places this beautiful can there be in all Ilbrea?"

"You'd be surprised." Ena lifted Adrial's arm and draped it over her shoulders.

Adrial tensed as his skin pressed against hers.

"Don't be frightened. I'm cold is all," Ena said.

"I'm not frightened." Heat flared in Adrial's face.

"Yes, you are." Ena nestled her head onto his shoulder. "And you should be careful about showing it. Making you uncomfortable is too much fun. I'm afraid it'll become a habit."

"I'm not—"

Ena cut him off, pressing a finger to his lips. "Shh, you'll ruin it."

The circle of light that beamed into the cave shifted, a tiny movement as the sun tracked its path through the sky.

The ray of light reached the blue at the bottom of the pool, and as though a thousand candles had been lit, the cave burst into light. Each of the streaks of blue on the walls and swirls on the ceiling shone with a dazzling glow. The entire bottom of the pool radiated a light so bright, Adrial had to blink before he could see it properly.

The light wasn't stagnant. It swirled and shimmered like a million tiny dancers come to life.

"There." Ena pointed to the center of the pool.

The water stirred, bubbling as though something beneath had awakened.

Adrial blinked again, trying to make sense of what he was seeing, as a tower of light reached the surface and continued to grow. Leaves of thin, blue crystal blossomed out of the tower, unfurling as they draped toward the water.

The tower stopped growing, and its petals fluttered open. A burst of powder like diamond dust puffed up into the air.

"Now it's my turn." Ena slipped into the water. Her skin didn't block the light from below. Rather, the glow enveloped her until her legs were a faint shadow.

As she swam forward, the pool echoed her movement, creating waves shimmering with what appeared to be the light of an unseen moon.

"Thank you, sweet flower." Ena stood on her toes to keep her head above the water as she reached up and plucked a petal. The flower shivered at the loss, but before a breath had passed, a new petal grew in its place.

"Come see." Ena beckoned Adrial into the water.

He slipped into the blue. A warm feeling, like life multiplied, buzzed against his skin.

In one stroke, he reached Ena's side and stood in the water.

"Not fair, you standing so easily," Ena said.

"Had to happen sometime." Adrial smiled as the water swirled around his shoulders, bristling with light.

"Hold it." Ena offered him the petal.

His fingers shook as he reached for it.

The thing will shrivel and die if I touch it.

But Ena placed the glowing petal into his hand. The heat of the flower kissed his palm, and vibrations tingled his flesh.

"Ever held magic before?" Ena whispered.

"No." Adrial lowered his hands until the petal touched the water. With a crack, the pool flashed bright white as a joyful ringing filled the cave. The sound vibrated Adrial's lungs but wasn't loud enough to throb in his ears.

"Told you there was life outside your books, scribe."

"Thank you, Ena."

She looked up to the pinpoint of light above them. "It's almost done." Looping her arm through Adrial's, she guided him to the shallowest part of the pool.

She tipped her head back onto his shoulder so her hair spilled over his chest.

"Now," Ena whispered.

With a flash brighter than any Adrial had ever seen, all the lights in the cave flared white before diming to shadows.

They stood in silence for a moment.

"We should build a fire before it gets too dark." Ena didn't leave Adrial's shoulder.

"We should." Adrial looked at the petal in his hand. The brilliant light of it had faded, but the sheen of magic still clung to the blue.

"I'll hold it while we jump." Ena gently lifted the petal from his palm. "If we lose this, we'll have to try again next month."

She dove down and swam to the far edge by the thundering falls.

Even without magic dancing in the water, she was perfect.

"Jump straight down, not out," Ena warned before stepping off the ledge and plummeting out of sight.

23

ALLORA

A wide, sweeping valley filled with spring flowers, growing all the way to the edge of a gentle river. Birds soared overhead, chirping their joy to the clouds. Sunlight kissed her face, but she didn't mind. Just as she didn't mind waiting for the man with dark brown hair as he slowly paced the narrow bank of the river, examining each tiny detail.

There was no jealousy in her heart for the care he gave the map, for as he turned to glance at her, a smile lit his eyes, as though her sitting on a rock waiting for him was the most marvelous thing in all Ilbrea.

A gentle tapping sounded in the distance.

Perhaps rain would chase them away from the valley. They'd find someplace warm to wait out the storm. A little haven, only large enough for two.

The tapping grew harder, more urgent and violent.

But the sky was still bright blue and calm.

"Lady Karron," a voice echoed into the valley. "Lady Karron."

Allora's eyes flew open as the voice ripped her from her happy dream.

Her room was dark, the curtains still drawn tight against the night.

"Yes," Allora called as the knocking began again.

"Lady Karron, you're needed at once."

Fear shot through Allora's heart as she leapt out of bed.

"What's wrong? What happened?" She shouted as she ran for the door, not caring that the freezing floor stung her feet or that propriety demanded she take the time to find her dressing gown.

Father. No, father is still here. Niko.

She wrenched open the door. A lone guard stood outside, lamp in hand.

"You've been summoned to the Royal Palace, Lady Karron." The guard bowed, kindly averting his eyes from Allora's lack of dress.

"The palace?" Allora repeated the words, trying to fit the phrase into the terrible imaginings of horrible things happening to her family.

An attack on the library. No, this house would be safer than traveling to the palace.

"You've been summoned at the Princess's request," the guard said. "You've been asked to go as quickly as you can."

"But why?" Allora's hand shook on the doorknob.

"The Queen is ill, Lady Karron. The Princess has requested you come for her comfort." The guard glanced up and down the hall before continuing. "I do not wish to speak out of turn, Lady Karron, but the soldier who delivered the message said the Princess was near hysterical."

"I'll be down in a moment." Allora dashed back into her room, pulling the simplest dress she owned from her wardrobe. The plain fabric wasn't fit to be worn to the palace, but it would be the quickest to slip into.

Guilt bubbled in her stomach as her fingers fumbled on the buttons. It wasn't her father, or Niko, or Adrial. The journey to the north hadn't been destroyed by a terrible storm, and Kai hadn't been lost at sea.

The Queen is the mother of all Ilbrea.

It's still better than losing one of my own.

Allora pressed her head to the door, willing herself to be strong enough and gracious enough to deserve the Karron name.

The guard waited for her in the hall, as though he'd been ordered to make sure Allora obeyed the Princess's summons.

Allora didn't speak to the guard as she walked down the corridor of the family wing as quickly as propriety would allow.

The soldiers waited for her at the bottom of the grand staircase.

"Lady Karron." A soldier bowed. "Thank you for attending the Princess."

Allora nodded to the soldier, her loose hair falling around her shoulders.

I should have pinned it back. I'll look like a merchant in the palace.

The carriage waited at the bottom of the front steps, door open and ready to swallow her.

Allora turned to the guard who had woken her. "Tell my father where I've gone."

"Yes, Lady Karron."

The night air cut through her dress, setting goose bumps all over her skin.

The driver didn't speak as she climbed into the carriage, nor did the soldier as he closed the door.

Allora had half-expected the matron Sara to be waiting for her in the darkness, stern face pursed with displeasure at Allora's appearance. But she would be with the Princess. Of course she would be with the Princess.

The carriage tore from the grounds, rattling and bouncing through the night. Allora closed her eyes, trying to ignore the swaying as they rounded each of the curves on the switchbacks down the cliffs to the city proper.

In a third of the time it normally took, the carriage rumbled across the bridge and onto the palace grounds.

It was the middle of the night. The grounds should have been still, save the soldiers who protected the royal family. But lights blazed in the front windows, and two other carriages sat at the bottom of the steps—one trimmed in healer red, the other in sorcerer purple.

The carriage door opened the moment the horses stopped.

A soldier reached up, offering his hand. "You'll be led to the Princess's suite."

"Of course," Allora said.

Four soldiers surrounded her, escorting her into the glittering entryway. Silence filled the house, though movement could be seen everywhere Allora looked. Servants flitting through the shadows. A young man in healer red darting down a long corridor.

Two soldiers flanked Princess Illia's bedroom door. One knocked before Allora had even reached the white wood of the entry.

"Is she here?" Illia threw open the door.

The moment she saw Allora, Illia ran to her, burying her tear-streaked face on Allora's shoulder.

"Your Highness." Allora held the girl as she trembled with tears.

"She's going to die, Allora," the Princess wept. "She'll be dead by dawn, I know it."

"Shh." Allora guided the Princess to her room. The death of a queen was not a thing to be discussed in a hallway. "Everything will be all right, Your Highness."

Princess Illia's bedroom was as grand as one would imagine a princess required. Larger than anyone could ever need, with a gilded bed as the centerpiece. Paintings of pastures and towering mountains interrupted the rich tapestry of the walls. A sparkling chandelier had been lit, sending its light blazing off every surface, despite the darkness of the night. Soft couches and chairs, offering seating for six, surrounded a large fireplace. Only one seat was taken, and the matron Sara looked to have chosen the least comfortable place.

At the sight of Allora, the matron's face pinched as though she had tasted something rancid.

"What's happening?" Allora asked as she escorted the Princess to a couch large enough to fit the two of them.

"The Queen is ill," Sara said, her tone devoid of emotion.

"She's been ill for days," Illia spoke through her tears. "At dinner tonight, she collapsed. It's happened before. She's never been well, not since she lost the first child."

"Princess Illia," Sara said, but Illia ignored her.

"I thought she had just fallen ill again," Illia pressed on, gripping the front of Allora's dress. "Then night came, and I heard my brother shouting. Then the sorcerers and healers came. They've lit all the lights in the palace. There are people everywhere. She's going to die, Allora."

Illia collapsed in a fit of tears, hiding her face in Allora's lap.

"Hush." Allora stroked the girl's hair. "Have they said anything about the state of the Queen?"

"No," Sara said. "The best healers and the Lady Sorcerer herself are here."

"They've turned on the lights." Illia sat up, glaring daggers at Sara. "They don't expect her to live."

"I'm so sorry"—Allora took Illia's hands—"but I don't understand what the lights have to—"

"It was the same when both my parents died. First Mother, then Father. All the lights on in the middle of the night. No one telling me what was happening. I found out my parents were dead when they blew the cathedral horns. No one came to tell me. The soldiers kept me trapped in my room. And now it's all happening again. Carys is going to die, and no one will tell me. I can't survive it again, Allora, I can't."

"Your Highness," Sara said, "I understand this has been a very distressing night, but you are speaking of family matters—"

"Don't tell me what I may and may not speak of to my friends. I am the Princess of Ilbrea, not you."

Sara's eyes narrowed as she leaned back in her chair.

"Your Highness," Allora said after a long moment, "if the Queen is badly ill, I'm not sure what I can do to help. I will sit with you for comfort, but I can't keep the horns from blowing."

"None but Saint Morelan and Dudia Himself can save Carys." Illia gripped Allora's hands. "But you can find out what's happening. The soldiers won't let me leave my rooms, and they won't tell me anything. Sara won't even go and try to ask for information since my brother ordered her to sit with me."

"You want me to find the sorcerers and ask after the health of the Queen?" A tremble of fear stirred in Allora's stomach.

"You are my only true friend, Allora," Illia begged, "and everyone in the Guilds knows your face. They'll know who you are. They respect you more than they do me."

"That's not true," Allora said.

"It is." Illia pressed Allora's hands to her tear-streaked cheeks. "I am nothing but a child to them. A child whose only worth is in being sold to another king. But you are Lady Allora Karron, who has stood at the head of her father's house as he brought the Map Makers Guild glory as it hadn't seen in centuries. You stand at the head of Ilaran society without fear. If anyone can help me, it's you. Please, Allora. I'm begging you."

Allora brushed the tears from Illia's face. "I've spent many nights terrified the people I love wouldn't be in this world come morning. If someone could have brought me peace, I would have begged them as well. I don't know if what I find will be anything good."

"Better to know than to wait for the horns," Illia said.

Allora nodded and stood. "I'll come back as soon as I know anything."

Allora started for the door, freezing in place at a *tsch* from Sara's corner.

The urge to swear at the old hag as Kai would, or to berate

her for being awful as Mara would, battled in Allora's mouth. But her father's words won out.

"It is so easy to forget that while some are born to great destinies and high positions, they are still only human, and a little human kindness can be needed to see them through the darkness."

Not looking back, Allora opened the ornately carved bedroom door and stepped out into the hall.

She longed to press herself into the shadows and riddle through how she had ended up in the Royal Palace in the dead of night. But soldiers surrounded the door, two seemingly waiting as her escort.

Pressing her shoulders back, Allora spoke to the group. "I need to see the sorcerers who have come to aid the Queen."

None of the men spoke.

"At the request of Princess Illia Willoc, I demand to be taken to the sorcerers who arrived to care for the Queen." Allora's voice rang through the hall. "I have no wish to see the Queen nor to interfere with her care. If you insist on keeping the Princess locked in her room, do not keep her proxy from doing her will."

One of the soldiers nodded. "Follow them."

The two soldiers standing away from the group turned to walk down the hall.

"Thank you." Allora followed the men, her heart racing as though she'd just been in a fight.

Scolding soldiers assigned to guard the palace was ill-advised. They had no right to keep the Princess trapped in her room, but Allora had no right to demand to see the sorcerers either.

The soldiers led her down a long, ornately decorated corridor—marble floors inlayed with intricate, swirling designs, and walls covered with mirrors and portraits. In daylight, the whole hall would have sparkled. Even with only the lamps for light, the effect was astounding.

The first floor of the Royal Palace might not have been

anything spectacular compared to the public rooms of the Map Master's Palace, but where Lord Karron had built the private rooms to be familial and comfortable, the Willocs seemed to have saved the best for the King and Queen.

Allora caught a glimpse of herself in a mirror. She looked more like a lost child than a woman capable of any task. Her loose hair and plain dress, her cheeks pink from fatigue and cold—it was hard to believe the girl in the mirror had actually come of age.

You are not a child, no matter how you look, Allora Karron.

A murmur of voices carried from the end of the long hall. Soldiers surrounded a set of closed doors large enough for a royal carriage to pass through. But the voices came from farther down the hall where a more modestly sized door stood open.

"Anyone who might be available to talk is in there," one of Allora's escorts said. "I hope you'll find good news for the Princess."

"As do I." Allora nodded and moved toward the door.

"Lady Karron," the soldier spoke again.

"Yes?" Allora turned back to the soldier.

She hadn't noticed before, but he was as old as her father. Gray streaked his hair, and as he looked at Allora, the lines in his forehead deepened.

"If it is the worst, I'm grateful you'll be here for the Princess."

Allora nodded and walked into the room.

The burst of color startled her eyes. Red and purple robes clustered together in the small space. Sorcerers and healers filled all the seats, their presence garish against the light hues of the room.

Everyone stared at Allora as she entered. Her green dress shone like a beacon, screaming to all of them that she was thoroughly out of place.

"I've come for news of the Queen." Allora's voice didn't waver as she spoke.

"Lady Karron." Petra Roo, the head sorcerer, stepped forward. "I'm surprised to see you here."

"I was sent for by Princess Illia," Allora said. "She wishes for news of the Queen."

Murmurs floated around the room. A whisper that could have only one meaning.

"I'm sorry to deliver such news, Lady Karron," Petra said, "but—"

Horns drowned out the rest of Petra's words, echoing through the city, shattering the last peace of the night.

24

KAI

Horns blared, jerking Kai from sleep. The thick wood of the ship dulled the noise enough the sound didn't seem urgent. But there was something in the tone that kept Kai from covering his head and rolling over in his bunk.

"What could the slitches at the cathedral be wanting at this hour?" The low groan carried through the dark.

"Keep quiet for a moment," Drew said as he lit the lamp in the middle of the bunkroom.

All the men froze in their beds.

Four long, mournful horns echoed slowly through the night.

"The Queen," Kai said. The horrible feeling that he should be doing something, but didn't know what that something might be, sank in his stomach. He pulled on his boots to give himself an excuse to move.

"Is she dead?" Shafer asked from his bed high up in the corner.

"They wouldn't have sounded the horns if she wasn't." Drew had already stood and yanked on his clothes.

"What should we do?" Shafer leapt down from his bunk.

All the men looked to Kai.

I'm not fit to give commands on how to handle the death of a Queen.

I shouldn't be the only Guilded sailor on the ship. The captain should be on the ship, not sleeping at his home halfway across the city.

"We need to get outside and protect the docks." Kai yanked on his deep-blue shirt and buckled on the belt that held his long knife. "If the chivving bastards who tried to attack the eastern mountains journey want another moment to damage the city, they'll not find a better one. These ships are too close to being sea ready. We're set to sail to try the builders' improvements in two weeks' time. The new ships were commissioned by order of the King. We've just lost the Queen. We can't risk any more damage to the spirit of Ilbrea."

A cheer rose up from the men, pounding off the walls of the ship.

"Right." Kai nodded and ran up the stairs to the main deck before the men could look to him for more words of comfort or inspiration.

Allora would be so proud.

A chill wind swept over Kai as he reached the deck.

Sailors, both Guilded and common, swarmed out of the other ships and onto the docks, lighting every lamp in sight, giving the night an eerie glow.

Kai headed straight for the newly raised mast, climbing the ropes of the rigging before most of the other men had even emerged from below. The height of the crow's nest gave him a view of the city stretching out to the base of the cliffs.

The white of the cathedral's tower shone like a beacon as the torches around its base flickered to life. A wave of light spread through the city as Ilarans woke to the news of their fallen Queen.

"The people will want to go to the palace," Drew called up to Kai. "They'll all want to be there."

"Good," Schafer shouted back. The young man had taken a place by the gangplank. "Let the soldiers deal with the masses. They're the ones who've caused problems, not us."

"Hush, all of you!" Kai shouted, holding a hand up to silence the crew.

The sounds of the city had changed.

Keening cut through the night. Wails of despair and pain.

Let them stay in their homes. For the love of the Queen, let them all stay safely in their homes.

Shouting echoed in the distance.

Not the shout of one solitary person. The clamor of a crowd, a horde united behind a common voice.

"Kai," Drew said. "Kai, we can't just stay here."

"Our place is to protect the ships." Kai squinted into the distance, trying to see where the shouting carried from.

"And if a gang who wants to blow things up comes here?" Schafer said. "Should I just poke at them with my knife?"

"If you're brave enough to risk a voyage to the southern islands, you should be brave enough to defend your ship," Kai said. "Or did Lord Nevon make a mistake assigning you to this voyage?"

"He made no mistake." Shafer pulled his knife from its sheath. "But I would rather die in a storm than burn to death a hundred yards from dry land."

"I agree," Kai muttered.

The shouting solidified as it moved closer to the docks, changing from a rabble of sound to words nearly clear enough to be heard.

A stream of light danced around the forms between buildings.

Kai's heart leapt to his throat as a flicker of fire appeared four blocks away. But the flames weren't licking the roofs.

Torches.

Dozens upon dozens of torches followed the chanting.

"The end of the gold! The end of the gold!"

Kai tightened his grip on the hilt of his knife.

If the ships were sent up in flames, he'd be able to swim far enough to find a safe place to come back to the shore. All the men on the ship would. But if they lit a blast like the one that had nearly gotten Allora and Adrial…

How many won't be fit to swim?

"We need soldiers," Kai called down. "There's a mob coming toward us."

"But the soldiers must know," a cabin boy called from the prow of the ship. "They'll be on their way."

Kai hadn't even noticed him there. The child couldn't have been more than eight, not much older than Kai had been when he'd started on the ships. The child gripped a knife in his hand, the short blade of it glinting in the night.

"They'll be too busy with the palace," Schafer said. "Why did we decide we didn't need the soldiers patrolling our docks?"

"Because the slitches kept getting in our way," Kai said.

"I'll go to the barracks," Drew said. "Make sure they know we've got trouble coming."

"How good of you to volunteer to be scalped by the mob," Schafer said.

"I'm common," Drew said.

"And if working on a ship makes you a traitor in their eyes?" Kai leapt out of the crow's nest, grabbing a rope that hung ten feet below.

The coarse fibers cut into his palms. He'd end up bleeding from it, but the pain was bracing. A jolt to remind him that danger lurked in the dark.

"I'll go. I'm the one with the Guild mark." Kai lowered himself hand over hand onto the deck. "I'll make quicker time, and the soldiers are more likely to listen to someone in blue."

"And if it's common folk coming at us with torches, they'll hang you." Drew caught Kai's arm.

"They'd have to catch me first." Kai smiled, the expression not touching his eyes. "Keep the men rallied to the ships. If a mob comes, don't let their flames get near you. Cast off and row out if you have to, but don't let them touch the ship."

"Saint Farrin carry you safely home." Drew clasped Kai's hand before turning to the crew. "Get the oars ready. The tide's with us. If it comes to it, we'll pull the ship from shore."

What a captain he could be if only he were Guilded.

No one questioned Drew as they rushed to their tasks.

Kai sprinted down the gangplank, wishing the Guilds would issue sailors better weapons in port than a knife.

At least the knife was mobile, a thing he could easily hold in his hand as he ran up the stairs at the back of the sailors' kitchen and leapt out the open window. The blade didn't bother his balance as he ran across the rooftops toward the ever-growing shouts of the mob.

"The end of the gold. The end of the gold."

The chant pounded through the streets.

The soldiers must have heard by now. How could anyone with ears miss this racket?

Kai paused at the edge of the tannery roof.

He could go back to the docks. The horde didn't seem to be moving closer anymore. They had all clumped together, rallying toward some point farther north.

Curiosity took hold of Kai's feet as he leapt north instead of south, running the length of the building before good sense could win out.

If they were angry with the Guilds, what could they be moving toward? Not the library or the Sorcerers Tower. Not the Royal Palace. They should have stayed toward Farers Way to get there.

Kai took the next leap at a run. Air swirled around him as he soared through the darkness.

But the night changed. The roar of the chant disappeared.

Kai stumbled, his feet sliding out from under him on the slanted roof. He caught the peak with his fingers, his own weight jarring his arms as he stopped his fall and a voice began to speak.

"People of Ilara!" the voice boomed through the darkness. "The gods have smiled upon us."

Kai dragged himself up onto the roof, his arms shaking from the effort.

"We are alive, and the Queen is dead!"

A roar sounded from the crowd.

"The Queen who mourned the loss of each unborn babe she could not carry but felt nothing as the children in the south starved. The Queen who lived in her gilded palace while the people of her city begged for coin to survive."

Kai crouched, inching forward on the roof. The street below him flickered with the light of a hundred torches.

"Too long have the Guilds prayed to their saints in their temple, thinking their god Dudia will listen only to those who wear fancy robes and have named saints to pray to, not understanding the common starving man doesn't care which god will aid him. Because all of us, we know the Guilds will leave us in the dirt to die. Too long have they lived in luxury, forgetting that no one in Ilbrea eats without the sweat and blood of the common folk!"

A cheer split the night, shaking the roof beneath Kai's feet.

"How much gold will the King spend to bury his barren bride?"

Kai lay on his stomach, peering out onto the street. Three hundred people filled the yard outside the stables.

"How many families would that gold feed?" A man stood on top of a pile of crates in front of the stable doors, speaking to the enraptured crowd. "No one will think of the children that could be fed when they buy diamonds from the east to bury with the Queen, that I can promise you."

People in the throng nodded their agreement.

It was easy to see why. The man was tall, with broad, imposing shoulders and unruly blond hair. He looked more like a painting of a saint than an actual living person. He turned his head, and the torches cast light upon his face.

The chivving slitch from the White Froth.

Kai curled his hands into fists, every ounce of him longing to charge the man. But the crowd would stop him before he could get close.

"The King won't listen when we beg for mercy as he taxes our brothers in the south until their children starve. The Guilds won't listen when we beg them to accept our children into their fold. They don't care that mothers weep, praying to any saint or god who will listen, that the Guilds will steal their children from them so their babes won't die of hunger." The man paused, his gaze scanning the crowd.

No one spoke. No one questioned the man or defended the King and the Guilds.

"Rise up with me, brothers. Rise up and prove the rotta the Guilds have trod on for so long are more than just vermin they can control. Rise up and prove Ilbrea does not need her Guilds as much as she needs her people. Rise up and make sure even the King hears our voices as he hides behind his stone walls. Rise up, stand beside me, and make sure every Guilded paun understands that if we die, they will all burn with us!"

The man pounded a fist into the air, and the crowd roared their approval. He grabbed a torch, and for a horrible moment, it looked as though he might touch it to the side of the stables and burn up all the animals within.

"Tell your neighbor. Tell your father. Tell your sons." The man stared deep into the flames. "Tell anyone who has been damaged by the Guilds the time is coming fast. Soon, the city will burn. And those who don't stand with us, those who betray their people to aid the Guilds, can burn alongside their precious King."

He touched the tip of his torch to the stone of the street. Flames sparked to life, scattering the people gathered closest to the barn.

He's a madman. He's going to burn his own people.

A woman shrieked as the flames streaked toward her, but they twisted before they reached her skirt, arcing back on themselves, bending toward another branch. The swirls of fire formed a pattern, searing itself into Kai's eyes.

A sun burned brightly on the street. The perfect circle of its sphere surrounded by arcing tendrils of fire.

"Let the Guilds imagine themselves far above us," the man said. "Let them imagine themselves heavenly perfection. Ilbrea will survive without a star reigning over it. But the common folk, we are the sun that protects this land. We bring food and life to all its people. It is time to rise up. When the flames of the sun call to you, rise."

The man handed his torch to a woman in the front row and strode off into the darkness.

"We will rise!" an old man in the back shouted.

"Rise!"

"Ilbrea must rise!"

Glass shattered somewhere below as Kai shimmied backward on the roof.

He clenched his eyes shut against the sounds of splintering wood.

A man wanted to bring rebellion to Ilbrea. He wasn't the first, and he wouldn't be the last. The man was capitalizing on the death of the Queen, catapulting his movement.

Tham would know what to do. He would run down into the fight and make sure a riot didn't start and hurt any of the animals. Niko would sidle his way into their midst and convince them they were wrong by oozing charm.

Kai was neither Tham nor Niko. He couldn't even recall some centuries old rebellion that had been thwarted and learn lessons from the forgotten mess as Adrial would.

"You're not a little boy," Kai whispered. "You're a Guilded sailor, not a cowering, chivving child."

A scream carried from a nearby house.

In one, swift movement, Kai pushed himself to his feet and ran the length of the building.

Someone shouted in fear in the house below him.

Kai said a silent prayer that whoever he'd scared would forgive him.

"There's someone up there!" a voice shouted from the street, but Kai didn't slow as he leapt to the nearest house, ducking under an oversized weathervane as he built up speed for the next jump.

This was where he belonged. Running. Doing something far from the normal world.

For a few blocks, pounding footsteps carried from the streets below as people attempted to follow him, but they couldn't match Kai's speed. Inhibited by houses and roads, how could they hope to catch him?

The streets widened, and the time of leaping unchecked through the darkness ended. Kai slid down from the low roof of a house and onto the street.

"Blow out your lights," Kai growled as he pressed himself into the thin shadows left on the streets.

Everyone in the city had been woken by the horn, and light cascaded out of every house.

Men, women, and children somberly walked the streets, all heading toward the palace, unaware of the man who had lit the night on fire not far away. As the crowds grew thicker, Kai joined their ranks, counting on numbers to lend him anonymity as they wound their way to the Guilded part of town.

How long had he been gone from the docks?

Long enough for every ship to burn.

Drew will protect the ships. He won't let the voyage fall to nothing.

You'd see the light in the sky if the ships caught fire.

Kai veered west, away from the crowd. He dodged back into

the shadows as they reached the Guilded section of Ilara, heading toward the soldiers' barracks.

Here, light shone from every window in every home, shedding the pretense that anyone would be able to sleep.

A line of blazing, sorcerer-made lights shone from the sides of the soldiers' barracks. Men in black uniforms were posted around the low stone building while other units moved out in packs toward the palace.

"Soldiers!" Kai waved both hands in the air as he ran toward the wide metal lattice blocking the barracks door. "Soldiers, I've come from the docks."

"Has there been an attack?" A man who looked older than Lord Karron stepped out of the shadows.

"Not that I know of," Kai said, forcing himself to speak calmly. "There was a riot by the merchants' stables. They were breaking windows when I came to find you. Sir, I think I may have just heard the beginning of a rebellion."

25

ADRIAL

The sun warmed the graying dawn. Their fire had settled to embers hours before, but Adrial didn't dare move to rekindle the flames.

Somehow in the night, Ena had drawn Adrial's arm over her shoulder like a blanket, nestling into his warmth. His arm gently rose and fell with each breath Ena took. Her hair splayed out behind her, touching Adrial's cheek.

There was comfort in the closeness, in feeling another person sleep. Adrial couldn't bear the thought of missing a breath.

He stayed frozen as the sky pinked, wishing there were some kind of magic in Ilbrea that would make the night last just a little longer.

A raven flew overhead, his cawing carrying over the rumble of the waterfall.

"Are you awake, scribe?" Ena asked.

"Yes." Adrial waited for her to toss his arm aside or shove away from him.

She did neither. She leaned her weight back into him, drawing him closer. "Sleeping outside isn't so bad when you choose it."

"No, I don't suppose it is."

"What would they do if you never went back to the library?"

"How do you mean?"

Ena rolled over. Her chest pressed against his.

Knowing what lay beneath her clothes sent an even brighter blush to his cheeks.

"Would they come after the inker for dragging you out of your shop?" Ena said. "Would they smash everything I own until they could prove I was gone forever? Would they send out search parties to find you?"

"I don't know. The only one who knows I'm with you is Taddy."

"Poor, sweet Taddy." A strand of hair tumbled across her cheek.

"Taddy's a good lad, and he doesn't know where we are. I didn't know where we were going." Adrial's heart forgot to beat as he brushed the hair from Ena's cheek.

"And if I decided not to take you back to the city? If I kept you out here in the wild forever?"

"I've no idea how to get home, so I don't suppose there's much I could do."

"But you'd miss it?" Ena sat up.

"I—" Adrial began to argue. His chest felt hollow in the absence of her warmth. "I truly don't know. I've spent most of my life in Ilara with the scribes. I don't know what else there is."

"There's this." Ena swept a hand toward their hidden paradise.

The morning sun glinted off the falls. Birds rustled high up in the trees. They could dive back into the water and pretend Ilara didn't exist.

"But then what would the scribes do without you?" Ena asked. "A foul paun like Travers would take your place. He'd sit on the Guilds Council, and the world would be a worse place for it."

"You really think I could make that large a difference?"

"I'm sure of it." Ena leaned over him, pressing her cheek to his as she whispered in his ear. "It's not fair that being good has sealed your sorry fate. But that's your place. There's nothing to be done for it."

"Ena—"

"Come on, scribe." Ena grabbed Adrial's hand, dragging him to his feet and shoving their blankets back into their bags. "All Ilbrea waits for you."

"They would survive without me. We could stay out here another day, or a week."

"The strong ones would survive, but not the ones who need you." Ena didn't look back at the waterfall as she slipped through the crack between the boulders and out of sight.

Pain squeezed Adrial's throat as he looked up at the waterfall.

May Dudia let me see such beauty again.

He didn't call for Ena as he slid through the passage and back out into the world. He made it through the rocks just in time to see the hem of Ena's skirt disappear from view.

The climb up the gully was nothing compared to climbing the falls. The pebbles shifted and tumbled under his feet, but he kept moving forward, a sense of dread growing with every step.

The stomping of hooves carried through the trees at the edge of the woods.

Ena already sat in her saddle. "I thought maybe you'd decided to stay."

"I considered it." Adrial didn't look to see if Ena returned his faint smile as he pulled himself onto his saddle. His back ached from riding and sleeping on the ground, and sharp pain tickled his bad leg from all the effort.

Ena kicked her horse forward. Bits of earth clung to the rich colors of her hair.

Adrial's fingers longed to free the tiny bits of twig that clung to her, but her horse had already begun to run.

Morning had burst over the wide valley, filling it with brilliant sunshine.

Adrial tipped his head up to the sky as his horse charged forward. He pictured every detail of the falls in his mind, every moment of the magical flowers' birth.

For the hundredth time in his life, he wished he were a map maker. This time, he didn't envy their adventures or acclaim. He only wished he could paint an image of what he had seen while his horse carried him.

Ena didn't speak as she let her horse drink from the same cool creek. A somberness had crept over her. The carefree twinkle of her eyes dimmed with every passing mile.

"Ena, please wait," Adrial finally said as their horses turned onto the proper road.

"We haven't time to wait, scribe." Ena slowed her horse enough for Adrial to ride alongside her. "You've a library to get back to and a vellum to create. I finally have the petal to finish the ink you needed for your perfect Ilbrean sky. Just imagine all the work we're already going to have to catch up on."

"It can wait a while longer."

"Easy for you to say. The Guild buys you your food. I have to earn coin, or I won't eat at all."

"Then I'll pay you extra." Adrial knew his mistake the moment the words left his lips.

"Thank you, Head Scribe." Ena gave a dramatic bow of her head. "How kind, Head Scribe. It's nice to see my wonderful plan worked. Show you a beautiful secret, let you see me naked, and now more coin."

"That's not—"

"If I wanted to earn gold by luring men with my tits, I promise you I could make plenty and never leave the city."

"I didn't mean anything like that, and you know it." Adrial turned his horse, blocking Ena's path. "I only meant if you ever need anything, you only need tell me. I won't ask for anything in return. Yesterday, the waterfall, you showed me magic, Ena. Real, true magic. Not the caged creations the sorcerers hoard."

Ena looked up through the trees that towered over the road.

"I can never repay you for that," Adrial said. "I don't have magic to offer, but I can promise you I won't let you starve or want for anything. All you need to do is ask. I will keep you safe, Ena."

Ena stared at him for a long moment before speaking. "I've been told that before. And it was a lie."

"I'm not lying."

"I know. You believe every word you're saying. That's what makes the hurt of it so dangerous. The hurt of it all so dangerous."

"I don't understand."

"The trouble with being happy is how horrible the pain is when it ends." Ena petted her horse's mane. "We'd better go. Waiting will only make it worse."

"Ena, I will protect you."

A bird swooped across the road, flitting through their path without even the ground giving it pause.

Ena kicked her horse forward, skirting the edge of the road to move past Adrial. "Come, scribe. You'll miss your supper."

You pushed too far.

Horrible doubt rang through Adrial's head as Ena urged her horse to move faster.

She isn't yours to protect. And what can you offer her anyway. Gold? Food?

A much more confident voice, one that had a tone more like Niko's, answered.

You have a position. You have a fine set of rooms to call home. She doesn't think you're a monster.

The walls of the city came into view in the distance. Pale smoke billowed high above.

"Ena, stop!" Adrial shouted.

"What for?" Ena halted her horse and twisted to look at him.

"White smoke." Adrial pointed to the sky.

"Unless explosions burn white now, I don't see why it's something to worry about."

"The death of a royal," Adrial said, moving to lead. "When a royal dies, the sorcerers light the steps of the cathedral on fire."

"What?" Ena laughed.

"It's not real fire. It's a ceremony. If there's smoke like that in the sky, one of the Willocs is dead."

"I wonder which one."

Adrial kept his horse to a somber walk as they approached the northern gate. Black flags lay draped over each seven-pointed star carved into the stone of the wall.

"Who is it?" Adrial asked the first soldier they reached without preamble.

"The Queen." The soldier's eyes were shot through with red, and his voice held the thickness of someone who'd just been crying. "Happened in the middle of the night."

"May Dudia watch over her." Adrial bowed his head.

"What's your business in the city?" the soldier asked.

"I work for the library," Adrial said, choosing to stick to a half-truth rather than tell a lie about farming and risk questions he couldn't answer. "I was out doing some research and am just coming back."

"You've picked a day for it." The soldier pointed behind Adrial. "Is that horse yours as well?"

Adrial glanced back. Ena's seat was empty. Her horse turned its head, blinking at Adrial.

"Yes." Adrial forced himself not to scan the trees around the road. "My research partner had some traveling on foot to do today, asked me to bring back her horse."

"Of course." The soldier winked. "Nice to have a horse obedient enough to follow you on the road."

"They train the library horses very well," Adrial said. "Scribes aren't known to be the best riders."

The soldier gave a chuckle and bowed Adrial past. "Travel safely."

Adrial didn't bother thanking the soldier.

Ena will be able to get into the city. She wouldn't have slipped away if she didn't have a place to be.

The sounds of the city were different than when Adrial had left only a day before. Low and mournful voices took the place of cheerful conversation. The music that normally drifted down from open windows in the Guilded section of Ilara had fallen silent. The clatter of wheels on the stone streets seemed too raucous to be allowed in a city overcome with mourning.

"Come on then," Adrial murmured to his mount. The second horse followed him without argument.

Black drapes covered the signs of businesses and hung over the front doors of opulent homes.

Duty urged Adrial to aim straight for the scribes' shop, but necessity steered him toward the library. He needed to return the horses and put on his robes before anything else could be done.

He'd planned to take his time and wait for the stables to be empty before depositing his charges, but with the city in mourning, it would be impossible to find a time when scribes wouldn't be asking for horses.

Adrial held his head high as he rode into the stable yard.

"Is there something I—" the scribes' guard at the gates began.

Adrial turned to face him.

"I'm sorry, Head Scribe." The guard bowed. "I didn't recognize you, sir."

"Don't apologize. That was rather the point." Adrial rode through the tall gates, sliding down from his horse before the stable hands could reach him and walking away before they could ask any questions.

Rumors of the head scribe riding into the stables in common clothes would fly through the library, but there was nothing to be done. If he had to answer questions, so be it.

He could tell them enough of the truth without having to mention Ena. As long as she was left out of it, he didn't mind whatever censure Lord Gareth might issue.

The steps leading to the residential wing of the library were thankfully bare. Adrial moved up them as quickly as his tired legs would allow, not giving himself the luxury of stopping to catch his breath.

The long hall of the scribes' apartments stretched out in front of him, offering nowhere to duck out of sight and no shadow to disguise his face, as a chambermaid slipped out of Vessa's quarters.

The maid froze, her mouth dangling open, as she stared at Adrial.

Adrial gave her a nod and kept walking down the hall.

You can do better than that, Adrial Ayres.

He turned back to the maid, who still stood frozen and gaping.

"Have a fresh tray of tea brought up to my rooms. Enough for two, please," Adrial said, his tone clear in the empty hall.

The maid bobbed a curtsy and ran out of sight.

Taddy would need a strong cup of tea. The poor boy was probably ill from lying, if he had managed to keep up the pretense of Adrial working at all.

Adrial paused outside the entrance to his own quarters. The plain wood of the door had been polished to perfection. The knob showed no sign of a hand ever having touched it. With a sigh, Adrial turned the handle.

"I've told all of you not to bother the head scribe," Taddy shouted as Adrial pushed open the door. "He didn't say to change—Head Scribe!"

The moment Taddy caught sight of Adrial, he bolted to him, threw his arms around his middle, and buried his face in Adrial's worn and dirty common clothes.

"It's all right, Taddy." Adrial tried not to grimace as the boy squeezed the air from his lungs.

"Head Scribe, I thought you were dead! When you didn't come back when the horns blew, I thought you must be dead as well as the Queen. But what if you weren't dead and I told people you were? Then I'd have failed you. But what if you were dead and I didn't tell anyone? Then animals would eat your corpse. I didn't know what to do, sir."

"I'm certainly glad you didn't panic." Adrial patted the boy's head. "You didn't tell anyone I'd gone?"

"I sent out the letters to Lord Gareth and the shop yesterday morning like you said." Taddy let go of Adrial and searched his pockets. "No one asked questions, and I took your meals in just like you said." Taddy pulled out a handkerchief and gave his nose a noisy blow. "But then the horns sounded last night. It was a terrifying sound to wake up to. I'd read of the horns for royal deaths, but it had never really occurred to me I would hear them myself."

"That's not a thing many consider." Adrial guided his apprentice to a seat at the center of the study. "Did anyone come for me after the horns sounded?"

"A scribe came from Lord Gareth. Said you were to go meet the Lord." Taddy's wide-eyes filled with horror.

"What did you say, Taddy?" Adrial sat opposite him.

Taddy bit his lips together.

"It's all right, whatever you said, but I need to know," Adrial said gently.

"I told them you'd taken ill at the sound of the horns. Told them as an Ayres born, you thought of the Queen as your own mother and were quite overtaken with grief. I begged their pardon and said, as there was nothing you could do to help the Queen, if we might let you rest as you mourned. I said"—Taddy turned his gaze to the ceiling—"I said I was afraid if we didn't let you rest, the scribes might end up mourning one of their own on top of our Queen."

"I'm not sure if I should be terrified of your brilliance or proud of your quick wit." Adrial sagged back in his chair.

"I didn't want to make you sound ill, but I didn't know what else to say."

"You did very well." Adrial stood. "You've helped me greatly, and I won't forget it. There's a tea tray coming up for you. I'm going to take a bath and dress, then we'll sort out what to do next."

"So you'll let me stay here as your apprentice?" Taddy stood so quickly, he knocked the chair out from under himself.

"Yes, Taddy"—Adrial gave a tired laugh—"I'll keep you as my apprentice, but try not to break any furniture." Adrial walked past the long wall of bookshelves, toward his bedroom door. "Or damage any of the books."

"Yes, Head Scribe. Absolutely, Head Scribe."

Adrial shut his bedroom door. The wood wasn't thick enough to block out Taddy's whoop of joy.

His bed was perfectly made and utterly inviting, but Adrial walked past its comfort and into the bathroom. A long tub took up the center of the room. Adrial turned the taps and breathed in the steam that filled the air.

Even knowing how the pipes worked, the instant comfort still seemed a bit like sorcerers' magic.

Stripping off his common clothes, Adrial folded them carefully. He'd need to have them washed on his own. They should be kept hidden in his room in case.

In case of what?

The answer was either too wonderful or too terrible to be considered.

Bottles of scents filled a tiny shelf near his tub. Each bottle represented a luxury lower scribes were not provided. None of their aromas held any appeal. They wouldn't fill his lungs as the fresh wind of the valley had, or make him forget to breathe at all as the blooming of the blue flower had. There wasn't a scent in the world like the perfection drifting from Ena's hair.

Adrial stepped into the bath, letting the hot water ease the pain in his hip.

There isn't a bath in Ilbrea that could be as perfect as swimming in the blue pool.

Squeezing his eyes shut, Adrial sank under the water, blocking out the world. Trying to lock every detail of the falls into his mind forever.

26

MARA

"We can't keep waiting forever," Smitter growled, staring high up to the top of the blue ice cliffs.

"Lamac went up," Rowls said. "What did you expect?"

"Not to have to wait the entire summer for them to come back." Smitter leaned back in his rickety, foldable seat. The thin wood growled in protest at the shifting of his abundant weight.

"Don't be so dramatic," Mara said. "They've only been gone for a day. If they found a path through, it could easily take them this long to know if it's worth all of us scaling up there."

"It's good to know it's not just the dogs who are getting impatient." Kegan strode over from the circle of dogs. Elle stood up, her tail thumping Mara's leg as she panted with glee at his approach. "If we don't see a sign of them soon, I'll have to hook the dogs up to a sled and run them just to keep the pack from tearing each other's fur out."

"If the louts would hurry it up, we wouldn't have to worry about waiting." Smitter crossed his arms, his face set in a near comical frown.

"How long do we wait before sending someone up after

them?" Tham asked. "They could be hurt or lost by now. The longer we leave Edder and Lamac up there, the worse things could get for them."

"Edder's a fine soldier," Smitter said, "and map makers have a compass marked on their skin."

"A compass doesn't do much good if you're trapped in an ice maze." Tham narrowed his dark eyes, gazing up to the ledge high above.

"Tham's right." Mara squinted against the light. "They could have fallen into a crevasse. Or found a cave and lost the path out."

"Then what do you think we should do, map maker?" Kegan gave an absurdly flourishing bow. "As Smitter says, we can't wait here until the winter storms come back."

"We'll give them today," Mara said. "If they haven't come back by morning, I'll go up and see if I can tell where they went."

"I'll accompany you," Tham said.

Mara bit the insides of her cheeks to hide her smile.

"I'll go run the dogs so they don't go mad." Kegan strode off through the snow.

Elle sniffed his heels before settling back down at Mara's side.

"You know, it's not something they tell you when you're assigned to journey with the map makers." Rowls settled himself into his seat. "They warn you about the awful food and the days of walking. They tell you to kiss your toes goodbye when you venture into the snow. But no one ever mentions the waiting. I hate waiting."

"I think we all do." Mara closed her eyes, trying to picture what Lamac had found on top of the cliffs. It could have been a hundred things that kept him up there overnight. They'd climbed with a tent, so there was a good chance they were still alive.

Mara snuggled deeper into her warm coat. With the sun beating down on them, the cold wasn't too unbearable. That was something to be grateful for.

Tham sat by her side—another wonder. Elle had taken to sleeping on top of Mara at night. It wasn't the most comfortable arrangement, but it was better than being alone. Having the dog's bright blue eyes staring at her every morning was something else to be grateful for.

Mara kept going down the list, trying to keep herself from making plans when planning was impossible without knowing what was happening on top of the cliffs.

She had a wonderful home at the Map Master's Palace. Allora would make sure she took a dozen hot baths when they returned to Ilara.

Mara kept building the list for hours.

Midday passed without any movement on the cliffs.

Mara left her seat to eat by the fire with the others. Then they all drifted back to their places. Some working on preparing climbing equipment and maintaining the dogsleds, the rest watching.

"At this point, Smitter's singing might actually be a relief," Rowls said when the length of the afternoon became tiring.

"I'm pleased to oblige." Smitter stood and turned to face the group.

"How thrilling." Mara kept her tone even, not wanting to admit that even Smitter's crass songs would be a welcome break in the monotony.

"There once was a dragon so fair,
She never came out of her lair,
For the moment she did—"

A shout from the top of the cliffs cut through Smitter's song.

"We leave you alone for a day and you resort to Smitter's singing?" Edder called down. "And here I was afraid you would all be pacing and worrying if we were all right."

"Got tired of worrying over your sorry hide," Smitter shouted back. "Where's Lamac?"

"I'm here." Lamac peered triumphantly over the edge of the cliff. "And you'd all better get packed up to join us. We've found a path into the mountains!"

A cheer sounded from the men as they all hurried to pack up the camp.

Only Kegan stayed standing next to Mara. "I was really hoping there was nothing up that way."

"Why?" Mara folded her short stool.

"I don't mind a bit of climbing myself, and the slings to haul the dogs up will work." Kegan rubbed his gloved hands over his stubble. "But those dogs aren't going to like the trip up, and that'll leave me with a pack of powerfully built, scared and unhappy animals, all of whom have very sharp teeth."

Mara's tent had already been rolled and stowed by the time she reached it. The fire trays had been slipped into their covers and packed away.

"Never see a camp packed up so quick first thing in the morning," Edder shouted from above, "but leave people stuck for a bit, and they'll be ready to go in no time."

"Easy for you to say," Rowls said. "You haven't been sitting in the snow, waiting."

In less than ten minutes, the crew stood at the base of the cliff. Piles of supplies had been tied into bundles to be hauled up on long, sturdy ropes. Kegan had the four slings ready to hoist the dogs.

"I should be in the first group." Mara clipped shining metal spikes to the toes of her boots. "The sooner I can review Lamac's map, the sooner we can make a plan for moving on from this cliff."

"So women get antsy just like men?" Smitter said.

"Of course we do." Mara gripped an ice axe in each hand. "We're just better at hiding it."

"Twenty feet apart?" Tham stepped up to the cliff, axes in his hands, spikes on his toes.

"That should keep the ice stable." Mara nodded.

A thrill tumbled through her stomach as she kicked her first toe into the ice. The jarring in her legs meant she was doing something. The ache in her shoulders as she pulled herself up with the axes earned her the adventure ahead.

"Good thing you aren't afraid of heights, Tham!" a voice called from below.

Mara held tight to her axes as she laughed. "I think Tham lives for heights."

"Perhaps," Tham said.

One foot, the next, one foot, the next. The pattern brought comfort.

The higher they climbed, the stronger the wind became.

Mara's calves twitched in protest. Careful to keep her weight toward the cliff, she glanced up. Fifty more feet until the ledge. She chanced a glance down. A sea of snow glittered beneath her.

How wonderful would it be to let go of the cliff and fly? To soar out over the ice and see the mountains from above?

With a sigh, Mara kicked her toe into the ice and pulled herself up another step.

"Starting up from behind," a voice called from below.

"We're bringing up ropes," Tham said. "Wait and we'll tie you in."

"Leave the ropes for the dogs," Kegan called. "If we don't start getting them up now, we'll have to wait until tomorrow to finish the job. And I, for one, am not sleeping down here with a pack of carnivores."

Just a bit more.

Mara's arms screamed with fatigue as she pummeled the axes into the ice.

"We've got you." Hands clasped around Mara's wrists, dragging her belly first onto the top of the cliff. Fatigue batted away the instinct to be insulted at that sort of help.

"Not too bad a climb, eh?" Edder helped Tham to his feet.

"I've done worse." Tham unhooked his pack and pulled out stakes and rope.

Mountains surrounded both sides of the ice where they stood. From up here, it looked as though the glacier stemmed from a point high up in the peaks. The cliff she'd just climbed ended the glacier, where the sun or an earthquake had sheared off the tip.

Streaks of cerulean blue shone through the snow, and bits of dark rock speckled the edges where ice met mountain. Boulders dotted the path that led up the saddle between two ridges and twisted out of sight.

Mara dropped her pack next to Tham's and headed straight for Lamac who stood at the far western side of the cliff. "May I see your map?"

"Want to see what took us so long?" Lamac raised an eyebrow.

"I'm not worried about how long it took so long as no one was hurt," Mara said, "but if you found something worth being gone for a day, I'd like to see what it is."

"Here." Lamac pulled a scroll from the tube at his hip. "We started by climbing up the glacier. As you so sagely suggested, I wanted to be sure there was something on the other side worth hauling up the whole camp."

Mara studied the map. The glacier cut between two unmarked peaks, but the top of the glacier hadn't been drawn. Instead, toward the end of the marked out ice, a swivel of darkness cut to the north.

"What is that?" Mara asked.

"Well, we started climbing up the glacier, but I found something more interesting." Lamac beamed smugly. "A system of caves that cuts into the mountain."

"How far?"

"Farther than we could travel without going back for the rest of the party."

Mara traced her finger along the dark line. The drawing of it was rudimentary. Mapping tunnels was no small task, but it should have been better done.

"Once we get everyone up, we'll head back into the caves," Mara said. "Map out the system."

"You mean you'll map out the system I discovered?" Lamac shook his head and wrinkled his nose. "I don't think so. We've been sent to chart the mountains, so we'll head to the top of the glacier. When we get back to Ilara, I'll show Lord Karron the map of the caves I discovered. I'm sure he won't mind sending out a journey next year to chart Lamac's Cave."

"Better tidy your map if you're planning on handing it to Lord Karron." Mara smiled. "There's an art to charting caves, and I don't think the map maker you studied under quite taught you the knack."

Grinding her teeth, Mara turned and walked north, up the glacier.

Careful, Mara. Telling him you're better trained will only make him antagonize you more.

She pressed her rough, cold gloves to her eyes, willing her anger to settle back into fierce determination. Wind swept past her, ruffling the snow around her feet as though the mountains themselves wanted to remind her how precarious her footing constantly remained.

"I know," Mara whispered. "Believe me, I know."

She opened her eyes and turned back toward the cliff. Half the men had made the climb, and from the terrible whimpering as Tham and Edder pulled on a rope, the first dog had begun the trip up.

A long row of gray rocks marked the edge of the ice sheet.

"A stone to hold Kareen." Mara bent down and chose two rocks. Both had seen a thousand winters. Both had survived the mountains.

Mara tucked the smaller rock into her pocket and headed

back to the cliff, where Tham knelt, untying the sling and pulling the blindfold from Elle's eyes.

Trembling, the dog ran straight for Mara, leaning against her legs with a piteous whimper.

"You're all right, pretty girl," Mara cooed, pressing a rock into Tham's hand.

Tham cocked his head, examining the stone.

"To bring back to Whitend," Mara said. "Best not to forget Bernate's warning."

"Want to pull?" Rowls asked as his rope caught two sharp tugs from below.

"Of course." Mara joined him on his line, dragging the squirming mass of dog up the cliff.

"Supplies are all up, and I'm damned sick of whining dogs," Smitter shouted from below, digging his axe into the wall of ice.

"You loved them when they were hauling your gear." Kegan wrestled another dog into a sling.

"Sure, sure," Smitter said. "But they'd be more useful if they were quiet."

The dog in Mara and Rowls' sling yipped and wiggled, bouncing himself against the ice.

"Hold still, mutt," Rowls grunted. "You're only making it worse for yourself."

"Imagine if we needed to hunt for meat?" Smitter said, his words coming out in a halting fashion as he climbed. "And there's no saying it won't come to that. How are we supposed to hunt with twenty howling dogs telling the whole range of the white mountains where we are?"

The wind picked up, tickling Mara through the thick fur lining of her coat.

"What would there be to hunt anyway?" Kegan said. "Have you seen anything worth eating?"

"You'd be surprised what food you can find when you're starving," Smitter said.

The dog in Mara's sling howled in terror as a gust of wind buffeted the cliff.

"Getch dog," Rowls said, but a scream cut over his curse.

A figure fell from the side of the cliff, plummeting toward the ground.

"Smitter!" The scream tore from Mara's throat, but there was nothing to be done as his body crumpled into the white.

27

ALLORA

"I don't look pretty enough." Illia threw her dress to the floor. "I won't look like a common girl walking in the procession of the Queen's funeral."

"I'm so sorry, Your Highness." The maid curtsied and picked up the dress. "This is the one you requested we have made, and—"

"Make another!" Illia shouted.

"Princess," Allora spoke gently, not moving from her seat in the corner, "the funeral begins in an hour. There isn't time to make a new gown. Even if every seamstress in the palace worked, it couldn't be done."

"Should I walk through the cathedral naked?" Tears streamed down Illia's face. "Should I borrow rags from a beggar?"

"What's wrong with the dress?" Allora stood and took the garment from the maid, who bobbed a curtsy and backed into the corner.

"It's too plain. It's terrible." Illia sniffed.

"It's quite beautiful." Allora held up the dress.

It was a well-made gown if not ornate. Delicate, silver stitching edged the cuffs of the long lace sleeves and neck. A fitted bodice led to a skirt, which, while lacking a train, had tiny, scalloped edges.

"I don't want to wear black." Illia's voice was thick with tears. "I am Princess Illia Willoc of Ilbrea, I should be wearing silver. It is my place within the Guilds." Illia coughed the last few words before dissolving into tears.

Allora laid a hand on Illia's shoulder, a motion that had become too common since the Queen's death, and one Allora wouldn't have dared before. "Princess, none of us will wear our Guild colors today." Allora patted her own plain, black dress. The thin green trim at her wrists and hem gave the only hint at her place as Lady of the Map Makers Guild.

"But you're beautiful." Illia viciously wiped the tears from her cheeks. "You could wear a sack from the docks, and you'd still be the most beautiful woman in Ilbrea."

"Don't be silly. You're positively stunning in whatever you wear."

At Allora's compliment, Illia crumpled into wracking sobs, burying her face on Allora's shoulder.

"Perhaps if you wait outside until the Princess is ready to dress." Allora looked to the maid who cowered with wide-eyed horror.

The maid curtsied and darted out the door.

"Princess," Allora said, "I know you're terribly sad, and the loss of the Queen weighs more heavily on you than it could on anyone outside the royal family. But Sara will come for you soon. I can only put her off for so long. If you aren't dressed when she arrives, she won't take a gentle hand with you."

"I don't miss her," Illia muttered the words into Allora's shoulder. "I'm a hateful girl, and I don't miss her."

"Princess—"

"She was the closest thing to a mother I've had for most of my life, and she never warmed to me." Illia let go of Allora to pace in front of the fireplace, worrying her hands. "I wanted her to love me, but she only cared for the children she couldn't have. I thought maybe she could be a sister to me as I got older, but she didn't want anything to do with me then either. She never cared for me, no matter how badly I embarrassed myself begging for her affection."

"I'm sure she cared for you in her own way."

"She would have said I looked dull and plain in the black dress. She would have said Dudia blessed me in being born a princess. Without a title to offer, I'm no good to any man."

A cold hand gripped Allora's heart. "I'm so sorry."

"She wasn't kind to me even before she lost the first child." Illia brushed her tears away again. "She preferred to pretend I didn't exist. That my brother was hers alone and there was no one else to share his affection."

"Your brother loves you fiercely."

"But it's not the same as having a sister. Sweet Allora"—Illia grasped Allora's hands—"you've been more a sister to me than Carys ever attempted to be. With Carys alive, at least I could pretend she liked me. Now I can't even fool myself into thinking I have someone to rely on."

"I am here whenever you need me."

"Then let me call you sister," Illia said. "Let me hear a female call me by my given name. Please, Allora."

"Of course, Illia," Allora said. "I would be honored to call you sister."

"Thank you, Allora." Illia flung her arms around Allora's neck. "You are everything I ever hoped for."

"Thank you, Illia." Allora held her for a long moment, letting the girl blubber all over her dress.

Too well Allora remembered the sad time in the Map Master's Palace before Mara had come to live with them. Too new was the sting of being alone in a massive house with no one who addressed her without her title.

"I suppose I should be brave and wear the plain awful dress."

Illia stepped away.

"It's how all of us will be dressed, and you will look lovely." Allora shook the gown out for Illia to see.

"Will you bring the maid back?" Illia sighed. "I'll have to powder my face to get rid of the red. Though I suppose it might be pointless as I'm likely to cry again."

"Whether you cry or not, you'll be beautiful. A true credit to the Willoc family name." Allora slipped out into the hall. "She's ready for you."

The maid bobbled a curtsy and scurried back into the room.

How under all the sky did you end up here, Allora Karron?

You were kind to a lonely child and have the title to suit.

A soldier strode down the hall, his gaze fixed on Allora. "Excuse me, Lady Karron?"

"Yes." Allora nodded regally.

"I've been sent to bring you to the carriages," the soldier said. "The King's carriage leaves in ten minutes, and all the others should reach the cathedral before his."

"Of course," Allora said. "I'm not sure if the Princess will be ready to leave so soon."

"I've only been asked to bring you down, Lady Karron." The soldier bowed. "But I can assure you the Princess will not be left behind."

Allora turned to one of the soldiers flanking Illia's door. "Please tell the Princess I've been called away and that I'll see her at the cathedral."

"Yes, Lady Karron."

Allora followed a soldier down the long hall of the residence wing, batting away the tendrils of guilt growing in her stomach at leaving Illia with only a maid and Sara for comfort.

A line of six carriages waited outside the entrance of the palace, ranging from ornately carved but ungilded, to the King's glittering conveyance. Black drapes obscured the sides of the royal carriage. Even so, the sun still found bare patches of gold and glinted off its shining surface.

A man stood near the royal carriage. For a moment, Allora didn't recognize him dressed all in black. But the man gave a sad smile that didn't reach his teal eyes.

"Your Majesty," Allora said as the soldier led her too near the King to warrant remaining silent. "I'm so terribly sorry for your loss."

"My loss?" The King shook his head. "It sounds rather like I misplaced the Queen, doesn't it?"

"Perhaps a little," Allora said. "Her death is a great loss for us all."

"She wouldn't have believed you." Wrinkles formed on the King's forehead.

Allora hadn't seen him up close since his wife's death. Gray had added its tint to his skin, and bluish bags under his eyes only made their brilliant color more noticeable.

"She thought the people hated her." The King lowered his voice, though it was impossible for the soldier standing four feet behind him not to hear. "She thought they despised her for not bearing an heir. She called herself a breeding mare. Said she should be put to pasture like a horse that is no longer fruitful."

"That's…" Allora tried to find words appropriate to be spoken in front of the King. "That's terrible. She was much loved by the people of Ilbrea. With or without an heir."

"Loved isn't the same as needed," the King said. "The people need an Ilbrean heir. My sister must marry Prince Dagon. Once she is gone, there will be no Willocs but me left in Ilbrea. There's a line of ascension, a dozen or so cousins and the like nipping at my heels to sit on my throne. A dozen who have never lived in a palace. Who have never sat in a meeting of the Guilds Council."

He stopped talking and stared at Allora as though she should have something useful to say.

"Perhaps you should take a cousin as an apprentice of sorts,"

Allora finally managed. "Train them in the way you would wish them to sit on the throne. It may not be the royal custom, but it has kept peace within the Guilds."

"You are a remarkable woman, Lady Allora. It's a brilliant idea." A tired smile touched his lips again. "A way to lift the weight of an heir from my shoulders, and one I have pondered before. But then what of the cousins not chosen? What might they do to the one who is to rule? If the heir were my child, there could be no question, but with a cousin, strife would become inevitable."

"There is a path forward." Allora tipped her chin up. "You will find a way to secure a smooth succession. You are not, by any measure, an old man. By the grace of Dudia, you'll have many years to riddle it out."

"I don't need years," the King said. "I know the answer. It's the one the Queen hated most. I'll marry a new wife. One who is young and healthy enough to make the people forget there was ever a sickly queen. One who will bear royal children that carry the Willoc name."

"Yes, Your Majesty." Allora glanced down the row of carriages, willing someone to beckon her away. "I suppose that would solve the problem."

"The trouble is I'm much pickier now than I was when I married the late Queen." The King stared into Allora's eyes so intently, the teal of them seemed to burn. "I won't listen to a pack of advisors prattle on about which family, or Guild, or country I need to forge an alliance with. I gave them the Queen they wished for. Now I will have the Queen I want. And I won't spend months in black waiting for anyone's approval."

Allora's heart hitched up into her throat. "You are the King, Your Majesty. You are the ruler of Ilbrea. I don't know whose approval you might be seeking."

"That is what makes you both smart, and lovely, Lady Allora." The King took Allora's hand and kissed her fingers before wrenching open the door to his carriage. "I am the King of Ilbrea. And my time of begging for goodwill has passed."

The King stepped up into his carriage and disappeared from sight.

Allora's knees threatened to buckle as the world spun.

Do not faint, Allora Karron. You have survived terrors and adventures. You have enough illegal maps hidden in your mother's tomb to be hanged a dozen times over. You will not faint.

Allora walked toward the other carriages, concentrating on the minute difference in the levels of the stones beneath her feet, trying to ignore the burn of teal eyes on the back of her neck.

"Lady Karron." Petra Roo of the Sorcerers Guild beckoned from her carriage. "We have room for you, if you wish."

"Yes please, Sorcerer Roo." Allora kept her pace even as she walked toward the carriage. "I would be honored to ride with you."

A sorcerers' guard offered her a hand at the carriage door.

Allora gave the purple-clad guard a nod and settled into the seat across from the sorcerer.

Plush, purple fabric covered every surface. The effect should have been stifling, but the deepness of the color instead brought comfort. Like a nice, dark corner where Allora might curl up and sleep until she realized the last week had been a dream.

"Is the King well?" Petra asked as the carriage rumbled forward.

The clopping of the horses' hooves rattled against Allora's words as she fought to form them. "He is as well as one could expect, given the day."

"He'll be better as soon as he has a new bride," Petra said without a trace of shame. "The sooner, the better really. A wedding by mid-summer would be best."

"The Queen's body still lies in the cathedral," Allora said. "Surely, the King has more time than the summer."

"An empty bed is a luxury that cannot be allowed to a king

who lacks an heir," Petra said. "Ilbrea needs stability. You've seen the trouble in the streets firsthand. How far would a royal baby go toward calming the people?"

"Surely—"

"You've grown up in the Map Makers Guild, Lady Allora," Petra cut in. "You've grown up with the notion that maps and exploration are the highest calling. I grew up with the sorcerers. We might be seen only for our magic, but our true calling is to protect the crown of Ilbrea. For centuries, we have sat at the right hand of the ruler, doing whatever is necessary to preserve the crown and our country."

Allora swallowed the dreadful taste of fear. "Then a sorcerer would be a perfect bride for the King. Have you had an audience with him? I'm sure he would find you charming."

"I am a trained sorcerer." Petra leaned back in her seat. "I am most useful to Ilbrea and the King in the Sorcerers Tower."

"And me?"

"If the wind stays its course, you will very soon need to decide how you can best serve Ilbrea, and *all* her people." Petra smiled as she spoke.

Does she think I'm in too deep to run from her trap, or that marrying a King would be a blessing?

"I'm sure you must be mistaken," Allora said as the carriage rattled to a stop. "I am a confidant of the Princess. I have no other relation to the royal family. It is my deepest wish that Ilbrea and all her people be safe and prosperous. I happily do my part, standing at my father's side."

Allora wrenched open the carriage door, not waiting for a guard to open it for her.

"Strange that a map maker's daughter should be so frightened of flying from home," Petra said.

Allora stopped, one foot out of the carriage.

"It is not fear that keeps me at my father's house," Allora said, "but knowing my place in this world. I hope when fate teaches you yours, she shall be kind in her lesson."

Allora's hands shook as she fought the urge to run. To find her father, or Kai, or Adrial. Any friend in the city.

Take a horse and ride east. Find Niko.

The thought was absurd, dangerous even. And pointless besides. The King could mean to marry any of a dozen women, and Petra wasn't even the head of her Guild.

A pawn of the sorcerers, that's all Petra was. A minion of the purple-clad usurpers who tried so hard to pretend they didn't think themselves more important than the crown.

Then why you? Why of all the Guilded would Petra imply you?

Allora barely noticed the heatless, white flames that licked the hem of her skirt as she climbed the cathedral steps. Black valances hung over the open, golden doors of the cathedral, somberly welcoming the elite of Ilbrea.

Lord Karron already stood at the tip of the map makers' point of the star, staring at the golden altar that had been placed at the center of the space.

"Father." Allora nodded, taking her place by his side.

The golden altar had a pattern running through the metal, thin wisps of silver that caught the afternoon light.

"I was worried you might not make it in time." Lord Karron did not look at his daughter.

"I was helping the Princess," Allora said. "I rode over with Petra Roo of the Sorcerers Guild."

The muscles in Lord Karron's neck tensed, his veins popping out against the dark green of his collar.

"I would have thought you would come in an earlier carriage."

"After I helped the Princess, I had an interesting conversation with the King."

Fear stung Allora's heart as her father glanced at her for a split second before looking back to the Queen.

They had dressed her in a white gown with gold stitching

around the neck, sleeves, and hem. A sole beacon of white in a sea of black-clad mourners.

"And how did the conversation go?" Lord Karron asked as the royal carriage stopped at the foot of the cathedral steps.

"Not well," Allora whispered as the talk around her dimmed. "It left me quite confused."

"Anyone who tries to riddle through the plans of sorcerers and kings is bound to become confused," Lord Karron said.

The King stepped out of his carriage, waiting on the street to give his sister his arm.

"Father, my place is with you. I cannot leave the map makers."

"Then we will not let them claim you."

Fear rose as bile in Allora's throat as the King entered the cathedral and the Queen's body burst into dazzling white flames.

28

ADRIAL

"It's down by the docks. She wasn't lying about that." Taddy pointed at the map of the city. "I asked around as much as I dared, and Ena lives somewhere on this street. Though no one said exactly what building, and there wasn't a sign for her shop."

"Thank you, Taddy." Adrial passed the boy another cookie. "You've done very well."

"You know," Taddy said, holding his cookie as though it were a grand prize, "being your personal apprentice is even better than I thought it would be."

"Thank you, Taddy." Adrial leaned back in his chair, staring at the vellum page in front of him. A wide cove and a peaceful blue seascape surrounded the ships of the first Willoc fleet.

Taddy swallowed the rest of his cookie. "And scouting for Ena is very good training. Scribes have to be able to do research, and I've definitely had a lesson in that."

"I'm glad you found the hunt educational."

He needed the pale blue to continue. Five pages of the vellum lay on his work desk, each awaiting a dazzling Ilbrean sky.

"I'm going to find Ena." Adrial stood, shrugging out of his white robes.

Taddy stared open-mouthed at the common clothes Adrial wore beneath.

He'd managed to find more common clothes to add to his hoard, constantly wearing them beneath his robes in case...

In case of what, you fool?

"Shouldn't you wait here?" Taddy asked. "She always comes back to the shop eventually."

"It's been more than a week." Adrial carefully folded his white robes.

"Then let me go find her and bring her here," Taddy said. "If you give me a few coins, I'm sure I could pay someone to tell me which door is hers."

"I'll take coin and pay them myself." Adrial walked toward the back door.

Taddy darted in front of him, blocking his path.

"It might not be safe, sir. There's all sorts of unhappy people in the city."

"Did you feel unsafe, Taddy?" Guilt squirmed in his stomach at having sent the boy out to the docks alone.

"Of course not, sir." Taddy tipped his chin up. "But I, sir, am a pudgy little nobody who's surprisingly fast for a boy with short legs. I can run and duck into corners and hide, and no one will think anything of it. You can't run, sir, and you're important besides."

"Taddy—"

"Let me go for you. I'm your apprentice. It's my job to help you. I'll go find her and get the ink. I can ask her to come here, if you like."

"I'm going, Taddy." Adrial took the boy by his shoulders and steered him away from the door. "The best way you can help me is to tell anyone who asks after me that I've gone for a meeting at the Map Master's Palace."

"But then you'd have gone in a carriage." A pink hue of panic crept into Taddy's face.

"Tell them Allora, Lady Karron, sent a carriage for me and had it come to the back for privacy." Adrial held up a hand as Taddy began to protest again. "And get to work on your transcriptions. I'll be checking them when I get back."

"Yes, sir." Taddy bowed, worried lines carving his forehead.

"I'll be back before you know it." Adrial hurried out the back door before his apprentice could come up with another logical protest.

The bright sun warmed Adrial's skin the moment he stepped outside. The wind swept away the fatigue of being trapped in his workroom.

Keeping his head down, Adrial moved through the city as quickly as he could, careful to hide his limp despite the pain it brought. He longed to look up to the sky, to watch the people he passed, but anonymity was his best defense.

A pack of workers scrubbed the side of the public stables, trying to rid the wood of the scrawled words *The End of the Gold.*

Adrial walked faster as he turned down a merchant lane, choosing speed over hiding his limp. Shattered windows that had been quickly patched with wood adorned more than one storefront.

"It's the chivving rotta of the city that will ruin us all." A man stood in front of a boarded up shop, smoking a long, black pipe and reeking of frie. "They'll destroy everything without even realizing they're burning themselves in the process."

"And the soldiers can't even seem to own there's a problem," a woman wearing fine merchants' silks answered. "Wait till the destruction reaches the Guilded part of town. They'll start paying attention then."

Adrial bit back the urge to ask who had broken all the shop windows and kept up his pace as he hurried down the street.

He could ask Lord Gareth what had happened. Surely, it had been reported to the Guilds Council, even if the Lord Scribe hadn't seen fit to tell Adrial.

A blackened ruin appeared at the end of the street. Charred beams and a half-burnt, smoke-stained counter were all that remained of the shop. The sides of the shops around it had been blackened by the fire, but some miracle had saved them from catching as their neighbor had.

Madness has taken Ilara.

The streets leading to the docks weren't marked by the same damage that marred the merchants' shops. Whether they were below the notice of the rioters or above their wrath, Adrial didn't know.

He reached a row of warehouses and homes jumbled together, cramming into the space just north of the Sailors Guild docks. The breeze carried the stink of fish, though the people bustling through the street didn't seem to mind.

Women selling vegetables sat next to men scaling fish. A stall offering roughly woven cloth sat next to a man selling shoes. Children ran through the streets with no one telling them to be careful of horses.

"Excuse me, miss." Adrial bowed to a woman who hunched over baskets of flowers, tying them into bundles with such quick movements, it seemed like all the petals should fall off the blooms. "I was hoping you might be able to help me find someone."

The woman narrowed her eyes, appraising Adrial from tip to toe.

"Who are you looking for?" the woman said, her eyes still squinted.

"I'm looking for a girl who makes ink." Adrial kept his voice light and casual. "I have a special project, and I hear she's the best. From what I'm told, she runs around looking rather like a rainbow."

"That one." The woman shook her head. "I know where she lives."

"I'm happy to pay if you'll show me where to find her." Adrial pulled a gold coin from his pocket.

The woman stared at the coin for a long moment.

"Smallish green warehouse just down from here." The woman pointed. "There's a black door with peeling paint on it. That's where she'll be if she's still in Ilara." The woman snatched the coin from Adrial's hand before continuing. "Girls like her don't tend to stick around long, so don't come back looking for your coin if she's gone."

"Of course." Adrial gave the woman a nod and headed down the street.

He passed a tavern with a sign so worn it was impossible to read. Tables had sprawled out into the street. Most of the seats were filled, and the occupants didn't seem to care if they were blocking the people passing by. A fiddler stood on top of a crate, playing music as men and women danced around him. Adrial scanned the dancers for signs of Ena. Her colorful hair was nowhere to be seen.

Just past the tavern, a rundown, green, two-story warehouse came into view. A wide, red door opened out onto the street, but tucked around the side sat a peeling, black door.

A wave of relief mixed with fear sent Adrial's pulse racing as he hurried to the door. He forced his hands to stop shaking before daring to knock.

Thump, thump, thump.

The wood of the door was far thicker than it appeared. Adrial's knocks echoed into the building.

A creak sounded overhead.

"Of all the chivving things for a man to do."

By the time Adrial looked up toward Ena's voice, the window had slammed shut.

"Ena?" Adrial called.

The pounding of someone running down stairs carried through the door, followed by the thunking of locks turning.

Ena swung the door open.

Adrial took a breath to speak, but before he could remember how, Ena grabbed him by the front of his shirt and yanked him stumbling into the dark.

"What do you think you're doing?" She shoved him aside and rebolted the three locks on the heavy wooden door.

"I came to be sure you were all right," Adrial panted as his heart returned to a normal rhythm and his mind discovered he was not in a tomb-like hold, but at the bottom of a shabby wooden staircase.

"I would be a lot better off if the head scribe didn't come knocking on my door." Ena grabbed his arm, dragging him up the creaking steps.

"No one knows I'm a scribe. I didn't wear my robes, and I never mentioned my position when I asked where you lived."

"You asked where I live?"

The staircase opened up into a room the size of the warehouse below. Dried herbs and flowers hung from the rafters. A wide, soot-stained fireplace made of chipped bricks took up most of one wall. A table with a mortar and pestle, knives, and dozens of little glass pots occupied the center of the space. A cot and tub sat in the back corner, next to a wide cupboard and a stack of crates.

"Scribe." Ena shook Adrial's shoulders. "Who did you ask?"

"A woman selling flowers," Adrial said, finding it difficult to form words with the delicious scent of the room blurring his thoughts. "I gave her a coin for helping me."

"What kind of coin?"

"A gold coin."

"What under the gods and stars made you do a chivving foolish thing like that?" Ena tore her hands through her teal and pink streaked hair. "Do you think anyone on this street has a gold coin, much less one to spare?"

"You do." Tendrils of anger curled in Adrial's stomach.

"I don't tell anyone about them."

"I was trying to be kind!"

Ena froze for a moment, her eyes wide with something between shock and amusement.

"Of course you were," Ena said, "and that'll mark you as not belonging here as quickly as anything else."

"But you're kind," Adrial spoke gently, "and I shouldn't have shouted. I'm sorry."

"I'm not kind." Ena turned to her worktable. She picked up a purple flower, ripping the petals from it and tossing them into a wooden bowl. "I'm tolerable to you, and you're so used to people being awful, you take it as kindness."

"That's not true."

"Anyway, I'm proud of you for shouting." Ena shot him a pinched smile. "Maybe I'm wearing off on you."

"Maybe."

Ena threw the flowers onto the table with such force, they sent the wooden bowl skidding across the surface and tumbling to the floor on the other side. "But what did you come here for?"

"I haven't seen you in more than a week." Adrial limped to the far side of the table, picking up the bowl and salvaging what torn up purple petals he could.

"So you just missed me?"

"I was worried about you." Adrial set the bowl back on the table. "You disappeared at the gate, and I haven't heard anything from you since."

"I didn't have anything to bring you."

"That isn't good enough." Adrial held her gaze for a long moment, glad the table between them tamped down his need to reach for her.

"They burned the shoe shop." Ena pressed her palms against the top of the table. "The cobbler that made all the shoes for the Guilds, they burnt his shop to the ground. He lived right above it. The shoemaker and his two children died."

"That's terrible—"

"All the shops that sell goods to the Guilds had their windows smashed as well. The bookseller who carried my ink had every pot of it smashed in the night. Most of his books torn to pieces, too."

"Ena—"

"He's got nothing to sell. I've been working my fingers to bleeding trying to give the poor man something he can earn coin with before his family starves."

"I'm sorry."

"Don't be. You didn't do it." Ena grabbed the bowl and began tearing apart a new bunch of flowers.

"Is there anything I can do to help?"

Ena laughed. The sound was broken, like some part of her had shattered. "It's not safe for you to be here, let alone to help. If they find out that poor man is taking help from the Guilds, they'll burn his book shop as quick as they murdered the shoemaker."

"Then you can't sell to me anymore." Adrial hated the words as he said them. "If they're doing that to shops, they'll come after you if they find out."

"So I'll just starve then?"

"You won't starve." Adrial moved to the other side of the table, keeping eye contact with Ena, willing her to understand. "I'll give you whatever you need. Coin, food, anything."

"You want me to be your whore?" Ena cocked her head to the side. "I'm sure the tilk will think much better of me selling you my body than my ink."

"I'm not trying to buy anything, I only want to take care of a friend. I ask for nothing in return."

Ena bit her lips together. "Then you're a better friend than most deserve. Certainly better than I deserve. But it's too late. Everyone knows I've been selling to you."

"How?" Adrial glanced to the gap in the floor that led to the stairs.

"People talk." Ena waved the flowers through the air. "They've all known since the chivving bastard broke everything in my basket. And there's no way to make people unknow anything. At least not that the sorcerers have shared with the rest of us."

"Then you can't stay here." Wild plans flitted through Adrial's mind.

We could run to the waterfall. I could bring her to Allora.

"You should come live at the library."

Ena laughed.

"You would be safe there," Adrial said.

"A rotta inker like me go live in the library? I'll marry the King next week."

"You're valuable." Adrial pulled the flowers from her hand before she could tear any more of them apart. "I need your help on the vellum. If I tell Lord Gareth, he'll find a place for you."

"Scribe"—Ena took Adrial's face in her hands—"I'd rather be buried in a tomb than lock myself in one while I'm still breathing. No matter how pretty and white it is."

"You'll get hurt. I saw what they did to the cobbler's shop. They could do the same to you."

"I've seen too much for a pile of ashes to scare me. Besides, they won't hurt me." Ena pressed her forehead to Adrial's. "He wants me too badly."

"He?"

A violent knock banged on the door below.

"I didn't think it would take him so long."

29

ADRIAL

"Ena!" a voice shouted. "Ena Bairn!"

"You've got to hide." Ena grabbed Adrial's arm, nearly yanking him off his feet as she ran toward the pile of crates.

"Who is that?"

Ena pulled a crate aside, opening up a hollowed out part of the pile larger than he would have thought possible.

"Get in," Ena whispered.

"Ena, if you're pretending not to be home, I'll just wait here till you've wizened up!" The voice carried through the wood of the building.

"If you value my life or yours, you will crawl into that dark hole and not make a peep, no matter what happens." Ena shoved Adrial toward the hole.

"Ena, if someone's here to hurt you, I can't just hide." Adrial grabbed her wrists to stop her pushing. "I won't."

"If you stay quiet, I promise we'll both make it out of this alive. If you don't, he'll kill you, and it won't make anything better for me."

"Ena, I'm not one for waiting," the man shouted from below.

"Promise me," Ena said, the hint of begging in her tone more terrifying than the man bellowing below.

Adrial nodded, his throat too tight to form words, and crawled into the hollow behind the crates. Before he could get his bearings, Ena shoved the loose crate back into place, throwing Adrial into near darkness.

A squeak sounded in the shop. "What do you want, Cade?" Ena shouted without any trace of fear in her voice.

"Finally decided you're home?" Cade called from below.

A slit of light cut through the darkness in Adrial's hiding place.

"No, I just finally got sick of your chivving shouting," Ena said. "I've got work to do, and it's terribly hard to get anything done with a slitch bellowing at you."

"Then let me up and we can talk. Come on, Ena. I just want to have a chat."

Twisting to face the room, Adrial found the source of the light and peered through the crack between the crate's planks.

"Fine," Ena shouted out the window, her hands planted on her hips. "But if you break anything up here, I will take it out of your hide. Do you understand?"

"Have I ever been anything but a gentleman?"

Ena slammed the window shut and headed for the stairs.

Propping himself up on his elbow, Adrial pressed his eye close to the crack.

The sound of the locks thunking open came a moment before they thunked closed again.

"Locking me in with you?" Cade's laugh boomed up the steps.

"I'd rather not be joined by any of your friends during our chat." Ena appeared at the top of the stairs and strode straight over to the table to rip apart more purple petals.

A powerfully built man with curling blond hair climbed two steps behind Ena. She didn't say anything as Cade circled the shop, sniffing the dried flowers that hung from the rafters and kicking the leg of Ena's cot, before leaning against the table where Ena worked.

"Aren't you going to ask why I'm here, Ena my love?"

"I'm more interested in when you're leaving." Ena didn't look up from her work as she spoke.

"You're always so blunt, Ena." Cade lifted her hair away from her cheek, revealing the pale skin of her neck. "And you never blush. I think that's why I like you so much."

"I'll have to take up blushing then." Ena didn't flinch as Cade leaned close to her ear.

"You never say thank you either." Cade's lips brushed her skin. "I protect you. If anyone else on this street sold to the Guilds as you do—"

"Dozens do."

"Not like you, going to their door, begging. If anyone else stooped so low, they'd have their home burned, like the chivving traitor cobbler."

"Were his children traitors, too?" The muscles in Ena's neck tensed. "Do you know how horrible a death flames offer? What kind of monster would do that to children?"

"Some people got too enthusiastic."

"You mean you lost control of the slitches who've decided to follow you, and they murdered a whole family." Ena dumped the rest of the petals into the wooden bowl.

"They've been disciplined."

Ena's hand froze as she reached for the pestle. "So you killed them?"

"I did what I had to do."

"Then you finally did something right." Ena pounded the pestle into the wooden bowl.

"Ena, I want what you want." Cade spoke over the thudding of Ena's work. "I want freedom for the common folk of Ilbrea. No more taxes that starve out the farmers in the south. No more watching children die when there are healers and sorcerers in this city who could help them. In aiding the Guilds, even with something as simple as ink, you betray your own people. And the time for abiding traitors has passed."

"And making a living is traitorous? So I should starve in the city as others do in the south?"

"I've told you before"—Cade placed his hand on top of Ena's, stopping her work—"I will protect you. You'll want for nothing."

Ena stared at Cade's hand on hers. "How many men in this life will offer to protect me? Do I really look like a girl who needs saving?"

"I'm giving you a chance to stop working for the paun."

"I won't have to work for the paun, just lift my skirts for you. How could anyone resist such an offer?"

"Ilbrea is changing. I'm giving you a chance to be on the winning side." Cade stepped behind her, wrapping his arms around her waist. "We are standing at the beginning of a whole new world."

"A world built on the deaths of innocent common folk?" Ena said, not flinching as Cade closed the tiny space between them. "I will see flames dance through the streets of Ilara, but I will not let them consume the thousands of tilk children who could be caught in the blaze. The paun are the ones who murder us, and you would have us crawl through common blood just like the Guilded monsters."

He pressed his hips to her back.

Pain shot through Adrial's hands as his nails dug into his palms.

Save her! Do something to save her, you coward!

"Freedom comes at a cost. If sacrificing common lives is the only way forward, so be it." Cade kissed Ena's hair.

"You must think me a child. A little girl lost in a cold, cruel city with no idea how to survive. But I've seen blood. I've seen fire. More than you'll ever live to suffer through. I've stood beside a man at the start of a new world. I watched him make speeches so great, those who followed him forgot their will to survive. I bandaged his wounds after battles and shared his bed as we plotted ways to save us all from the Guilds. I will not make that mistake again."

Cade dropped his hands to the sides of Ena's skirt, bundling the fabric in his fingers as he raised the hem. "Then you bedded a fool who didn't deserve you." He kissed the side of Ena's neck. "I will free Ilara and drive the Guilds out of our country. I will show you how a real man leads a revolution."

In one swift movement, Ena punched the pestle over her shoulder, hitting Cade in the temple.

Before he could scream, Ena had spun around, knife in her hand. The tip of her blade kissed Cade's throat.

"I don't want your protection," Ena growled. "I will not share your bed."

"You're a fool of a whore." Cade pressed his hand to the blood that trickled from his temple.

"A fool of a whore who will never have the likes of you." Ena stepped toward him, digging her knife into his neck.

"I will have you, Ena Bairn." Cade's eyes glinted in his rage. "I will free Ilbrea, and I will have you by my side."

"And I will cut your throat," Ena whispered, a smile curving the corners of her lips.

Cade pressed his throat to the blade. A drop of blood ran down his neck. "Of all the people who want me dead, I fear you the least."

"Then your revolution is worse off than I feared." Ena dug the knife in deeper.

"I'll come back for you, beautiful Ena." Cade stepped away, his tone conversational, as though he weren't bleeding from his head and neck. "When the people come after you with torches, you'll beg me to save you." He dipped his finger into the blood dripping down his neck and dragged it across Ena's lips, painting them red. "And I'll take you, Ena. You'll be my prize for saving the world." He walked halfway to the stairs before stopping. "And if I see the Guilded Cripple anywhere near you, I'll beat him before I burn him alive in the middle of the street."

Ena kept her knife in her hand as heavy footsteps thudded down the stairs, the locks thunked open, and the door slammed shut. She carried her blade with her as she ran down the steps, thunking the locks back into place.

Adrial didn't move as she walked slowly back up the stairs and straight for the basin next to the tub. She dipped a cloth into the water and wiped the blood from her lips.

"You can come out now, scribe. Just stay away from the window."

Pressing with his feet, Adrial shoved away the crate that had trapped him.

"Ena, are you all right?" He crawled to freedom, letting the cool air of the room fill his lungs.

"Me?" Ena scrubbed her lips with the cloth. "I've been through worse than that chivving slitch could ever offer."

"I shouldn't have come." Adrial dragged his hands over his face.

"I told you as much." Ena tossed the bloodstained cloth aside. "But I guess you can't be blamed since you spend too much time with paper to know what's going on in your own city."

"I'm still sorry." Adrial took Ena's hand in his, half-expecting she'd press her knife to his throat, knowing full-well he might deserve it.

Ena stepped closer to Adrial and rested her forehead on his shoulder.

He wrapped his arms gently around her. It wasn't until then that he noticed her shaking.

"Don't be sorry, scribe. If you hadn't been hiding over there, watching, I would've cut his throat. Then his men would have come for me and I'd be dead before dawn."

"We need to tell the soldiers." Adrial pressed his cheek to her hair. She still smelled of fresh winds. "They can find him and stop him."

"No." Ena stepped away and went back to her worktable. "I can't stop you from telling them what you know, but I won't say a thing."

"Why not?"

Ena wiped the specks of blood off the end of the pestle before pounding it viciously into the petals. "Because what if he really is the one to end all this? What if that slitch is the one who can get rid of the Guilds forever?"

"Is that really what you want?"

"Of course it is!" Ena slammed the wooden bowl down on the table. "I'd go hang myself outside the palace right now if I thought it would do an ounce of good toward freeing the people of Ilbrea. You survived Ian Ayres. If that's what the Guilds do to babies no man will claim, what do you think they do to farmers whose fields won't grow enough? Or to men who can't pay their taxes? You all sit in your comfortable palaces and never think that the people who grow the food on your tables might be starving.

"I hate Cade. I hate what his men have done. And if it's anything like the rebellions that have come before, it'll end with the lot of them dead and no change at all for the price of the blood spilt. But if there is even the tiniest shred of hope that Cade and his men might help the common folk, I won't be the one to stop them."

The color drained from Ena's cheeks as ferocious anger glimmered in her eyes.

"Is that what happened to the man you stood beside before?" Adrial asked. "Did he try to overthrow the Guilds and fail?"

"Trying to get enough for the Guilds to hang me? I can offer you a dozen reasons for the paun to murder me if you want a list."

"I would never let them hurt you." Adrial stepped forward,

holding both hands low as though approaching a frightened dog. "I would do anything to protect you."

"Why does everyone think I need protecting?" Ena laughed. "Like I'm not capable of choosing what's worth risking my neck for."

"I don't think you need protection, but that doesn't stop me wanting to give it."

"You're a worse fool than Cade, scribe. But I can't bring myself to hate you for it."

"Thank you."

Ena took Adrial's hands, wrapping them around her waist as she brushed her lips against his cheek. "I can forgive you for being naïve, but never ask about before. I may be strong, but I'm not strong enough for that. Finding the words would destroy me. I'd shatter, and I don't think I'd ever recover."

Adrial wrapped his arms around her and held her tight, as though the foolish notion that if he held her tightly enough he could keep her from shattering had been deemed true by Dudia Himself.

"I'll never ask."

Ena buried her head on his shoulder, finding a place where she seemed to fit perfectly.

"Promise me one more thing, scribe."

"Anything."

"When the Guilds fall, you won't give your life to try and stop it. Stay with your books, stay in the library."

"Ena—"

"The world can't afford to lose another good man. Promise you won't be fool enough to stand in front of men with swords."

Adrial tried to picture it. Cade coming with his band of angry men, all of them bearing torches as they stormed the library, determined to burn the legacy of the scribes. Murdering the people who served knowledge.

"I don't know if I can," Adrial said.

"I didn't think so." Ena pulled away from Adrial. "It was worth a try, I suppose." She picked up the mortar and pestle, pressing them into Adrial's hands. "Get to work then."

"What?" Adrial glanced down at the bowl of pulpy petals.

"I'm not going to be able to smuggle you out of here until dark, so you might as well help me work. It's a bad drop through the floor to the warehouse below, and a tiny crack to get into the water. We're in for a cold swim tonight, but there's nothing else for it."

"Will we be keeping our clothes on?" Adrial said, unable to keep a hint of humor from his tone.

"This time, scribe." Ena tossed a handful of flowers at his face. "I have enough trouble around here without any of those slitches seeing me naked."

30

MARA

She'd filled twelve scrolls as they journeyed up the glacier. Eight days they'd walked since burying Smitter in the snow.

The white will drive me to madness. Not the grief, not the pain. The white itself will end us all.

The crunch of the others following her kept Mara moving forward one step at a time, chasing the dogs who pulled the supply sleds but never seemed to tire even with their burden.

Kegan mushed the first sled, while the rest of them took it in turns to run the second.

Not run. None of us have the strength to run.

The snowshoes on her feet added effort to every step. The shoes were better than sinking into the snow pack, but Mara longed for unfrozen ground. She forced her gaze up to study every angle of the mountains they'd spent days passing between.

We should turn back.

The crushing thought came at least once an hour, making each step forward more difficult to take. The journey's orders were to map the edge of the mountains and search for signs of life, not to journey down an endless path of ice that could lead to the other side of the world.

Sheer mountainsides with no breaks surrounded them, all with peaks too high for even the best of their climbers to reach. Even Lamac seemed to know they should turn back.

But that would mean they'd climbed the cliffs for nothing. Smitter would have died for nothing.

Tham walked two steps behind her.

Mara could feel him watching her every move, keeping her safe.

If only I could hold him for a moment.

"Whoa!" Kegan shouted from the head sled. A chorus of barks followed his command as his sled slid to a stop.

"Whoa!" Elver shouted, his sled slipping as the dogs clamored to a halt. "Whoa!"

"Get them back!" Kegan said. "Move the dogs back."

"What's going on?" Mara ran as fast as her snowshoes would allow.

The dogs had stopped at the top of a rise. Whatever Kegan had kept the dogs from reaching lay hidden behind a mound of snow.

"I think we've found the place to turn back." Kegan shouted commands, ordering the lead dogs to turn the sleds around.

"We're not turning back," Lamac said. "We're farther inside the white mountains than any man has ever reached."

"Well, when you learn to fly, you can feel free to keep going," Kegan said.

Legs burning, Mara made it to the top of the rise.

Tham grabbed her arm, holding her back as the dogs pulled past, but there was nowhere for Mara to go.

Great cracks split the earth, blocking their way forward. Dazzling blue sparkled from the ice walls of the crevasse, sending the sunlight dancing in a mesmerizing way, until black swallowed the depths of the pits.

"There's no getting the dogs over that," Kegan said. "Dudia himself blocked our path."

Mara looked to the other side of the ravine more than a hundred feet away. Other cracks shot off from the gap, some large enough to swallow a person whole, others barely wide enough to slice through the layers of snow.

"We could climb around on the mountainside." Lamac pointed to the east.

The mountain rounded out to meet the cracks. While the angle of the slope was far from vertical, it would still be too much for the dogs.

"We're not going," Tham said. "We've gone as far as we can, and now we go back."

"You are not a map maker," Lamac snapped. "You are a soldier—"

"The soldiers are here to protect us," Mara said. "Even if it's from ourselves."

"We can make it!" Lamac reached toward the slope, as though wishing to embrace the mountain.

"The soldiers will not be going any farther." Tham placed himself between Mara and Lamac.

"I don't think you have the authority to decide what the soldiers will do." Rowls stepped up to the top of the rise. "I'm the second in command."

Tham took a breath before speaking. "In the city, you outrank me. But the rules on a journey are different. I've traveled with the map makers more than the rest of you combined. With Smitter gone, that gives me rank. As the ranking soldier, we aren't going."

Rowls seethed for a moment, his jaw clenching as though he were preparing to fight.

"Do you really think we could all survive that?" Mara asked. "If the snow slips, we'll fall into the crevasse. There's no point in making a map if no one survives to deliver it to Ilara."

"This is mutiny," Lamac spat.

"I don't think it is," Kegan said. "See, Mara is the same rank as you. You're meant to work as a team. I think it would only be mutiny if I told you I'm taking the dogs and leaving your slitching hide to the white if you're fool enough to try and make it around that."

"I'll bring all of you in front of the Guilds Council." Lamac pointed a trembling, gloved finger at the group that had formed behind Tham.

"Feel free to tell them it was me who stopped you," Tham said.

"Chivving cact of a slitching…" Rowls muttered. "Tell them I stood with him. I don't want it brought to the council that I got outranked."

"Let's see how far back we can get before dusk," Kegan said. "I'll bet we move faster going back. There's just a touch of a downhill."

A blue glimmer caught Mara's eye, something at the edge of the ice.

"What's that?" Elver asked, pointing to the glint Mara had seen.

"That's not just ice." A manic smile split Lamac's face. "There's something down there."

"And whatever it is can stay there," Kegan said. "Do you have any idea how fast the ice can swallow a man? About as fast as a fall can kill one."

Everyone but Lamac froze as he ran to the sleds and grabbed a long line of rope. "Tie me off. I'm going to the edge of the crevasse to see what there is."

"Lamac, don't," Mara said as he tied a knot around his stomach.

"Afraid I'll take even more of the glory?" Lamac sneered.

"Lamac!" Mara caught his arm. "There are some things in this world best left untouched."

"We're map makers." Lamac yanked his arm free, tossing the end of his rope to Edder. "It's our job to tear through the world and find all its secrets."

Rowls and Elver joined Edder on the rope as Lamac dropped to his knees, crawling to the edge of the crevasse.

"There's something moving inside the ice," Lamac called back. "A light of some sort. It must be some kind of animal, but it's moving too quickly for the ice around it to be solid."

Stop him! Aximander, stop him.

"We can report what you've seen to the council," Mara said. "You shouldn't get too close to the edge."

Lamac pulled an axe from his belt. "This is why women shouldn't be allowed into the Map Makers Guild. They're more fit for worrying like mother hens than achieving anything of value." His torso hanging over the edge of the crevasse, Lamac struck the ice with his axe. "Come on, little beast, let me grab you."

Tham took Mara's arm, drawing her back as Lamac pounded the ice again and again.

"What a beauty!" Lamac scooted back and turned to sit, holding out a chuck of ice for the party to see.

Something glowed within the ice. A bright light that was not a reflection of the sun. The thing squirmed, as though fighting to free itself, wriggling from one end of the ice to the other.

"Think they'll name it after me, lads?" Lamac laughed and held the ice over his head as a crack sounded beneath him.

Time seemed to slow as the ground split and Lamac tumbled back, disappearing into the black.

The dogs howled and barked, and the three men on the rope screamed for help.

Tham leapt onto the line, pulling with a strength the other men couldn't match.

But the ground continued to split, slices of nothing reaching toward the journey.

"Move back!" Kegan shouted, running to the dogs to keep them from bolting. "You have to move back!"

"Tham!" Mara screamed as the cracks reached Edder on the front of the rope. His feet slipped out from under him.

Rowls let go of the rope, grabbing Edder before the ice could swallow him.

"Help!" Elver screamed as the rope jerked him forward without the aid of the two other men.

"Tham!" Mara ran toward him as the line dragged Elver to the edge of the abyss. The ground split, blocking her path.

She ran along the side of the still-growing crack as Tham seized Elver around the middle, jerking him back as more of the ice crumbled into the earth.

"Get back!" Kegan bellowed from down the glacier.

Mara turned away from the gaping slice in the ice and ran toward the side of the mountain, praying the rest would have the sense to do the same.

Tham!

The need to scream for him burned past her fear for herself, but she couldn't make a sound. Couldn't risk him losing a second to look for her.

A scream carried from behind her, then another as she clawed through the ice and snow up the side of the mountain. A boulder stuck out of the slope. Mara grabbed the edge, pulling herself up onto the safety of the rock as a rumble sounded beneath her.

Something hit her in the back, driving her face first into the white as a cascade of snow tumbled on her from above.

"Tham!" Mara screamed against the noise.

A sheet of ice shook free beneath the rock, tumbling into the abyss beyond.

"I'm here." Tham arched his body, covering her head with his heart.

Mara counted as the rumbling continued, waiting for the ice to swallow them or the snow to crush them.

One, two, three.

Allora had made her play the game when she'd first come to the palace. When Mara was sure Allora and Lord Karron would disappear forever and she would get sent back to that horrible island.

Thirty-one, thirty-two, thirty-three.

Count as high as you dare and see if the world still hasn't ended.

Seventy-five, seventy-six, seventy-seven.

A little bit of control, a wager against her own daring, even if she'd never be strong enough to stop the Guilds from sending her back to Ian Ayres or keep the white from devouring her.

Ninety-three, ninety-four.

The sound stopped, as though all the noise in the world had been shut off.

Mara held her breath, waiting for Tham to move, for a sign he was all right.

"Are you hurt, Mara?" Tham's words reverberated through her.

"I'm fine." Tears burned in Mara's eyes. "Tell me you're all right and mean it."

"I'm not hurt." Tham shifted, letting Mara up.

The whiteness of it all burned her eyes as she tried to riddle out what she was seeing.

A chasm split the center of the glacier, sixty feet wide and reaching as far back as she could see. A figure huddled on the rock beneath her, sniffing back tears. Two men clung to the mountainside opposite. To the south, at the edge of the ravine, Kegan waved from the back of the dog pack.

"Who fell?" Mara asked.

"Rowls and Edder," Elver sniffed. "I saw them go."

"We have to get to the others." Mara looked to the western slope. Layers of snow had slipped away. Mara opened her mouth to shout to the others, but common sense won out. A sound could bounce between the mountains, sending a new sheet of snow tumbling down upon them.

Mara waved her hands at the two across the way.

Danny and Vance waved back to her.

Mara pointed south to Kegan. Both men nodded and turned to the slope they needed to move across.

"We're not going to make it." Tears dripped down Elver's cheeks, freezing as quickly as they formed. "There's no way this snow will hold."

"Yes it will, Elver," Mara said. "We're going to move carefully, and we'll get there just fine."

"We need to move quickly, or we won't get anywhere." Tham pointed to the sky north of them, where a bank of dark clouds gathered, overwhelming the sea of white.

The white mountains do not like our invasion.

"Right." Mara pulled off her snowshoes and clamped spikes to the toes of her boots. "Follow me then, and we'll move as fast as we can. It'll be just like climbing up, only sideways."

Mara let out a long breath as she dug her toes and axes into the packed snow.

It held out while the other sheets fell, it'll hold for you.

She sidled along one slow step at a time, her body protesting her every movement.

She chanced a glance to the side, gauging her distance to solid ground.

For one horrible moment, she thought Kegan had abandoned them. Taken the dogs and run away. Then he came back into view, pitching their tents south of the cracks in the ice and as near the side of the mountain as he could, stopping every few moments to glance at the storm that chased them.

"Dudia love that man," Mara whispered, picking up her pace as the storm clouded the sky above them.

"Dudia wants to kill us," Elver said from his place at the back of the line as snow drifted down around them.

Neither Tham nor Mara answered him.

The truth was both too simple and too much to be spoken.

There were some things in this world best left untouched, and Lamac had punched a hole into one of them.

Mara swallowed her anger as she dug her axe into the slope, pulling herself sideways.

She should have done more to stop Lamac. Lamac shouldn't have been a fool who'd refused to listen to her. The sorcerers shouldn't be so determined to keep magic outside their control hidden. Then maybe Lamac would have understood the dangers of disturbing the ice.

Snow slipped out from under Mara's axe, raining down onto her body. She froze, waiting for a great sheet of white to sweep her to her death. Her axes stayed firmly in the ice even as Tham reached for her.

"I'm fine," Mara whispered. "You and Elver go higher."

She continued sideways, keeping in front of the men, watching the slope for signs of disintegration with every move.

It really was the sorcerers at the end of it all.

The sorcerers who had rejected the first map Niko ever made because it held signs of magical places. The sorcerers who had tried to keep Mara from joining the map makers because she, too, had known magic in the wild. The sorcerers who made them all traitors by forbidding any map that showed magic outside the Lady Sorcerer's control. The ground held magic, animals held magic, the air in Ilbrea itself held magic.

How many have to die to keep their pride intact?

Mara freed her axes, lowering herself gently onto the glacier. The ice beneath her feet held firm as she switched to her snowshoes and Elver and Tham lowered themselves beside her.

The snowfall had grown harder. Mara had to squint against the swirling white to see Danny and Vance still skirting their side of the glacier.

"Keep to the edge," Mara warned Elver as they moved toward the camp.

Kegan had staked out three tents on the very edge of the ice and set up the pen for the dogs on the side of the slope. He'd pitched the two remaining tents within the boundaries of the silver stakes, with a fire already blazing in each.

"I won't let the dogs freeze," Kegan said as they reached the tents. "We're all dead without them, and it would kill my heart besides."

"I agree," Mara said as Elle bounded toward her, knocking her face into Mara's knees.

"Do you have supplies in your pack?" Kegan asked Tham and Elver.

Both nodded as Danny and Vance started across the glacier toward the camp.

"Keep to your tent until the storm passes." Kegan grabbed Elver by the back of the jacket. "Even if it's days, keep by your fire. If you leave your tent, you could freeze in the white three feet from safety or fall into the black. Stay inside!"

Kegan dragged Elver into a tent.

"Do you know what to do in a storm?" Mara raised her voice over the howling wind as Danny and Vance reached them.

"Stay inside," Danny shouted. "Or the white monster will swallow you whole."

"Saint Dannach be with you!" Vance said as both men dove into their tent.

Mara looked up toward the clouds, their gray barely visible through the sweeping snow. The storm had swallowed the sun as surely as the ice had swallowed Lamac.

"We have to go, Mara." Tham grabbed her gloved hand in his and dragged her into the tent, Elle chasing Mara's heels.

31

KAI

The salty wind whipped across Kai's face, flooding his lungs with the perfect scent of the sea. Eyes closed, he stood on the bow of the ship, feeling the faint rocking of the deck beneath his feet.

Home at last.

"This is a chivving waste of time," Drew said.

"Quiet. I'm enjoying the wind." Kai didn't open his eyes.

"A pleasure cruise now?" Drew asked. "Is that what we're going to do? Run about the Arion Sea for the fun of it?"

"We're out at sea." Kai opened his eyes, taking in the glorious sparkling of the sun off the water. "We're not trapped on the docks. We're not worrying about someone coming to burn our ship. Enjoy the time we've got out here. In a few days, we'll be back in Ilara, and you'll wish we were at sea."

"Our duty, as ordered by the King himself, is to find a way to sail through the southern storms." Drew gestured to their deep violet sail pulled taut by the wind. "The sorcerers make us a fancy new sail that even gods aren't supposed to be able to rip apart and decide we have to sail out right now to test it. Now. When there's not any sort of storm on the horizon. A lady's skirt would hold as a sail in this wind."

Kai laughed, and Drew scowled at him.

"We should be in port, finishing work on the ships to prepare to sail south. If those purple-clad, interfering slitches make us test every *improvement* they make to our ships with five days at sea, we'll be ready for the run south when Princess Illia's daughter is looking to get married." Drew puffed as though he'd just finished a fistfight.

"Done?" Kai failed to hide his smile.

Drew pounded a fist on the rail and nodded.

"The sorcerers are making all sorts of changes to the ships," Kai said. "I don't think they understand enough about ships to know if their magic will actually improve anything. They made a pretty purple sail and wanted us to test it. Lord Nevon wanted to keep the peace, so he sent us out."

"Catering to the purple lady." Drew pointed back up at the sail. "You do see we're sailing under sorcerer colors now. Not the King's gold, not the sailor blue."

Kai stared up at the sail, squinting at the light filtering through the fabric. "Lord Nevon was none too pleased by the color. They shouldn't have made it purple. But that's how it came. If the thing works, I'm sure they can make one in blue or gold. And you should be glad we're testing it. Some of the sorcerers' magic can go terribly wrong, and you wouldn't want a sail with some spell in it that pulls down lightning."

"And how are we going to know if lightning has a taste for the pretty plum sail without a storm to test it in?"

Kai took Drew by the shoulders. "I agree, but we're out here and we might as well enjoy it. A short trip in fine spring weather? What sailor can't find pleasure in that?"

"One who doesn't like being made to feel beholden to magic," Drew said.

"Aren't we all beholden to magic?" Petra Roo appeared next to them, her purple robes billowing in the breeze.

"Head Sorcerer." Kai gave a bow, kicking Drew in the ankle to make him do the same.

"Head Sorcerer." Drew's tone didn't hold the same level of neutral politeness Kai had managed.

I'll have to ask Allora to give him a lesson in dealing with slitches.

"I suppose I must be more beholden than most." Petra stepped around Kai, taking his place at the bow. "I was born in the south to a common family. If I didn't have magic in my veins, I would probably still be there. Toiling all my days to force a living from the land."

She turned back to Kai and Drew, leaning against the rail and smiling. The expression wasn't kind, but rather that of a cat preparing to pounce.

"But I was given the great gift of magic. They brought me to the Sorcerers Tower and trained me. Years of education far beyond what anyone who hasn't the gift could possibly dream up. It may seem cruel to only shower such riches of knowledge on those who are magical by providence of birth, but giving you the spells would do Ilbrea no good." She pointed from Kai to Drew. "You aren't sorcerers. It would be a waste. But"—she held a finger in the air—"my magic does do Ilbrea good. The sorcerers forge the weapons that keep Ilbrea strong. The sorcerers build things that would be impossible by any other means."

Sparks of light appeared around Petra's finger, zinging in and out of existence.

"The sorcerers heal when all normal means fail. The sorcerers guide and protect the King and all Ilbrea. We are the ones to make sure famine doesn't kill the land."

"Really?" Drew said. "From what I've heard, there isn't very much food in the southern farmlands. Maybe we should steer the ship there and you can magic those poor common folk more crops."

With a smirk, Petra flicked her finger. A bright light burst from her hand, streaking toward the sail. The bolt of lightning struck the fabric.

Kai's lungs seized with fear, sure the whole ship would burst into flames.

But the material absorbed the force of the strike, sending a shimmer through the sail.

Cheers and clapping chorused around the ship.

Petra gave a nod and a wave to the crew before continuing. "See what we've given you? I don't blame you for your bitterness. Jealously is only natural when you've been born with no talent save the ability to pull a rope. You see the world from your place close to the ground, only capable of knowing the next tiny step on your insignificant journey. From the top of the tower, we see all. A path to a greater Ilbrea you cannot even begin to comprehend.

"You have been given the honor of being aboard the first ship with a spellbound sail." Petra's smile returned. "What a great voyage this is for the Sailors Guild! These few days at sea are an important step for the fleet of Ilbrea. Soon, all ships will carry sorcerer-made sails. All ships will be capable of sailing around the horn, a voyage you could hardly even dream of accomplishing without the assistance of the Sorcerers Guild."

"I am sure we're all very grateful for the sorcerers helping us in accomplishing the task laid out by the King." Kai forced the words to sound conversational, though his jaw was clenched so tight he could barely speak.

"We in the tower have unfortunately grown used to outsiders not appreciating our gifts as they should. But—" Petra clapped her hands.

A scream sounded from the deck. Kai spun to see what was wrong. The man screaming hadn't been struck by a bolt of the sorcerer's magic. Instead, he stared up in horror at the sail.

The fabric curled in on itself, narrowing until the purple was nothing more than a strip barely wider than a rope.

The speed of the ship slowed as the captain ran up onto the deck.

"Never forget, the gifts the sorcerers give can just as easily be taken away." Petra clapped her hands again, and the sail unfurled, catching the wind and pulling the ship forward with a jerk. "Sailor Saso, you are the captain's second on this voyage?"

"Yes," Kai answered through gritted teeth.

"Wonderful," Petra said. "I actually need to speak to you and the captain. I'm sure he won't mind seeing the two of us in his cabin. And you"—she smiled at Drew—"I thought being a deckhand was meant to be a busy job. Haven't you something to clean?"

Kai stepped in front of Drew before he could respond. "I'm sure the captain would be pleased to see you. After that magic show with the sail, he must be very intrigued to see what else the sorcerers have planned."

"Wonderful." Petra took Kai's arm as if they were going for a stroll. "But I've never liked the term *magic show*."

"And what is your preferred term, Head Sorcerer?" Kai asked.

"Demonstration of power."

"Sorcerer Roo, what happened to the sail?" the captain asked before they'd gotten within twenty feet of him.

"I apologize for any alarm, captain." Petra let go of Kai's arm, walking straight toward the captain's cabin. "Sailor Saso required a demonstration of the attributes of the new sail."

The captain glanced at Kai, who gave the tiniest shake of his head, before following Petra into the cabin.

The deep wood of the walls absorbed the afternoon sun, leaving the room dim. Maps of the Arion seacoast covered one wall while the Ilbrean seven-pointed star marked the other.

Petra stood in front of the captain's desk, blocking him from sitting in his own chair.

"I think we need a better test of the sail," Petra declared without preamble.

"Well, as you've demonstrated you can make it useless to us without warning or cause," the captain said, "I think we should bring our report back to the council as soon as possible."

"What report?" Petra asked. "The sails were designed to be stowed easily in case of emergency at the wisdom of the King and by the power of the Lady Sorcerer. I'm sure they'll be pleased to know it went so smoothly, but I don't think it worthy of a report. What we need is to head south and test the sail in the conditions it's been designed to conquer."

"Our orders are to take a five-day sail and head back to Ilara." The captain's jaw barely moved as he spoke.

"We'll only be gone for, what, an extra ten days or so if we wish to kiss the southern storms with the sail?" Petra said.

"Our orders came from Lord Nevon himself. I have no intention of disobeying the Lord Sailor."

"You needn't worry about disobedience." Petra waved a flippant hand through the air. "I'm perfectly willing to give you the order to sail south. If there's any trouble, I'll accept full responsibility."

"But you see"—the captain gave a small bow—"I am the captain of this ship, the ranking officer on board. You don't have the authority to give any orders at all."

Kai gripped his hands behind his back, barely resisting clapping the captain on the shoulder.

Petra stood, meandering over to the map. "This ship is equipped with oars, correct?"

"Yes," the captain said.

"We're about here, aren't we?" Petra pointed to the map. "How long would it take to row back to Ilara from where we are right now?"

"A while," the captain said.

"Longer than to sail down, touch the storm, and run right home?" Petra asked.

"Yes."

"Then I suggest you sail south." Petra smiled. "Or you might find rowing to be your only option."

"Are you threatening to take down our sail?" the captain growled.

"Not threatening, no. I'm simply offering you a choice."

"This is mutiny," Kai said. "You'll be jailed for interfering with the course of this voyage."

"You call it interference. I call it ensuring productivity." Petra dusted off her hands as though she'd dirtied them by touching anything in the captain's quarters. "You don't have a place you can contain me. You don't have a sail I can't control. Therefore, you will do as I say and sail south."

"I will have you brought before the council for this," the captain said.

"Please do." Petra headed for the door. "We stand at the brink of change. The sailors need magic to succeed. For too long the sorcerers have sat idly by, giving you gifts and saying nothing when you fail to utilize them for the good of Ilbrea. That unfortunate era has gone."

"We don't need sorcerer help to sail our ships." The captain stepped in front of the door. "We can do it all on our own."

"Make it through the storms to the southern islands with any sort of reasonable consistency?" Petra laughed.

Pain shot through Kai's jaw as he bit back the words he longed to shout.

"Make trade runs around the Horn quickly enough to allow real commerce? I don't think you can, and neither does the King," Petra said. "All ships will soon be equipped with sorcerer-made sails, and all royal voyages accompanied by sorcerers. Now get out of my way, *captain*. I need to observe the running of the ship. Very soon, it will be the sorcerers who command the voyages."

The captain froze, seeming to teeter on the edge of rage, before stepping aside and letting Petra open the door.

"Do enjoy your cabin while you can," Petra called over her

shoulder. "You'll have to vacate it on the next voyage for the sorcerer in charge."

The door slammed shut behind her.

"That evil, horrible," Kai fumed as the captain went to his desk, "chivving cact of a slitching paun."

The captain opened his desk drawer, pulling out a bottle of frie and two glasses. "Sounds about right."

"How dare she think she can give orders on this ship!" Kai spat. "And the Sorcerers Guild trying to usurp the power of the Sailors Guild?"

The captain pressed a glass into Kai's hand.

Kai took a sip, letting the heat of the drink singe the edges of his rage.

"It would destroy the sanctity of the Guilds," Kai said. "Each of the Guilds controls its own people. Even the King can't interfere with the inner workings of a Guild without agreement from the council. And that hasn't happened since the rebellion of the scribes four hundred years ago."

Kai paused, waiting for the captain to jump in with a tirade of his own.

"Sit, Kai." The captain sank into his own chair.

Legs shaking, Kai followed suit.

They sat in silence for a long moment, Kai clinging to his glass almost to the point of crushing it, the captain staring into the depths of his frie as though looking for the secrets of time herself.

"Can you honestly say you're surprised?" the captain asked.

Kai didn't look at the captain as he answered. "No."

"They've wanted control for years." The captain downed the rest of his glass. "They imply it at every council meeting. How they could help with *this*, relieve the stress of doing *that*. With the 777th anniversary coming, it's the perfect opportunity. So many things to be done, so many ways to be useful."

"So many ways to stick their fingers into every pie in the

kingdom." Kai drank the rest of his frie in one burning gulp. "We can't let it happen, captain."

"We won't," the captain said. "I'd rather burn than be a slave to the purple lady."

"Then what do we do?" Kai leaned forward, the promise of a plan raising a bubble of purpose above his anger.

"Do as she says for now." The captain leaned back in his seat. "We can't row the ship back, that's for sure. If I weren't afraid of being hanged for murder, I'd shove the lady overboard."

"I wouldn't mind doing it," Kai said.

"I won't see you hanged either, Kai. We'll play along for now, and when we get home, we'll make sure those purple beasts never lay hands on one of our ships again." The captain stood, slamming his empty glass on the desk. "Come, Kai. Let's find some rough seas and see how ill we can make the violet paun."

ADRIAL

You know I wouldn't bother you, but it's horribly important to the Princess. Please ask your wild little inker girl to come meet me. I promise to keep a civil tongue if she promises not to bite. If you were to believe Princess Illia, this is practically averting a terrible war that will rip apart all Ilbrea.

Thank you, sweet Adrial,

Allora

Adrial stared down at the letter on his desk. Allora's tidy scrawl sent fear stabbing through his gut, which made it utterly impossible to concentrate on the vellum.

He had the ink now—the perfect blue with a hint of pink for the Ilbrean sky—but he couldn't do a damned thing with it.

Ena would be safe getting to him. She'd sent a note with a flea-ridden boy, saying to keep the back door unlocked and tell the guards not to hang her.

It was the very thought of Ena and Allora in the same room that shook his hands too badly to work. Adrial looked to the three teacups in the corner, grinning at the thought of what Ena would say to such fancy china.

"They'll tear each other apart." Adrial pinched the bridge of his nose. "It'll be a miracle if Ena doesn't pull a knife."

"Head Scribe, sir," Taddy called from the outer office, the sternness in his tone enough to tell Adrial Ena hadn't decided to use the front door. "There's a lady to see you."

"Thank you, Taddy." Adrial grabbed Allora's letter, tucking it into his pocket as the door swung open.

"Adrial." Allora held both hands out to him as she entered the room. "Thank you for helping me, for helping the Princess, really."

Taddy stood in the doorway, staring at Allora as she kissed Adrial's cheek.

"You can go, Taddy," Adrial said.

The boy jumped a bit as though he hadn't realized he'd been gaping open-mouthed at the Lady of the Map Makers Guild.

"Don't let anyone else in without asking," Adrial added as Taddy swung the door closed.

"Is this what you've been working on?" Allora tucked her hands behind her back as she examined the pages.

"Yes," Adrial said. "A wedding gift fit for a princess."

"You really are quite remarkable," Allora said. "I've always known it, but it is nice to see it laid out where it's impossible for anyone to deny."

"Thank you, Allora." Adrial pulled himself up to stand as straight as he could as she examined him.

"To think the little orphan who hid in a cupboard turned into the head scribe," Allora sighed. "I'm just so amazingly proud of you."

"Proud of me?" Adrial turned to the tea tray, unable to look Allora in the eye as she praised him. "Aren't you the little girl who climbed into the cupboard to teach the little boy how to read?"

"It was a very clean cupboard." Allora lifted the teapot from Adrial's hand, pouring two cups and mixing in the spices. "Is the girl coming?"

"*Ena?*" Adrial emphasized her name. "Probably."

"Unreliable and intrusive?" Allora sipped her tea through pursed lips.

"It's not easy for her to come to the Guilded parts of town," Adrial said. "If you haven't noticed, working for the Guilds isn't safe at the moment. If she's seen coming in, they could hurt her."

"You like her." Allora tipped her head to the side. "You're not just giving me a lecture on ignoring the plight of the common people. You're worried about the little inker girl because you care for her."

Heat rose in Adrial's cheeks. "Ena is strong, and brave, an incredibly talented inker, and kind. And—"

A tiny laugh carried from the corner by the window, which had somehow been opened.

Ena stood beneath, leaning against the wall, arms crossed and biting back a smile. "Please don't let me interrupt you, scribe. I do love hearing how wonderful I am, though I'm not sure you've the right girl with the *kind* part."

"Ena," Adrial spoke over Allora's, "How did she get in here?"

"I know I told you to leave the back door open." Ena pushed away from the wall, heading straight to Adrial and completely ignoring Allora. "But it didn't occur to me there would be an entire pack of soldiers prowling about. I didn't feel like chatting up a horde of black-clad paun to get in here."

Allora gasped at the word *paun.*

Ena took the tea from Adrial's hand, staring Allora down as she took a sip. "You didn't make it today." Ena wrinkled her nose and passed the teacup back to Adrial.

"Allora made the tea." Adrial set the cup back on the tray.

"Pity." Ena went to the table, examining Adrial's work. "You should add a darker blue to the edges of the sky."

"Allora—" Adrial began.

"Lady Karron," Allora corrected.

"Lady Karron," Adrial began again over Ena's laugh, "is here to ask for your help."

"My help." Ena spun to face Adrial. "My help?" She shifted her glare to Allora, her gaze moving slowly from Allora's perfect blond plait to her deep green dress. "And what can someone like me do for the Lady Map Maker?"

"It's more for the Princess," Allora said.

Ena laughed again and moved back to the tea tray, placing the empty cup into Adrial's hand.

Adrial turned to the teapot to pour a fresh cup, grateful for the excuse to look away from the women.

"And what can a common inker do for Her Highness?" Ena asked.

They're going to kill each other. I've just sentenced them both to death.

"I'm sure you've heard of Princess Illia's engagement to Prince Dagon of Wyrain," Allora said.

"I heard they sold the poor child to a man she's never met," Ena said.

Adrial added a dash of sugar to the tea, mixing the granules in as slowly as he could.

"The Princess is thrilled with her engagement," Allora said, her voice tight. "She has been writing to Prince Dagon. It is her desire to embrace her future home. She wants ink in the colors of Wyrain's flag with which to write her letters."

Adrial pressed the cup into Ena's hands.

"Thank you, scribe." Ena took a slow sip, staring at Allora.

"From what I've been told," Allora said, "you should be able to match the colors for the Princess."

Ena continued to stare.

"She can match anything," Adrial said. "She's made all the ink for the vellum."

"Then it should be easy work for her." Allora gave a pinched smile. "The Princess is, of course, willing to pay. And she specifically requested the ink be made by the one working on her vellum."

Ena took another sip of tea.

"However, if you don't think you're up to the task—"

"Did she come here to ask me to make three colors of ink?" Ena looked to Adrial.

"Yes." Adrial widened his eyes, willing Ena to agree and be done with it.

"She came all the way down here to ask me to make violet, gold, and emerald ink any northern chivving inker could have made?"

"The Princess wants them to be an exact match. She wanted it made by the best, which I've been told you are." Allora glared at Adrial.

"She is the best," Adrial said.

"Then there's one thing we can all agree on." Ena went to the table, pulling little jars of ink from her pocket. "I've brought what you should need for the next bit, scribe. Even the deep blue to finish your sky." She held a bottle of dusky blue ink up to the light. "Is there anything else you want?"

"A red," Adrial said. "An orangish-red."

Ena stepped forward, holding her arms out for Adrial to search the plethora of colors that adorned her skirt.

"Couldn't you just…" Adrial's words faded away as Ena smirked at him. "Right."

Ena turned in a slow circle.

"There." Adrial pointed to a patch on the backside of her hip.

Ena looked over her shoulder, raising an eyebrow at Adrial.

"This one." Adrial touched the patch that seemed so like burning coals that, for a childish moment, he thought he might burn his finger.

"I'll have it for you in a few days." Ena winked. "I'll take the coin for this lot and be back out the window if you don't mind."

"What about the Princess's ink?" Allora stepped forward.

"What about it?" Ena took Adrial's money pouch and shoved it into her pocket.

"Well, are you going to be a proper citizen of Ilbrea who serves the crown and the Guilds or not?"

Allora froze as Ena stepped toward her, looking for all the Guilds like a wolf set to attack.

"A proper citizen," Ena whispered, "who helps you sell a child's future, shoves her out of her home to land in a stranger's arms when her country is about to burn? A proper citizen who risks her neck to help paun scum like you push the child to it?" She stopped, her face so close to Allora's, it looked as though she might kiss her. "I will never be a proper citizen of your Guilds, Lady Paun. I'd rather starve than serve slitches like you."

Ena strode to the back door, flinging it open. "I'd thought better of the company you keep, scribe."

"Ena, wait!" Adrial shouted, running after her as fast as his leg would allow. "Ena!"

She didn't stop as she stormed through the back hall and onto the narrow street beyond.

"Adrial!" Allora called after him.

"Ena, please stop!"

The soldiers at the end of the alley glanced back.

Ena didn't turn but slowed her pace enough to let Adrial catch her arm.

"Ena, please," Adrial whispered. "I'm sorry for Allora. She doesn't mean—"

"Don't you dare make excuses for that paun who thinks you're her pet," Ena spat, still refusing to look at Adrial.

"You won't have to deal with her at all," Adrial said. "Make the ink for me, and I'll pay triple the regular rate."

"Triple?" Ena spun to face him so fast her hair slapped him across the cheek. "It took me three hours to cut far enough around not to be caught bringing you ink today. You know full well what would have happened if they'd seen me coming to you."

"I know," Adrial said. "I was terrified you'd be caught."

"But you want me to make ink for the Princess?"

"I'm sorry," Adrial begged as Ena yanked her arm from his grasp. "I'll send her away. You'll never hear of it again."

"Not good enough." Ena looked over Adrial's shoulder.

Adrial glanced back.

Allora stood in the doorway, glowering at the two of them, looking more like Lord Karron than Adrial had ever seen her.

"I don't have to come back here," Ena said. "I'll earn my living somewhere else."

"I'll find a safer way for you to deliver the ink." Adrial's mind raced. "I can meet you outside the city."

"Nowhere in Ilbrea is safe."

"I'll do anything," Adrial said. "I swear to you I will. Please, whatever you want."

A dangerous glint sparked in Ena's eyes.

"What?"

"Kiss me."

Adrial's heart stopped for a moment as he tried to understand the two simple words Ena had spoken. "Sorry?"

"Kiss me." Ena stepped forward. "You want me to keep risking my neck for you, then kiss me."

"I—I can't." Adrial's heart raced.

"You want to." Ena laid her hands on the front of his robes. "You've wanted to since the first time you saw me."

Surely, his heart would explode from beating so impossibly quickly. "Ena, no."

She leaned in, brushing her cheek against his, pressing her chest to his.

Heat surged through Adrial's body. He was going to catch fire. He would burn from the inside out.

"If you don't kiss me now, you'll never see me again. I'll disappear, and you won't find me. You'll spend your whole life wondering what happened to the rotta inker girl." Ena stepped back, a smile curling her perfect mouth. "Goodbye, scribe."

Adrial seized her waist, pulling her back to him, pressing his lips to hers.

All Ilbrea stopped as he tasted the sweetness of her lips. As she twined her fingers through his hair, pulling herself closer.

A wolf-whistle sounded from the end of the alley as Adrial wrapped his arms around Ena, molding his body against hers.

Dudia save me.

Ena pulled away, brushing her lips gently against his. She kept her fingers twined through his hair as she rested her forehead against Adrial's.

Adrial took her waist in his hands, trying to memorize the feel of her.

"I'll make your ink, but not for the Lady Paun. I'm doing it for the poor child in case it can bring her a happier life after being sold." Ena stepped back, shooting a wink over Adrial's shoulder. "It'll be five times the normal rate or nothing. The silver Princess can afford it."

Ena strolled out of the alley, waving at the soldiers who smiled gapingly as she passed.

Follow her. Follow her so she'll never leave.

Adrial turned at a *tsch* from behind him.

Allora stood in the doorway, her face having transformed from Lord Karron's collected anger to Mara's all out rage.

Adrial swallowed as the joy inside him flickered away.

Allora turned without a word and disappeared into the shop.

"Allora," Adrial called after her, chasing her as quickly as he could. "Allora."

"She's common," Allora stormed, pacing the small length of Adrial's workroom.

"Allora—"

"She kissed you to be cruel to me." Allora stomped to the back door, shutting it with unladylike force.

"I'm sure you don't care who I kiss." Adrial reached for a cup of tea before stopping. He wasn't ready to lose the taste of Ena's lips.

"I care about everything you do because I adore you." Allora flapped her hands through the air. "I care if someone hurts you. Adrial"—she took his shoulders—"do you think that mad excuse for a woman cares for you?" Allora's eyes widened, and she dropped her chin. "I don't say it to be cruel. You're worthy of the love and adoration of a thousand women, but she'll hurt you. She is as wild as a deathly storm. Women like that aren't meant for men like you."

"She doesn't care for me," Adrial said slowly, waiting for one of his words to sting. "Not in the way you mean. I don't know if she can. But she trusts me, and she doesn't hate me, and I think that's as much as she can give."

"So nothing at all." Allora let go of Adrial.

"It's enough for me."

"She will hurt you, Adrial. No matter what you say."

"I'm not afraid of pain, Allora. I've felt it all before."

NIKO

"But have you ever heard of a person switching Guilds?" Amec asked, walking so close on Niko's heels, the soldier kicked the back of the map maker's ankles every fifth step. "I mean to say if a person joined one Guild, and found themselves better suited to another, and knew there would be years of work ahead but were willing to do it—if all those things happened, do you think a person could change Guilds?"

Niko leapt up onto a boulder, moving his ankles out of harm's way. "I've never heard of such a thing, but I'm not really the one to ask. I'm a map maker, not an expert in Guild law."

Amec's shoulders sank.

"I have heard of soldiers spending most of their careers guarding map makers' journeys, though."

Amec stood a little straighter at Niko's words.

"It's not an easy life," Niko added. "This journey has been comfortable and calm compared to most I've been on. Stay with the map makers long enough, and you'll learn to hate the sight of fire trays and tents. You won't find the glory of battle tramping through the wild either."

"I've never been one for glory." Amec shook his head. "I like the woods better than the training fields, and I don't know as I could raise a sword to anyone who wasn't threatening my mother's life."

Niko swallowed his laugh at the soldier's earnest speech. "Make it through this journey first. If you still want to be a soldier assigned to the map makers, I'll put in a word with Lord Karron."

Amec beamed at Niko like he was Saint Aximander himself.

"I can't guarantee it will get you the assignment you want." Niko held up a hand to stop Amec's thanks. "But I'll put in a word, and that's the best to be done."

"I won't disappoint you, Niko." Amec looked as though he might do a jig. "I'll earn your recommendation, I promise you that."

"Good." Niko looked out onto the vista, hiding the smirk on his face.

Too well he remembered his joy at joining the Map Makers Guild, desperate to see the world and make maps to be cherished by the ages.

A wide valley reached up to the foothills of the mountains. Far beyond, the terrain changed as the farmers who braved the land nearest the eastern mountains tended their fields. Even from a distance too great to make out the houses Niko knew must be there, he could see the marks on the terrain the farmers had made. Clearing out trees, planting crops instead of letting the grass and flowers grow wild.

"Do you think any of them have been this high up in the mountains?" Amec asked.

"Almost certainly."

"Even with all the legends of bandits and ghosts roaming the forest?"

"Myths of danger lurking in the shadows would make the climb more alluring to some." Niko studied the base of the foothills, searching for signs of a frequented trail. "People have lived in this region as long as there have been men in Ilbrea. Someone's come to these woods before. They just didn't bring a map maker with them."

"Niko!" a voice shouted from the south. "Niko, I think we've found a path."

"Just a moment." Niko spent another minute staring at the line of trees that edged the mountains, memorizing the arc of the woods as they reached out toward the fields, feeling the tickle of magic as the map at his hip filled itself with new details.

"Should we set up camp here?" Tarrum laughed. "Let you spend a whole afternoon staring at trees?"

"Staring at trees is my job." Niko jumped down from the boulder and cut through the thick forest toward Tarrum's voice. "And if this path is anything like the other three you've found this morning, then there's nothing but deer awaiting us. A game trail doesn't interest the King."

"We haven't discovered anything at all to interest the King," Tarrum said as Niko spotted him through the trees. "Certainly not another path to Wyrain. Unless we convince the sorcerers to make flying carriages and train mountain goats to pull them."

"Fair enough." Niko didn't have to ask what path Tarrum thought he had found.

Tarrum and Jerick stood on either side of a bare streak of earth wide enough for two men to walk side by side.

"I don't think this one looks like a game trail," Jerick said smugly.

"You're quite right." Niko knelt, running his fingers through the dirt of the trail.

The earth was dryer than it should have been. The soil of the mountains was rich enough to keep forests growing on its sweeping slopes with deep roots to anchor the trees in the vicious winds of winter.

"A lot of people must have walked this trail to leave it so bare." Amec knelt next to Niko, copying his movements.

"Indeed." Niko peered into the trees above and below the trail.

Down the slope, grass and moss encroached on the sides of the barren dirt. Up the mountain, the path stayed wide as it cut straight through the trees. From the look of it, no vegetation had even attempted to grow on the path. Rather, the plants had left the barren strip alone.

A knot of fear settled in Niko's throat at the exact same moment excitement leapt in his heart.

"We should turn back." Niko stood, carefully brushing the dirt off his hands.

"But we've found a trail," Tarrum said.

"If this many people have traveled it, surely there must be something worth getting to." Excitement danced in Amec's eyes.

"My best guess would be a pond or some other source of fresh water clinging to the side of the mountain." Niko kept his eyes on the dirt on his hands. "But if we follow it up, we might not make it back to camp tonight, and that's the plan we gave Rollands this morning."

"And you're afraid Rollands might worry himself sick over his babes lost in the scary wood?" Tarrum barked out a laugh.

"We can come back tomorrow prepared to spend the night if needed," Niko said.

After I've had time to think.

"But it might lead to something just out of sight." Amec bounced on the balls of his feet. "It could be just through those trees. Shouldn't we at least follow the path for a while?"

He would have done well as a map maker.

"I'm not worried about sleeping a night in the woods if it comes to it," Jerick said, "but I am tired of climbing this chivving mountain every day. We've only just gotten up the beast, and we can't do anything else until we've followed this trail. I don't fancy going straight back down before we've seen if this path is useful."

"I agree," Tarrum said. "Best to see what we can see and not waste the hours we've spent scaling this monster since dawn."

Niko's mind raced for a moment, trying to find a good reason to leave the trail. But the men were right.

"We'll follow it a ways," Niko said, "but when it comes time to go back to camp, we're turning back and trying again tomorrow when we're better prepared."

"That's the way of it!" Amec turned up the trail as though ready to bolt into the trees.

"I'll head up first," Niko said. "If there are marks on the trail to tell us who uses it, we can't risk disturbing them."

"Anything you say, map maker," Amec said. "I'm right on your heels."

"Not literally, please," Niko said.

The trail stayed wide enough for two to stand side by side as they followed it up the mountain. The unnatural dryness of the dirt didn't change.

If you could only pour water onto the dust.

It would be the simplest way to test the dirt. If the soil stayed dry, his journey had undoubtedly stumbled upon some sort of magic. If the trail turned to mud, they had found a path someone tread almost daily.

If it was the latter, this might be the break they'd been searching for these past four weeks. If it was the former, then the last thing he needed was three soldiers walking right behind him.

Aximander, let it be nothing. And if it is something, give me the presence of mind to steer them away from it.

"If we discover a way across, will they name something after you?" Amec asked. "Will we have Niko's Peak?"

"If it's something truly amazing, they might give me the honor of a namesake," Niko said. "Though I'm assuming the Lord Map Maker might want to be a bit more formal, maybe Endur Mountain." A flutter of pride tickled Niko's chest. To have a mountain named after him…

"I'm not sure if we've just found your wildest dream or a pile of stones," Tarrum said.

Niko's hopeful pride crumpled and shattered.

Four giant slabs of rock sat before them, forming three stone walls and a stone roof. The chest-high, covered space was big enough for one large man to lie down in and not get pelted by rain.

"What is it?" Amec strode past Niko, leaning in close to the stones. "You don't suppose someone lives here, do you?"

"Can't." Jerick peered into the space. "Nothing in there to keep warm or comfortable. No bedding, not even straw. If someone lived here, it was a very long time ago."

"But if no one's been here, why is the trail worn down?" Amec asked. "Niko, hold your fancy light in there."

"We can see in there perfectly well." Niko shook his head. "It looks like a long-abandoned shelter to me. Animals must be using it."

"There's no tracks for animals." Jerick bent double as though about to walk right in. "Come on, shine a light in the corners. Maybe something's been left behind."

"Go on, Niko." Amec beamed with excitement.

Dudia, I know I'm not the most faithful. But let us find nothing, and I'll do better. I'll be kinder and better. I'll be more faithful and never curse again.

Niko pulled the criolas from its pouch. Even in the midday sun, the orb shone brightly.

"I'll crawl in first," Niko said. "If a monster slithers out of the shadows, send my love to the Queen."

Niko held his light in front of him as he ducked beneath the stone roof.

Bare gray rock surrounded him.

Niko let out a sigh of relief. "Whoever built this thing is long gone, and it doesn't lead to Wyrain."

"Niko!"

Niko swiveled toward Amec, bashing his head on the stone roof.

Lights danced in front of Niko's eyes as he looked to Amec, who'd ducked into the space and crouched, pointing at the wall.

Niko blinked, trying to get the spots out of his eyes. But the glittering grew every moment, sparkling and shimmering in waves across the stone as distinct patterns formed something like letters in a language Niko couldn't read.

"What is this place?" Amec whispered.

"It wasn't built for sleeping, that's for sure." Tarrum leaned into the entryway. "This is sorcerer work."

"If it's sorcerer work, then why isn't it marked on any maps?" Jerick asked. "Unless it is and our Niko didn't bother to check."

"Of course he checked," Amec said.

The text expanded, moving from one slab to the next, each new letter glowing a glittering blue.

"This isn't on any maps." Niko hovered his fingers over the writing. A vague warmth radiated from the inscriptions.

Magic.

"Maybe it was a rogue sorcerer." Amec followed Niko's motions, holding his fingers close to the letters.

"There's no such thing as a rogue sorcerer," Jerick said. "All magic in Ilbrea is held by the Sorcerers Guild."

"Then why did the Sorcerers Guild build something up the side of an unnamed mountain?" Tarrum asked, skepticism filling his voice.

The letters reached the end of the other wall.

How much is written on these stones? What lost knowledge did someone try so desperately to hide or preserve?

Adrial would know how to read it, but without recording every symbol on the scroll that held his true map, there was no way to get the writing to Adrial, and if the sorcerers found him with that writing, how steep would the penalty be?

A shiver of cold wound around Niko's neck, as though he could already feel the noose that would be his end.

"We should leave this be," Niko said. "We tell no one back at camp what we've found. I'll bring it to the Sorcerers Guild myself when we return to Ilara."

"But the others would be thrilled to hear about this," Amec said. "We've been out here for four weeks, and the most exciting thing we've found is the old spring I fell into."

"We can't risk word of this spreading." Niko tucked his criolas back into its pouch. "What if someone disturbs the site? We tell no one until the sorcerers release the location."

"Look at this." Amec ignored Niko and pointed at the back wall.

In the center of the writing, a circle shone, drawing light from all the unreadable words around it.

"Shouldn't the writing have faded when you put away your criolas?" Jerick took a step back.

The circle devoured more of the light, adding to its own brightness.

"But it's magic." Amec leaned closer to the stones. "Things don't have to make sense with magic. That's why we're never supposed to talk about it. We don't understand what the sorcerers do, so we'd just get it all wrong." Amec reached toward the blue circle of light as it grew brighter still. A pulse echoed through the glow, as though it were alive. "What sort of wonder could do all this?"

"Amec, don't!" Niko shouted a moment too late.

Amec's fingers grazed the stone.

A rumble cracked under Niko's feet. He opened his mouth to scream, "Run!" but the word never made it out.

The ground beneath him split. Darkness swallowed him. Before true fear could seize him, he hit hard ground. The impact knocked the wind from his lungs. He flung his arms over his head, protecting himself from the mountain of earth that would surely crash down on him.

But the pain of being crushed by stone didn't come.

A single crack shook the air before everything around him

froze.

Niko lay in place for a moment, willing breath to return to his body and his heart to start beating a rhythm that would allow coherent thought.

"Hello," a voice sounded in the dark by Niko's head. "Is...is anyone else—"

"I'm here, Amec." Niko's hand shook as he reached for the criolas pouch on his belt.

"Praise to Saint Dannach," Amec coughed. "Jerick, Tarrum, you all right?"

Silence filled the darkness as Niko fumbled the light from its pouch. "Jerick, Tarrum, sound off!"

Blue light filled the space. Stone surrounded them.

"Where are they?" Amec stood, swaying as he searched the shadows.

Niko didn't stand. He didn't need to. There wasn't anywhere for them to search.

A solid stone ceiling above solid stone walls stretched into the distance on one side. And on the other side, where they had just fallen into the darkness, a slanted slab of stone blocked their path.

"They're not here," Amec said. "Did they get crushed by the rock? Help me, Niko." Amec dove toward the slanted slab, knocking his shoulder into the stone. He cried out in pain, but the thing wouldn't budge. "Jerick, Tarrum!"

"They might not have fallen through." Niko pushed himself to his feet and ran his fingers along the edge of the stone. Fresh earth caught in the corners, making Niko sure this was the way they'd gotten into the tunnel, but there was no break in the rock to mark a way out. "They might still be aboveground. They were outside the rocks when we fell. They're probably standing up there right now, screaming for us and trying to find a way to get us out." Niko pressed his criolas to the stone, hoping against hope the light would work some magic and set them free.

"Then we should just wait here." Amec's voice trembled as he spoke. "Wait here, and they'll let us out."

"Right." Niko traced his hand along the bottom of the stone slab. Moisture greeted the tips of his fingers.

"What if they did fall through?" Amec asked.

The moisture was warmer than the earth. Deep red mixed in with the soil on Niko's fingers.

"Niko, what if the stone fell on them and crushed them?"

Niko wiped away the blood with the inside of his sleeve.

"We'll just have to wait for them." Niko unhooked his pack and sat against the smooth stone wall. "Just settle in and wait."

MARA

Tham's chest rose and fell under Mara's head, keeping a steady rhythm even as the wind whipped the sides of their tent.

Elle lay curled up on Mara's feet inside the layers of blankets they'd cobbled together to share. The weight of the dog numbed her feet, but it was better than the biting cold.

The flames of the fire tray licked the air, not caring how long it had burned. How long they'd been stuck in the tent.

I don't even know how long it's been.

The light hadn't changed through the storm. Day and night had disappeared in a sea of waiting.

Squeezing her eyes shut, Mara tried to imagine she'd found her way back to Ilara. She was safe in her bed, Tham beside her. A fire crackled in the fireplace. The sun would rise to bring the morning...

And Tham would leave.

Mara bit her lip, pushing back the tears that threatened to spill onto Tham's chest.

You brought him into this. If he freezes in the storm, it will be your fault.

A gust of wind smacked the sides of the tent.

Elle whimpered and squirmed at Mara's feet.

"Hush, dog," Tham murmured, pulling Mara closer to his chest, tucking the top of her head back into the warmth of the blankets.

Elle whimpered again, wiggling her way up to hide behind Mara's knees.

The three of them lay in silence for a moment, waiting for the wind to return to its usual pummeling of the tent.

"We're going to make it," Tham said. "Past the storm, back to Ilara. We'll make it through."

"Because we're Karrons," Mara laughed. The tiny movement pushed a bit of the cold away.

"No," Tham said. "Because we're together."

"We're together because I dragged you out here. You should be home in Ilara."

"Going south to demand the farmers pay their taxes? I'd be terrible at that."

"You'd be safe." Mara kissed Tham's chin. "You wouldn't be freezing in a storm."

"It's not so bad in here." Tham pressed his cheek to the top of Mara's head. "The tent is strong, the fire is magic, and we've food to last."

"And if the storm never ends?"

"All storms end. You only have to be brave enough to wait them out."

They lay in silence for a long while.

"If anything happens to you, the guilt will chase me into death itself."

"I made my choice, Mara. Better to suffer the storm with you than savor the sun without. Don't make me so small as to take my choice away."

"I love you." Mara wrapped her arms around him as tightly as she could. "More than all the stars ever made."

"Sleep, my love." Tham kissed her forehead. "I'm with you through the storm."

Tham hummed a tune. One she'd heard him hum before, though he said he didn't remember the words that went along with it. His chest rumbled with each note, dampening the wail of the wind.

Before he'd made it to the end, Mara had drifted to sleep.

Kareen will find you, a voice whispered in Mara's dream. *Through the snow of the dead, she'll find you.*

Scraping claws ripped Mara back out of sleep.

"Lie still, Elle," Mara murmured.

"We need to get up," Tham said. "All of us."

The urgency in his tone woke Mara in an instant. "What's happening?"

Tham held a finger in the air.

Mara listened for the howls of wolves come to kill them, or the rumble of the mountainside crashing down upon them.

"It's silent," Mara whispered, wriggling free of the cocoon of blankets. "Is the storm over?"

"No idea." Tham yanked their coats from the bottom of the bedding and tossed Mara hers.

Elle yipped and ran toward the tent flap, pawing at it to be opened.

"Just a moment, Elle." Mara tugged on her boots, gloves, and thick hat before reaching for the tent flap. Her hands froze on the knots. "What if they're all gone? What if the rest of them blew away or the storm is only pausing for a moment?"

"We can't know without getting out there. And we've got to know to help."

Mara nodded and pulled the ropes, opening the flap of the tent.

A world of white greeted them, the bright blue of the sky stinging Mara's eyes after so long in the darkness.

"Hello?" Mara called as loudly as she dared. "Kegan. Danny."

At her call, a faint sound of barking carried from up the slope.

Mara grabbed her snowshoes as Elle scrambled out into the snow that surrounded the tent.

"It sounded like there would be more snow." Mara pushed herself to her feet. Only a few inches had piled up in front of their tent flap.

"The wind blew too hard for it to stick." Tham pointed to the north side of the tent, where a solid bank of snow leaned against the thick material.

A chorus of barks echoed from the pegged-in area. Both tents had made it through the storm. Elle whined, knocking her nose against the invisible barrier.

"Where's Kegan." Mara searched the blanket of white. Two mounds poked through the snow just south of their tent.

"Kegan, Elver!" Mara ran toward the nearest mound. "Kegan!"

"In here," a faint voice answered. "We're in here. Please tell me it's over."

"It is." Mara pulled at the knots of the tent. "The sky is clear."

"Truly?" Elver's face appeared through the tent flap.

"I told you it would pass," Kegan said, shoving Elver aside to get out of the tent. "How are the dogs?"

"I came to you first."

Kegan headed up the hill. Five dogs stood clustered by the stakes, barking to bring down the mountain.

Please let there be more alive.

"Mara." The tone of Tham's voice sent a shock of fear up Mara's spine. "They're gone."

"Gone?" Mara ran to the last tent as Tham dropped to his knees, searching the ground. "What do you mean *gone*?"

Mara peered into the tent. The fire tray still burned brightly. Two sets of bedding lay rumpled as though the occupants had climbed quickly free.

"Their boots are gone." Tham stood, scanning the area. "Danny and Vance dressed to leave."

"To go where?" Elver asked, his face gray and his eyes bloodshot, as though he'd been sick for a week. "There was nowhere to go. Nothing but endless white."

"Did they panic?" Mara asked. "I never spoke to them much. Did they seem the type to spook in a storm?"

"Everyone's the type to spook in that sort of storm," Elver said. "They could be anywhere."

Mara opened her mouth but couldn't form the words.

Wherever they are, they're dead.

"We should find their bodies if we can," Tham said. "See them buried properly."

"Bodies? They could be alive. They could have…" Elver's gaze swept over the white. "We should see to the dogs first."

"We need to get the supplies packed," Mara said. "We need to move before another storm hits."

"We'll do it." Tham grabbed the bedding from the tent, pressing it to Elver's chest. "In case we find them."

Elver nodded.

"I'll get the sleds ready." Mara headed toward the two lumps in the snow just below the dogs' enclosure.

"Four dead," Kegan said as Mara began digging in the snow. "Four dead, seven in good shape, one half-dead."

"What about the other eight?" Mara scanned the distance for a sign of the dogs. "Something couldn't have come out in the storm to eat them."

"No idea." Kegan clutched one of the dogs to his chest as tears welled in the corners of his eyes. "But it was a demon of a storm that took them."

Mara's gloves scraped something hard in the snow. "We need to head back to Whitend. The journey is over."

"I hate to say you're right." Kegan checked the fastenings on the remaining dogs' harnesses. "But the chivving white mountains won."

Mara shoved aside a chunk of snow. "Danny."

The word came out before her mind could truly understand. The lump in the snow wasn't a sled but a person, frozen as solid as the ice, curled up in a ball like a child hiding from the white monster.

Mara tore at the other pile of snow. "Tham, help me!"

Elle reached her first, using her paws to dig.

A sled emerged from the white, but no sign of Vance.

"What did he think he was going to find out here?" Elver knocked the snow from the sled to stow the tents.

"You can't know what a man thinks in a storm." Kegan laid a portion of food in front of each dog as he clipped them to the sled.

"Should we just cover him back up?" Elver asked.

"It doesn't seem right, but I don't think there's anything else for it," Mara said.

Elver's hands shook as he reached for Danny.

"I'll do it." Tham carefully pushed snow to cover Danny's face.

"Vance took the other sled?" Mara said.

"Maybe." Kegan shrugged. "Don't know where else it could have disappeared to."

"Where did he think he could go?" Mara asked, watching as Danny disappeared beneath the snow.

We shouldn't leave him here. Shouldn't leave any of them.

Mara moved up to the tents that had sheltered the dogs. If they couldn't give Danny a proper funeral, it was best to be gone as quickly as possible.

Fur and mess covered the bottoms of the tents. They wouldn't be fit for human habitation, but if they needed to shelter the dogs again…

Don't think of it, Mara. What will come will come.

It took less than twenty minutes to pack up the whole camp and load the lone sled. Kegan had bundled up a jet-black dog and nestled him in with their supplies in the sled. "He might not make it through the day, but I won't be the villain who leaves him."

Mara nodded, not begrudging the dog his place of comfort.

"Let's go," Tham said.

The dogs plodded forward at a slow pace. None of them seemed up to much more.

Mara, Tham, and Elver all walked side by side behind the sled.

"We should look for signs of Vance," Elver said. "He might be down this way."

"Perhaps," Mara said.

Or he could have fallen through the earth and landed miles below.

She turned her gaze to the mountains, trying to muster the focus to draw a proper map. This glacier might be all their journey would chart, but she could at least make the record a good one. Something that would be of use to the Map Makers Guild.

"Eat." Tham pulled hardtack from his pack, handing chucks to Elver and Mara.

They had been so careful with their rations. They'd needed enough to last the season. But now, even one sled down, they would have plenty when they made it back to Whitend.

Mara felt the weight of the stone in her pocket.

To keep Kareen at bay.

"What time do you think it is?" Elver asked.

"We'll know when it gets dark," Kegan called from the front.

At least we're moving. Better than being stuck.

Up ahead, a blue glimmer sliced through the base of the mountain, catching the sun and shining like a mirror.

"Was that there before?" Kegan asked.

"No," Mara said.

"Didn't think so," Kegan said. "Guess it doesn't take a map maker's eye to know there didn't used to be a thirty-foot high streak of shining blue in the side of the mountain."

"We're not going to touch it, are we?" Elver said.

"We won't disturb it." Mara squinted at the hollow.

At six feet wide, the opening was plenty big enough for a man with a sled to hide in.

"We need to look for Vance," Tham said as though reading Mara's thoughts. "I'll check inside."

"No," Mara said as the party drew level with the cave. "If it's anything of interest, I'll need to see it for the map anyway."

Mara started toward the opening.

"I'm coming with you," Tham said.

"Tham—"

"You can't stop me," Tham cut her off.

Mara bit her lips together and nodded.

"I'll be happy to wait here with the dogs." Kegan drove the sled up onto the base of the slope a hundred feet from the cave opening.

"Me too." Elver sat on the edge of the sled.

"We're just going to make sure Vance isn't in there, and then we're leaving." Mara pulled her criolas from its pouch, holding it out toward the blue walls of ice.

Lights didn't dance in the ice as they had in the crevasse. The walls glistened like glass, perfectly smooth as they reached toward a peak high overhead. The blue of the walls was the same as the glacier they'd been walking on, but there were no faults to be seen, not a single hint of imperfection.

The sheer beauty of it stole Mara's breath away.

"Wait." Tham grabbed Mara's arm, pulling her back from the mouth of the cavern. He pointed to the ground.

Just inside the entrance, fresh snow had drifted in from the storm, but beyond the pull of the wind, paw prints and two solid tracks marked the ground.

"Vance," Mara called. "Vance!" Her voice echoed off the solid ice.

"Did you find him?" The sound of footsteps crunched up behind her.

"No." Mara took a step into the cave. "But he came in here."

In a flash bright enough to blind her, the walls of the cave reflected the glow of her criolas.

Tham caught her under the arms as she stumbled backward.

"Thanks." Mara blinked at the light, forcing her eyes to focus.

The walls seemed to have absorbed the light of her criolas, carrying the glow farther back than the single orb should have been capable of reaching. The cave stretched off into the distance, maintaining its high-peaked arch as the path led down and out of sight.

Mara stepped forward, testing each footfall as the snow disappeared, leaving nothing but blue ice beneath her feet.

"How far back do you think it goes?" Kegan stood firmly outside the cave entrance.

"Could be miles," Mara said.

"It's like the caves Lamac found," Elver said. "Except ice. The two don't join together, do they? Are they part of the same thing?"

"It's"—Mara teetered on the edge of the easy lie—"possible." She didn't need to turn to see Tham's look of worry. She could feel his concern radiating off of him. "It was magic we saw in the ice. It was magic that took Lamac and the men when the ground collapsed."

"Magic squirming around in the ground?" Elver said from his place ten feet behind Mara and Tham. "So the magic in the ground made the walls in here all smooth like craftsmen carved them?"

Mara finally turned to Tham. There had already been too many disasters to risk the safety of a lie. If Vance was alive and down below, they couldn't leave him.

"Natural magic with no person helping wouldn't have made something like this," Tham said. "People used magic to build this tunnel. There's no other way."

"The sorcerers built something like this and just forgot it in the mountains?" Elver reached toward the wall.

Tham caught his hand. "I wouldn't touch anything."

"It wouldn't be the sorcerers so far north," Kegan said. "This land is barely Ilbrean. We only claim it since it touches the rest of the country and no one's ever said no. It wasn't our Sorcerers Guild that built this. It was something else."

"Have you heard of such people, Kegan?" Mara walked back to the mouth of the cave, wanting to watch Kegan's face.

Kegan twisted his mouth and narrowed his eyes. "Do you want me to say I've never heard of anything on the ice to offend the Guilds? That there's nothing but wolves and bears and things to fill their stomachs living out past Whitend?"

"I want the truth," Mara said.

"I don't know the truth," Kegan said. "I know men have come back, ranting about women who run naked through the snow. I've heard men talk about an underground city with more beauty than all of Ilara stacked together. And I've never heard of those men again once they've talked."

"So there is something out here." Mara buried her face in her cold gloves.

"We should leave if there are people down there." Panic tightened Elver's voice.

"We can't leave Vance," Mara said.

"He's a traitor who stole a sled and dogs and made a run for it. If it's really him who's here," Kegan said.

Mara looked to Tham.

Tham stared at her, his eyes unreadable. "Whatever Vance might have done, we have to see if the dogs he took need our help. Mara and I will go in a bit farther, see if we can find Vance. Elver and Kegan stay out here and protect the dogs. If there are signs of another storm, pitch the tents in the cave. Agreed?"

"Agreed," Elver and Kegan said together.

"May whatever god who will listen to fools who brave the ice grant you protection," Kegan said.

"May the gods hear your words and shelter you from the cold." Mara nodded and turned back down the tunnel.

She followed the path as it arced down and out of sight without glancing back. There was no need with Tham walking beside her.

"Do you really think there are people here?" Mara's fingers itched with the childlike need to hold Tham's hand while walking into danger.

"I'm sure of it," Tham said. "Vance wasn't smart enough to steer the dogs here on his own. If he's here at all, someone helped him."

Mara's hand drifted to the hilt of the knife strapped to her hip.

The ice walls around them moved gradually closer together, like they were being pressed into a funnel.

Tham stepped behind Mara when it was no longer possible to walk side by side.

"This is too narrow for a sled to fit. They couldn't go forward, and they didn't go back." Mara turned sideways, careful not to touch the ice of either wall.

Tham didn't answer. Instead, he pulled his knife from its sheath.

Mara did the same, taking comfort in the weight of her blade.

A knife will not protect you from magic.

Her elbow brushed the ice behind her.

Instinct told her to freeze. Her breath caught in her throat as she waited for the ceiling to crumble down upon them.

A heartbeat passed. Then another.

She turned to look at Tham, and too many things happened at once.

Terror filled his face as something jerked Mara back into the wall. She braced herself for pain, but her head didn't smack against the ice.

Tham reached for her as she passed through the wall, the world around her blurring in a blaze of blue as Tham screamed.

"Mara!"

NIKO

"I used to be afraid of the dark, you know." Amec didn't open his eyes as he spoke. "I drove my mother crazy with it. Wailing my head off as soon as she turned out the lamp. My father was a Guilded soldier, did you know that?"

"No," Niko answered, though he knew it wasn't necessary.

"He was captain of his unit before he was killed in the fighting down south. My mother decided I would be a soldier before I was old enough to not soil my pants. I'd cry in the dark every night, and she'd get so mad. *How are you going to be a soldier if you cry like a babe in the dark?*

"My grandmother was kind, though. Batty as a fairy-loving healer, but still kind. She told my mother not to be so angry. We were all born with a fear. Some from things so far in the past, only the stones remember the terror. Some from horrors of days that haven't yet come. Days only Dudia Himself can see."

"Your grandmother sounds like a kind woman," Niko said after Amec had been silent for a full minute.

"She was." Amec gave a wan smile as he opened his eyes. "She was right, too. Spent all my years terrified of being trapped in the dark, and here I am, buried alive in a tomb."

"This isn't a tomb."

"And it's not blood that dripped from the wall either. And Tarrum and Jerick aren't dead. They're really searching for a way get us out of here. It's kind of you to pretend, Niko. But I think we can both be sure no one's coming down to save us."

Niko dug his fists into his eyes.

Mara should be here. She'd be better at this.

"You're right." Niko stood, brushing the dirt off his pants. "There is no one coming down here to save us and no way I can find to reopen the hole that swallowed us. We've got two choices. We can sit here and feel miserable while we wait to starve. Or, we can follow this tunnel and see where it goes."

"Where do you think it goes? Paradise?" Amec didn't get up even as Niko refastened his pack.

"We've been waiting down here for at least a day and haven't run out of good air to breathe." Niko took a bracing breath to demonstrate. "That means this tunnel goes somewhere. I don't know how far that may be or if we can reach it, but there is something down this tunnel to be found. It won't matter to the world above if we wait here to die since I doubt they'd find our bodies even if the Guilds cared to try, so we might as well keep moving. Who knows? We might find a way out of this yet."

"Do you really think so?" Amec picked at the top of his pack. "Or are you just saying that so I won't be such a bother as we slowly starve to death?"

"Amec, I honestly don't know what's going to happen to us. But I've been in worse binds than this. Believe me, waiting for something horrible to happen is much more painful than just going out to find the disaster for yourself."

"I suppose that's a map maker thing." Amec reached for Niko's hand. "Keeping going when you're lost beyond redemption."

"It's more a Karron thing." Niko dragged Amec to his feet. "You can't spend years in the Map Master's Palace and get away without feeling obliged to keep fighting till your last step.

Besides, I promised someone I would make it back to Ilara, and I don't care what sort of stone and shadows I have to claw through to keep my word."

"Let's go then." Amec hoisted his pack onto his back, letting Niko take the lead down the dark passage.

The walls stayed the same. Smooth and carved in an unnatural, arching pattern.

"What was it like, being the Lord Map Maker's apprentice?" Amec asked.

Niko trailed the fingers of his free hand along the wall as he searched for an answer.

"The truth? Brutal." Niko laughed. The sound carried down the tunnel, echoing off rocks far out of range of the light of his criolas.

"He's not a nice man?" Disappointment sounded in Amec's words.

"Lord Karron is a great man." Niko slowed his pace as the tunnel sloped down at a steep angle. "And I would never call him unkind. Me being a child from the eastern foothills and being dumped into the Map Master's Palace, it was bit like jumping from a puddle into the Arion Sea."

"Is it true there are two ballrooms in the palace? Both large enough to swallow a ship whole?"

"No." Niko laughed again, taking comfort that the walls held strong against the sound. "There's one ballroom and one parlor Allora likes to use as a second ballroom. And neither of them could eat a ship. Though they are large enough to fit a healthy stable of horses."

The tunnel ended, and the ground in front of them dropped away.

Niko stopped suddenly, and Amec ran into his back. Niko gripped the wall to hold his balance. "Wait a moment."

He inched closer to the ledge, holding his criolas low. A path led sideways along a wall of dark rock then twisted and cut sharply down, switch-backing its way to something far below the reach of Niko's light.

"What's down there?" Amec whispered.

"No idea." Niko stepped half his weight onto the path, bouncing a bit to test the stone's stability. Whoever had created the walkway had kept the stone smooth and symmetrical as it sloped down. "Keep back a few feet and stay away from the edge."

"Will do. I'm not afraid of heights as such, but I have a healthy enough fear of them to stay away from ledges."

"Good." Niko started down the slope, carefully testing every footfall. The path was wide enough for a person to walk without fear of tipping over the edge, but two people would be hard-pressed to pass.

"What in Ilbrea could have built this?" Amec asked as they reached the sixth pass down. "It must have been sorcerers. No normal pick dug this, and it was a magic stone that sent us falling down here."

Allora, please forgive me.

"There is more magic hidden in Ilbrea than has ever been held in the hands of the Sorcerers Guild," Niko said.

"What? Whoa!"

Niko turned to see Amec pin wheeling his arms as he tipped toward the darkness.

"No!" Niko reached out, snatching the sleeve of Amec's coat and yanking him toward the solid wall.

Amec hit the wall with a thud and crumpled to his knees.

"Thank you, Niko." He pushed himself to his feet with a groan, wiping the sweat from his forehead with his sleeve. "After all we've been through, I don't think I could take another fall."

"Agreed." Niko made sure Amec was steady on his feet before continuing down the path.

"But what did you mean? About the magic."

"I've seen magic in the ground, in plants, in animals…" Niko paused, making sure Amec wasn't going to tip again. "I've met a dragon."

Amec stared blankly at him for a moment. "A dragon?"

"Yes." Niko cut around the corner and onto the next leg of the path. "She flew, breathed fire, and glittered with blue scales to rival the sea herself."

"But dragons are only legends. Storybook things for children."

"I promise you she was very real. The stories of the floating land in the south are true, too. There are a fair number of children's stories I've seen come to life with my own eyes."

The sound of Amec's footsteps stopped. Niko looked back to find him standing on the path, hands planted on his hips.

"So the map makers have found all sorts of wonderful magical things and they've lied to all of us?" Amec said. "How could they keep things that wonderful from the people of Ilbrea?"

"It's not the map makers." Niko looked to the dark ceiling high above the reach of his light. "It's the sorcerers. They don't want anyone to know there's magic in Ilbrea outside their control."

"Why?" Amec narrowed his eyes.

"Think, Amec. You were raised Soldiers Guild. You can't tell me you never heard complaints of the sorcerers putting themselves above all other Guilds."

"The Lady Sorcerer thinks she's in charge of the army. She's learned she can't issue orders, but what comes down from the King is just him parroting what the purple lady wants done."

"And how does the Lady Sorcerer get away with it?" Niko waved Amec to follow.

"There's no way to fight the sorcerers. They've got all the magic. Even with our army, we couldn't break into the Sorcerers Tower, and only our nightmares can tell us what the sorcerers could do in battle."

"Exactly. But what if the King, and the soldiers, and all the people in Ilbrea knew there was power outside the Sorcerers

Tower? Power that might be even stronger than the Lady Sorcerer herself."

"She'd lose her place lording over the King. She'd have to be a regular member of the council instead of pulling all the strings and watching us jump for her."

"Right in one," Niko said. "The sorcerers aren't the source of all magic in Ilbrea. They hoard all the children who show any magic. They make the map makers destroy all the maps that might have any signs of rogue magic on them. They've spent centuries hiding the truth about magic from the people of Ilbrea. Now it's all been turned into fairy stories, myths, and legends. And anyone who dares to argue disappears."

Niko walked around the next switch, and the path leveled out onto a flat surface. He stomped on the ground. The thump of it sounded thick as bedrock.

Holding his criolas high, Niko peered through the dark. The walls on either side of them were more than twenty feet apart, and the ceiling towered high out of reach of his light. Ahead, a solid sheet of shadows with no visible break greeted them.

"Onward then." Niko nodded to Amec to follow.

"If dragons are a fairy story and you found them," Amec said slowly, as though he were trying to unspool a lifetime's worth of lies, "and the floating islands were a story and you found them, then what story have we fallen into?"

Niko stayed silent for a few moments, examining the walls as he walked, checking for cracks that might send stones tumbling down upon them.

"Niko? What story?"

"There are a several options," Niko said. "There's the tale of the city beneath. The tale of the Dark Hall. The tale of the buried wanderer. The tale of the Black Bloods. The tale of the city of death."

"Which one do you think we're in?"

"In my opinion, some combination of the five."

A shape loomed in the darkness, pushing its form through the shadows.

Niko held up a hand to silence Amec.

The shape didn't move. The thing towered in the dark, three stories high and as wide as his light could catch. A sound whispered from the shadows, like water running through a tiny fountain.

Slowly, Niko crept forward, holding his light out toward the shape.

Cut stones had been stacked into a high wall, blocking the passage in front of them. Windows of a sort had been fashioned into the rock.

The feeling of a thousand eyes staring from the shadows prickled the hairs on the back of Niko's neck.

"Are there people in there?" Amec whispered.

"No idea."

A door, the size of one from a common house, hung off its hinges at the bottom of the wall.

"If there are, they don't seem too concerned with defense."

Niko's heart thundered in his ears as they crept toward the door. He reached for the knife at his hip.

A rasp came from behind him as Amec drew his own blade.

Niko touched the door. The edges of the wood crumbled under his fingers.

The hinges squealed in protest as he swung the door open wide enough to squeeze through.

A tunnel barely tall enough for him to stand in waited on the other side. Niko held his light in front of him as he crept forward. The feeling of being crushed lasted only a moment before the tunnel opened up into a dark courtyard.

It looked for all the world like the walled garden of a rich man's country estate. Stone walls surrounded them. A crumbling walkway with decorative arches peered down from above. A fountain made of black stone gurgled at the center of it all.

Niko stepped forward onto, not stone as he had expected, but something soft. Pale moss covered the ground. Plants with broad leaves grew around the edge of the fountain, with mushrooms peering up between the stalks.

"Bring the light here." Amec stood in the corner, touching something on the stone wall. "Are these flowers?"

Black blooms climbed a gray vine.

"Yes, they are." Niko touched the petals to assure himself the flowers weren't carved from stone.

The soft blooms trembled at his touch.

"Do you suppose the water's safe to drink?" Amec ran to the fountain and dipped his hands into the water.

"Might as well try it. If we don't drink something, we won't live long enough to work our way out of this place."

ADRIAL

Pain shot through Adrial's leg with every step. He hadn't slept the night before. The clatter of soldiers riding through the streets carried up to his bedroom windows. Worse than the noise was not knowing why there were so many soldiers on the move. Visions of fire eating the palace, the cathedral, the docks, had raced through Adrial's mind all night.

Or maybe men were rioting and hauling innocents out of their homes. Or soldiers and commoners were clashing on the streets of the city they all shared.

Each possibility was as frightening as the next, and he had no way of knowing what had truly happened.

Lard Gareth's note had almost been a relief when it arrived with his breakfast.

Taddy had gaped at the well-known script.

Come to my study at your earliest convenience.

Adrial made his way down the stairs to the ground level of the library. The Lord's study stood at the far end of the great room, as separated from the rabble of the rest of the scribes as the space within the library would allow.

Adrial paused with his hand on the polished wooden door to the great room, taking a breath before swinging it open.

The space remained as awe-inspiring as the first time he'd seen it when he was only a child. A room large enough to swallow the cathedral whole. Rows and rows of tables sat under enormous skylights, providing the scribes perfect sunlight for their work.

Stacks of common reference books wound around the easy-to-access sections of the walls, but the vast shelves of books reached five stories high.

Too well, Adrial remembered starting the third year of his apprenticeship and being allowed to climb to the second story of books and explore the wealth of knowledge on the next level. The exams at the end of every year brought the best prize—access to the next flight of books.

Adrial breathed in the scent of the thousands of volumes as he made his way down the center aisle, trying not to blush as each of the scribes he passed laid down their work to bow their head as he walked by.

You could make them stop when you take charge.

And break a centuries-old tradition in doing it.

Hiding his limp as best he could, he moved through the library.

The apprentices at the end of the aisle stood as he passed, most hiding their hands behind their backs.

Adrial smiled kindly, recognizing the fear of being caught with ink on his skin.

Even the thought of ink brought Ena dancing into his mind. Ena, with hair that smelled better than old books or new. Whose laugh was sweeter and more dangerous than all the fairy stories the library allowed.

Too soon he reached Lord Gareth's study.

A pen matching the mark on Adrial's arm stretched across the double doors.

He knocked gently, not wanting to disturb the Lord Scribe if he was busy with more important guests.

"Come in," a voice that did not belong to Lord Gareth answered.

Steeling himself, Adrial opened the door and entered Lord Gareth's study.

The Lord sat behind his wide desk, with better color in his cheeks than Adrial had seen in weeks. A trickle of relief began as Adrial glanced from the familiar painting of Saint Alwyn to the shelves of books locked behind thin metal grates, blocking unworthy hands from the texts. The only unusual thing in the room was the towering, black-clad figure of Rictor Nance.

"Good morning, Adrial." Lord Gareth beckoned Adrial to sit in front of his desk, waiting for Adrial to sink into the chair before continuing. "It is my understanding you've met Soldier Nance?"

"Yes, Lord Gareth." Adrial nodded. "He was the soldier who sent me to the safety of the Sorcerers Tower after the blast at the start of the eastern mountains journey. It's a pleasure to see you again, Soldier Nance."

Rictor nodded. "I only wish it were under better circumstances, Head Scribe."

A knot of dread curled in Adrial's stomach.

"The state of the city is becoming worse by the day." The color faded from Lord Gareth's cheeks as he spoke. "Soldier Nance came to report there were five fires last night. Unfortunately, there were some commoners caught in the blazes. With that—"

"Where were the fires?" Adrial turned to Rictor. "Who was harmed?"

"They were all in the merchants part of town," Rictor said. "Three homes and two shops. Elias Fent and his family didn't make it out of their house in time."

Guilt surged in Adrial alongside his relief.

"We found the men who set that fire," Rictor said. "We know

they're a part of something larger, but they'd all rather swing than talk. They'll be hanged for destruction and murder this afternoon."

"That's terrible," Adrial said. "I'm so sorry."

"The fires were too close to the scribes' shop to be allowed," Lord Gareth said. "Only two streets away from one of the blazes. The villainous men who are committing these crimes have moved from common alleys to merchants' homes. We can only assume they'll be coming for the Guilds themselves next. As such"—Gareth took a rattling breath—"I can no longer justify the risk of allowing the scribes' shop to remain open."

Adrial searched Gareth's words, trying sort out where he had gotten confused. "You're going to close the scribes' shop?"

"At my recommendation," Rictor said. "If that fire had spread east, the entire shop would have been lost, including the scribes living above it."

"It's far too dangerous to leave our own out there unguarded," Gareth said.

"But Lord Gareth, with all due respect, they aren't unguarded," Adrial said. "There have been soldiers surrounding the shop for weeks."

"There's only so much soldiers can do against fire," Rictor said. "A blaze is not an enemy we can fight with swords."

"What of the people who need the services of the scribes' shop?" Adrial asked. "Will they be allowed to come to the library for help?"

"Goodness no." Gareth waved a hand in the air, as though batting away the foolish notion. "Inviting people who have nothing to do with the scribes into the library is tenuous at the best of times. It is absolutely too dangerous to be allowed now."

"Then, sir," Adrial said, "you can't close the shop. I'm sorry, but it would be wrong. A horrible blow to the people of Ilara."

"The people of Ilara will have to make do," Gareth said.

"Has the King passed down an order allowing marriage

without a scribe-written certificate?" Adrial asked. "Will people be able to purchase property, or gain a plot to bury their dead?"

"Of course not. If we allowed just anyone to write those forms, there would be inconsistency in the official records," Lord Gareth said.

"Then without the scribes' shop, life in the city would come to a halt," Adrial said. "Dead would go unburied."

"The commoners did it to themselves," Rictor said. "They're the ones starting fires. If it disrupts their lives, so be it."

"But it's not all of the common folk." Adrial took a breath, aligning his words in a way that couldn't be argued against. "A small group of violent rebels is trying to convince the common masses that the Guilds care nothing for them. The commoners didn't hold a council. There wasn't a vote. We can't punish the masses for what a few vicious men have done. If we abandon the commoners now, we're confirming what the rebels are saying. We will be telling the people of Ilara we care for nothing beyond the Guilds.

"It's not the men who've started the fires we'll be punishing. It's the young couple expecting a baby, rushing to be wed before it's too late. It's the grandson who wants to bury his grandfather in a decent way. The Guilds' purpose is to serve the people of Ilbrea. If we shut down the shop, we've already lost to the rebels, whether they know it or not."

"If intelligence weren't so vital in a scribe, I would wish for a less discerning heir." Lord Gareth tapped his finger on his pursed lips, gazing from the ceiling to the window overlooking the street. "I'm sorry, Soldier Nance, but the scribes' shop will remain open. I want all the scribes escorted back to the library each night. I'll not have any of you sleeping in the city, but during the day, the shop will conduct business as usual."

"At your order." Soldier Nance bowed and moved to leave the room.

"Wait a moment." Adrial stood. "You haven't found the leader behind all this mess?"

"No." Rictor's shoulders tensed as he turned around. "As I've said, no one wants to talk."

"But surely you must know something?" A spark of guilt shook Adrial's nerves.

You've seen the man's face. You've heard his name.

But only with Ena.

"We've been patrolling and searching, but whoever is leading this chaos seems quite skilled at scaring the people around him into silence."

Images of Cade's hands as he raised the hem of Ena's skirt flashed through Adrial's mind.

"His name is Cade, I believe," Adrial said. "Tall, broad fellow. Curling, blond hair."

"How do you know?" Rictor narrowed his eyes.

"It's a rather embarrassing story that involves me hiding under a crate," Adrial said.

"Adrial, what under the sky were you doing?" Worry creased Gareth's face in a near comical way.

"I went to the docks to see off a friend who was sailing," Adrial said.

Gareth's eyes widened in shock.

"It was a poor choice, but I didn't realize how poor until I was hiding under a crate. Cade was there, made a few threats. It sounded as though he were in charge, though I'm sure he could have been bragging," Adrial said.

Rictor and Gareth stared at him.

"I would have said something earlier, but it honestly didn't occur to me the soldiers wouldn't know who to look for. I apologize for not speaking sooner and for my misjudgment in walking through the city alone."

"You will see it does not happen again." Gareth pounded a fist on his desk.

"It won't, Lord Scribe." Adrial bowed to Gareth before looking back to Rictor. "I don't know if having the name of the man will help."

Adrial swallowed the sour taste of panic.

I didn't mention Ena. There's no way for anyone to know I saw Cade in her home. The sooner that man is gone, the safer she'll be.

"I'll speak to Lord Kearney," Rictor said. "Thank you for the information. Though I don't know if anyone but Dudia can truly help us."

Adrial's chest sagged as Rictor left the room, closing the door behind him.

"Going down to the docks?" Gareth said.

"I've been a hundred times before," Adrial said. "I didn't imagine it to be a dangerous place in the daylight."

"We are too sheltered, all of us who wear the white. We see our books, always there, assuringly consistent, and we forget the world is anything but unchanging. We forget the bloody histories in our books could happen again if we don't tread carefully."

"Yes, sir," Adrial said.

"You need to understand how very important you are, Adrial." Lord Gareth pushed himself to his feet. His face shifted from pale white to gray. "When I die, which only Dudia can know how much time I have left"—Lord Gareth held up a hand as Adrial opened his mouth to speak—"you will take my seat. You will be one of the seven to rule the Guilds. Do not let me die without the security of knowing you will be there to take my place.

"The troubles upon us are greater than a few fires and a mob of angry men. The storm has been building in Ilbrea since the drought in the far south began twenty years ago, and it's only gotten worse since. Soon, fires the rains cannot put out will begin to blaze. We need someone with a cool head reminding the Guilds what it will take, not only for the Guilds to survive, but for the people of Ilbrea to survive as well."

Tell him he's not allowed to die and leave you to face a world that's growing dark and burning.

"Yes, sir," Adrial said.

"You are my choice, Adrial. You are my legacy." Gareth sank back into his seat. "You are my hope. Guard yourself carefully."

"I will, Lord Gareth." Adrial bowed. "And be careful with yourself as well. We still need you."

I'm not ready.

Gareth smiled, shooing Adrial toward the door. "I'll always be needed. That doesn't mean I'll always be here."

Adrial gave a final bow and turned to leave, the weight of every book in the library pressing down on his shoulders.

The door to Lord Gareth's study seemed heavier than ever.

Make it back to your quarters. Don't let the weight crush you until you're alone.

Adrial shut the door. Before he'd made it two steps into the great room, a figure in green ran toward him, blond hair flying behind her.

"Adrial," Allora whispered, seizing his hand and dragging him toward the balcony. "They let me into the great room, but they wouldn't let me into Lord Gareth's study to get you."

"What's happened?"

Allora shoved open the door to the narrow balcony that overlooked the street.

Four scribes sat in the sun, enjoying the morning air.

"Send them away." Allora's voice shook as she spoke.

"If you would all give us a moment," Adrial said.

The four scribes obediently stood and filed back inside, each surreptitiously glancing at Allora's pale, panicked face as they passed.

"Allora, what's the matter?" Adrial asked as soon as the door closed.

"It really is a wonder they let me in." Allora paced the small length of the balcony. "The soldiers almost didn't allow it.

Though I suppose they'd have some trouble explaining turning away the Lady of the Map Makers."

"Allora." Adrial took her shoulders, holding her still.

"A soldier came." Allora's voice dropped. "He brought me a letter. One for me and one for Father. Father isn't here. He's out with his new apprentice to test the boy on mapping the peaks. The soldier gave me my letter and rode out after Father. He's chasing him with a letter."

The beat of Adrial's heart echoed in his ears, thudding a terrified rhythm. "What did the letter say?"

"I didn't open it." Tears glistened in Allora's eyes. "I stood by the door, holding it for nearly an hour, but I couldn't do it."

Reaching into the folds of her skirt, Allora pulled out an envelope. The paper had wrinkled, and filth marked the corners. The green of the unbroken map maker's seal shone like a beacon on the tattered parchment.

"Where did he come from?" Adrial's mouth had gone completely dry, making speech near impossible.

"I couldn't form the words to ask." Allora pressed the letter to Adrial's chest. "I can't do it. I'm not strong enough."

Adrial's hands shook as he took the letter. The thundering of his heart drowned out the sounds of the street below as he tore open the envelope.

"Read it." Tears streamed down Allora's cheeks.

Adrial unfolded the letter, fighting to pull in air as his eyes took in the script at the top of the page. "From Bertrand Rollands, Map Maker. Eastern Mountains Journey as ordered by King Brannon Willoc."

Allora gasped, her hand flying to her mouth as she swayed. "Keep reading." Her whisper was barely audible.

"Lady Karron, it is my sad duty to inform you Map Maker Nikolas Endur will not be returning with the eastern mountains journey." Each word tore at Adrial's throat as tears streamed down his face. "In scouring the mountains for a path to Wyrain, his party of four were lost to unknown circumstances. He made known his wish that you be informed should he fall while carrying out his duty to the Map Makers Guild.

"Niko was a friend to all, and he served Ilbrea with dedication and honor. His name will sit in glory with the other map makers who gave their lives for Dudia and the greatness of the Guild. May Saint Aximander bring you strength and Dudia bring you comfort."

Allora sank to the ground, her sobs echoing through the streets around them.

Adrial knelt, holding Allora tight. Speech he could not understand mixed with her tears. Only one word cut through the horrible scream of grief in his mind.

Niko. Niko. Niko.

ALLORA

The sun shone brightly. Obscene in its joy. Filtering through the windows into the map room, casting light on the dust motes that drifted through the air. The sun didn't know the world had stopped. Dudia had forgotten to tell her days should stop coming.

Allora sat on the floor at the center of the room, staring up at the maps. She'd never allowed herself to sit on the floor as a child. Such behavior was unbecoming of a lady.

The smoothness of the floor under her fingers surprised her. Seeing the difference from one piece of wood to another and not being able to feel it.

The other side of grief. I can feel it, but I can't see it.

The maid had handed her a green dress as always. The cook had sent up breakfast.

The map room hadn't changed. The most beautiful maps of Ilbrea ever created still coated the walls. Perfect details, glorious lines, all works of art in their own right.

Her fingers itched to tear the maps from the walls. To make sure the room's glory would never be the same again. But she hadn't the strength to stand.

The sun drifted along its path through the sky. Moving its beams from one part of the great maps to another.

The fields by the river. Where Niko had snuck her out of the city for an adventure when she had passed out of childhood and should have known better than to go.

The Arion Sea. They'd been on a ship the first time Niko really spoke to her.

Allora's eyes burned as if with tears, but there were no more tears left for her to cry.

The thumping of horses' hooves pounded up the drive.

It could be Father.

The rattle of carriage wheels dissolved the tiny thread of will she had to get up. Her father wouldn't arrive in a carriage. Kai wasn't back yet. Mara and Tham…

A scream of frustration tore from Allora's throat, the sound of it frightening as it echoed off the walls of the empty hall.

I should be doing something.

But there was nothing to do. No plans to make. No tasks to organize. Just a sea of endless nothing.

She couldn't even wear black.

A map maker's funeral couldn't happen until the journey returned. It would be months before the time to wear black came. Months before his name would be carved with the other map makers who had given their lives for the calling of exploration. Months before her place in the Guilds granted her permission to grieve.

A bubble of burning rage swelled in Allora's throat.

The Guild had stolen the simple act of grieving from her. Her family, her childhood, her love taken for the good of the map makers.

Months of nothing. They've condemned you to months of nothing.

A life of nothing.

Allora's rage vanished as her whole body shook with a fresh round of tearless sobs.

INKER AND CROWN | 349

"Lady Allora."

A man stood in front of Allora, his black boots shining.

Don't look up. If you look up, he'll hand you a letter.

"Lady Allora, are you all right?" The man knelt.

Allora squeezed her eyes shut tight, willing him to disappear.

"Lady Allora?"

His voice had a familiar resonance. His words perfectly enunciated.

Allora opened her eyes to see the King kneeling in front of her, concern etched in the creases of his brow.

"Your Majesty." Allora tried to push herself up but found she didn't have the strength.

"Don't," the King said. "It's all right. I asked them to let me in without warning you. I heard about Map Maker Endur. I've been told the two of you were close."

Allora nodded. The knot in her throat had tied itself too tight to allow words to pass.

"I'm so terribly sorry he won't be returning with the journey."

Allora nodded again. Tears had found their way back to her eyes. A fresh stream of them trickled down her cheeks.

"He gave everything he had for Ilbrea. For the Guilds." The King looked up to the maps on the ceiling high above. "I suppose there comes a time when each of us can be called to give everything we are for the good of the people. You and I, we sit so close to the center of the star, our moments come more often. Lady Allora. Allora."

The tender familiarity in the King's voice sent a shiver down Allora's spine.

"The people are unhappy." The King spoke slowly, as though testing every word. "With the death of the Queen, the city, the country has fallen into despair. A group of horrible men are using the Queen's death to their advantage. Spreading the lie that the royal Willoc family is done for. In the Guilds Council this morning, with Head Map Maker Train standing in for your father, it was the advice of the council that I remarry. An immediate engagement to be announced as soon as possible with a wedding to take place at mid-summer."

The room swayed and spun.

The King's words echoed as if spoken from far, far away. Beyond the reaches of all the maps.

"The council agrees with me that the best choice to help save the city from chaos is you, Allora. The people love the map makers, and they love you. You'll bring peace to the city, and my sister will find great comfort with you in the Royal Palace. As for me…I cannot imagine a worthier woman to stand by my side or a better Queen for Ilbrea."

A shattering split the air, but the King didn't flinch at the sound that shook every inch of Allora. His mouth kept moving, forming words Allora fought to hear.

"…until your father returns, I understand. Even being the King, I wouldn't want to override the wishes of a father. Especially in taking the Lady of the Map Makers."

"No." A silence filled the hall of maps, even worse than a storm of sound. It would have been kinder if the whole world had started screaming. Then she wouldn't have been alone. "I'm not waiting for my father. The map makers have taken enough from me. I'm done."

"Allora—"

"I'll marry you. As soon as you like. I can't be in the Map Master's Palace anymore."

"As you wish, Allora." The King took her hand. "I can have you moved to a private room in the palace today."

"Now." Allora stood, swaying.

The King wrapped an arm around her waist, steadying her as the maps swirled above.

"I'll have someone collect your belongings," the King said. "You can ride back in the carriage with me."

"Yes. I never want to see this place again."

"The people of Ilbrea will love you, Allora. You've saved us all."

Allora didn't flinch as the door to the hall of maps slammed shut behind her.

ADRIAL

"Is she really going to marry the King?" Taddy asked, taking a long time shifting everything on the tea tray into perfect lines. He moved the mugs for the fourth time, squinting at the handles to be sure they were exactly parallel.

"You were there when we sent out the announcements to be posted." Adrial squinted at the copse of trees he'd drawn on the top corner of the page.

I need something darker for the shadows.

"And you were raised in the house with Lady Karron." Taddy poured tea into a mug, stirring it slowly before adding anything in. "Like you were her brother."

"I suppose she's as near to being my sister as anyone could be." Adrial tipped the slanted portion of his worktable back, searching for a different angle of the light.

"So if your *near* sister is going to be the Queen, that makes you *near* a prince." Taddy dumped two giant spoons of sugar into the tea.

"No, Taddy." Adrial limped over, removing both mug and sugar spoon from Taddy's destructive grip. "Lady Karron will become Queen Allora Willoc, and I will remain Head Scribe Adrial Ayres. Now go see to your work."

Flushing pink, Taddy headed to the door, hesitating with his hand on the knob. "You are going to get to go to the wedding though, aren't you?"

"As head scribe, I will. Now out."

Guilt simmered in Adrial's stomach before the door had closed behind Taddy.

It wasn't his apprentice's fault Adrial hadn't heard the news from Allora herself and had only found out when the message had come to make the announcements.

Allora hadn't answered his letters.

Lord Karron was refusing visitors.

Adrial had been left alone with a stack of papers, grieving his friend who couldn't even be deemed properly gone until well past the end of summer.

And now Allora was marrying the King.

Adrial dug his knuckles into his eyes, wishing he could go back to his rooms and hide far away from people. Or run to the docks and find Ena, forget everything and everyone in the scent of her hair.

You've work to do, scribe. Curling up and forgetting is a privilege you aren't allowed.

Adrial turned back to his work. He'd completed twenty pages of the vellum. The images lay in a long line across his table. Brilliant skies and soaring birds lay beside ferocious storms and fields caught in terrible blazes.

"It's all a part of our history. The chaos and the wonder, all laid out in ink."

Adrial picked up his pen, the familiar weight of it comforting in his hand.

The late afternoon sun gleamed down through his window, casting the paper in a warm light. Another hour, and the soldiers would bustle all of them back to the library. Then time for sleep.

Then back to the scribes' shop. Back to hoping Ena would climb through his window.

Adrial dipped his pen into the pure black ink.

Saint Galen wandered through the forest, searching for a cure for engalscrof. Every moment that passed on her journey brought the weight of another innocent she had failed to save. In the sixth month—

Adrial's desk shook under his pen, sending dots of ink spattering across the page and onto his fingers.

"Chivving—"

A terrified scream cut over his curse as the desk rattled again and a boom shook the windows.

Adrial froze, pen in hand, looking dumbly at the walls for the source of the noise.

Chimes tinkled brightly the moment before a voice shouted, "All of you out, now! We have to go!"

Adrial dropped his pen, which fell on the knees of his robes, leaving a long, black streak.

"The pages." Adrial ran to the side of his desk, reaching for the precious sheets of paper.

"Head Scribe, we have to go!" Taddy shouted from the doorway. "Head Scribe!" Taddy grabbed Adrial's arm, trying desperately to yank him toward the door. "There was an explosion, and now there's a fire. We have to go!" Frightened tears glistened on the boy's pale face. "Please, sir!"

Adrial pulled his hand away from the parchments, letting Taddy lead him to the front room of the shop.

Two soldiers stood at the door, ushering the last of the scribes onto the street.

"Head Scribe, we need to get you back to the library," one of the soldiers said in an urgent, clipped tone.

"What's happening?" Adrial asked.

The second soldier clamped a hand around Adrial's arm, dragging him onto the street.

"What's going on?" Adrial didn't fight against the soldier's grip.

Natalia and Travers disappeared down the street with the rest of the scribes, three soldiers a step behind them.

"There were two explosions nearby," the soldier said, not letting go of Adrial as they hurried toward the library. "We don't have time to wait for a carriage. We're going to have to run."

"Take Taddy and go," Adrial said to the other soldier. "You'll move faster than I can."

"I can't leave the head scribe, sir," the soldier said at the same moment Taddy shouted, "I'm not leaving you!"

"We'll all make it there fine if we move quickly," the soldier gripping Adrial's arm said.

Another boom shook the street. Screams echoed in the distance.

"We should help them." Adrial took a single step toward the screams.

A twang and a whoosh sounded the instant he moved. A grunt of pain came from behind Adrial. He spun toward the sound.

The long shaft of an arrow stuck out of the soldier's chest.

The remaining soldier grabbed Adrial and Taddy by the backs of their necks, shoving them toward a narrow alley between houses.

"We have to help him," Taddy squeaked as the ground quaked and the windows above shattered.

Adrial grabbed Taddy, covering the boy's head with his body as shards of glass rained down on them.

Adrial looked up when the shower of glass stopped. The soldier who'd been shot lay on the street, unmoving.

"We should help him." Taddy's words came out as a whimper.

Adrial held Taddy back as he tried to run for the fallen soldier.

"Our orders are to protect you," the remaining soldier said. "We're going to have to cut around the other way."

Adrial pulled off his robes. If the soldier was shocked at the common pants and shirt Adrial had grown accustomed to wearing under the white, he didn't show it.

"I only have my whites, sir," Taddy said shakily.

"It's all right, Taddy." Adrial tossed his robes to the side and struggled out of his shirt.

Taddy gasped at the scar on Adrial's shoulder.

"Cover your robes, Taddy."

Taddy nodded and yanked on the worn shirt.

"Good to know there's some sense in the scribes." The soldier moved to the other end of the alley as a fresh wave of screams carried from the north, in the direction of the library.

The clang of metal striking metal greeted them at the end of the alley. Two streets down, a group of soldiers clashed with men in common clothes. The shining Guild-made swords glinted in the dimming light. Time had eaten the polish off the blades in the hands of the commoners, but the men still swung them viciously.

"Stay close." The soldier charged onto the street, heading to a gap between houses across the way.

Two commoners broke free from the fight and ran, bellowing, toward Adrial's party.

"Get to the alley and stay out of sight." The soldier planted his feet, his sword ready to meet his attackers. "Go!"

Adrial grabbed Taddy, running toward the alley as fast as his bad leg would allow.

"They saw us come in here." Taddy winced every time the swords clanged together. "They'll come for us."

"We'll go to the next street and find a place out of sight."

A horrible scream echoed behind them.

Adrial didn't stop to see who had made the awful sound.

The chaos on the next street was worse than what they'd just left. A woman lay on the cobblestones, a pool of blood blossoming around her. The front of a home had collapsed, and men dug through the rubble, screaming a name Adrial couldn't understand.

"This way!" The call came from the alley behind them.

Adrial scanned the street for a place to hide.

A bright bloom of orange burst into being, searing the air as a wave of heat and sound knocked Adrial off his feet.

Pain shot through his shoulder as he hit the ground, and the world fell silent.

Taddy. Adrial's mouth formed the word, but sound didn't join his cry. *Taddy.*

He forced himself to his knees.

The street swayed.

Adrial took a deep breath, sucking in the smoke-filled air as he tried to make the stone houses hold still.

Taddy crawled toward him, blood dripping from a gash on his head.

Adrial pushed himself to his feet, his legs wobbling beneath him. He wrenched Taddy off the ground, keeping the boy's hand in his as they ran away from the blast.

He dragged Taddy through another alley and out onto a narrow street of lesser merchants' homes.

There were men holding planks of wood, but no swords or flames in sight.

"Taddy"—Adrial's voice sounded distant and muddy to his own ears—"I need you to run for the library as quickly as you can. It's not far from here. I know you can make it."

"We can make it." Taddy clutched Adrial's hand.

"You're going to run ahead of me." Adrial pulled free of Taddy's grip and took the boy's shoulders. "You're going to run as fast as you can and go straight to the library."

"I won't leave—"

"I'll be fine. I've got no white on. I'll grab a board and pretend to be one of them. That won't work if we're traveling together, and I'm too slow to outrun them."

"I can't." Tears streamed down Taddy's cheeks.

"You have to. I need you to warn the soldiers outside the library that I'll be wearing common clothes. If you want to help me, Taddy, you'll run as fast as you can and get to the library."

Taddy wiped the blood from his forehead with Adrial's sleeve and nodded.

"I'll tell them you're coming." Taddy took two deep breaths and took off running up the street.

He made it nearly to the men with the boards before they turned toward him.

"Where are you running to?" One of the men reached for Taddy.

"A bunch of rotta filth mucking up the streets"—Adrial stepped out into the open and shouted at the men—"I can't wait to see how badly the soldiers make you bleed!"

Taddy darted past the men, who had all turned their glares toward Adrial.

Keep going, apprentice.

"Did I offend you?" Adrial asked. "Sorry, I didn't know you were smart enough to understand speech."

Adrial bolted back down the alley before bothering to see if the men would chase him.

His ears caught a hint of the rumble of their footsteps behind him before he'd reached the next street. He couldn't tell how close they were with the sounds of the world still so strangely muted.

But there was no panic in Adrial's chest as he raced along the front of a house and darted into the next alley. His hip screamed its pain. His shoulder throbbed. But he had no fear.

The pounding footsteps of the men grew louder as they reached the street.

Adrial threw himself to the ground behind a sack of rotting

vegetables and curled up like a drunk too bad off from the night before for even the explosions to wake him.

He kept his breathing even, despite the sharp scent of the rotting food bringing bile to his throat. He'd survived Ian Ayres by hiding. He'd made an art of being indistinguishable from the filth around him.

After he'd been beaten and his hip ruined, Adrial had learned that violent men rarely looked toward the quiet, still places for their victims. Those who wanted to hurt enjoyed watching their prey run.

Another explosion shook the ground beneath Adrial's head.

Joyful whooping came from the streets.

The horrible sound wasn't muffled in Adrial's ears.

The shouting of battle cries and the clanging of swords carried from both ends of the alley.

Adrial waited while the sounds of the fight shifted, moving closer to the library and the Guilded section of Ilara.

Let Taddy have reached safety. If you have any mercy, give it to the boy. Adrial tossed his plea up to Dudia.

He'd never make it to the library, and with dusk fast approaching, he'd need to find shelter for the night in case the fighting spread.

But if violence devoured the city, there would be no safe place to hide. Everyone in Ilara would be in danger.

Ena.

Adrial pushed himself to his feet, glancing to both ends of the alley before heading west.

He stuck to the narrow side streets as much as he could, ducking into the ever-growing shadows whenever people came too near.

None of the men bearing swords, axes, knives, or clubs seemed to care much about the half-naked cripple creeping between the alleys.

The homes in the common part of the city were all dark.

Shutters closed, no candles to be seen. Whether the residents were hiding from the violence or had gone to join in the bloodshed, Adrial didn't know.

His pressed his back to the cold stone of a house and kept his chin tucked as four men carrying torches ran down the street.

He waited for them to round the corner before darting through the next alley and out to the long row of warehouses.

The stench of fire and fear had replaced the usual odor of fish.

Flowers and vegetables had been trampled on the ground, as though the rioters had torn through the sellers' stalls. Some businesses had been locked up tight, leaving nothing that could be stolen or ruined. Everything else had been preyed upon by the mobs.

The tavern's windows had been shattered and the tables torn apart.

Adrial wondered if any of the wood had been turned into makeshift weapons and how much blood a simple table leg might spill.

Bile stung his throat, and the cold air froze the sweat that slicked his skin.

A woman crept through the shadows, clutching a bundle in her arms.

Adrial tried not to think about what the woman might be holding.

Ena. Just find Ena.

If he could get to her, be sure she was safe, they'd find a place to wait for the fires to be put out. They'd huddle together in the dark until this horrible nightmare ended.

The dark green walls of the warehouse came into view, and he picked up his pace, his gaze fixed on Ena's black-painted door.

But there was no door, just a dark opening.

"No." Adrial ran toward the open space that should have been blocked by all Ena's locks. "Please, no."

Splintered wood hung from the hinges, and the smashed door had been cast aside on the street.

"Ena!"

The stairs thudded under his uneven footfalls as he pounded up the steps to her home, wishing for the first time he had a weapon. Not to defend himself, but to kill whoever had harmed Ena.

The world spun as Adrial tried to make his mind understand the wreckage of Ena's workshop. The table had been flipped over. Shattered glass jars covered the ground. Ink of every color had spilled onto the floor, the brightness of the hues obscene against the decimation around them.

"Ena?" Adrial called over the crunch of glass beneath his feet. "Ena?" Red stains marked a corner of the floor.

Let it be ink. Please let it be ink.

"Ena."

Her bed was made. She'd gotten up and started her day.

And then they came for her.

"Ena!"

A scrape and a thump sounded from the open window.

Adrial spun to see Ena, clean and unharmed, swinging down from the roof and into her shop.

"Chivving gods and stars, scribe, what do you think you're doing here?"

Adrial ran to her and pulled her into his arms, his need to feel her safe and whole pushing past the absolute terror of the city around them.

"You're alive," Adrial whispered. "You're alive."

"Scribe"—Ena wriggled free, taking Adrial's face in her hands—"what are you doing here?"

"They attacked near the shop." Adrial pushed Ena's purple and blue streaked hair away from her face. "There were explosions, they tried to evacuate us, but my guards were killed. I couldn't get through the fighting to get to the library, and the fires are spreading. And I had to make sure you were safe, and—"

"We have to get out of here." Ena seized Adrial's hand, dragging him toward the stairs. "I have a place nearby. You can wait there until the soldiers retake the city."

"Do you think they will?" Adrial tried to keep his pain out of his voice as they ran down the steps.

Ena paused just inside the door and peered out onto the street. "Cade's a fool. You want to set explosions and draw the soldiers away from their barracks? Fine. Lure the paun out and fight them on the street. It'll give the tilk a better chance against them. But there are too many soldiers in the city. Even if hundreds of brave tilk join Cade's men, they'll still be fatally outnumbered.

"There are scribes' guards, and royal guards, and a tower filled with sorcerers. You can't end the Guilds' rule by killing a few hundred soldiers. Cade is going to bring the wrath of the Guilds down on the people of Ilara. Ridding Ilbrea of the Guilds can't be done with one night of rebellion. It will take more than that to end our torment."

"Do you really think the Guilds should fall?"

Ena met Adrial's gaze.

There was pain in her eyes, a deeper agony than what he'd seen before. There was a fire in her eyes, too, more deadly than the flames that ravaged the city.

"I will see the paun burn. I will see the Guilds crumble to ash." She brushed her lips against his cheek. "But I will not toss the innocent into the flames."

"But there—"

"Run, now." Ena grabbed his arm, dragging him onto the street, heading north toward the orange that danced in the darkening sky.

They cut across the alley and around the nearest warehouse.

Ena kept to a pace Adrial could match. He wanted to tell her to go on without him, but the idea of facing the darkness without her hand in his stole his breath away.

Clack.

The sound echoed up the street, ringing crisply in Adrial's ears.

Clack.

Ena didn't glance behind or slow her pace.

Adrial dared to look back.

The silhouettes of twelve men walked up the street behind them. A few carried torches. The rest carried weapons.

One of the men struck the stone street with his club.

Clack!

Adrial's heart thundered in his ears. "Ena, you have to go."

She turned down an alley and bolted through an open warehouse door.

The scent of horses, wet wood, salt, and rotting hay filled the dark. She let go of his hand and shoved him toward a line of barrels against the back wall.

"Get behind the barrels and hide." Ena tore through the darkness to the far side of the warehouse.

Adrial ran to the line of barrels. There was barely any space behind them. To fit, he'd have to lie on his side. He'd have no chance of getting out quickly. No hope of defending himself.

Ena kicked open a door on the far wall, but didn't run through it.

"Get down." Ena sprinted back toward the door they'd entered through.

"Ena, please run."

"Hide, now." Ena squared her shoulders and faced the door. She didn't pull her knife from her boot or search for any sort of weapon. "I need you to trust me, scribe. Promise you'll trust me."

"Always."

Ena kept her gaze fixed on the doorway.

Forcing all the air out of his lungs, Adrial squeezed into the tiny space behind the barrels.

Clack. Clack.

I'm useless. The horrible truth pounded through Adrial's head as he lay pinned on his side. *She is in danger, and I am useless.*

Clack. Clack. Clack.

A flicker of light shone from the doorway.

Adrial searched the warehouse, trying to find some aid, some savior hiding in the shadows.

"I thought I'd have to chase you longer."

Cade's voice sank painful dread into Adrial's stomach.

"If I'd known you were chasing me, I would have run faster," Ena said.

"Where's the Guilded Cripple?"

"In the library, I'd expect," Ena said.

The light in the warehouse brightened as boots thumped across the floor toward the door Ena had kicked open.

"Don't lie to me, Ena," Cade said. "When you hid from me this morning, I decided to pay to have your warehouse watched. Cost me a pretty coin, but they came running to me when the paun limped to your door."

"I wonder what he wanted," Ena said.

"I saw him running here with you. You are already guilty of aiding the paun. Don't make your crimes worse by lying to me."

"Crimes? Do you get to decide what's considered a crime now? What will the punishment for my crimes be?"

Ena gasped.

Adrial tried to shift his chin to see what was happening, but the gap between the barrels was only wide enough to give him a view of the abandoned cart.

"Where is the scribe?" Cade asked.

"So you can kill me now?" Ena laughed.

Smack.

Terror raced through Adrial, setting his every nerve on fire.

"Give me a reason to show you mercy," Cade said.

"I can't," Ena's spat. "Cut my throat if you like. Beat me if you like. I'd rather die by your hand than let the monster take out his vengeance on me. You don't know what he'll do to me. What he threatened…I'd rather be dead."

"What did the paun do?" Cade's voice lost a hint of its edge.

"Nothing."

"Lying helps no one, Ena. What did the monster do?"

"He hasn't hurt me. Not yet. But if I don't do the work he asks, if I betray him, he'll send the soldiers for me. He'll lock me in the library so I can make his chivving ink. And once I'm there, do you think he'll leave me alone? Just let me work in peace? I'll be stuck in a cage, and that monster will come for me."

"Why didn't you tell me?"

"Because I won't survive being locked in with the paun!"

Silence followed Ena's shout.

Adrial's pulse thumped in his ears. He tried to calm his heart. He needed to listen for the sound of a knife rending flesh, for…

It would already be too late.

"I can protect you," Cade said.

"From the Guilds?" Ena spoke barely loudly enough for Adrial to hear. "From the soldiers he'll send after me? He is going to be the Lord Scribe. There is no safety for me, Cade."

"You'll find safety by my side. The Guilds will fall. It's already begun. The soldiers won't be able to reach you. I've offered you my protection before, Ena. The offer still stands."

"I can't."

"You will be safe."

"For how long?"

"Always."

"Promise that monster won't come near me?"

"No paun will ever touch you again."

Adrial held his breath as the silence dragged out.

The light shifted.

A torch crackled.

A little gasp and a sigh carried from just out of sight.

No. Please no. Adrial wanted to scream, but he promised to trust her. *Promises don't matter. Nothing matters but keeping her alive.*

Two figures stumbled into view.

Ena with her fingers twined through Cade's hair as she kissed him.

Cade running his hands up Ena's thighs.

He pressed her against the abandoned cart and lifted her onto the back. He kept kissing her as he raised her skirt, exposing the pale skin of her legs. He trailed his fingers up her thighs, up her breasts, to the knot at the top of her bodice.

Adrial dug his nails into his palms as rage burned through him.

But she wasn't fighting back.

She kept her fingers locked in Cade's hair as he untied the laces of her bodice. She arched her back as he yanked the fabric down, exposing her breasts. The dark stone of her pendant shone in the torchlight. He pulled his lips from Ena's and lowered his mouth to the skin that should have stayed hidden.

Adrial shut his eyes. The anger and fear in his chest swelled into a horrible pain.

Ena gasped.

Adrial tried to picture himself in the great room of the library, surrounded by silence and sunlight and peaceful books where everything made sense.

But no thoughts of peaceful places could drown out the creaking rhythm of the cart.

ADRIAL

The warehouse had gone silent.

Adrial pressed his head against the wall behind him, needing the pain in his body to keep him present despite his despair.

"Are you going to lead the fight?" Ena asked.

Hearing her speak soothed a bit of Adrial's fear but heightened his hatred.

"We're going to burn the barracks," Cade said. "The charges have already been set. Once the paun are wounded, we'll slaughter them all."

"What about me?" Ena said. "I can't go back to my shop. The scribe could send soldiers there."

"Stay here. My men will protect you."

"I don't know them. I don't want them near me."

"They're good men."

"I don't trust them. I only trust you, Cade. Please."

Silence followed.

Adrial pressed his head against the wall so hard he thought he might split his own skull.

"I'll have my men stand guard outside," Cade said. "You can lock the doors."

Boots thumped toward the wide warehouse door.

"When will you be back?" Ena asked.

Light footsteps chased after the boots.

"When the Guilds have fallen," Cade said.

"Don't die," Ena said. "Do not abandon me. You've promised me your protection, and—"

Adrial longed to scream as another silence tortured him.

"I'll be back. And I'll prove to you why you should have accepted my protection long ago."

The boots thumped away.

The bang of wood on wood made Adrial open his eyes. The light in the warehouse had nearly disappeared.

A rasp carried from out of view before a figure ran to the other side of the warehouse.

A scrape and a thump came from that door.

Adrial stayed frozen, waiting for some new form of torment to greet him.

The barrel near his head shifted.

"You can come out now," Ena whispered.

With a thump, something dropped to the floor.

Adrial tried to push himself up but couldn't get enough leverage.

Chill water splashed on his forehead.

"I've bought us time, but we still have to get you out of here," Ena said. "I don't trust Cade's men to leave me alone for long. And I can't be here if he survives the barracks."

Adrial wriggled his way along the wall, inching to freedom. He legs broke free, and he let all the air out of his lung as he pushed himself sideways and sat up.

Starlight and the dim flicker of torches fought their way through the high windows, casting dull shadows into the warehouse. Still, the light was enough for Adrial to be able to see Ena drop her skirt and tear off her bodice and shift.

She leveraged herself up and into a barrel. Water flooded the floor as she submerged her whole body.

"Ena." Adrial forced his legs to hold his weight as he took a few steps toward the barrel.

But she was still beneath the water, huddled inside the barrel where he could not reach her.

"Ena."

Her head broke through the surface, and she gasped for air.

"Ena, are you all right?"

"There's another way out of here." She scrubbed her hands over her neck. "They won't know to guard it. If we can make it that far, you should be safe to hide."

She climbed out of the barrel. Water dripped off of her, but Adrial couldn't see her face—the light was too dim.

Ena grabbed her boots and knife but didn't reach for her clothes before heading to the farthest corner of the warehouse.

She stopped, facing the wall. "Are you coming or not?"

Adrial reached toward her clothes.

"Leave them," Ena said. "You'll need both hands to climb."

He tucked his hands at his sides and hurried toward Ena.

"I'm sorry it won't be an easy path," Ena said. "But it's the only safe place I have left."

"I don't care about my safety." Adrial reached for her arm.

"Don't touch me." Ena pulled away from him.

"I'm sorry." Adrial swallowed the pain that pressed into his throat. "Did he hurt you?"

"I can smell him." She started climbing up a ladder that had been built into the wall. "I don't want that stench on you."

A void grew in Adrial's chest.

No, not a void. A pain he didn't have a name for. It wasn't anger or fear. It wasn't even grief. Just a helpless, hollow feeling that devoured every bit of strength he'd thought he had.

"Come on, scribe," Ena said. "Cade will come back."

Adrial gripped the rungs of the ladder and began pulling himself up.

Ena made the climb seem easy, even with her boots and knife in her hands.

For Adrial, every step up meant negotiating with his arms, begging them to accept his weight, and battling against his bad hip, which seemed determined to see him tumble to the ground.

He moved one rung at a time, refusing to count, or feel any sympathy for himself. He didn't deserve pity or kindness, only loathing. For bringing more trouble to Ena. For failing to protect her from Cade. For wondering if she wanted to be protected from Cade.

When he reached the last of the rungs, Ena grabbed his hand and pulled him to the top.

Rough wood scraped against his bare chest as she dragged him into the narrow loft above the warehouse floor.

"That should be the worst of it." Ena hauled him to his feet.

Shapes loomed in the darkness—things that looked like crates and wheels and oddly shaped piles.

He gripped Ena's hand as she weaved through the shadows.

"Watch your head, and stay silent." Ena stopped and let go of him.

Starlight filtered through the roof as she pushed open a slanted trapdoor.

The bottom lip of the square opening was barely over waist-high, and she easily leveraged herself through.

Adrial gritted his teeth, determined not to show his pain as he followed her.

She steadied him as he stood on the pitch of the roof, three stories off the ground.

From so high up, it was easy to see how far Ilara had fallen.

To the south, bright light glowed from the docks, as though the sailors had lit every torch they could find to ward off the shadows that swallowed the city. But to the north, near the cathedral, library, and barracks, fires raged. The blazes had spread beyond the Guilded section of the city to the rows of merchants' homes.

Ena shut the trapdoor and tugged on his hand, drawing him toward the edge of the roof.

The light glistened off her wet skin. Goose bumps dotted her arms, but she didn't shiver as she stepped up to the ledge.

Another roof waited two feet away and a few feet down.

She pressed her lips to his ear. "Sit on the edge and climb across."

She let go of his hand and jumped to the other roof, landing without a sound.

Adrial stood on the roof alone. Above the burning city. Helpless and cold. Useless. Hurting the girl who wanted to help him.

A faint creak sounded from across the way as Ena opened a trapdoor in the other roof.

Adrial looked down to the ground far below. If the arrow had struck him instead of the soldier trying to protect him, Ena would have stayed safe. Cade wouldn't have touched her. Taddy would have been escorted to the library.

"Scribe." Ena's whisper pulled his gaze back to her. Her perfect face. The confidence in her stance as she stood, wearing only her black stone pendant, on a roof above a crumbling city.

Adrial sat and scooted forward until his legs hung over the edge of the roof. A moment of terror filled his chest as reason said he would fall to his death, but stepping on top of the next building over was no harder than getting up from a chair.

As soon as he'd gotten to his feet, Ena climbed down into the trapdoor. He crept toward the opening and sat again, shifting his legs through the opening before dropping to the other side.

"Stay down." Ena reached above him, lowering the door and closing them in.

Adrial had expected to land in a space like the one they had left, a storage loft cluttered with things, but this space was pitch black.

"Don't move." Ena spoke a little louder than before, as though she trusted the safety of wherever she'd led him.

A faint scraping sounded in the corner, and then a lantern began to glow.

He'd been right. They weren't in a loft. Solid wood surrounded them on every side, with the only breaks being the trapdoor they'd come through, another in the floor, and a hinged slat of wood on the southern wall.

Ena set the lantern down and dug into a bag in the corner.

"What is this place?" Adrial asked.

"A little warren I found a few months ago." Ena pulled a shift, dark skirt, and black bodice from the bag. "I went exploring on the roofs, and no one seemed to have been in here for a while."

"So you left clothes here?"

Ena froze with her shift in her hands. "I've learned too much about death, and fighting, and evil men. I was not foolish enough to think my home would be untouched when the flames came for Ilara."

She yanked her shift on and grabbed her skirt.

"Ena, I'm sorry. I shouldn't have come here. I shouldn't have—"

She pressed her fingers to his lips. "Don't." Her hand shook as she pulled it away. "Your safety is what matters. Everything else—Cade—it will all burn away."

"My safety isn't more important than yours."

"Yes, it is." Ena pulled on her skirt. "A hundred men like Cade will try to save Ilbrea from the Guilds and leave thousands of dead in their wake. I know. I've seen it happen. Even the good leaders, the ones who are kind and brave and should lead people to freedom, they aren't strong enough to defeat the paun. But you are."

"I'm not." Adrial sank to the ground. "If that's what you think, if that's why you kept Cade from finding me—"

"Cade doesn't matter. I don't matter. You are worth a thousand of me." Ena knelt in front of Adrial. "You have stood in the cathedral, lived in the Map Master's Palace and the library."

"But that doesn't mean—"

"You are a good man, Adrial." Ena took his face in her hands, forcing him to meet her gaze. "You have known the pain the tilk suffer every day. You know what it's like to be hungry and abused and left for dead."

"That doesn't mean I can change anything."

"It does." She kissed his forehead. "Maybe you can't see it yet. But one day you will, and you will save us all."

She let go of him and dragged the black bodice over her head. "When you hear the soldiers coming to this part of the city, call to them. Tell them you're here. They can take you to safety. You'll be able to watch through the gap in the wall." She pointed to the hinged planks of wood. "Make sure you blow out the lamp before you look outside. As long as you're careful, no one should be able to find you."

"Find us. You'll be here, too. If this place is safe, you've got to stay here with me."

"I can't." Ena tugged on her boots. "If Cade survives, he'll come back for me. I bought us time, but not my freedom. I can't let him touch me again."

Adrial touched the back of her hand. "I…thank you."

"Make sure it was worth it." Ena slid her hand from beneath his and tucked her knife into her boot.

"The soldiers will stop Cade. He won't be able to come near you again."

"I don't consider paun soldiers to be any safer than Cade." Ena pulled a coat and another knife from her bag. She gripped the hilt of the blade. "He let his men watch us. If he dies, one of them will try to claim me. I'll not be passed around as the whore of the rebels. I have to get out of Ilara." She pulled on the coat and tucked the knife into her pocket.

"Where will you go?"

"I don't know."

For a tiny moment, Adrial thought he saw her hands trembling, but then she lifted them and began weaving her wet hair into a braid.

"I have work that can't be left undone. I'll find a place to go and a way to be useful," Ena said.

"You're useful here."

"There are more important things than ink and papers."

"When will you come back?"

She tossed him a blanket. "Keep yourself warm while you wait. It might be hours before the soldiers make it out this far."

She gripped the handle on the floor.

"Ena, please." Adrial scrambled toward her. "Please don't go."

She leaned forward and brushed her lips against his.

Adrial wanted to savor the taste of her and the warmth of her lips.

"You can be the one to stop this, scribe. I'm sure of it."

The trapdoor squeaked as she pulled it open. And then she dropped out of sight.

Adrial stared into the dark patch of floor where she had vanished as the faint sounds of her movement disappeared.

The horrible hollow in his chest grew, swallowing his lungs, making it impossible to breathe.

He crawled to the lamp and blew it out before fumbling for the hinged slats of wood. He pulled them open, trying to catch just one more glimpse of her. The shadows on the street held no hint of Ena.

A man with a torch stood by the door to the warehouse where Cade had found them. The glow from the docks stayed steady.

He wished he could see the Guilded section of the city, but the window only let him look south.

Adrial stared at the warehouse that had been Ena's home. She'd lived there. Made him inks there. And now he'd never see the mad inker again.

The hollow threatened to crush him.

He closed his eyes and forced himself to breathe. "You are the head scribe, heir to the Lord Scribe. You were raised by Lord Karron. And you will not let Ena down."

But what could she want from him? From a man whose world was made of books and ledgers? He'd never even lifted a sword, let alone led a battle.

The coarse fabric of the blanket itched his skin as he wrapped it around his shoulders and leaned his forehead against the wall.

She was right. It could be hours until the soldiers came. There was no fire and mayhem here. The Guilds would secure the rest of the city before making their way out to the warehouses.

While the city burned, the head scribe would huddle in the dark, waiting to be rescued.

A scream rent the night.

"No! Please. I'm not here to hurt anyone!"

Adrial opened his eyes.

"I'm not fighting," the voice screamed. "I'm just...just trying to find my friend."

"Taddy?" Adrial peered out the window.

Long shadows filled the street near Ena's warehouse. He couldn't see any people, but he was sure he'd recognized Taddy's voice.

Taddy screamed.

Adrial scrambled across the floor to the open trapdoor.

There was no ladder or stairs. He couldn't see anything but a gaping blackness below him.

He couldn't jump down. He couldn't fight.

"Please don't!" Taddy screamed.

He couldn't sit in safety and listen to his apprentice being murdered on the street.

Adrial sat on the edge and leaned across, gripping the far side with his hands to soften his fall as he dropped into the darkness below.

Pain shot up his legs as he landed, but he managed to stay on his feet.

Another scream carried from outside.

"I'm coming, Taddy." Adrial fumbled through the dark, searching for a path down to the street.

He banged into a wall, and something else that jabbed into his ribs, before finding a narrow staircase with a wobbly handrail. Gripping the railing, he made it down the steps as quickly as he could.

The sound of cruel laughter came from outside.

Adrial found solid ground and stood, squinting in the dark, searching for a way out.

A slim bit of light peeked through the wall. He ran toward it.

Something caught his foot, and he fell hard, cracking his forehead against the ground. He pushed himself to his feet and lunged toward the light, gripping the side of the door and tossing it open.

An empty alley awaited him.

He breathed in the cold night air, taking one moment to revel in the beauty of working lungs and a steady body. Then he wiped the blood from his forehead with the back of his hand and ran down the alley toward the street.

Taddy screamed again.

The pain in Adrial's leg didn't matter. The men with torches didn't matter. Nothing in all Ilbrea mattered but keeping his apprentice away from the demons.

He reached the street and tore south toward Taddy.

"It's the scribe!" a man shouted behind him.

Adrial didn't stop.

He could see Taddy, arms held wide by two grown men while a third punched the boy in the face.

"Let the child go!" Adrial shouted as he stumbled to a stop. "I'm the one you're looking for."

The man who'd been hitting Taddy turned toward Adrial.

"Do you want to be known as monsters who beat children," Adrial said, "or would you rather capture the head scribe?"

"Looks like we can do both."

Adrial looked behind him.

Four of Cade's men prowled up the street toward him.

"Let the boy go," Adrial said, "and I will walk with you to the cathedral square. I will stand on the steps and tell all of Ilara how wrong the Guilds are to oppress the common folk."

The two men holding Taddy tossed the boy to the ground.

Run. Please, run.

Taddy lay on the street, coughing. Blood covered the boy's swollen face.

One of the men drew his knife. The other picked a bloodied board up off the street.

The seven men prowled toward Adrial.

Adrial took a deep breath, readying himself for pain and death. He would never be able save anyone. He was not that brave or strong. He couldn't make the Guilds serve the common folk or fix the wrongs the sorcerers had committed. But if he could buy Taddy time to escape, that would be enough.

"We don't need pretty words from a scribe." Cade stepped out of the shadows. "We've heard enough lies from your kind."

One of the men reached down, grabbed Taddy by the back of the shirt Adrial had given him, and tossed the boy forward.

Taddy landed at Adrial's feet with a whimper.

"Taddy," Adrial said. "Get up, Taddy."

Cade stepped in front of his men as they formed a ring around Adrial. "It will be nice to finally kill you."

A strange little gurgle came from Adrial's right as one of Cade's men tipped forward and fell onto the street.

Ena stood behind him, a bloodied knife in her hand.

The whole world seemed to stop.

The next man didn't even raise a hand to fight as she sliced through his throat.

That man dropped the board he'd been holding.

Ena kicked it toward Adrial as Cade screamed his rage and charged her.

Adrial grabbed the board and stepped in front of Taddy as two men lunged toward him.

One carried a torch, the other a sword.

The man with the sword swung first. His blade sliced into Adrial's poor weapon, carving a chunk off the top.

Adrial swung the board again, but the man with the torch hit him in the back of the legs. Heat seared Adrial's skin as he fell to the ground. His head struck the pavement, but he managed to hold on to the board and swung it at one of the men's ankles.

Shouts filled the air, but one scream carried over them.

Adrial looked toward the sound.

Ena wrenched her blade from one man's gut while kicking away another that tried to grab her from behind.

Pain shot through Adrial's hands as a boot kicked the board from his grip.

Adrial punched forward, catching the man with the torch in the knee.

Cruel laughter filled the street.

Adrial looked back toward Ena.

Another of Cade's men had fallen, but the last one had pinned Ena to the ground.

Cade knelt over her, reaching for her throat.

"No!" Adrial screamed.

A blow to the stomach knocked all the air from his lungs.

Ena.

There were sounds in the world, shouting and chaos and thunder that rumbled through the street, but he couldn't manage to scream her name.

A blow to his hip brought agony that stole his sight.

Something hard struck his back, pain enveloped him, and the world faded away.

As he dove into the black, the scribe only carried one word with him.

Ena. Ena. Ena.

ENA

I remember the first man I ever killed. He had a scar on his lip and gray-blue eyes.

He should have been an ally, but he broke the rules of the envoy. A finger grazed across my breast had forged his doom.

I didn't want to kill him. I didn't want the weight of his death on my shoulders. But I didn't have a choice. So I took the knife they gave me, and I sliced through his gut.

I remember the warmth of his blood pouring over my hand.

I don't think I will ever forget that feeling.

But I have grown accustomed to it.

The others gathered in the cathedral square did not wear such armor.

I weaved through the crowd toward the cathedral steps, ignoring the stares of those I passed.

I hadn't tried to hide the marks the battle had left on me. The bruises, the cuts—they proved I had survived. I pulled my hair back, letting them all see the handprint Cade had left on my throat.

A woman in fine merchant silks gasped and backed away from me.

I held her gaze as I walked by.

The others had tried to disguise the pain the rebellion had caused. They'd dressed in their finest clothes, like they could prove how little damage the flames had done to them.

Fancy clothes could not hide the fear on their faces.

I wound my way closer to the cathedral steps, toward the forty-three pikes the Guilds had erected. Monuments to prove to the common folk that rebellions would not earn freedom, only beheading.

It was the head mounted on the center pike I'd come to see.

Cade's blond hair had turned brown with dried blood. Carrion birds had pecked out his eyes before landing on the cathedral roof to caw their displeasure at being deprived of the full corpses of the dead.

"Miss." A soldier held out a hand, blocking my path up the cathedral steps.

I hadn't even realized I'd made it to the front of the crowd. I'd been too busy staring up at Cade's head, trying to prove to myself that it really was him.

"Miss, are you all right?" the soldier asked.

"I'm fine." I swayed as I looked away from Cade to meet the soldier's gaze.

He had a cut on his cheek that had pinked around the edges as though the healers hadn't bothered to properly care for the paun.

"You should go, miss." The soldier's forehead wrinkled, like he was worried I'd faint.

I'm not afraid of blood and death. I've spent too long living with them. They are home to me.

"This isn't the sort of thing people should see," the soldier said.

"Then why put them up?"

"To prove the city is safe from the monsters," the soldier said. "That doesn't mean a girl like you should be here. Go home."

I nodded to the soldier and pushed my way back through the

382 | MEGAN O'RUSSELL

crowd. I couldn't stay in the square any longer. Not without screaming the truth to the common folk who packed in to stare at the pikes like they actually believed the Guilds would protect us.

We were not safe. This rebellion had died, but another would come. Maybe their leader would be a good, wise man who would protect the people of the city as he fought against the Guilds.

But I had no hope that such a man would step out of the shadows to save us all.

The flames would come again, and more innocent blood would be spilt. If not by the rebels' hands, then by the Guilds'.

We were trapped in a tale where our role was to die, and the common folk did not control the pages of the story that needed to be rewritten.

At the back of the crowd, a pack of common men stood together, staring at the Guilds' horrible display. They bore signs of fighting, but their shoulders were not rounded in grief or defeat. Their faces held no trace of fear.

The man at the front stood tall and proud, like a leader posing for a portrait.

A spark of hope glimmered in the man's eyes.

It had already started again. Men were forming grand plans. Flames would devour the city.

I shoved my pain beneath the embers of my rage.

I would set my own blaze in Ilara. I would see the flames dance through the streets as the Guilds crumbled from within.

I would not let the innocent be consumed by the fire.

The Guilds of Ilbrea series continues with Myth *and* Storm.

Ena's story began long before she journeyed to Ilara. Turn the page for a glimpse into the Inker's past.

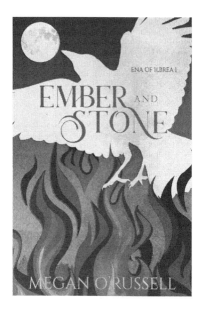

Uncover the mysterious past of Ena Bairn in the *Ena of Ilbrea* series. Turn the page for a sneak peek of book one, *Ember and Stone*.

1

The crack of the whip sent the birds scattering into the sky. They cawed their displeasure at the violence of the men below as they flew over the village and to the mountains beyond.

The whip cracked again.

Aaron did well. He didn't start to moan until the fourth lash. By the seventh, he screamed in earnest.

No one had given him a belt to bite down on. There hadn't been time when the soldiers hauled him from his house and tied him to the post in the square.

I clutched the little wooden box of salve hidden in my pocket, letting the corners bite deep into my palm.

The soldier passed forty lashes, not caring that Aaron's back had already turned to pulp.

I squeezed my way to the back of the crowd, unwilling to watch Aaron's blood stain the packed dirt.

Behind the rest of the villagers, children cowered in their mother's skirts, hiding from the horrors the Guilds' soldiers brought with them.

I didn't know how many strokes Aaron had been sentenced

to. I didn't want to know. I made myself stop counting how many times the whip sliced his back.

Bida, Aaron's wife, wept on the edge of the crowd. When his screams stopped, hers grew louder.

The women around Bida held her back, keeping her out of reach of the soldiers.

My stomach stung with the urge to offer comfort as she watched her husband being beaten by the men in black uniforms. But, with the salve tucked in my pocket, hiding in the back was safest.

I couldn't give Bida the box unless Aaron survived. Spring hadn't fully arrived, and the plants Lily needed to make more salves still hadn't bloomed. The tiny portion of the stuff hidden in my pocket was worth more than someone's life, especially if that person wasn't going to survive even with Lily's help.

Lily's orders had been clear—wait and see if Aaron made it through. Give Bida the salve if he did. If he didn't, come back home and hide the wooden box under the floorboards for the next poor soul who might need it.

Aaron fell to the ground. Blood leaked from a gash under his arm.

The soldier raised his whip again.

I sank farther into the shadows, trying to comfort myself with the beautiful lie that I could never be tied to the post in the village square, though I knew the salve clutched in my hand would see me whipped at the post as quickly as whatever offense the soldiers had decided Aaron had committed.

When my fingers had gone numb from gripping the box, the soldier stopped brandishing his whip and turned to face the crowd.

"We did not come here to torment you," the soldier said. "We came here to protect Ilbrea. We came here to protect the Guilds. We are here to provide peace to all the people of this great country.

This man committed a crime, and he has been punished. Do not think me cruel for upholding the law." He wrapped the bloody whip around his hand and led the other nine soldiers out of the square.

Ten soldiers. It had only taken ten of them to walk into our village and drag Aaron from his home. Ten men to tie him to the post and leave us all helpless as they beat a man who'd lived among us all his life.

The soldiers disappeared, and the crowd shifted in toward Aaron. I couldn't hear him crying or moaning over the angry mutters of the crowd.

His wife knelt by his side, wailing.

I wound my way forward, ignoring the stench of fear that surrounded the villagers.

Aaron lay on the ground, his hands still tied around the post. His back had been flayed open by the whip. His flesh looked more like something for a butcher to deal with than an illegal healer like me.

I knelt by his side, pressing my fingers to his neck to feel for a pulse.

Nothing.

I wiped my fingers on the cleanest part of Aaron's shirt I could find and weaved my way back out of the crowd, still clutching the box of salve in my hand.

Carrion birds gathered on the rooftops near the square, scenting the fresh blood in the air. They didn't know Aaron wouldn't be food for them. The villagers of Harane had yet to fall so low as to leave our own out as a feast for the birds.

There was no joy in the spring sun as I walked toward Lily's house on the eastern edge of the village.

I passed by the tavern, which had already filled with men who didn't mind we hadn't reached midday. I didn't blame them for hiding in there. If they could find somewhere away from the torment of the soldiers, better on them for seizing it. I only hoped there weren't any soldiers laughing inside the tavern's walls.

I followed the familiar path home. Along our one, wide dirt road, past the few shops Harane had to offer, to the edge of the village where only fields and pastures stood between us and the forest that reached up the eastern mountains' slopes.

It didn't take long to reach the worn wooden house with the one giant tree towering out front. It didn't take long to reach anywhere in the tiny village of Harane.

Part of me hated knowing every person who lived nearby. Part of me wished the village were smaller. Then maybe we'd fall off the Guilds' maps entirely.

As it was, the Guilds only came when they wanted to collect our taxes, to steal our men to fight their wars, or to find some other sick pleasure in inflicting agony on people who wanted nothing more than to survive. Or if their business brought them far enough south on the mountain road they had to pass through our home on their way to torment someone else.

I allowed myself a moment to breathe before facing Lily. I blinked away the images of Aaron covered in blood and shoved them into a dark corner with the rest of the wretched things it was better not to ponder.

Lily barely glanced up as I swung open the gate and stepped into the back garden. Dirt covered her hands and skirt. Her shoulders were hunched from the hours spent planting our summer garden. She never allowed me to help with the task. Everything had to be carefully planned, keeping the vegetables toward the outermost edges. Hiding the plants she could be hanged for in the center, where soldiers were less likely to spot the things she grew to protect the people of our village. The people the soldiers were so eager to hurt.

"Did he make it?" Lily stretched her shoulders back and brushed the dirt off her weathered hands.

I held the wooden box out as my response. Blood stained the

corners. It wasn't Aaron's blood. It was mine. Cuts marked my hand where I'd squeezed the box too tightly.

Lily glared at my palm. "You'd better go in and wrap your hand. If you let it get infected, I'll have to treat you with the salve, and you know we're running out."

I tucked the box back into my pocket and went inside, not bothering to argue that I could heal from a tiny cut. I didn't want to look into Lily's wrinkled face and see the glimmer of pity in her eyes.

The inside of the house smelled of herbs and dried flowers. Their familiar scent did nothing to drive the stench of blood and fear from my nose.

A pot hung over the stove, waiting with whatever Lily had made for breakfast.

My stomach churned at the thought of eating. I needed to get out. Out of the village, away from the soldiers.

I pulled up the loose floorboard by the stove and tucked the salve in between the other boxes, tins, and vials. I grabbed my bag off the long, wooden table and shoved a piece of bread and a waterskin into it for later. I didn't bother grabbing a coat or shawl. I didn't care about getting cold.

I have to get out.

I was back through the door and in the garden a minute later. Lily didn't even look up from her work. "If you're running into the forest, you had better come back with something good."

"I will," I said. "I'll bring you back all sorts of wonderful things. Just make sure you save some dinner for me."

I didn't need to ask her to save me food. In all the years I'd lived with her, Lily had never let me go hungry. But she was afraid I would run away into the forest and never return. Or maybe it was me that feared I might disappear into the trees and never come back. Either way, I felt myself relax as I stepped out of the garden and turned my feet toward the forest.

2

The mountains rose up beyond the edge of the trees, fierce towers I could never hope to climb. No one else from the village would ever even dream of trying such a thing.

The soldiers wouldn't enter the woods. The villagers rarely dared to go near them. The forest was where darkness and solitude lay. A quiet place where the violence of the village couldn't follow me.

I skirted farmers' fields and picked my way through the pastures. No one bothered me as I climbed over the fences they built to keep in their scarce amounts of sheep and cows.

No one kept much livestock. They couldn't afford it in the first place. And besides, if the soldiers saw that one farmer had too many animals, they would take the beasts as taxes. Safer to be poor. Better for your belly to go empty than for the soldiers to think you had something to give.

I moved faster as I got past the last of the farmhouses and beyond the reach of the stench of animal dung.

When I was a very little girl, my brother had told me that the woods were ruled by ghosts. That none of the villagers dared to cut down the trees or venture into their shelter for fear of being taken by the dead and given a worse fate than even the Guilds could provide.

I'd never been afraid of ghosts, and I'd wandered through the woods often enough to be certain that no spirits roamed the eastern mountains.

When I first started going into the forest, I convinced myself I was braver than everyone else in Harane. I was an adventurer, and they were cowards.

Maybe I just knew better. Maybe I knew that no matter what ghosts did, they could never match the horrors men inflict on each other. What I'd seen them do to each other.

By the time I was a hundred feet into the trees, I could no longer see the village behind me. I couldn't smell anything but the fresh scent of damp earth as the little plants fought for survival in the fertile spring ground. I knew my way through the woods well enough I didn't need to bother worrying about which direction to go. It was more a question of which direction I wanted to chase the gentle wind.

I could go and find fungi for Lily to make into something useful, or I could climb. If I went quickly, I would have time to climb and still be able to find something worth Lily getting herself hanged for.

Smiling to myself, I headed due east toward the steepest part of the mountains near our village. Dirt soon covered the hem of my skirt, and mud squelched beneath my shoes, creeping in through the cracked leather of the soles. I didn't mind so much. What the cold could do to me was nothing more than a refreshing chance to prove I was still alive. Life existed outside the village, and there was beauty beyond our battered walls.

Bits of green peeked through the brown of the trees as new buds forced their way out of the branches.

I stopped, staring up at the sky, marveling at the beauty hidden within our woods.

Birds chirped overhead. Not the angry cawing of birds of

death, but the beautiful songs of lovebirds who had nothing more to worry about than tipping their wings up toward the sky.

A gray and blue bird burst from a tree, carrying his song deeper into the forest.

A stream gurgled to one side of me. The snap of breaking branches came from the other. I didn't change my pace as the crackling came closer.

I headed south to a steeper slope where I had to use my hands to pull myself up the rocks.

I moved faster, outpacing the one who lumbered through the trees behind me. A rock face cut through the forest, blocking my path. I dug my fingers into the cracks in the stone, pulling myself up. Careful to keep my legs from being tangled in my skirt, I found purchase on the rock with the soft toes of my boots. In a few quick movements, I pushed myself up over the top of the ledge. I leapt to my feet and ran to the nearest tree, climbing up to the highest thick branch.

I sat silently on my perch, waiting to see what sounds would come from below.

A rustle came from the base of the rock, followed by a long string of inventive curses.

I bit my lips together, not allowing myself to call out.

The cursing came again.

"Of all the slitching, vile—" the voice from below growled.

I leaned back against the tree, closing my eyes, reveling in my last few moments of solitude. Those hints of freedom were what I loved most about being able to climb. Going up a tree, out of reach of the things that would catch me.

"Ena," the voice called. "Ena."

I didn't answer.

"Ena, are you going to leave me down here?"

My lips curved into a smile as I bit back my laughter. "I didn't ask you to follow me. You can just go back the way you came."

"I don't want to go back," he said. "Let me come up. At least show me how you did it."

"If you want to chase me, you'd better learn to climb."

I let him struggle for a few more minutes until he threatened to find a pick and crack through the rock wall. I glanced down to find him three feet off the ground, his face bright red as he tried to climb.

"Jump down," I said, not wanting him to fall and break something. I could have hauled him back to the village, but I didn't fancy the effort.

"Help me get up," he said.

"Go south a bit. You'll find an easier path."

I listened to the sounds of him stomping off through the trees, enjoying the bark against my skin as I waited for him to find the way up.

It only took him a few minutes to loop back around to stand under my perch.

Looking at Cal stole my will to flee. His blond hair glistened in the sun. He shaded his bright blue eyes as he gazed up at me.

"Are you happy now?" he said. "I'm covered in dirt."

"If you wanted to be clean, you shouldn't have come into the woods. I never ask you to follow me."

"It would have been wrong of me not to. You shouldn't be coming out here by yourself."

I didn't let it bother me that he thought it was too dangerous for me to be alone in the woods. It was nice to have someone worry about me. Even if he was worried about ghosts that didn't exist.

"What do you think you'd be able to do to help me anyway?" I said.

He stared up at me, hurt twisting his perfect brow.

Cal looked like a god, or something made at the will of the Guilds themselves. His chiseled jaw held an allure to it, the rough stubble on his cheeks luring my fingers to touch its texture.

I twisted around on my seat and dropped down to the ground, reveling in his gasp as I fell.

"You really need to get more used to the woods," I said. "It's a good place to hide."

"What would I have to hide from?" Cal's eyes twinkled, offering a hint of teasing that drew me toward him.

I touched the stubble on his chin, tracing the line of his jaw.

"There are plenty of things to hide from, fool." I turned to tramp farther into the woods.

"Ena," he called after me, "you shouldn't be going so far from home."

"Then don't follow me. Go back." I knew he would follow.

I had known when I passed by his window in the tavern on my way through the village. He always wanted to be near me. That was the beauty of Cal.

I veered closer to the stream.

Cal kept up, though he despised getting his boots muddy.

I always chose the more difficult path to make sure he knew I could outpace him. It was part of our game on those trips into the forest.

I leapt across the stream to a patch of fresh moss just beginning to take advantage of spring.

"Ena." Cal jumped the water and sank down onto the moss I had sought.

I shoved him off of the green and into the dirt.

He growled.

I didn't bother trying to hide my smile. I pulled out tufts of the green moss, tucking them into my bag for Lily.

"If you don't want me to follow you," Cal said, "you can tell me not to whenever you like."

"The forest doesn't belong to me, Cal. You can go where you choose."

He grabbed both my hands and tugged me toward him. I tipped onto him and he shifted, letting me fall onto my back. I caught a glimpse of the sun peering down through the new buds of emerald leaves, and then he was kissing me.

His taste of honey and something a bit deeper filled me. And I forgot about whips and Lily and men bleeding and soldiers coming to kill us.

There was nothing but Cal and me. And the day became beautiful.

Order your copy of Ember and Stone *to continue the story.*

THE GUILDS OF ILBREA SERIES RETURNS
WITH MYTH AND STORM

Now available for preorder.

ESCAPE INTO ADVENTURE

Thank you for reading *Inker and Crown.* If you enjoyed the book, please consider leaving a review to help other readers find this story.

Dive deeper into the world of the Guilds on MeganORussell. com/ilbrea, where you'll find exclusive Ilbrean content, a peek behind the scenes, and updates on new books.

As always, thanks for reading,

Megan O'Russell

Never miss a moment of the magic and romance.

Join the Megan O'Russell readers community to stay up to date on all the action by visiting https://www.meganorussell.com/ book-signup.

ABOUT THE AUTHOR

 Megan O'Russell is the author of several Young Adult series that invite readers to escape into worlds of adventure. From *Girl of Glass*, which blends dystopian darkness with the heart-pounding danger of vampires, to *Ena of Ilbrea*, which draws readers into an epic world of magic and assassins.

With the *Girl of Glass* series, *The Tethering* series, *The Chronicles of Maggie Trent*, *The Tale of Bryant Adams*, the *Ena of Ilbrea* series, and several more projects planned for 2020, there are always exciting new books on the horizon. To be the first to hear about new releases, free short stories, and giveaways, sign up for Megan's newsletter by visiting the following:

https://www.meganorussell.com/book-signup.

Originally from Upstate New York, Megan is a professional musical theatre performer whose work has taken her across North America. Her chronic wanderlust has led her from Alaska to Thailand and many places in between. Wanting to travel has fostered Megan's love of books that allow her to visit countless new worlds from her favorite reading nook. Megan is also a lyricist and playwright. Information on her theatrical works can be found at RussellCompositions.com.

She would be thrilled to chat with you on Facebook or

Twitter @MeganORussell, elated if you'd visit her website MeganORussell.com, and over the moon if you'd like the pictures of her adventures on Instagram @ORussellMegan.

Mountain and Ash

Ice and Sky

Feather and Flame

<u>Guilds of Ilbrea</u>

Inker and Crown

Myth and Storm

Made in the USA
Middletown, DE
21 October 2020